The
WEDDING CRASHER
and the
COWBOY

At Entangled, we want our readers to be well-informed. If you would like to know if this book contains any elements that might be of concern for you, please check the back of the book for details.

To all my readers, new and returning,
thank you from the bottom of my heart. xoxo

ALSO BY ROBIN BIELMAN

Entangled Publishing, LLC
10940 S Parker Road
Suite 327
Parker, CO 80134
Visit our website at www.entangledpublishing.com.

Amara is an imprint of Entangled Publishing, LLC.

Edited by Stacy Abrams
Cover design by Elizabeth Turner Stokes
Cover art by Shutterstock/Oleksandr Lysenko and
Shutterstock/WeddingVideoThailand,
Interior design by Toni Kerr

Print ISBN 978-1-64937-094-5
ebook ISBN 978-1-64937-114-0

Manufactured in the United States of America

First Edition November 2021

AMARA

The
WEDDING
CRASHER
and the
COWBOY

ROBIN

USA TODAY BESTSELLING AUTHOR

BIELMAN

CHAPTER ONE

Five days until the wedding

Rookie mistake number two for crashing a wedding: allowing an official guest to take her picture.

Too late, Kennedy realized, she'd just handed over evidence of her presence. With a thumbs-up and an overly wide smile to boot, because why not really stick out among the more calm and cool attendees?

Mistake number one: losing track of her coconspirator.

Her best friend handled mischief much better than she did. He blended in to any situation with confidence and ease. Case in point: there he stood across the beautifully decorated outdoor welcome brunch talking to the man of honor without a care in the world. Andrew did incognito like Tom Brady threw a football—effortlessly. She, on the other hand, lingered at the periphery of the event, awkwardly trying to appear casual and hoping to get the groom alone for an urgent conversation.

Much to her dismay, the groom and his bride-to-be hadn't arrived yet. At least fifty other people mingled around the "backyard" of the three-story inn, talking, laughing, and filling their plates with food. (There was a doughnut cake! Of course there was. The groom loved glazed doughnuts. As did she.) The inn and ranch stood on acres of land, and a tall decorative fence surrounded this particular grassy area. *To keep the ranch's animals at bay,* she'd overheard someone say.

She smiled to herself. She'd accidentally met one of those animals yesterday.

White tables and chairs, ocean-blue umbrellas, flower arrangements inside mason jars, and small shrubs in burlap bags tied with white silk ribbons painted a beautiful picture personifying the *sea meets the trees* image that made this particular Northern California ranch unique. The bride loved the ocean and the groom loved the forest and mountains, and they'd found the perfect destination to offer both. This morning, a cloudless sky kept Kennedy's sunglasses on her face, while a slight breeze carried the scent of salty air and pine and kept the summer day at a comfortable temperature.

She walked along the fence line toward the mimosa bar. A drink ought to help her blend in—standing by herself like a fish out of water was no way to get in the wedding spirit. She poured equal parts orange juice and champagne into a glass flute and added a splash of pineapple juice.

"Cheers," an older woman beside her said.

"Cheers," Kennedy answered, clinking glasses and blowing out a small sigh of relief. *That went well.*

Drink in hand, she found a quiet spot to stand beside the fence with a clear view of the deck and steps that led down to the first of many pre-wedding gatherings. From this position, she'd for sure see the groom's arrival. Hopefully sooner rather than later, because she was positive she had "wedding crasher" written all over her face.

"Caught you."

Ugh. That deep, masculine voice belonged to her least

favorite person and startled her into choking down her sip of citrus bubbly.

She turned around to find Maverick on the other side of the fence, a cowboy hat on his head, his blue eyes pinned to her with a sparkle that annoyed as much as it galvanized.

"Not too hard to do," she told him, "since I'm not trying to hide." Not *really*.

He stood above the top of the fence and looked down at her with a mix of interest and displeasure. "Then what *are* you doing?" he asked.

The gentle wind carried his scent to her nose, and the combo of man and soap upped his rugged appearance beyond fairness. She twitched her nose to try to get rid of it.

"Brunching, obviously. What are *you* doing?" He couldn't see her eyes through her sunglasses, but they were narrowed at him anyway.

He chuckled.

"What's so funny?"

"I like your shades, but you get a little crease in your forehead when you frown at me."

She instantly relaxed her face. "It's such a common occurrence, of course you'd notice."

"I'm pretty sure I should be the one giving *you* a dirty look." He took quick stock of the event behind her. "Given you haven't been invited to this wedding."

"Shh!" At his raised eyebrows, she reluctantly added, "Please."

So began a staring contest, just like they used to do in college when they'd each stand their ground, unwilling to see the other's point of view. Only this time, Maverick held all the power. Damn him.

A bell tinkled. Someone declared, "They're here!" And a ripple of excitement stole over the celebration.

Kennedy spun around to watch the engaged couple join their family and friends. The bride-to-be wore a shimmery aquamarine shift dress while the groom-to-be wore a Stetson with his khaki pants and collared shirt. *Huh*. She had no idea he had a bit of cowboy in him. Glancing over her shoulder at Maverick, she could admit that he wore the hat a hundred times better. Not that she *liked* it or anything.

"Remember what I said, Shortcake." His tone, while friendly, brokered no compromise.

Grr.

If Maverick called her that one more time, she'd put cow dung in his boots. Or itching powder in his boxer briefs. (Not that she knew what he wore under his Wranglers.) Or better yet, beat him at his own game. Cause *him* a little bit of trouble.

Guests tapped their forks and spoons to their glassware and chanted, "Kiss, kiss…"

The smiling couple obliged, the groom dipping his bride for a dramatic lip-lock. Family and friends cheered and whistled. Kennedy stayed quiet. The kiss ended with Reed plopping his cowboy hat on his future wife's head. Then, from across the bright green lawn, his gaze collided with hers.

He shook his head. Not enough to draw attention, but enough to say, *Not now*. She tried to use telepathic communication to ask, *When?* But his focus turned to someone else.

"They look happy to me," Maverick said from over her shoulder.

"Oh, are you still here?" She twisted back around. Big mistake. He'd folded his arms on top of the fence, his tanned, sinewy forearms on display in a relaxed pose. His easygoing composure did not help her novice wedding-crashing skills.

"I'm here all week," he reminded her, a lilt to his voice indicating he had the leg up on their little cat-and-mouse game.

She might be on his ranch, but she never gave up on a goal she set for herself. Kennedy looked beyond his wide shoulders toward the mountains and reminded herself of the rules of wedding crashing that she and Andrew had discussed this morning:

1. Act the part. Not much of a stretch, since she did honestly know the groom. So she lacked an actual, physical invitation. At five feet nothing, it wasn't like she took up much room.

2. Hang with the crowd. Okay, she needed more practice at that. Standing at the fence line with Maverick might look suspicious.

3. Have a backstory ready. Andrew was playing the part of her boyfriend and they'd faked it before, so it should be easy as long as he stuck to the plan. Plus, she and Reed *were* doctor friends and had plenty of history.

4. Pay attention to the staff and security. Maverick could be considered both, since ownership meant wearing many different hats. He knew she didn't belong here, but he didn't know the profound impact she might have on the event. And best to keep it that way. Which made her feel awful, but necessity trumped honesty in this situation.

"You're thinking really hard over there." Maverick's

voice brought her focus back to him. "Don't hurt yourself," he teased.

She smiled up at him. "Worried?"

"Hardly."

"I should get back to my party."

"Or I could call the police and have you arrested for trespassing."

She huffed out a breath. "You wouldn't dare."

He lifted his arms off the fence and tipped his cowboy hat in a show of brawn and authority. "You know the deal, Shortcake. No funny business." With that, he turned and walked away, leaving her to fume.

How had she landed herself in this much hot water so darn soon?

CHAPTER TWO

Two days earlier…

The man on the computer screen had salt-and-pepper hair and Paul Newman eyes. And for the past fifteen minutes, he'd made Kennedy Martin's palms sweat. "Why emergency room medicine?" he asked.

Finally. A question she had a quick and easy answer for. Make that two answers.

She ran her hands along the bottom of her crisp white collared shirt. It was the only material available, since she wasn't wearing any pants. (Comfort was key with big interviews and, since she was visible only from the chest up, she'd opted out of clothing her lower body. Not her best decision, however, given her sweaty palms.)

"The first reason is there's never a dull moment. A man once came in to the emergency room via ambulance with burns on his lower extremities. His tennis shoes were charred and the bottoms of his jeans were burned away, but thankfully his skin wasn't too bad. He'd been in his backyard using a propane weed burner and things got out of control. I smelled alcohol on his breath and asked him if he'd been drinking, and he said, 'Nooo, ma'am.' I was practically tipsy just from standing next to him, so I looked him straight in the eye and as professionally as possible said, 'Sir, you are a liar, liar, pants on fire.' The paramedics standing beside me cracked up, and the man was so drunk, he did, too."

Dr. Weaver, chief physician at the most respected hospital in Boston, laughed. *Excellent.*

She wanted this job more than anything. Needed it. A new start, a different big city. She'd miss Los Angeles, but an opportunity like this didn't come along very often.

"A sense of humor is always good," he said.

"The second reason is more personal. When I was fourteen, an emergency room doctor saved my life. Long story short, scar tissue from a surgery I had as a newborn broke off and triggered a bowel obstruction. No one could figure out why I was in pain, since things seemed generally fine. Until they weren't, and I went into sudden heart failure. An ER resident discovered I was crashing and alerted the attending minutes before I would have passed out. They rushed me into surgery just in time to save me.

"I was really scared, and the ER doctor in particular made me feel like everything was going to be okay. When there was a complication after the surgery"—Kennedy closed her eyes for a moment and took a breath—"I remember picturing Dr. Hawkins's overconfident expression and hearing him say I was strong and had my whole life ahead of me, and that made me fight to survive. Once I recovered, I knew I wanted to give that same hope and assurance to people facing medical emergencies."

Dr. Weaver nodded from behind his desk. He jotted something down on a notepad before glancing at the thick black watch on his wrist. "Having been through something like that definitely gives you a special perspective."

"It does."

"Where do you see yourself in five years?"

"Running an emergency room," she said without hesitation. She almost said "running *your* emergency room" but didn't want to be presumptuous.

"Is that all?"

She took a second to study him. Was he asking about her personal life? Was he a family man, a proponent of a strong work-life balance? "I'd like to get married and have kids, but there's no guarantee on love." She pressed down on her knee to stop it from bouncing. After what happened with her ex, the mere mention of the L-word still made her twitchy.

He gave a brief nod—in commiseration or dismissal, she wasn't sure—and she hoped she hadn't given the wrong answer. "It was a pleasure speaking with you, Miss Martin. I'll be in touch within a week if we'd like you to fly out for a final interview."

"Thank you very much for your time and consideration, Dr. Weaver. I sincerely appreciate it and hope to hear from you."

"Take care," he said and ended the video chat.

Kennedy closed her laptop and relaxed in her chair, relieved to be done with her second interview. If she got that third, in-person invitation, she'd be another step closer to her dream job. She played their conversation over and over again in her mind as she stared out her bedroom window. A lone cloud in the August sky shaped like an anchor gave her hope. She wasn't about to sink. Not yet anyway.

"Ned!" Ava called out, arriving inside Kennedy's room like a tornado and flopping down on the bed. "I can't take it anymore!"

Kennedy stood and dropped next to her younger sister on the white comforter. They lay shoulder to shoulder on the queen-size bed, being close their preferred position. "*It being...?*"

"Homework! *Duh*. I hate summer school. Why did I think this was a good idea?"

"You didn't. Mom and Dad did."

"Oh, right. The broken parental unit who decided to band together and force their youngest daughter to take classes *so I graduate on time*."

Kennedy thought about the extensive med school loans she'd be paying off for the next gazillion years. "It might suck now, but you'll be glad later."

"I need you to save me." Ava rolled onto her side, propping her head in her hand. "Can we get pad thai and watch a movie?"

The number of times Kennedy had *saved* her sister were too many to count, but that was okay. Saving people—literally and figuratively—kept her heart and head in a happy place.

"Sounds good."

"Yay! Thank you. Want to go pick it up now? I missed lunch." Ava glanced down Kennedy's body, her brows knitting in confusion. "Did you just do an interview without any pants on? Oh my God, you're my hero. That is totally badass and awesome."

"That's me, an awesome badass."

"And how rude of me not to ask how it went."

"No worries, and I think it went well."

Ava jumped to her feet. "That's great! Can I borrow your black baby tee I love so much?" She didn't wait for an answer, instead ransacking the top drawer of Kennedy's dresser like a dog looking for a bone.

"What's wrong with yours?" she asked, scooting to the foot of the bed. Ava had the same ruffle-edged tee in white.

"It's in the laundry. Found it!" Ava waved the shirt in the air and turned around. "Thank you. I'll be ready in ten."

Kennedy smiled as she watched her sister skip out of the room. Why Ava needed to wear that shirt to walk down the block to pick up food to bring back to their apartment, Kennedy didn't know.

She swapped her interview blouse for a soft crew neck T-shirt, then pulled on a pair of drawstring linen pants. And because she always liked to add a few inches to her slight, five-foot stature, she slipped her feet into her favorite black strappy four-inch sandals. Being taller gave her an extra boost of confidence. People always thought she was years younger than she actually was, which, in medicine, didn't really do her any favors.

"I'm ready! You ready?" she called out from the living room a few minutes later.

Glancing around the room, Kennedy saw Ava had textbooks and college-ruled notebooks strewn all over the coffee table and couch. Despite her protests, her sister loved school and really wasn't that sad to be taking up some of her summer before her senior year at UCLA on women's studies and global healthcare.

"Ready!" Ava flounced into the room with a giant grin. She looked adorable in a pair of beige capri pants and the ruffled tee. Her hair, a shade darker than Kennedy's blond, hung in waves around her shoulders.

They linked arms and left their apartment.

"I don't know what I'd do without you, Ned. Thanks for letting me move in with you this year and for taking such good care of me."

"I'm happy to, but you know…"

"I know. If you get the job in Boston, I'll be without you. Which, for the record, will suck immensely, but I hope you get the position anyway."

"Thanks, kiddo."

"Please do not call me that while we're out. It's bad enough I still get carded for R-rated movies."

"*I* still get carded for R-rated movies," Kennedy admitted.

"The curse of Martin genetics. Speaking of, have you talked to Mom or Dad lately?"

"No. Dad was away on business and I haven't connected with him since he's been back, and Mom is busy with wedding planning."

Ava squeezed her arm. "Wow. I think that's the first time you've mentioned the wedding so nonchalantly."

"I guess enough time has passed that I'm not as affected as I used to be." The wedding being their middle sister Victoria's.

"That's good."

"Very good. Now, let's talk only about happy things for the rest of the night. Deal?" Only the two of them—thick as thieves since they were young—thought their sister's upcoming wedding lacked a happy occasion vibe. Although, given the circumstances, Kennedy was sure a poll of strangers would agree she had every right to be upset.

"Deal."

They had a great time eating pad thai on the couch and

watching *27 Dresses* for the umpteenth time. Afterward, they talked and giggled about everything and nothing until they repeatedly caught yawns from each other.

"Good night," Kennedy said, heading to her bedroom.

"Sleep tight," Ava said, walking to hers.

"Don't let the bed bugs bite," they said in unison.

Kennedy washed her face, brushed her teeth, and slipped on her comfiest nightgown. Crawling under the cool covers, she gave silent thanks for Ava. They might be eight years apart in age, but they always looked out for each other.

Right in the middle of a fantastic dream starring Anthony Mackie—who was just about to unzip his Captain America uniform—a phone rang. It took her a fuzzy second to recognize it wasn't dreamy Anthony's phone but one actually near her ear. She sighed and reached for her cell on the nightstand with one eye half open to see the screen. *Reed.*

She closed her eye and rolled over. She and her exboyfriend had remained good friends over the years, but that didn't mean he could wake her at 1:07 in the morning. They definitely didn't have *that* kind of a relationship anymore.

The phone slipped from her fingers as she tucked her hands under her pillow and hoped she would fall back asleep.

After a moment of wonderful silence, the phone rang again.

Because there was always the weird chance her best friend or someone in her family had an emergency at the exact same time she'd been woken by another call, she looked at the phone. Still her ex. Maybe *he* had an emergency?

She bolted up, phone to her ear. "Hello?"

"Ken-*ned*-eee," Reed greeted-slash-slurred.

She slouched, elbows on her thighs. Not a crisis, just a drunk dial.

"Hi, Reed. How are you?" The last time they'd talked rather than texted had been three weeks ago. His engagement to Elle, a woman she'd seen pictures of but never met, had reshaped their close relationship. As happened with major life changes.

"I dunno," he said.

Hmm. Not exactly the answer she wanted to hear. "Where are you?" Music and voices blared in the background, suggesting a bar.

"Bash-ler party."

"*Your* bachelor party?"

"Uh-huh."

"Okay, go find your brother and tell him it's time to go home."

"Not at home. In a wind song."

What? "Reed, where are you?" He must mean Windsong, the small town where he was getting married. His entire family was flying in from Baltimore for the big day. The background noise ceased, followed by the sound of… running water?

Reed sighed in contentment. Oh no. He did not take her into the bathroom with him. "Ew, Reed!"

"Sorry," he said, at least having the decency to sound contrite. "For a lot of things."

She had no idea what that meant. They were good.

They'd dated forever ago and come out as far better friends than lovers. "Okay…" If he needed someone to just listen, though, she could do that.

She put the phone on speaker, gathered her hair to tie in a knot on top of her head, and closed her eyes.

"Wedding's in seven days?" he said. It sounded like a question, even though she knew it wasn't. Saturday, August fourteenth, in the evening, a weeklong destination wedding on a ranch up north. That's what Reed had told her, along with apologies for not inviting her because 1) they were keeping it fairly small, and 2) his fiancée wasn't all that comfortable with it. Kennedy was bummed she wouldn't get to share in his special day but hadn't let on. Her sister's upcoming wedding supplied more than enough drama.

"Yes," Kennedy said, covering a yawn with her hand.

"Not sure it's a good idea," he said softly.

"What are you talking about?"

"I don't want to get *mare-eed*."

Kennedy brought the phone back to her ear. "You don't want to get married?" she asked gently. She didn't know Elle, but Reed had only great things to say about her. "Did something happen between you two?"

"It's too late," he slurred.

No. No. No. It wasn't too late. But… "It's normal to feel nervous, you know. Are your feet cold?" she joked, hoping he'd laugh and tell her that's all this was.

The sounds of a busy bar punctured their silence before a guy said, "Dude, get back out here. We can't celebrate without the man of the hour."

"Wish you were here," Reed said.

"Is that Elle again?" the guy asked. "Tell her I've got you, bro."

"One sec," Reed said, and Kennedy pictured him holding up his finger. The background noise ceased, the only sound a deep breath from her friend. "I gotta go. Sorry to bother you."

"You didn't bother me. Reed—"

"S'okay. Forget I called."

"But Reed—"

He disconnected, leaving her with unanswered questions that made her heart pound and her mind race with worry. She called him right back. He didn't pick up. She tried again. No luck.

An uneasy knot lodged in her stomach. Did Reed have cold feet or was it something more? In med school he'd dated a lot, gaining a reputation as fickle, so when he got engaged, Kennedy knew Elle had to be special. They'd been together less than a year—had his feelings suddenly changed so drastically that he didn't want to get married at all now?

She lay back and stared up at the ceiling. Reed was one of the few people she could count on for anything and who she'd drop everything for in return. Spending four years of medical school and three years of residency together, they had each other's backs. Blinking repeatedly, she recalled the time he'd saved her from an addict who pulled a knife on her in the ER. Reed's arm took the brunt of the weapon and required stitches to repair.

Then there were her mom and dad. They'd divorced during her teenage years, and the repercussions had been painful. Still were, since her parents barely tolerated each other. While there were never any guarantees in marriage, she hated the idea of divorce possibly happening to Reed. His parents had been happily married forever, so he had no idea what divorce did to a person, let alone a family.

Which meant if he had doubts about marrying Elle, she owed it to him to talk this through before it was too late. She could help him see he *had* found the woman of his dreams. The glaze to his doughnut.

Wish you were here.

Lucky for him, she could make that happen.

CHAPTER THREE

Six days until the wedding

Maverick Owens hefted another bale of hay off the back of his pickup. The stack inside the barn tilted slightly to the right, enough so that Magnolia poked her head through her stall and touched her nose to the golden straw. She did it to nudge the stack back into alignment. Swear to God, his horse was a genius.

She had a treat coming her way in thanks.

He continued to unload and, when he got to the last bale, that's when his younger brother Hunter showed up. Some might say that meant his brother was also a genius. Maverick liked to call him lots of other names instead— troublemaker, nuisance, mini-me. Completely out of love, mind you.

"Need any help?" Hunter asked.

Maverick didn't bother answering. Instead he gave him a look that said, *What do you think, dumbass?*

Hunter let the look roll off his shoulders as usual, and seated himself on the edge of the open tailgate. Great. He wanted to talk. "You should have come out with us last night. Guess who was at Sutter's?"

This time of year, with tourists and college kids home from school, the local bar in town packed in more than the usual crowd. Maverick leaned against the tailgate. Lifted his hat and wiped the sweat off his forehead with the back of his hand.

"Who?" he asked, even though he already knew the answer. His brother was about as transparent as the side of a barn.

"Callie." Cue the floating hearts above Hunter's head. He'd had a crush on their sister's best friend for as long as Maverick could remember.

"Did you talk to her?"

"No."

Maverick hated hearing the sound of defeat in his brother's voice. Plain old love was hard enough, but unrequited love sucked a hundred times worse.

"But," he said, his tone leveling up to its normal buoyancy, "there was a bridesmaid there who decided I was the guy."

"The guy?"

"To show her around when there weren't any wedding obligations. She's from back east and this is her first time in California."

"The wedding at the ranch this week?" Maverick's family owned and operated The Owens House Inn and Guest Ranch in the small town of Windsong, California. They ran the property with the help of a dozen or so part-time staff, and in the past few years, weddings had become a popular event, most notably in December, but other months were booking up as well.

"None other."

"Bad idea, Hunt."

"Why is that? You jealous I've got the attention of a beautiful woman and you don't?" This ridiculous question was accompanied by a smirk.

"It's best not to break any guests' hearts."

"I'm not going to do anything to upset her."

"Not on purpose." Hunter was one of the best people Maverick knew, kinship aside, but the guy didn't know the power he wielded over unsuspecting females. "Plus, you're going to be busy with extra work this week."

"I can multitask."

"All right. Have fun, then."

"Plan to." He slipped down from the tailgate. "I do wish you'd join us out sometime. The hermit thing is getting old."

Maverick nodded. He appreciated that his brother and friends wanted his company, but he preferred to spend time by himself on the couch with his dog or in the pasture with his horse. He ventured to town plenty on his own when it suited him.

"I'll see you later." Hunt waved over his shoulder on his way toward the main house for lunch, no doubt. A glance up at the sun told Maverick it had to be around noon. That meant a full meal waited for them in the kitchen.

He walked back into the barn, postponing food for now. Grabbing a carrot, he nuzzled up to Magnolia. "Think I can get away with laying extra low this week?" he asked her.

Magnolia made a noise of agreement as she chomped on the vegetable.

"Thanks for the support. I'll count on you to keep me busy and hidden—how's that? I don't think there're any scheduled lessons or horseback rides, so it's just you and me."

Another short, sweet *neigh*.

"That's my girl." He rubbed down her mane, camaraderie invading his body. Leave him alone with his horse, and Maverick felt at peace. Something he'd struggled with for the past three years.

He spent the next half hour checking on the three other horses they stabled, then looking in on the rest of the ranch's menagerie. Their family of animals was small but mighty. Just one look at George, their smart-as-a-whip mule who half the time thought he was a dog, had visitors at the ranch gushing and enjoying themselves, whether they were animal lovers or not.

"Hey, George." Not two seconds later, the mule stood all up in Maverick's personal space, stepping on Mav's toes—literally—nibbling on his arm in affection, and demanding ear scratches. George had absolutely no boundaries when it came to physical contact, which five times out of ten delighted people.

"You keeping an eye on Barley for me?"

George nodded. Seriously. And admittedly, the animal had a yes answer for every question, but the gesture still went a long way to bringing smiles to people's faces.

Maverick canted his head to look around George. His sweet Barley lay in her usual spot in the sun, sleeping. The golden-shepherd mix was due to give birth in the next week, and everyone looked forward to having puppies on the ranch again.

The timing wasn't exactly perfect for Mav, since he had a plane to catch in two weeks, but they'd be loved enough without him there. He gave George one last pat, then stepped around him to take a seat on the ground next to Barley, legs straight out in front of him.

If things had gone according to plan, Maverick would have a veterinary practice right about now. Most days he didn't let the thought bother him, but seeing the dog he'd rescued on the side of the road, then nursed back to health, and knowing what anniversary loomed next week, he couldn't help but let a moment of melancholy creep into his head.

Sensing his presence, Barley shifted and laid her head on his thigh. He gently petted her, her soft fur running through his fingers. "How you feeling, girl?" Her body temperature this morning registered normal, and she'd had no loss of appetite when fed, both signs labor hadn't started yet. "We've got a pool going, you know. Date of birth and number of puppies." He resisted the urge to palpate her tummy for a count. Chances were he'd miss one or two anyway and not know for sure until the little wigglers started coming out. "I'm down for five puppies on the tenth. Think you could make that happen? The stakes are high."

Winner received a homemade pie from Baked on Main. And considering Maverick was leaving town for at least two months, he *really* wanted that pie.

Not that it was the best pie in town. No one baked better than his mom.

He should tell her that.

Maybe he would.

Probably he wouldn't. Compliments from him made her tear up. Especially lately, since she knew he might not be back on the ranch for longer than those eight weeks.

He pulled down his cowboy hat to better shield his face from the warm sun, let out a deep breath, dipped his chin, and closed his eyes. He dreamed about what he always did when he felt especially wistful: a deep green meadow, long blades of grass beneath his feet, and the beautiful, extraordinary woman who laughed when she put her toes in the cold creek, and who had loved him until her last breath.

CHAPTER FOUR

Six days until the wedding

"Wake up, sleepyhead. We're here."

Kennedy opened her eyes in time to see a sign on the side of the road that read Windsong: Population 9230.

"I'm not sleeping. Just resting my eyes," she clarified, staring out the passenger-side window. Rolling green hills dense with trees reminded her she wasn't in the City of Angels anymore but on a mission—Operation Talk-To-Reed-Before-It's-Too-Late. She'd tried again and again to reach him before hatching this out-there plan, but he still wasn't answering any of her phone calls or texts.

"Sorry, Charlie, but the snoring gave you away," her best friend, Andrew, said.

She rolled her head to the side to look at him in the driver's seat. "I do not snore."

"That's what everyone who snores says." He took his eyes off the road to flash her the smile that had earned him his first toothpaste commercial. Then, returning his attention to the road, he made a very loud, very objectionable snorty-grunty sound.

"Shut up! I do not sound like that." *Hopefully*.

Friends since she saved him from choking on a hot dog in high school, they both knew his teasing was nothing new. They'd road-tripped numerous times over the years and he always drove so he didn't get carsick. Which left Kennedy to passenger, and okay, occasionally sleep a little. Not that she'd just been sleeping. *Or* snoring.

She sat up taller as he slowed to drive through the quaint town of Windsong. Charming shops and restaurants lined both sides of the street. Massive oak trees stretched above rooflines, their branches grazing blue-striped awnings. Late-afternoon summer sunlight glistened off store windows. A line of people stood outside a shop called Baked on Main.

"Cute town," she said. "Thanks again for coming with me."

"No way was I missing this. You know I have a crush on the man."

Kennedy laughed. Andrew had been way more upset than she was when she and Reed had broken up. "I hope I'm not making a mistake coming here, but I need one heartfelt conversation with him to make sure he's okay."

"We'll make it happen." Andrew made a right turn, leaving Main Street, then a quick left. Less than a minute later, a gorgeous three-story building with wraparound porches and white columns came into view. The deep blue Pacific Ocean added color in the distance. Hanging ferns and the American flag decorated the B&B, as did a traditional sign in the shape of a pine tree with the words, The Owens House Inn & Guest Ranch.

Andrew parked the car in a designated spot for check-in. Gazing out the windshield, he said, "I think one night here is just what the doctor ordered."

She shook her head. Like she hadn't heard his "just what the doctor ordered" cliché a hundred times before. She quickly slid out of the car, more than ready to stretch her legs after the six-hour drive from home. The first thing to hit her was the quiet. The peacefulness. She took a deep breath, the scents of mountains, the ocean, and flowers all filling her nose.

One night away, even on a ranch, *would* be good for her soul. Provide a nice distraction from thinking about the job in Boston.

Andrew came to stand beside her. "Okay, so our cover is we're boyfriend and girlfriend here for a night to celebrate our one-year anniversary. You've never been to a ranch, so I surprised you."

She was pretty sure she was allergic to ranches, being that the one time she'd visited a farm, she couldn't stop sneezing. (It *may* have been a cold, but either way, she'd felt miserable.) But here they were to help Reed if he needed it.

"Let's hope we don't have to fool anyone before I find Reed. You know I'm a terrible actor," she said.

"But you're excellent at small talk and putting people at ease. You did it every day in the ER with your patients and their families."

"I guess," she said, her heart squeezing at his use of the past tense. She'd finished her residency two weeks ago and said goodbye to the hospital she'd originally planned to work for. No way could she accept their job offer when her ex-boyfriend slash future brother-in-law worked there. *Please,* please *let me get the job in Boston.*

"And you'll do it again somewhere bigger and better." He gave her a quick side hug, which she gratefully reciprocated. Andrew always knew just what to say.

"Thanks." They walked toward the inn. As they got

closer to the curved staircase, boisterous voices punctured the quiet.

"Someone's having a good time," Andrew said just before a group of people spilled out the glass front door. At the sight of Reed with Elle on his arm, Kennedy stopped mid-step. Maybe if she didn't move, no one would notice her.

Too late. Reed's eyes widened in…surprise? Horror? She couldn't decide.

"I'll catch up with you guys in a minute," he said, gently extricating himself from the group. He marched toward her and Andrew, meeting them in the middle of the staircase. "Kennedy?"

"Hi, Reed."

"What are you doing here?"

"Making sure you're okay. After your phone call last night—"

"I was drunk."

"Is what you said true, though? You don't—"

"Reed?" Elle stood at the top of the stairs, her brows furrowed. Her gaze jumped from Reed to her to Andrew and back to Reed.

"Stay in town," Reed whispered to Kennedy before turning and bounding up the stairs to his fiancée. "Hey, sorry about that." He took Elle's hand and led her away.

Kennedy let those words sink in. Her friend *did* need her.

"I'll go check us in," Andrew said.

While he did that, she took a deep breath and let her gaze wander. Lost in concern for Reed and why he wanted her to stay, she found herself walking down the stairs and across a large expanse of grass, her four-inch heels sinking every so often in the soft ground. Straight ahead stood a brightly colored rose garden with a pond and small, white-painted bridge. Beyond it, a large barn with a brown patina roof. To her left and right were dirt walkways lined with ginormous trees.

"George! Get back here!" someone shouted.

An adorable someone about three feet tall, wearing a T-shirt with a Disney princess on it, shorts, and bright yellow rain boots, was chasing a miniature horse. Or maybe it was a donkey. Whatever the animal was, it definitely did *not* want to be caught.

"Don't be afraid," the young girl shouted, just as George stopped about an inch from Kennedy.

Kennedy didn't move a muscle. She didn't blink. Or breathe. She'd faced cardiac arrests, severed limbs, gunshot wounds, drug overdoses, and baby deliveries without so much as flinching, but this seemingly harmless animal had her at a loss.

She had no idea what to do. Except freeze, apparently.

Just as the little girl reached them, George took off. "Sorry, lady!" the child said, taking off, too.

Kennedy watched them run across the bridge, their game of chase one they'd obviously played before. The tension in her shoulders lessened. Jeez. It's not like the animal had wanted to take a bite out of her.

There should be a P.S. on the inn's sign: *Beware of wildlife.*

Turning to walk back toward the inn, she bumped—*oomph*—right into a man. She teetered, her heels stuck in the grass so she couldn't take a step back, arms flailing to catch her balance. Mr. Brick Wall placed his hands on her shoulders to steady her.

Then *he* stepped back, blocking the sun with his height. He stood well over six feet, considering she found herself eye level with his broad chest.

"Sorry," she said, tilting her head to look up at his face. "I didn't hear or see you."

He lifted an eyebrow and stared down at her with an unreadable expression on his face. She almost fell flat on her butt. *No, no, no.* It couldn't be. "Maverick?"

"Hello, Shortcake."

She ground her teeth together at the nickname he'd tortured her with in college. "Please tell me this isn't your family's ranch."

He smirked down at her as he crossed his arms. "When have I ever lied to you?"

Great. Not only was she crashing her ex's wedding, but she was on *his* property. Maverick Owens. The bane of her small, private undergrad existence.

He'd played the part of Captain Obnoxious annoyingly well while they tried to best each other—always jockeying for the number one and number two spots—whenever they were in the same premed class, or even in the same vicinity. One of their favorite games was who got to the campus coffee shop first and snagged the leather armchair by the window. She couldn't put her finger on exactly what had started their animosity toward each other, but his constant teasing about her small size contributed. She was a *doctor*, for goodness' sake, not a *shortcake*.

"It's been seven years—maybe you've changed."

He remained stoically quiet, telling her nothing yet

everything. He hadn't changed.

She tried to casually dislodge her heels from the cement-like ground so she could be on her way, but no go. Instead, her subtlety heightened Maverick's attention. He glanced down her body, taking in what felt like every inch of her.

"Problem?" he asked, a playful glint in his eye.

"No." She ran her hands down her white linen pants.

"You sure? Looks like you might be stuck."

"I'm fine. Don't you have somewhere else to be?"

His eyes moved over her head for a second before returning to hers. "Looks like Jenna and George made it to the barn."

"Jenna?" Did he have a daughter?

"My niece."

"And George is a...?"

One corner of his mouth quirked up ever so slightly. "Mule."

She nodded like *I knew that* and was only making polite conversation. Which must be some sort of maturity side effect, since they had rarely been nice to each other in college. From the second they'd met, they'd rubbed each other the wrong way and made sport of it rather than try to be friends.

There's a fine line between love and hate, Andrew always said.

Whatever. She knew which side of it she was on.

Since Maverick stood there staring at her, she stared back. Light blue jeans, black cotton T-shirt stretched by wide shoulders, scuffed cowboy boots. His light brown hair curled around his ears and was creased along the sides of his head like he'd recently taken off a hat. Unfortunately, the past several years had made him even more handsome. Not that she'd ever dwelled on his looks. Anyone would appreciate his appearance. Objectively.

"What brings you here?" he asked, his tone toeing the line between cordial and unsociable. Nothing new there, either.

"An overnight stay."

His brows pinched. "Voluntarily?"

"What is that supposed to mean?"

He scratched the back of his neck. "You hate the countryside."

That he remembered this fact rattled her. "Well, for your information, *I* have evolved, and my boyfriend surprised me with a night away for our anniversary." Huh, maybe she *could* act her way through this, considering that lie had rolled off her tongue easier than she thought it would.

Right on cue, Andrew appeared at her side. He slid off his sunglasses and hung them on the V-neck of his shirt. "Hey, Maverick."

The tall, distractingly good-looking cowboy in front of her moved his gaze to her best friend.

"I believe you've met Andrew before," Kennedy said.

Maverick put out his hand. "I have. Hey, Andrew."

Andrew shook hands, holding on a little too long. Jeez Louise, could the guy keep it together please? "It's good to see you again," Andrew said.

"I didn't realize friends celebrated anniversaries."

"Oh, we're not just friends." Kennedy wrapped both arms around Andrew's muscled biceps and leaned into him.

"Really?" Was it just her or did Maverick sound like he didn't believe her? Andrew had the kind of outgoing, affable, and confident personality that made both men and women fall for him. It just so happened he preferred the former over the latter. She didn't think Maverick knew that, though.

"Really." Kennedy gave Maverick the stink eye before turning her head and softening for Andrew. "Is our room ready, honey? Since we're here for only a short time, I don't want to waste it standing in this one spot."

"Yeah, about that," Andrew said. "Can I talk to you for a minute?"

"Sure." Only when she tried to step away, her heel stayed stuck, so rather than put distance between herself and Maverick, Andrew simply canted his head and lowered his voice.

"What do you think about staying for the week? We're both free and already here."

Reed's plea floated through her mind. *Stay in town.*

"Is there a room available for that long?" she asked.

"Funny thing happened when I got to the reception desk. The man in front of me checking in was the brother of the bride and the man of honor, and we started talking and then in a stroke of luck, the person who reserved our room starting tomorrow called this morning to cancel, so the room is available for the next week. Friends and family on both sides of the wedding party are the only guests at the ranch right now. The woman at the reception desk said she'd be thrilled if we'd like to keep the room."

Stay.

The only way to stop a wedding was to be at the wedding.

"I know that wasn't the plan. But Liam—the man of honor—was really friendly, and there was something about him that made me hot all over. I haven't felt that since…"

Joaquin. Andrew's ex, and the reason Andrew had fun but kept himself guarded.

"It's up to you," Andrew said. "But this gives you more time to make sure Reed truly wants to get married."

She and Ava had watched *Wedding Crashers* at least half a dozen times. She could pretend to be Andrew's girlfriend *and* a second cousin or something, right?

Andrew raised his brows, and his expression said *pretty please*.

"There's something else, isn't there?" she asked.

"I don't know what you're talking about."

Yes, he did. He knew exactly what she meant. She knew him better than he knew himself. He might be in insta-love with the man of honor, but his eyes were sparkling like they did after one of his stage performances.

She thought back to the improvisational acting workshop he'd mentioned he missed last week. He clearly saw this situation as an opportunity—a chance to be someone else and hone his skills, and she couldn't fault him for that. Not when it was her fault he'd missed the workshop. He'd rescued her from a disastrous dinner with her sister where Victoria couldn't have cared less about hurting Kennedy's feelings, taking dig after dig.

"The man of honor is Elle's brother," she whispered. If she had a red flag, she'd be waving it. She didn't want to stir up any trouble or cause undue harm for the bride-to-be, no matter what Reed decided.

"I realize that," he said like it wasn't a problem.

For him, maybe. She mentally kicked herself for even thinking about staying the week. She could barely fake a stomachache. But she also never turned her back on a friend. "Okay, let's—"

"*Ahem.*"

Oh, crap. She'd forgotten about Maverick, standing there this whole time, and no doubt overhearing bits and pieces of their private conversation. "I don't suppose you tuned all that out, did you?" she asked him.

"Nope."

At his smug expression, she pressed her back straighter. Maverick Owens didn't think she had what it took to enjoy herself on a ranch, and she'd like nothing more than to prove him wrong. She'd have a heart-to-heart with Reed, root for her best friend and the MOH to have a good time together, *and* put this country boy in his place.

"Looks like you're stuck with me for the week now," she said, matching his stance by crossing her arms.

"Awesome," Andrew said from next to her. "I'll go finish checking in and then grab our bags from the car and put them in our room. We're in the main house, room number six. Meet you there in a few minutes." He kissed her cheek and took off, leaving her alone with the one man on the planet she'd hoped never to see again, let alone be stuck with on the same property.

"I should go, too," she said, more than ready to walk away.

"What's really going on?" Maverick asked, always so suspicious.

"What do you mean?"

"There's a far greater chance of Andrew and me

celebrating an anniversary than the two of you. You guys are like brother and sister."

He knew. Of course he knew.

The man was annoyingly smart and intuitive and paid attention to everything around him.

"It's none of your business," Kennedy said. Especially since she was crashing a wedding *and* possibly stopping it from happening.

"Not true. The ranch is my business."

"Okay, but I'm not. Just pretend you never saw me. It sounds like the ranch will be overrun with wedding guests this week, so you can focus on them." She would be—at least in the sense of blending in. She bet there were daily activities, each an opportunity to sneak in a conversation with Reed and/or gather intelligence on the engaged couple.

His chiseled jaw tensed. "You're really staying?"

"Yes."

He looked further dismayed.

"What?" She objected to his visible malaise and put her hands on her hips in case her tone of voice wasn't clear enough. What did her length of stay matter to him?

• • •

What indeed? Maverick Owens had planned to do what he always did when there were big events on the ranch: make himself as scarce as possible, keeping to the animals rather than the people. But five minutes in Kennedy Martin's surprising presence had him changing his mind. Suddenly, there was nothing he wanted more than to once again ruffle her pretty feathers. In college she'd proven a worthy adversary, their competitions some of his favorite days.

He didn't like feeling this way. Correction: he didn't *want* to feel this way. This urgent desire to have some fun with her, to pick up where they'd left off all those years ago. That her caramel-colored eyes sparkled with intelligence and defiance didn't help matters.

"Well?" she said, clearly impatient with his silence.

Which only made him want to stay quiet. She'd been a thorn in his side from the first day they'd met in Biology 101, always offering unsolicited advice and vying for the best grades. The only time she'd given him some peace and quiet was when he got a TA position over her. Yeah, she hadn't liked that.

The antagonism between the two of them became something of a spectator sport, classmates taking bets on the country boy versus the city girl. But now they were on *his* turf, not the urban collegiate environment she'd thrived in.

"Fine," she said, intruding on his memories. She struggled to lift one heel, then the other, from the confines of the damp grass, so he offered his arm for leverage before he could rethink it. She reluctantly wrapped her soft hand around his forearm and freed herself. Her touch warmed his skin.

"Fine?" When a woman said "fine" it meant anything but.

"That's right. It's clear we can't remain in the same space together, so like I said, pretend you never saw me." She took one step and almost sank back into the earth.

Impossible. He still saw her occasionally in his thoughts, even after all these years. "I hope you brought some appropriate footwear," he countered, falling in step beside her. He didn't want her to trip and dirty those nice white pants. *Yeah, you do*, the devil on his shoulder said.

"Don't worry about what I did or didn't bring with me."

"I give consideration to every guest who stays on this property." Technically, guest relations fell to his older brother Cole and sister-in-law Bethany, but Kennedy didn't need to know that.

"Isn't there a mule you need to see to?" she huffed out.

Eventually. Not while he had Kennedy exasperated. Which got him thinking further… "Jeans and cowboy boots don't seem like your style."

"You know nothing about my style."

He knew something. In college, Mondays were black pencil skirts and heels, like she had a corporate job to go to after class. Fridays were casual pants and heels. On the occasion he ran into her over the weekend, she'd wear a flowery dress and heels. Not that he ever took notice of those things…much.

"I know the wedding we have scheduled this week is the reason you're here."

"You don't *know* that."

"Okay, I suspect that's the reason, given what I overheard."

She stopped dead in her high-heeled tracks. Pushed her shoulders back like that might gift her a few inches in stature. Nice try, but nope. She still came eye level to his chest. "It's very rude to eavesdrop."

"Is it eavesdropping if I'm standing in clear view a few feet away?"

"What exactly did you overhear?"

"You know the groom and…" He studied her pretty face. "You're worried he's making a mistake."

Her lips parted in surprise, her head tilting a few degrees to the left. A couple of seconds of silence ticked by before she said, "Please disregard everything you heard."

Something in her tone had him heeding her dismissal instead. "I can't do that."

"You mean you won't."

He ran a hand through his hair. He didn't want any trouble, and he was certain he was looking at it. She hadn't been *invited* to the wedding, yet here she stood. She and Reed obviously had history. The kind of history to warrant questionable, albeit compassionate behavior. She cared about people, always had, but what were her motives here?

Maverick should just walk away. Take her suggestion and forget they'd ever crossed paths. The problem was, the ranch had a reputation to uphold. Weddings were a lucrative business, and his family prided themselves on top-notch service that delivered on the happily ever after.

Kennedy looked up at the trees, down at the blades of grass, past the inn toward the ocean. He wondered what she saw as she looked around. The ranch had been in his family for over one hundred years. Three generations of blood, sweat, and tears to make it a multi-award-winning inn in the heart of the "happiest seaside and mountain town in California."

The people who came revered the rural setting like they'd found a slice of heaven.

"I mean we can't afford to have any drama," he said.

She held his gaze with confidence. "You won't. I…"

"Promise?"

Contemplating her response before speaking again, she said, "Remember that time in college when we had a PowerPoint presentation for Professor Banks and I crashed your group because mine wasn't taking it seriously, and I promised to play nice?"

He nodded. He remembered everything about their interactions.

She smiled up at him. "This is like that." Meaning she'd *try* to abide by his rules.

"You do remember I watched you like a hawk."

Her face scrunched into a skeptical expression. "You did?"

"Of course I did. I didn't trust you for a second."

She waved away his opinion. "There's no reason not to trust me now. You keep doing your ranch thing, and Andrew and I will do the wedding thing."

"And never the two shall meet?"

"Exactly."

He did prefer to keep his distance. And it really wasn't any of his business how she knew Reed. But it all came back to the inn's professional standing. "There's one main problem with that."

"Which is?"

"The two are intertwined. I can look away, but if I catch you doing something unforgivable, we'll have a problem."

"You won't catch me," she said with a small grin.

Maverick inwardly groaned. His wedding crasher had just issued a challenge whether she realized it or not. One he found impossible to ignore.

Three years ago…

Dear Nicole,

At night I fall into bed and imagine you're still here with me. That if I just turn my head, I'll find you on the pillow next to mine, looking at me with love in your eyes before you drift off to sleep. It always amazed me how quickly you could fall asleep. Two seconds after your head hit the pillow, you'd be out.

I never told you this, but I'd often just watch you sleep, feeling so lucky to be the man in bed with you. I miss that so damn much.

It still doesn't seem real that you're gone. It's been a month and I've picked up my phone to text you every day. I keep expecting you to walk through the door with takeout. Yesterday, I swear I heard your voice in the kitchen, humming your favorite song while you made coffee. There's so much heaviness in my heart it's crushing, and I don't think it will ever go away.

Miss you like crazy,

Maverick

CHAPTER FIVE

Six days until the wedding

Kennedy fell onto one of the two queen-size beds in room number six. "That man is the worst," she complained to Andrew. "He thinks he knows everything, and okay, in this case, he knows we're crashing the wedding, but as long as we behave, he claims he won't say anything."

"What do you mean by 'behave'?" Andrew asked, lying on his bed, a guilty edge to his voice.

She blew a strand of hair off her face. "Please tell me I don't have anything to worry about."

He turned to his side to face her. "You don't have anything to worry about."

"*Andrew.*"

"Okay, don't be mad, but I used my Australian accent when I met the man of honor and I might have told him I was Chris Hemsworth's stunt double."

"I knew it!" She threw one of the pillows on the bed at him. "I knew you'd decided to get into some character when you came back looking like you'd won an Academy Award."

"Sorry," he said sincerely. "The accent just came out so I went with it. And like I said, Liam made me feel something. This is the perfect opportunity to hone my improv skills and get over Joaquin at the same time."

"Where does this leave us with Maverick? If he hears

you using an accent…"

"He won't. I've got this. But speaking of Maverick, holy mother of cowboys, did he always look that good?"

She buried her face in the covers. "I don't want to talk about him," she mumbled.

"What?"

"Let's not talk about him," she voiced, rolling onto her back.

"Okay, let's talk about tonight, then. The wedding party is meeting at a bar in town called Sutter's, and I thought we could crash it."

"Andrew. You don't seem to understand the concept of talking to Reed in private. I don't want to upset him or his fiancée. We can't crash something like that."

"He and Elle won't be there. I heard Liam say they're having a romantic dinner alone, so we're free and clear. It's a good opportunity to get some intel on their relationship, though, don't you think?"

"I think you want to see Liam again."

"That too."

"I don't know." She laid her hand over her pounding heart. Once again, cool as a cucumber in an ER, but at a country inn where everyone suddenly knew everyone, she couldn't seem to keep her pulse in check.

"Come on, I've got your back. You know that."

"I know, and thank you." Her breathing slowed. "Do I have to use an Australian accent, too?"

"I haven't worked that bit out yet, but…maybe."

"Then there's no way I can go. I could milk a cow before I could speak with an accent."

"Look at you," he said with enthusiasm, "embracing this

ranch crashing like a champ."

She waved him off with an exasperated *pfftt*.

"You can do anything you set your mind to, you know that, but I understand. This is all on me."

"Not *all*. I did drag you here."

"Not even close. I'm happy to be here, and to help make things easier for you, I'll be your caffeine and doughnut dealer every morning."

"You're the best."

"I know." He grinned. "Do you mind if I go tonight?" His sweet tone combined with his puppy dog eyes made it impossible to say no. Not that she would anyway.

"Of course not. I want you to enjoy yourself."

He bounced off the bed. "You're the best, too. Love you." He kissed her cheek. "I'm going to take a shower and then head out."

At the sound of running water, Kennedy sat up to call Ava. "Hey," she said to her sister.

"Hi! Did you get there safe and sound?"

"We did. How was your day?"

"Good. I finished my term paper so *yay*!"

"Congrats. So, there's been a change in plans and Andrew and I are staying for the week." She went on to explain the situation.

Ava laughed. "Yesterday you did an interview without wearing pants, and today you're crashing a wedding. I'm a little worried about tomorrow."

In all honesty, so was she. "I'll keep you posted. In the meantime, would you mind feeding Mrs. White's fish? I told her I'd do it while she was visiting her grandson. Her key is on the hook in the kitchen. She said the food is next to the fishbowl and to drop in only two tiny flakes a day."

"No problem."

"Thanks. I'll call you tomorrow."

"Okay. Love you."

"Love you, too." Kennedy placed her phone on the nightstand, then walked to the single French door. The ground-level room, decorated in classic country blue and white, included antique furniture and plush rugs on the hardwood floor. She opened the door and stepped onto a private patio overlooking a garden. A woman in her early to mid-twenties with garden shears in her hands worked among the rose bushes.

"Hi!" the woman said.

"Hi." Kennedy gave a short wave. The small gate to her left stood open, so she ventured out for a closer look at the garden. Rows and rows of flowers formed a circle around a large three-tiered fountain. She took a deep breath in through her nose, enjoying the floral scent.

"It's beautiful here," Kennedy said to the woman.

"Thank you. I'm Nova Owens. It's nice to meet you." She dropped her shears and slipped off her heavy-duty gardening glove for a handshake.

"Nice to meet you, too." Kennedy knew nothing about Maverick's family, but this was obviously his sister, given the last name and startling blue eyes like her brother's. It seemed weird to think she'd spent four years at college with the man, and the only personal information she knew about him was that he came from a ranch in a small town. *Wait*. She also knew he loved animals. While they were both premed, he'd had plans to go to veterinary school. Had he done that?

"Are you here for the wedding?"

"Y-Yes." *Get a grip*. She *was* here for the wedding. Or at least the days leading up to the wedding.

"Well, I hope you enjoy your stay, and if there's anything I can do, please let me know. The garden is my specialty, but I'm good for suggesting places to see, restaurants to check out, and getting you acquainted with the ranch and all its offerings."

"I'll keep that in mind. Thanks."

Nova slipped her glove back on and took a step back. She immediately teetered, then hissed as if in pain. Kennedy looked down. Nova had stepped on the gardening shears with her bare foot, the long, sharp tip of the tool poking through the top of her foot at an angle. Nova fell onto her bottom and pulled her foot free before Kennedy could give a warning to wait. She winced in sympathy for Nova and glanced down at her high heels, feeling a ghost of sharpness in her foot. Most puncture wounds to that part of the body didn't cause much bleeding, but if an artery was nicked…

Blood spilled out of the gash as Nova wrapped her arms around herself. "Ow, ow, ow," she cried in pain.

Kennedy dropped to her knees. "Can I help?" she asked. "If you were going to do this in front of anyone, you picked the right person. I'm a doctor."

"Please," she said through a wince. Tears spilled down her cheeks. "I can't believe I did that. My mom is going to kill me. She's always telling me to put shoes on and I never listen."

"Can I have the bandanna in your hair?" Kennedy didn't wait for an answer. She quickly slipped it free from Nova's head. First things first; she had to stop the bleeding.

She tied the bandanna around Nova's foot and applied pressure. "I'm sorry if this is uncomfortable."

"It's okay." Clearly it wasn't, though, as Nova sucked in her bottom lip and the color drained from her face.

"If I can get the bleeding to stop, we'll take a look at it. If not, we're going to have to inspect it after we get you to the ER."

"The closest ER is thirty minutes away, but Dr. Choi can help. His office is in town."

"Okay, good." Kennedy glanced at the shears. They were dirty, slightly rusted. *Not good.* "Have you had a tetanus shot in the last few years?"

"I don't know. I don't think so, though." She brought up the knee on her injury-free leg and squeezed her arms around her shin.

"No worries. I'm sure Dr. Choi can give you one. Tell me about him." In Kennedy's experience, if she could keep a patient's mind off their injury, the easier it was to treat them.

"He's been the town's doctor since before I was born. He does it all, and everyone loves him. He's also going to yell at me for not wearing shoes so if it's possible to keep that part between us, I'd be grateful."

"I'll do the best I can."

"Everyone in town likes to be up in his business, too, so no doubt they'll all know about my stupidity if we head to his office."

"I wouldn't call it stupidity, not at all. Accidents happen. Besides, I think this is partly my fault. I distracted you and you put the shears down. If I hadn't done that, you'd still be pruning away." Blood soaked through the bandanna, the wetness reaching Kennedy's palm. The direct pressure seemed to be doing very little.

"Thanks," Nova said softly.

"Unfortunately, the bleeding isn't stopping, Nova. And with the brief glance I got, the wound looked deep. The shears aren't clean, either, and that combination can lead to infection, so we need to get you to the doctor's office where they've got the proper medical supplies. Think you can stand if I help?"

"What if Doc Choi came here?" She took off her gloves, then lifted her bottom and pulled a phone from the back pocket of her cutoff shorts. "Please? I really don't want to move."

Kennedy nodded, applied a bit more pressure.

Nova made the call, and luck sided with them: Dr. Choi said he could be there in five minutes.

"Can you hold this for a minute?" Kennedy asked, nodding at the soaked bandanna. "I'm going to go grab a washcloth inside the room." She wiped her hands down her pants, then pressed on the back of Nova's hands so she'd know how much pressure to apply.

Not thirty seconds later, she returned and took over, placing the washcloth on top of the bandanna. "Thank you," she told Nova. "You did fantastic. When Dr. Choi gets here, we'll have you fixed up in no time."

"This is the last thing I need with a wedding here this week. I've got so much to do and a florist to coordinate with and"—she let out a defeated sigh—"the timing really sucks."

"Your foot is going to be tender and sore for a few

weeks, but we'll get you up and walking around by tomorrow, okay?"

"Promise?"

"Yes." She pictured Nova in a medical walking shoe for several days, and if Kennedy had to drive to the nearest city to get one herself, she would.

After a few minutes of quiet camaraderie, Doc Choi arrived with a large black medical bag in his hand. "Good afternoon, ladies. What have we got here?" His kind, optimistic voice and aura of compassion immediately made Kennedy feel at ease. She imagined he'd seen just about everything if he was the only doctor in a twenty-mile radius.

Kennedy introduced herself and filled him in. Once they got the bleeding to stop, Kennedy grabbed the nearby hose so they could rinse the wound until it appeared dirt free.

"What do you think, Dr. Martin?" Doc asked.

Grateful for the question, she didn't hesitate. "The cut is deeper than a quarter of an inch and the lateral plantar nerve is visible, so stitches are required."

"Agreed. Would you like the honors?" He opened his bag of medical tricks.

"I would."

She donned sterile gloves and got to work, cleaning the wound with Hibiclens, placing sterile drapes around Nova's foot and ankle, numbing the site with lidocaine, and sharing every step aloud with Nova. Kennedy zoned in on the task at hand, so in tune to Nova's comfort level that when she lifted her head after the last suture, she was surprised to see they had an audience.

"My family," Nova said, affection so apparent, it made Kennedy's chest warm.

"Hi," Kennedy said. At a quick glance, there were seven in all—including Maverick, who looked at her strangely. "I'm almost done." She dropped the needle into a small sharps container, then bandaged the wound with clean dressing and Coban around Nova's foot to keep the dressing in place. Dr. Choi gathered all the waste into a small red biohazard bag.

Introductions were made as she and Doc got Nova to a standing position. Doc told her to keep off her foot for the rest of the day and he'd have a special shoe for her tomorrow when she came into his office for a tetanus shot. She hugged Kennedy in thanks, and then her brother Hunter, who could have been Maverick's twin, scooped her up and walked away.

"You're an angel. Thank you," Mrs. Owens said from beside her husband, who nodded in agreement. Similar appreciation came from Cole Owens and his wife, Bethany.

Little Jenna, however, decided to ask a question. "My mommy says if I stick my finger up my nose, it will get stuck. Is that true?"

"Jenna," Bethany groaned as everyone else chuckled.

Kennedy knelt down to her level. "Well, what your mom meant was germs that are on your fingers can get stuck in your nose and then you might get sick, and if that happens, you won't be able to chase George around."

"That would be atrocious," Jenna said with a straight face.

"It would," Kennedy agreed with a grin.

Doc and the family dispersed after that, except for

Maverick. He stood there quietly, staring at her like she'd sprouted wings to go along with his mom's sweet remark.

"Got something on your mind, cowboy?"

"That was…nice work, Martin. Thanks for helping my sister."

"It's what I love to do."

He nodded. "You've got"—he glanced down at her pants—"some stains on your clothes."

She looked at herself. Blood. Dirt. A smashed flower petal. So much for her nice white pants surviving the ranch, but that was okay. Getting dirty didn't bother her. She'd had way worse sully her scrubs. "Yeah. I guess I won't be wearing these again." She lifted her gaze back to his.

And the strangest thing happened. She'd swear his mind went right to the gutter and he was picturing her in her underwear. Which was ridiculous. They didn't imagine each other like that. He probably had someplace to be and was mad he was running late now.

Thinking about her clothes, she grumbled under her breath. She'd brought only a nightgown and one other outfit with her, assuming she and Andrew would drive home tomorrow. "You don't by any chance know of a clothing store in town, do you?" she asked.

"I know every store in town."

"Is there one that sells clothing?"

"Yes."

Could he be any more exasperating? "Well, then how about you give me the name so I can go buy some clothes?"

"Wildflower."

"Thanks. Oh, shoot. I'm sure Andrew already left and took the car. Is there a trolley or shuttle that goes into town? Not that I couldn't walk, but it's getting late in the day and I have a feeling I'll be ready to collapse soon, so—"

"I can take you."

"Really?" she asked, glaring right at him. "What's the catch?"

"No catch."

"With you, there's always a catch."

"Or maybe I've *evolved.*"

She pretended not to notice his extra emphasis. "Okay, then. Give me a minute to change?"

"I'll meet you in front of the inn in ten."

• • •

Nine minutes later, because God forbid one of them be late, Maverick opened the passenger side door of his truck when she stepped onto the circular driveway. He'd changed his T-shirt from black to royal blue, and she caught a whiff of soap and man that momentarily had her wondering things about him she shouldn't be wondering. Like what did he look like without his shirt on? What did he do at night once the sun went down? Did he live nearby? Did he live alone? Did he have a wife? A girlfriend?

None of those things mattered.

Only, as soon as he climbed into the driver's seat beside her, she did her darnedest to notice if he wore a wedding ring. His fingers were all bare. Not that that meant he was unattached.

"So, do you live on the ranch?" she asked.

"I do."

"And are you the local veterinarian as well?"

His hands tightened on the steering wheel. "I take it you're an MD now," he said in lieu of answering her.

"Did my fine suturing skills give me away? Or was it Dr. Choi's use of the name 'Dr. Martin'?"

"What field are you in?"

"Emergency medicine. And you? I'm guessing big animals. That's a specialty, isn't it?"

"It is."

"And that doesn't answer my original question. Again." She pulled her seat belt away from her body so she could turn to face him. Make him a little nervous with plenty of unwanted attention. He'd hated it in college when she stared at him in their lecture halls because she always won their silent contest when he looked away first.

Out of the corner of her eye, she did note his truck was clean, on the newer side, and a smooth oval rock about three inches in diameter sat in the cup holder. A worry stone. What did Maverick stress about?

"How long have you been practicing?" he asked.

"How long have you?" She was almost certain their advanced education included the same number of years, but were vets required to do a residency, too?

He pulled into a parking spot on Main Street and cut off the engine.

At his silence, she kept going, genuinely interested in knowing more. "And what kind of practice do you do?" She may have disliked him in college, and wasn't particularly fond of him now, but he'd always been intelligent and thoughtful and she didn't begrudge him achieving his dream of being a veterinarian. She wished him well even if he'd been a thorn in her side.

"I don't. I didn't finish vet school."

"Really?" This was hard to believe—he was such a go-getter in college. "How come?"

"Long story." He got out of the car and strode around the back of the truck, effectively blocking her view of him. It shouldn't matter to her why he didn't elaborate, but it did.

She opened the car door and slid out, the skirt of her green sleeveless wraparound dress gaping slightly open at her knees. Her heels hit the curb with a dull thud.

"I recommend a pair of closed-toe shoes while you're here," Maverick said, his gaze not on her feet but on her legs before his eyes jumped up to lock on hers.

"That is one recommendation of yours I think I'll take."

"The shop is on the corner." He helped close her door, then led her down the street. A middle-aged couple walking toward them smiled warmly at Maverick. "Hi, Barb. Hi, Chris," he said.

"Hi, Maverick." Barb's gaze quickly zeroed in on Kennedy. "You must be Dr. Martin." She stopped to give Kennedy a quick arm squeeze. "It's so nice to meet you. Doc sang your praises."

"He did?" She glanced at Maverick.

"Small town. News travels fast," he said.

"I better be on my best behavior, then," she teased, and hoped the lies piling up didn't come back to bite her in the ass.

"You're here for the week? For the Carson wedding?" Barb asked.

"I am. Did Doc tell you that, too?"

"No, that came from Mary Rose. I just got off the phone

with her." Mary Rose Owens: Maverick's mom and apparent purveyor of wedding news. "Chris and I own the local vineyard and we're supplying the wine for the reception. Of course your name came up."

Kennedy was about to ask why that was when Maverick said, "It was nice seeing you both. Have a good night." He took her elbow and practically dragged her away—no doubt he didn't like news of her attending the wedding any more than she did.

She opened her mouth to tell him to chill out when an older gentleman crossed their path and tipped his cowboy hat at them. "Hello, Maverick. Dr. Martin."

Was she in the *Twilight Zone*? Had she fallen asleep when she'd changed her clothes and this was a dream? Small town aside, she'd been in Windsong for all of three hours. "Hi," she muttered.

Maverick let go of her arm. "Hey, Uncle Tim, how are you?"

Uncle? That explained it. And once again, Maverick didn't seem the least bit surprised his uncle knew who she was.

He did, however, let out a faint breath of annoyance. "Good. It's nice to see you out with a pretty lady. Been a long time."

"It's…not really like that," Maverick asserted.

This was too good an opportunity to pass up. Ruffle Maverick's feathers? Yes, please. "It's not? What would you call it, then?" she asked as she batted her eyelashes up at him.

His brow wrinkled. "An escort."

She made sure to overplay her stunned expression, her

mouth dropping so far open, it hurt her jaw. "I had no idea you charged for your services. Uncle Tim, did you know—"

"That's enough."

Maverick could reprimand her all day, but she wouldn't stop until she was good and ready.

"I mean, isn't it customary to let a client know before you—"

"Kennedy." The way he said her name, like she had a tongue-lashing coming, made her giggle.

Uncle Tim laughed, too. "You've got your hands full with this one. I'll leave you both to it. See you later, Mav."

"Yeah." Maverick put his hand on the small of her back and ushered her forward, most likely in hopes of getting her off the street as quickly as possible.

"No more conversations for you," he teased as the delicious smell of bread and chocolate wafted out of Baked on Main. "It's bad enough my whole family now believes you're here for the wedding."

"That *is* why I'm here." She spun away from his too-close proximity and practically pressed her nose against the window to check out the inside of the bakery. A line of people stood at the counter. Her stomach growled.

"No, you're here for the groom."

"Potato, potahto."

"The shop's this way, Shortcake."

"Or…" She stopped herself. She'd come back for something sweet another time. When she didn't have the company of an impatient six-foot-something ranch owner and could enjoy herself.

They walked into Wildflower, a catchall store with high wood-beam ceilings and aisles of different offerings.

Besides clothes, she spotted everything from snacks to home goods to body lotions. She hurried over to the clothing area, thankfully losing Maverick along the way.

She decided on several pieces she could wear on the ranch and at home: jeans, shorts, a few plain T-shirts, and two sundresses—one with wildflowers and the other a pretty plum color.

She moseyed over to the shoe section and grabbed a pair of white tennis shoes and some black flip-flops. A package of socks and underwear completed the shopping spree.

The sales girl at the counter chatted nonstop, asking where she was from, what brought her to town, and suggesting she buy a pair of boots, too. "I know just the pair," she said, taking in Kennedy's heels as they walked back to the shoes. "They'll look great with everything. Size six, right?"

"Right." The brown boots with a classic cowboy heel were embroidered with a white floral design and decorative braided boot straps. The leather construction made for a sensible choice, and the embroidery made them feminine. She couldn't recall ever owning a pair of cowboy boots, plus they were comfortable, so she splurged and added them to her purchases. *When in Rome.*

Bags in hand, Kennedy pushed open the glass front door with her hip to exit. Maverick hadn't reappeared since they entered, so she figured he'd left, his duty to get her to the store complete. She'd find a ride back to the inn somehow or just walk. Or maybe track down Andrew at Sutter's.

To her surprise, though, Maverick stood waiting for her

outside the store, leaning against the building, one leg crossed over the other like he didn't have a care in the world. "Looks like a success."

"It was. But you didn't have to wait for me."

"A gentleman never leaves a lady without a safe ride home."

She looked around for said gentleman. He didn't seem fazed by her obvious confusion to his statement. Instead, he took the bags out of her hands, proving he was every bit the gentleman he claimed to be.

"I can…" It was no use; he had the packages and turned to walk back to his truck. "Do you have somewhere to be?" she asked, having to quicken her steps double-time to keep up with him.

"Yes."

"Home to your wife?"

He looked sideways at her. "Funny question coming from someone who thirty minutes ago accused me of being a paid companion."

She waved off her previous teasing. "It's a legitimate question anyone would ask."

He opened the rear passenger door of his truck and placed her bags on the seat.

"So no wife," she stated, climbing into her seat. "And I'm betting no girlfriend, either." Was she trying to get his goat? Yes. Yes she was.

It didn't work. He situated himself in the driver's seat and casually said, "You're awfully interested in my personal life."

She shrugged. "Only trying to figure out who I'm dealing with."

"Just a guy who doesn't want you hurting his family or the ranch's reputation. In less than a day, you've got everyone interested in you."

"This will either be the greatest crash of all time or the worst."

Maverick frowned and pulled away from the curb.

"But I sincerely promise my intentions are good. I would never do anything to upset your family." Not on purpose, anyway.

At the corner stop sign, he gave her a withering look. Maintained it. She couldn't hold his gaze, a terrible feeling of guilt overtaking her sincerity.

"You have nothing else to say?" Kennedy asked, moving her attention to the road ahead.

"Nothing you'd want to hear."

She crossed her arms over her chest and silently stewed. He didn't know her or anything about her relationship with Reed. Wedding crashing wasn't a crime. (She didn't think.) Neither was helping a friend in need. Maverick Owens could keep his thoughts to himself all night long for all she cared.

He pressed a button, and her window rolled down. The setting sun cast broad strokes of orange and yellow across the sky. A cool breeze rustled her hair.

"What are you doing?"

"Thought you might need some air."

"How nice of you," she said, over-the-top sweetly. She refused to let him get the best of her. "It is a beautiful night," she added out the window, changing her disposition with one beat of her heart.

The minute they pulled up to the inn, she hurried out of

his truck. He was faster, though, and grabbed her bags to hand to her, his biceps noticeably muscled.

"Thanks," she said, aware of his arms only because she was a doctor and the body happened to be her specialty.

And he did what he often did best. Stayed inexplicably silent as she turned to walk away.

CHAPTER SIX

Five days until the wedding

Maverick took a minute to enjoy the early morning fog rolling over the mountain. This time of day, before everyone else had woken, always filled him with a deep sense of calm. Just him and the land, making peace with yesterday and forging ahead with today. By midmorning, blue sky for miles would guide his way through the trees he had to inspect.

"You gonna stand there all morning lollygagging or get your ass in gear?" Hunter called out.

Maverick turned in surprise. Hunt rarely appeared on time on Monday mornings, so something had to be up. He closed the gap between them and met his brother at the barn door, taking one of the buckets full of grain from his hands. "You okay?" Maverick asked.

"Yep. You?"

"Yep."

Okay, then. Maverick might be unsettled by a brown-eyed, blond doctor with freckles across her nose, but he could live with it indefinitely. His brother, on the other hand, would most likely talk about what was on his mind by this afternoon. Until then, they got to work feeding the horses, then George. The chickens, goats Molly and Mo, and Bessie the cow were next. The ranch had long ago given up cattle, and they kept only a handful of animals now. It could be argued they were farmers more than ranchers, but no one cared about the difference.

Done with the feedings, they hightailed it to the inn for breakfast, entering the expanded kitchen through the back door. The family gathered every Monday morning for a hardy breakfast, per Mom's order. Mary Rose Owens liked to start the week with her loved ones, so that's what they did. Today would be a quick one, given that later this morning they had a welcome brunch scheduled for the wedding guests.

"Morning," he and Hunter said at the same time.

"Smells good in here," Hunt added, kissing their mom's check. He was a total mama's boy.

Their dad, John, sat at the head of the table next to Cole. Bethany and Jenna were next to him. "Where's Nova?" Maverick asked. "She okay?"

"She's fine," Mom said. "She's staying off her foot as promised. I'll take her something after we're through, then Dad will drive her into town to see Doc this afternoon."

The whole family lived on the ranch. The inn, along with two other buildings—The Cottage and Pine House— included a total of twenty-two rooms for guests. But beyond the immediate grounds, down a private dirt road, were their residences. A restored house dating back to the early 1900s for Mom and Dad. Cole, Bethany, and Jenna had a newer home near the lake. Nova lived in their guesthouse. Hunter made himself comfortable in the old bunkhouse, remodeling it in his spare time. And Maverick had his own cabin, set the farthest away from the inn, at the base of a hillside.

"Speaking of doctors," Cole said, "it looked like you and

Dr. Martin already knew each other."

Maverick sat across from his brother at the rectangular pine table. "We met earlier when Jenna was chasing George."

"I don't think that's it," Cole said, lifting his coffee mug to take a sip, a decidedly defiant gleam in his eyes. "I seem to remember you mentioning a Kennedy Martin back when you were in school."

Damn his brother and his steel-trap memory.

Rather than answer, Maverick filled his plate with scrambled eggs, bacon, and toast. The less he talked about the wedding crasher, the better.

"I knew it!" Cole said, Maverick's silence an error in judgment. "She's the girl you loved to hate, isn't she?"

"You and Kennedy went to college together?" his mom asked.

"Undergrad, yes," he said. "And I didn't love to hate her."

"Loved her, then, whatever." Cole had a punch to the face coming if he didn't shut up.

"Didn't love her, either."

"You something'd her," he insisted. "I vividly remember you complaining about her to me. You guys were always at each other. I thought for sure once you graduated, you were going to bring her home as your girlfriend."

"I didn't like her, Cole. And she didn't like me."

"I like Dr. Martin," Jenna said, taking a bite of bacon. "She's nice and she didn't freak out like some people do when George says hello."

"What were you two, then?" Mom asked thoughtfully.

Maverick didn't meet her eyes. He knew if he did, he'd see more than he wanted to. More questions. Questions like, *Are you ready to move on yet?* Leave it to Kennedy

Martin to not only crash his professional life, but his personal one as well.

"Rivals," he said. Plain and simple.

"What's a rival?" Jenna asked.

"An opponent. Someone you compete with," Bethany told her.

"Did you win, Uncle Mav?"

Maverick finished chewing his food, buying himself a minute to think. If you'd asked him the day after graduation who had won their frequent battles, he would have said himself, no question about it. But over the years, those battles had faded into fond memories rather than hateful ones. Nicole had taught him that. She'd encouraged him to look back with gratitude, that being challenged was a gift, and that he should hold on to the positives rather than the negatives. Kennedy had pushed him to do and be better. He'd always strived to do well, but be the best? Not until he'd met Kennedy.

She brought something out in him no one else had.

"We tied," he said, reaching over and ruffling his niece's hair.

Cole chuckled. "Right. The real answer is she kicked his butt."

"Any other answer is none of your business."

"Boys." One word from their dad and they both shut up.

"Whatever she was or wasn't," his mom said, "she's lovely and we owe her a debt of gratitude for coming to Nova's rescue like she did."

"I'm happy to show her some appreciation," Hunter piped in, his plate free of food. He always ate first, talked after.

"Don't even think about it." Maverick didn't need his brother putting the moves on Kennedy. And the reason for that was one he did not intend to examine.

Hunter grinned. "Why not? You planning to show her some personal thanks yourself?"

Maverick pushed his chair back to stand. "Thank you for breakfast." He took his plate to the sink, rinsed it off, and placed it in the dishwasher. He'd been reacquainted with Kennedy for less than twenty-four hours and, since seeing her again, memories of the two of them were constantly popping up and taking the place of others. The instant connection, if he wanted to call it that, made him... he didn't know. Confused? Interested? Happy? His jets cooled when he reminded himself exactly *why* she'd arrived at the ranch.

"Aw, don't run off," Cole said. "We're just happy to see you actually look at a woman again."

"I'm not looking," he grumbled.

"It's okay if you are," Hunter added.

"Uncle Mav looks at Mommy and Grandma all the time," Jenna said.

"That's right." Maverick's sour mood lifted. His seven-year-old niece always knew just what to say to help an uncle out. He had a good idea how to show her how much he appreciated her—and how to irritate his older brother at the same time. A win-win after Barley had her puppies and he gifted one to Jenna before he left on his trip. "See you later," he called over his shoulder, pushing open the door.

"Love you!" his mom called out.

"Love you, too," he answered.

As much as he looked forward to leaving the ranch for a while, he would miss seeing the faces of his family, even when they butted their noses where they didn't belong. *It means we care*, his mom liked to say. He understood that, but the last thing he needed was his mom caring about a certain wedding crasher.

. . .

A few hours later, it took him only a second to pick Kennedy out of the crowd gathered for the welcome brunch. Sunlight caught her wavy blond hair just right, and she wore the same green wraparound dress she'd worn last night. Green was his favorite color.

Her most obvious feature, however, was the fact that she stood alone near the fence line. He didn't know the first thing about crashing a wedding, but blending in seemed to be a wiser decision. That she appeared a little lost shouldn't affect him in the least. He had non-wedding things to do.

And yet, he couldn't get his feet to move toward the barn. Not yet. Not when he could—should—spare a couple of minutes to make sure trouble hadn't followed her to the brunch.

"Caught you," he whispered in her ear, leaning over the fence and also catching a whiff of her feminine scent.

She choked on her mimosa—he felt bad about that— then turned around. Even though he couldn't see her light brown eyes behind her sunglasses, he had a strong feeling they were sparked with annoyance.

"Not too hard to do," she said, "since I'm not trying to hide."

He stood well above the top of the fence and looked down at her with a mix of interest and disbelief. "Then what *are* you doing?"

She wiggled her nose, like she needed to sneeze. "Brunching, obviously. What are you doing?"

He chuckled.

"What's so funny?"

"I like your shades, but you get a little crease in your forehead when you frown at me."

She relaxed her face. "It's such a common occurrence, of course you'd notice."

"I'm pretty sure I should be the one giving you a dirty look." He took quick stock of the event behind her. "Given you haven't been invited to this wedding."

"Shh!" At his raised eyebrows she added, "Please."

So began a staring contest, just like they used to do in college, each of them unwilling to concede to the other.

A bell chimed. Someone called out, "They're here!" And a wave of excitement settled over the fifty or so guests.

Kennedy spun around to watch the engaged couple step down from the deck to enter the party. A few seconds later, she glanced over her shoulder at him, her lips pressed together.

"Remember what I said, Shortcake." He kept his tone friendly but firm.

"Grr." Her grumble was cute. She loved when he called her Shortcake. *Not*.

Guests tapped their forks and spoons to their champagne glasses and chanted, "Kiss, kiss..."

The smiling couple obliged, the groom dipping his bride for a kiss. Family and friends cheered and whistled, but

Kennedy stayed quiet. With her back to him, he couldn't read her expression, so he relaxed his arms atop the fence and leaned forward, hoping for a glimpse of her profile.

"They look happy to me," he said from over her shoulder.

"Oh, are you still here?" She spun back around, wobbling slightly.

He glanced down her body to see if her heels were stuck in the grass again. But to his surprise—and unwelcome delight—he found her wearing cowboy boots.

"I'm here all week," he reminded her.

Her gaze moved somewhere beyond him. The sunglasses hid her eyes, but she had another tell: worrying her bottom lip. She wanted him to think she had the situation under control, but she didn't.

"You're thinking very hard over there. Don't hurt yourself," he teased.

She grinned up at him. "Worried?"

"Hardly."

"I should get back to my party."

"Or I could call the police and have you arrested for trespassing." Yeah, he went there. The truth was, the ranch was private property and that meant he had every right to call the authorities. Not that he really would.

She huffed out a breath. "You wouldn't dare."

He lifted his arms off the fence and tipped his cowboy hat to show her who was boss. "You know the deal, Shortcake. No funny business." With that, he turned and walked away, no doubt leaving her to fume.

• • •

He wouldn't call the authorities, would he? Mr. Tall and Teasing just wanted to remind her to keep things on the down low. She could do that. And—wait a second. Was it trespassing if she was a guest of the inn? She didn't think so. *Grr…* He could take his warning and shove it up—

"Rule Number Two, hang with the crowd," Andrew said, coming up beside her.

She drained her mimosa, pushed a certain cowboy from her mind, and spun around. "You're right. Let's mingle."

Andrew gave her his elbow, so she linked their arms. "By the way, you look great in those boots and dress. Country singer vibe all the way."

"More like country winger, since I'm improvising this, but thanks."

"Stick with me, Carrie Underwood, and you'll be fine."

"I'll be fine with a glazed doughnut in me and a minute alone with Reed." She steered Andrew toward the buffet table and the doughnut cake. "Doughnut first."

"Hello," said a woman, standing near the table with her own doughnut in hand. "I don't believe we've met."

"Hello, I'm Andrew. And this is Kennedy." No Australian accent on Andrew's part. *Phew.*

"Hi." Kennedy grabbed a doughnut and took a quick bite, not to be rude but because Andrew was much better at this than she was. "Oh my God. This is the best doughnut I've ever eaten."

The woman smiled. "I know. This is my second one. I'm Connie, Elle's aunt. You must be friends of Reed's."

Kennedy almost choked. Nothing like meeting the bride's aunt their first day crashing.

"We are," Andrew said, cool as a cucumber. "Hospital friends."

"You're doctors, too?"

"Therapists. We run the dance therapy program, second floor, physiotherapy department."

Kennedy stuffed more doughnut in her mouth. Um, hello? She *was* a doctor. Why make this more difficult? At least the lie rolled off his tongue with ease and sounded believable.

"Kennedy hates when I share this, but were you a *Seinfeld* fan?"

Uh-oh.

"I was, yes," Connie said.

"You know the episode where Elaine dances?"

"How could I forget?"

"That was our Kennedy."

Connie laughed. "No!"

Kennedy stepped on Andrew's foot with the heel of her boot. He let out a little grunt. "Yes. After dislocating her hip, she took dance lessons to correct those awkward body mechanics of hers and the rest is history. Dance became her passion and a way to help others."

"You two will have to lead us in a dance at the reception."

"Of course," Andrew deadpanned.

Too bad he was going to be dead when Kennedy killed him long before the reception.

"Connie, it was nice meeting you," Kennedy said, eager to escape. "Excuse me, would you?" She gave Andrew her empty champagne flute and a look that said, *I'll deal with you later.*

She walked toward Reed, willing him to step away from

the person he was speaking with to have a quick word with her. When he didn't, she lingered nearby, waiting for the opportunity. Finally he turned her way.

"Hey," he said, moving closer. "Thanks for sticking around."

"Hi. How are you?"

He searched the party, his gaze settling on Elle across the grass. She looked over at them. "I can't really talk now."

"Okay. When?"

"I'll text you tonight or tomorrow."

"Reed." She put her hand on his forearm. "I'm worried about you."

"I know, but you don't need to be."

"Are you saying you do want to get married?"

"I'm saying—"

"Reed? Sorry to interrupt, but we need you for a couple of pictures." The photographer wore a camera with a large lens around her neck. "I've got some perfect natural lighting I want to take advantage of."

"Sure," he said, giving Kennedy a small smile in goodbye.

Damn it. Something still wasn't right, and she hoped they got a chance to talk sooner rather than later. The not knowing where he stood gnawed at her.

A tall, dark-haired guy around her age sidled up beside her. "Hey, Elaine, right?"

She glared at Andrew on the other side of the party, laughing like he was the funniest person on the ranch.

"Right," she said, torn between who was the worst right now, her best friend or Maverick.

CHAPTER SEVEN

Five days until the wedding

Maverick tacked up Magnolia for a ride to check the property lines. A Morgan horse, her shiny black coloring and expressive head were but two of her many attributes. Ten years old now, she showed no signs of slowing down, instead happy to stretch her legs at a trot or jump logs and harness race. Her great temperament made it easy on him.

The smell of pine and dirt, wildflowers and ocean, filled his nose as they rode across fields of grass, up and down tree-lined hills, along dirt paths, and finally around the edges of the property.

"Looks good," he said to Magnolia, eyeing the fencing while they trotted alongside it. He and Hunter had fixed a few broken places earlier in the summer, and he'd be hard-pressed to locate those spots now. On the rare occasion Cole ventured this far out, he'd compliment them until his face turned blue. The last thing their older brother wanted was to have any part of maintaining the physical property. Cole's expertise was running the inn, from financials to reservations to greeting guests and making sure they enjoyed their stay. Bethany handled the front desk, marketing, and their social media presence.

It was important to Maverick that before he left for his trip, everything was running as smoothly as possible, without any hint of neglect or worry. He'd be back by

Thanksgiving at the latest, to help with the influx of work, but that meant for three months nothing could go wrong. In moments like this, if he thought too hard about it, he almost changed his mind about leaving. The guilt of traveling weighed on him, but if he didn't go, he worried he'd never forgive himself.

"What do you call a horse that can't lose a race?" he asked aloud.

Magnolia gave a little shake of her head, like she always did.

"Sherbet."

She nickered, again like always, the weekly joke between them part of their routine. Yep, his horse understood jokes, too.

By midafternoon, they were back at the barn. Maverick led Magnolia to her stall, acutely aware of the woman standing two feet back from George's enclosure. She'd changed into jeans and a pale pink T-shirt, brand-new white sneakers on her feet. He wouldn't call it an improvement over her dress, because she always looked pretty, but it was definitely more practical.

He freed Magnolia of her tack and loved on her for a minute before taking off his cowboy hat and walking over to Kennedy.

"Hey," he said to his surprise intruder.

"Hi."

They stood side by side as poor George waited for some tangible attention. Kennedy stood even shorter without heels or the boots, and he couldn't help but inwardly smile, thinking once again how much she hated being called Shortcake.

"What brings you to my barn this afternoon, Shortcake?"

She ignored the nickname. "I was curious."

"About mules?"

"Among other things."

He wasn't opening that can of worms. No way. "You can touch George if you'd like. He likes ear scratches."

"He won't bite?"

"No."

She kept her feet planted in place and tentatively stretched out her arm, fingers extended.

"He's more of a nibbler," Maverick added as George pushed his nose through the gate, startling Kennedy. She whipped her arm back so fast, she almost toppled over.

"Jerk," she said. He was pretty sure she meant him and not George.

He took her hand in his and brought it to George's ear. "He really does love to get scratched right here, and his nibbles don't hurt."

Her breath caught when he let go, leaving her to rub George on her own, but she kept her hand in place. Her shoulders slowly relaxed.

"How about you take George for a ride?"

"No thanks."

Hmm…it couldn't be that easy, could it? "You're not scared, are you?"

Her jaw tensed. "No."

"Prove it."

"Hey, you two." Hunter strolled into the barn, standing a little straighter than normal, his chest puffing out.

Maverick glared at him. His timing, not to mention posturing, was damn annoying.

Chuckling under his breath, Hunt came to a stop right next to Kennedy. "Nice to see you again, Kennedy."

"Hunter, right?"

"Right. You thinking of riding George? He's fantastic with beginners, but i'm afraid he and I have a date."

"Oh?" Kennedy glanced away from Hunter and shot Maverick a quick glance, one that said, *Guess I can't prove it now*.

"Where are you headed?" Maverick asked.

"To the pen. A couple of bridesmaids want to give riding a try." Hunt looked directly at Kennedy when he added, "Mules are super smart and surefooted, and like I mentioned, great with novice riders. George, here, has been in the pen enough times that he knows exactly how to behave."

Maverick opened the gate. "Have fun."

"We will." Hunter and George took their leave. "Oh, Kennedy," Hunt called over his shoulder before rounding the barn, "you should go with Mav on his circuit today. He'd love the company."

That rat fink. The last thing Maverick wanted was company, and his brother knew it.

"Circuit?" she asked.

"It's nothing you'd be interested in." He almost followed that with, *Don't you have a groom to talk to?* But he bit his tongue. If she hung out with him, that meant she couldn't stir up any trouble with the wedding.

She followed Maverick out of the barn. "You're not worried I'll ruin your circuit, are you?"

"Not at all. You want to tag along, it's fine with me." He climbed into the all-terrain golf cart he drove when checking on the trees. "Hop in."

She sat down in the passenger seat. "No seatbelts?"

"Nope. Worried you'll fall out?" A part of him did worry she might, so he'd drive a little slower than normal.

"No. I'm… I'll just hold on here." She wrapped her small hand around the metal seat handle. "Did you know, though, that all moving vehicles are supposed to be equipped with safety belts? They save lives."

The worry in her voice hit him square in the chest. He imagined she'd seen her share of accidents in the ER, and her apprehension was justified.

"Noted, but we won't be going very fast."

"Have a helmet by any chance?"

He fought a smile. *Again.* She kept speaking and the corners of his mouth kept pressing up. "No helmet, either, but I promise you'll be fine." He reached under the seat for the red ball cap he'd left there.

"I better be." She looked straight ahead, through the small windshield that kept bugs from flying into their faces.

"I've got this." He offered her the hat. She shook her head so he ran a hand through his hair and put it on himself. "Hold on," he said, taking it extra slow at the start. He'd never seen this side of Kennedy before, this more reticent side that offered a glimpse of someone who wasn't as superhuman as she so often seemed.

"Where are we going?" she asked.

"You'll see." He drove them away from the inn and the barn, down the wide, bumpy dirt road that saw a lot of traffic during the holidays. He hadn't realized how bumpy until he noticed Kennedy's white knuckles. To her credit, she didn't say a word.

Wisps of her blond hair escaped her ponytail, and she sucked on her plump lower lip, so much so that he worried she might break the skin. He eased his foot off the accelerator. In theory, he had the rest of the afternoon to do this, so there was no reason to make her any more uncomfortable than she already was.

They rode up a hill, down the hill, up another, and at the peak, Kennedy let out a gasp. "You have Christmas trees. A million Christmas trees."

He stopped the golf cart at one of the best views on the property, one he never got tired of taking in. The trees had more growing to do, but row after row of pine, their triangular shape pointing to a blue sky, took a person's breath upon first sight.

"Not a million. But a lot."

She spared him a quick glance as she said, "This is a Christmas tree farm, too?"

"It is. It makes up a huge part of our business in the winter."

"How is that possible in such a small town?" She slid out of her seat to stand in front of the cart for an unfettered view.

He came to stand beside her. "We send trees all over the country."

"To anyone famous?"

"Maybe." They stared into the distance in comfortable silence for several minutes. When Kennedy wasn't bombarding him with questions or combative looks, she wasn't so bad. "Come on."

They took the cart down the hill to the base of the tree farm.

"Wow," Kennedy said, standing among the trees. "It's so green and smells like Christmas on steroids."

He glanced at her white sneakers. "Hope you don't mind getting those dirty."

"Not at all."

Her answer surprised him. "Follow me, then." He led her along the first row of trees at a slow pace as he examined each one they passed.

She watched him carefully. "What are you doing?"

"Looking for anything that can harm the trees."

"Like?"

"Aphids and bark beetles mostly."

She shivered, not because she was cold, but because her mind must have immediately gone to bugs landing on her—it happened to everyone he brought out here for the first time. They felt the phantom feet of insects on their arms, or the back of their necks, their ankles.

"Don't worry. They'd much rather suck on bark than you."

"Suck?" Her voice shook now, too. Hmm. Seemed Dr. Martin really didn't like bugs.

"Just a figure of speech. They're harmless to humans." He slyly reached behind her and traced a fingertip along the back of her neck.

She jumped and shimmied around, her arms flailing, one hand wiping at her neck. "Get it off! Get if off!"

His chest rose and fell in silent laughter. Score one for the country boy.

Finding him amused, she stopped, narrowed her eyes. "You did that. Oh, you are so going to regret it."

"Doubtful. Want to leave the ranch now?"

"No."

"Too bad."

"For you," she asserted, her entire demeanor changing right before his eyes. "Now, keep going. Are these a certain type of pine tree? What happens if you find bugs are infesting a tree? Do animals, like skunks or possums, get in here? What about birds? Do they make nests? What happens then?"

He pressed a finger to the side of his head. She peppered him with question after question, knowing full well it drove him crazy. *Relax, dude. This is your backyard. You can talk about this in your sleep.*

A change in his attitude did wonders. For one, it calmed him down. And for two, Kennedy no longer had the upper hand, and she knew it. She saw the minute he adjusted his composure meter—her steps had a little less pep and her questions were tempered with long seconds of blissful silence.

When he spotted a tear in the irrigation system, he kneeled to fix it. She knelt, too, her arm brushing his. This close, he caught a whiff of her scent again, a combination of vanilla and strawberries. She'd smelled the same back in college.

She watched him mend the hose with the tape he carried in his pocket. He'd come back later for a more permanent fix.

"Do you use pesticides on the trees?" she asked as they stood.

"We use our own."

"Your own?"

"I've developed a safer substance, using salt in the

irrigation system instead of chemicals."

"Wow, that's great. How does it work?"

They cleared a row, turned down another. "The salt absorbs the fluids that come from an insect's body and they succumb to dehydration before they can damage the trees. It works especially well on spiders."

"And it doesn't harm the trees?"

"No."

"So, you might not be an animal doctor, but you are a tree doctor."

He knew she meant it as a compliment, but it reminded him of what he'd lost. Who he'd lost. "That's it for today," he lied, because all of a sudden the thing he needed most was space and time alone.

Two years, nine months ago…

Dear Nicole,

It's the first Christmas since you've been gone, and my family is waiting for me at Mom and Dad's. I don't know if I have the strength to go. I don't know if I can be around Cole and Bethany and Jenna and not begrudge them something that was never in the cards for us. It's not their fault, and yet it helps to find blame in safe places. My brothers have never loved me harder, no matter how awfully I speak to them. They put a damn Christmas tree up in my living room last week to knock some cheer into me. It didn't work, but for them I pretended it did.

All the happy faces on the ranch this past month have been torture. It's been our busiest tree season yet, and all I can think is I'm not supposed to be here. I'm supposed to be with you, working in our veterinary clinic during the day and sharing dinner in our tiny apartment overlooking downtown at night. That was our dream. It's impossible for me to think of a new one. At least right now. Merry Christmas, Nicole.

Miss you like crazy,

Maverick

CHAPTER EIGHT

Five days until the wedding

Kennedy held on to the seat handle for dear life and pressed her feet flat on the floor of the golf cart to keep herself from bouncing. She'd never ridden a mechanical bull, but this seemed like a pretty close simulation. "Jeez, could you drive any faster?"

"I could," Maverick said, not the least bit bothered by the bumps in the dirt road.

Grr. Whatever bug had crawled up his ass, it was lodged way up there. One minute they'd been having a polite, educational conversation and the next he'd turned rigid and quiet, clearly anxious to be free of her. He'd never been this hot and cold in college. Something besides herself, she'd hazard to guess, bothered him. He needed the worry stone in his car in his pocket today. "This isn't the way we came."

"It's a shortcut."

She laughed. It was either that or insult him for being the jerkiest of jerks. The man obviously wanted her out of his sight. He scowled at her, making her laugh harder.

The barn came into view. The ocean. A small hill to the south covered in pink and white flowers.

When Maverick came to an abrupt stop near the entrance to the inn, she almost asked him for that ride on George, just to mess with him.

Instead she said, "Thanks," even though she didn't think he deserved her good manners at the moment. "I liked seeing the trees and learning more about what you do here." It had been a nice way to kill time until Reed texted her.

Maverick's reply came in the form of a curt nod before he hit the gas pedal a half second after she'd cleared the cart. A puff of dust literally blew up into her face. She coughed and lifted her hand to give him the middle finger, but then the golf cart stopped.

He got out, his long, jean-clad legs eating up the distance between them. He lifted the faded red ball cap off his head, jammed his fingers through his light brown hair, and put the hat on backward. He wasn't hiding his striking blue eyes. Wasn't avoiding the glare she shot him.

"I'm sorry," he said, coming to stand an arm's length in front of her. His sincerity made it difficult to stay angry with him.

"You should be," she said, crossing her arms over her chest.

His eyes dipped down to her V-neck, then jumped back up to her face. "I am." They stared at each other. "I'll, uh, see you later. Enjoy your afternoon."

She turned away at the same time he did, not sure what had just happened. She walked toward a random path to focus her thoughts on Reed instead of Maverick. At brunch earlier, he and Elle had looked in love, but she, better than anyone, knew that looks could be deceiving. She'd thought Trevor had loved her when in reality he'd been biding his time, waiting for *someone special*, and that someone turned out to be her sister. At least he'd had the decency to break up with her before dating Victoria. And the whole "it's not you, it's me" speech dropped the sting of rejection from a ten to a seven. But still. He'd damaged her trust, and if that was Reed's issue, she could more than relate.

"And, Kennedy?" Maverick said, stopping her in her tracks. "I think you should stay out of it."

She twisted back around. "It?"

"The wedding. You need to leave Reed and Elle alone. Let them make their own decisions."

"Don't you have trees to get back to?"

"They're not going anywhere."

"No, but I am. Away from you, in case you couldn't tell."

"The inn has a reputation to uphold. "

"I know, but is that more important than someone's happiness?"

"I didn't say that."

"You implied it."

"Okay, how about this… What makes you an expert on Reed?"

"He's my friend and…" She didn't want to talk about the details. She didn't owe Maverick an explanation. "He's confided certain things to me."

"Was he drunk when he did?"

How did he know that? She kept her face blank. "Now you're the expert?"

He walked toward her. "I know a thing or two."

"About love and marriage?"

His step faltered. It was subtle, barely there, but she saw it. More importantly, she felt it. Like the ground had shifted under his feet against his will.

Working in the ER had been her entire life for three years. And during that time she'd learned to read people. What they said and didn't say. Their expressions. Their body language and involuntary motions. Had Maverick been married?

"Don't." One word. That's all he gave her before turning to leave.

Good.

She didn't want to know what nerve she'd struck. Or what exactly he meant by "don't." Don't talk to him anymore? Don't talk to Reed? She strode down a wide, tree-lined path and took a seat on a wooden bench, forcing her thoughts back to Reed's confession. His asking her to stay. *Thanks for sticking around.* She might not be invited to the wedding, but he wanted her close by. And if he needed her reassurance that Elle was the one, or to drive the getaway car if she wasn't, Kennedy would put the pedal to the metal.

A text sounded on her phone, interrupting visions of speeding down the highway, Reed grateful she'd helped him run away. She pulled the cell from her pocket and grinned at the names on the screen.

Hugo & Maria

Hugo had come into the ER with his mom after fainting while at a birthday party. He'd been jumping in a bounce house and collapsed—not a typical occurrence for an otherwise healthy twelve-year-old. Then while sitting on the hospital bed telling her all about the party and how Iron Man was the greatest of all superheroes, Hugo fainted again, only this time it was accompanied by a seizure.

When Hugo came to, Kennedy immediately listened to

his heart. Fast, chaotic beats had told her they needed an EKG stat. If Hugo's heart beat erratically for too long, it could cause sudden death. Memories of her own near-death experience had hit her so swiftly at that moment that there was no way she was leaving Hugo's side until they got a diagnosis and knew how to make him better.

It turned out Hugo had long QT syndrome, or LQTS, a heart rhythm condition that occurs during physical exertion or emotional excitement. He'd been a trouper through test after test until she was satisfied with a course of action. Luckily, one of the best pediatric cardiologists in the country worked at the hospital, and she'd put the two of them together.

She and Hugo had bonded over more than superheroes and heart scares at a young age. They also shared a love for quesadillas, hip-hop music, and magic. Maria always had a deck of cards in her purse, and to kill time while they'd waited for test results and kept a close eye on Hugo, he'd dazzled them with card tricks. For the past year they'd kept in close touch, talking almost weekly.

Kennedy hoped to one day be invited to *his* wedding.

Hi Dr. Martin, mom got me the new Criss Angel Ultimate Magic Kit!

Hi Hugo! That is awesome.

Are u still coming to my birthday party? I'll do some of the new tricks for u

Of course I'll be there. I'm bringing the disappearing ice cream.

He texted back a zany face emoji. Much better than the face with rolling eyes he sent last week.

Say hi to your mom and I'll see you soon. You're

staying out of trouble, right?

Mostly

Mostly?

I rode my bike a little too much yesterday

Because Hugo's heart had never returned to a normal rhythm by itself, two days after his visit to the ER, he had a pacemaker put in. His heart wasn't strong enough to withstand future physical activities without some support, and even then they had to be kept to a minimum. He'd been devastated to hear he had to give up playing soccer, but the good news was he would continue to grow and thrive with the condition. He just had to be aware of his limitations.

Happens to the best of us. And he was the best. She loved him and felt protective of him like she would a younger brother.

She placed her phone on the bench and put her hand over her heart. Back then, she hadn't told Hugo and Maria the whole truth about her experience in the ER, only what they'd needed to hear to form a connection. What she'd needed to share to let Hugo know he wasn't alone. Feeling the slow beat inside her chest now, she could still remember both the erratic beat of her heart and the plummeting, free-fall feeling. The "Code Blue."

"Hey, you okay?"

She blinked and looked up in surprise at Maverick. He didn't look like he wanted to fight anymore. Instead, he kneeled down in front of her and swiped his thumb across her cheek, wiping away a lone tear she hadn't realized had fallen.

His touch wasn't unwelcome. It didn't make her flinch.

Or want to push him away. This close, his blue eyes brandished a ring of light green around his pupils. And he had a tiny scar, probably from chicken pox, on his forehead.

"Yes," she said, even though she felt certain she wasn't. Not when Maverick's presence put her at ease.

• • •

She didn't look okay. One minute she'd been texting on her phone with a smile on her face, and the next she'd zoned out and he'd swear her breathing had stopped. It had scared him. Not that he'd ever admit it aloud.

He'd come back to apologize more directly for being rude and stared at her from afar for a few moments. He couldn't help himself. She possessed some serious magnetic mojo, grown more powerful since college.

"You sure?" he asked.

She nodded.

Which wasn't the reassurance he needed. He told himself she was a guest of the inn and while not technically his job, he should see to her well-being. In reality, he didn't believe her being a guest had anything to do with it.

Damn, but his emotions were all over the place with her near again.

He slid her phone over and sat down next to her. A large oak tree supplied shade, a slight sea breeze carried the scent of gardenias. Nova loved the white flowers, so she made sure there were plenty around.

"Want to talk about it?" He had no idea where those words came from, but they were out and he had to live with them now.

"Are you the same man who practically pushed me out of his golf cart twenty minutes ago?"

"No," he answered honestly. Because somewhere between her calling him a tree doctor and looking like she'd just lost her best friend, he'd softened. Definitely against his will, but softened, nonetheless.

"I was texting with a friend of mine, Hugo, and he reminded me of what I went through when I wasn't much older than he is."

Maverick settled a little deeper into the bench. If she wanted to talk, he'd listen.

Kennedy relaxed on a sigh. "I was born with my stomach twisted in a knot. I should have died, but I didn't. Then when I was fourteen, I was rushed to the emergency room. They didn't know what was wrong with me at first, just that I was in a lot of pain. Turned out scar tissue from the stomach surgery I had as an infant had broken off and caused a bowel obstruction. The obstruction triggered sudden heart failure."

Jesus. To go through something like that as a kid.

"Thanks to the ER doctor, I was rushed into surgery just in time to save my life. The surgeons were able to fix the obstruction."

"For good?" he asked, praying she didn't suffer any lingering complications.

"Yes."

He sensed a "but" coming.

"After surgery, though, my heart rate continued to drop and I was in critical condition. My parents were in the waiting room when they heard 'Code Blue Room 327' and knew it was me. They rushed to the room, and my dad insisted the medical staff let him inside. He screamed at me so loud to keep fighting that my mom later told me every nurse on the floor had gravitated toward the window of the room."

Maverick knew the story ended well. Kennedy sat beside him healthy and strong, her hair smelling like strawberries and her skin glowing from being outside, but he didn't want to hear any more. He didn't want to be reminded of his own cries, coaching Nicole to fight harder, to hang on a little longer. To stay with him because life meant more with her in it.

"I had been flatlining for almost a minute when the ER doctor, Dr. Hawkins, rushed into the room and told me I wasn't fighting hard enough and that I had to live because I had great things to accomplish. Then everything got quiet for a second and my dad begged the doctor not to call it. Another second later, the beeping on the portable monitor started again and Dr. Hawkins said, 'we have a pulse.' In that moment, I opened my eyes and gave everyone a thumbs-up."

Maverick swallowed the thick lump in his throat, and without thinking too hard about it, he squeezed Kennedy's hand. A silent acknowledgment that he was happy she'd survived.

Then, because he had to do something to mask this deluge of gratitude, he said, "I'm glad you fought back, otherwise who would have bugged the crap out of me in college?"

"Ha! I think it's the other way around." She spared him a quick glance. "I can't believe I told you all that. Not many people know the entire reason I became an ER doctor."

"I'm a good listener."

She *pfft*ted.

"It's amazing you remembered all that detail." If that were true, then maybe Nicole had heard the last words he'd spoken to her. He hoped so. Unlike Kennedy, Nicole didn't have a chance of coming back.

"Yeah. It was like an out-of-body experience."

"Did you see a white light?"

She laughed. "No, nothing like that. It was more like an...awareness. A feeling that I wasn't alone and that there was a ton of optimism and love in the room, and those strong feelings are what brought me back. The sad thing is that I survived, but afterward, my parents' marriage didn't."

Her phone dinged. She looked at the screen and smiled. "This is Hugo." She showed Maverick a picture of a boy with a deck of cards fanned out in his hand, between his fingers.

"The kid's got some dexterity."

"He does. He's also super smart and very special to me."

Unmistakable affection resonated in her voice. "How do you two know each other?"

"We met in the ER. He's also had to deal with a heart issue. His, though, is chronic."

"I'm sorry." The tear he'd wiped away—was it for Hugo? "He looks healthy now."

"He is." She stood. Stretched her arms over her head. Her T-shirt shifted, revealing a thin patch of smooth, pale skin above the waistband of her jeans. "Want to grab lunch?" she asked, pulling his gaze back up where it belonged.

He had a list a mile long of things to do around the

ranch and yet found himself saying, "Sure, but I should make it quick."

"I'm happy with anything."

They strode toward the inn. "Really? You'll eat a plate of hot wings with me?"

"Ugh. No." She looked at him with wide eyes. "Wait. You remember that?"

"That you don't eat anything off a bone? Yeah." Their junior year of college, they'd been assigned to the same study group, and on more than one occasion they'd met at the local pub. Kennedy couldn't stomach eating any kind of meat that came attached to a bone.

"I can do boneless," she offered helpfully. This more amenable Kennedy must be due to hunger.

"Actually, I know just the place."

He took her around the inn to the back door of the kitchen. "Hey, Mom," he said, gesturing for Kennedy to enter first.

"Hello! What a nice surprise." Maverick knew his mom would enjoy seeing Kennedy again and showing her more gratitude for her treatment of Nova.

"Hi, Mrs. Owens."

"Please call me Mary Rose." She wiped her hands on her apron. Freshly baked cookies were plated on the counter — an afternoon treat for guests that they served with homemade lemonade.

"It smells delicious in here," Kennedy said.

"Thank you. Can I give you two some lunch? Have a seat."

Maverick pulled out a chair at the table for Kennedy. Her long lashes swept down over the tops of her cheeks in thanks as she sat. "It's not too much trouble?" she whispered to him.

He shook his head at the same time his mom said, "Not at all. I love feeding my children and their friends."

Kennedy raised her eyebrows at him. He shrugged. They could call a temporary truce for the benefit of his mom.

"So, Kennedy, are you married? Have a boyfriend?"

"Mom," he groaned. Man, he kept underestimating his family and their endless interest in Kennedy.

"I'm just curious." She put two plates and a large bowl of cold pasta salad on the table.

"I'm single," Kennedy said easily enough. "And happily so."

"Oh?" Mom said.

"The last boyfriend I had turned out to be... I don't even have the right words. Not who I thought he was, that's for sure. We were together when he met and fell in love with my sister."

His mom's hand went to her chest. "You're kidding."

Kennedy shook her head. "No. They're planning to get married next year."

"That's awful." His mom placed sliced apples, homemade rolls, cloth napkins, and silverware on the table.

"Thank you for saying that." Kennedy spooned some pasta onto her plate. "My mom and sister don't understand how weird it is."

"Do you have any other siblings?" His mom poured them each a glass of water from a pitcher and then took a seat at the table.

"Another sister, Ava. She and I are best friends, so I've

got someone on my side."

"And your dad?"

"He stays pretty neutral when he's around."

"I'm sorry you're dealing with all that."

"Me too, but fingers crossed I'll be on the other side of the country by the end of the month."

Oh? Maverick's ears perked up.

"Oh?" his mom echoed aloud. She had this way about her that made a person talk about anything and everything. She genuinely cared and set people at ease with her kind voice and friendly expression.

"I've been interviewing with a hospital in Boston. They have one of the best ERs in the country, and I've never wanted a job so badly."

Maverick could sympathize. There was a time when all he wanted was to have his own veterinary practice. He hoped Kennedy's wish came true.

"I'll keep my fingers crossed for you," his mom said.

"Thank you. I should hear this week if I've been invited for an in-person interview. If so, I'm pretty sure that means I've got the job." She took a bite of apple.

"Have you ever been to Boston?"

"No," Kennedy said, eyes remaining on his mom. It was like he wasn't there, which suited him just fine.

Until his mom said, "You've been to Boston, haven't you, Mav?"

He finished chewing his food, two sets of eyes on him. "I have. It's a fine city."

"What were you doing there?" Kennedy asked.

He had no intention of going down that path so said simply, "Vacation." He met his mom's gaze, silently imploring her to let it go. That she'd even brought up his travels was enough to make him want to run out the kitchen door. He rubbed a hand over the back of his neck.

Thankfully, Kennedy did let it go. "In all honesty," she said, "I chose it because of its great reputation, but also because it's far from L.A."

"That's where you're from?"

"Born and raised. I love it there, but I'm ready for a change."

"Being on a ranch isn't exactly Kennedy's idea of fun," Maverick said.

"True." She pointed her fork at him. "But I am finding it to be more interesting than I thought it would be." She turned her attention back to his mom. "And the people are beyond nice. How is Nova, by the way? Have you seen her today?"

"I saw her this morning and she was doing well. A little grumpy because the bottom of her foot hurts. But that's what she gets for gardening barefoot. My husband took her to see Doc and they're due back anytime. Thank you again for everything you did."

"It was my pleasure. And this lunch is delicious. Thank you."

"What's on your agenda for the rest of the day?"

"I'm not sure," Kennedy said.

Maverick had a feeling her plans were predicated on if she could get a minute alone with Reed. Thankfully, the topic of the wedding hadn't come up with his mom.

"Well, don't forget tonight is the 'S'more the Marry Her' event around the firepit near the pond. We put on a mean s'mores event."

So much for avoiding that subject.

Kennedy cut him a quick glance. "Right. Of course I'll be there. I can't remember the last time I had s'mores." She looked around the kitchen. "Do you do all the cooking here?"

"My husband and I, yes. He worked the ranch up until he had an accident five years ago. He was thrown from a horse and broke his leg and pelvis. During his recovery he started taking cooking classes and found he enjoyed it. I've been stuck with him ever since."

Maverick inwardly smiled at the term *stuck*. His parents had been happily married for the past thirty-four years. His dad doted on his mom, and vice versa.

"We have additional help when we hold weddings and other large events. There's another kitchen on the property."

"How long has the ranch been in your family?"

"Over a hundred years." His mom looked fondly at him. "We've carried on traditions and started a lot of new ones."

"The Christmas trees are a newer one?"

"You've seen the trees?" Her eyes darted between him and Kennedy.

"Maverick showed them to me. It must be magical here around Christmastime."

"It is. You'll have to come back for a visit."

"She'll be in Boston," he said matter-of-factly.

Kennedy gave him a sidelong glance. "Thanks for the vote of confidence. I think that's the nicest thing you've ever said to me."

"You're a good doctor," he said.

"Wow, you're on a roll. Please don't stop." She made a

circular motion with her hand to *keep going* and looked at him expectantly, those brown eyes of hers way too keen and appealing for his liking.

He turned his head to his mom. "Thanks for lunch. It was great as always."

His mom, clearly enjoying the exchange between him and Kennedy, looked ready to swing from the ceiling fan in joy. "Come back tomorrow. I'd love to continue this conversation then."

Or he could keep as far away as possible from his well-meaning but too-inquisitive mom. "We'll see," he said, knowing he'd at least be back alone. With travel plans of his own, he cherished time with his family even if he didn't always show it.

"Before you go, I have something I want to give you, Kennedy." His mom stood and moved to a drawer on the far side of the kitchen. He picked up his and Kennedy's plates and took them to the sink to wash.

"Thanks," she said to him as she got to her feet.

"This is just a small token of friendship for you to take with you," his mom said.

He watched over his shoulder as his mom placed a small glass ladybug in Kennedy's hand. She had a collection of the handmade pieces of art and didn't give them out readily. Bethany and Jenna each had one. His aunt. Their head housekeeper. Nicole.

"It's lovely, but I can't—"

"You can." Mom closed her hand over Kennedy's. "Around here, we believe that ladybugs are good luck charms, and I hope this one brings you luck in your job, and in love."

Kennedy blinked furiously, sucked her bottom lip between her teeth. "Thank you so much." She wrapped his mom in a hug. The embrace lasted for a long time. As they broke apart, Kennedy added, "I don't have a lot of friends, so this means more than I can say."

"You have a friend in me," his mom replied.

Maverick kept his back to the women as he dried his hands on a dish towel. If he looked at Kennedy now, he was afraid he'd fall into friendship with her, too.

She made it easy.

CHAPTER NINE

Five days until the wedding

The smell of roasting marshmallows should be made into a candle. Actually, it probably was, and Kennedy made a mental note to find one. She'd think of tonight, and the ranch and wedding, whenever she lit it. Nothing beat an in-person cookout, though, and she stuffed her mouth with her second s'more.

"Do you know something I don't?" Andrew asked from beside her.

She frowned at him, not understanding why he'd ask that.

"You're eating that like Hershey bars are about to become extinct."

"Shut up," she said around a mouthful of deliciousness.

"I'm not judging, just don't want you to bite off a finger."

She waved her hand at him. "All here, Mr. Stunt Double slash Dance Therapist."

"Andrew, hello again," a man said, coming to stand next to them.

"Hi," Andrew said. "Kennedy, this is Nathan and his wife, Jacqueline. They're friends of Reed's parents."

Kennedy quickly rubbed her knuckle over the corner of her mouth. She hoped she didn't have marshmallow or chocolate there. "Hi." Again no Australian accent from Andrew.

"Your brother told us some great stories earlier," Nathan said. "We've never met a bounty hunter in person before, and he had us in stitches."

Oh my God. It took every ounce of strength she had to keep her expression neutral. So Andrew was her brother now, in addition to her work partner? Had he stuck to their original boyfriend-girlfriend plan at all? Probably not, given his crush on Liam. And bounty hunter? *Bounty hunter!* He'd obviously decided to take improvisational acting another step further, much to her dismay. "That's Andrew, always telling stories to make people laugh."

Andrew put his arm around her. "Don't worry—I didn't tell them the one about your ex." He turned his face away from hers, cupped his hand around his mouth, and half-whispered, "Talk about funny."

"Oh, you have to tell us now!" Jacqueline's eyes widened in interest.

Kennedy slapped *her brother* on the chest. "Andrew, I thought your job was confidential." He just loved making her the butt of his jokes, didn't he? And how in the world was she going to keep track of his different personas? She made a mental note to steer clear of all guests. Or maybe come down with a debilitating case of laryngitis.

"Nate and Jackie aren't going to tell anyone," he said back with a wide grin, "are you?"

"Our lips are sealed," Jackie promised.

Kennedy would like to seal Andrew's.

"Long story short," Andrew started, "I'm waiting for her ex when he gets home from work, and when he tries to run, I grab him before he's even hit the sidewalk. My car is parked right there at the curb, back door already open like

I had it all planned." He winked at Nate and Jackie. "Not my first rodeo, ladies and gentlemen. So, he puts up zero fight since he knows me, and knows there's only one way this ends. Still, I have to follow protocol, so I lay him down on the back seat where I can cuff him. He asks if that's necessary and I tell him it is. Then I ask him to bring his ankles to his butt. He's barely stretched when he argues, 'That's as far as I go! You think I do yoga?'"

Nate and Jackie laughed.

"It gets better. Eventually I get him handcuffed and drive him to jail. Since we have history, I feel inclined to ask him if there's anyone I should call. I park the car and before we get out he says, 'yeah, my sister.' I didn't know he had a sister, so I say, 'no problem, what's her name?'"

Andrew paused (for dramatic effect, no doubt) and pulled his metal skewer out of the fire, his marshmallow burned to a crisp. "I look at him over the seat, and he's staring at me with a straight face when he says, 'Anita Weiner.'"

Everyone cracked up, even Kennedy. She had to hand it to her best friend—she didn't know where he came up with this stuff.

"Seriously?" Nate asked.

"Seriously." Andrew gave Kennedy his marshmallow. She took it without a second thought to make one final s'more.

The couple saw someone else they knew and walked away with smiles on their faces. No doubt they'd be sharing that story a time or two over the course of the week. Kennedy bumped Andrew's shoulder. "I love that you make people happy, but I hope you can keep all your personas straight."

"Piece of cake." Andrew playfully nudged her back.

She looked at their beautiful surroundings. Spread out around the large fire pit were white Adirondack chairs and small tables with benches. There were maybe fifteen people enjoying the firelight and sweet treat, each person receiving their own s'mores kit in a brown paper bag. A couple dozen kits remained for guests who ventured over later. Unfortunately, she'd yet to see Reed or receive a text from him.

Across the way, Liam gave a chin-up to Andrew. Andrew had been right about the man of honor—he was very attractive. And by all appearances, as interested in Andrew as Andrew was in him.

"I hoped Reed and Elle would be here," she half whispered. "With it being so dark, now would be a good time to try to talk to him without any notice."

Andrew lifted his chin back in Liam's direction, paying her no attention.

"Did you hear what I said?"

"What? Sorry."

"Never mind. Go on," she said. "Go have fun with your new BFF."

"I have only one BFF and you know it."

She did know that. "Don't forget your accent," she whispered.

"I won't." He handed her his s'mores bag and strode away. This was another reason they got along so well—she had the sweet tooth and he had the salty one.

"Hey, Kennedy."

She turned to find Hunter on the other side of her. "Hey."

"Two bags?" he teased, nodding at her hands. "Don't tell me this is your first time having s'mores."

"Not my first, but it's been a long time. This one"—she lifted the bag in her left hand—"was my friend Andrew's." She put both bags down on the Adirondack behind her, staying close to the fire to keep warm.

"I hear you and my brother had a good time today."

"How did you hear that?" Certainly not from Maverick. She doubted he'd characterize their time together as "good."

"I guess it was more of an observation. I asked him how it went with the tour of the trees and he got an annoyed look on his face."

She laughed.

"Which, for the record, I hope means you weren't annoyed, too. What's the story with you two?"

"No story." She didn't want to be rude and tell Hunter his brother had been an A-plus jerk in college.

"There's some story there. Only one other girl has ever gotten him worked up like you do."

She stared at the yellow and orange flames of the fire, unsure what to make of that. Her cheeks heated, from the heat but also—weirdly—from the pleasure of knowing she affected Maverick on more than a superficial level. That saying about knowing your enemy and keeping them close might be true for reasons she'd been afraid to examine too closely.

She was about to ask Hunter about this other girl when a man cleared his throat from behind them. That she knew without a glance it was Maverick sent a string of goose bumps up her arms.

"Hey, big brother, we were just talking about you."

Maverick frowned. "I came to find you. I think it's time."

"Yeah?" Hunter's voice rose an octave, excitement clear as the star-filled sky.

"Time for what?" Kennedy asked.

"Barley is having her babies," Hunter said. At Kennedy's confused expression, he added, "Barley is Mav's dog."

"Oh, wow. Can I come? I've never seen puppies being born before." She might not be keen on horses and mules, but she liked dogs and loved the practice of medicine in all its forms.

"Sure," Hunter said, while Maverick pressed his nice lips together in coolness.

Nice lips? She must be on a sugar high if she was assigning an adjective to his mouth. For the rest of the night, she vowed *not* to notice them again.

"Come on," Maverick said. "I've got my truck."

"Where are we going?" Kennedy asked, following the men at a good clip. With Reed nowhere in sight and no communication from him, she couldn't think of anything better than watching puppies come into the world.

"My house." Maverick opened the front passenger-side door for her, effectively directing Hunter to the back seat. Rather than complain, Hunter simply smirked at his brother.

Kennedy clicked her seat belt into place. She had a million questions. Was the vet meeting them there? Were home births common? How long was labor? Was this Barley's first litter? But when Maverick slid into his seat and looked at her, he must have seen the curiosity written all over her face because, before she could get out a single word, he pressed his finger to her lips. So surprised to feel his calloused skin on one of the softest parts of her, she stayed absolutely silent.

"All your questions will be answered there," he said calmly.

She managed a small nod, and he dropped his arm.

They drove down a private road (so noted by a sign) for maybe two minutes, before coming to a cabin—a log cabin!—nestled at the bottom of a hill. Lights shone from inside, and outside was a porch and stand-alone fence—the kind used to tie a horse to.

Maverick parked and they went inside.

In the corner of the homey and spacious living room, her eyes landed on a large wooden enclosure about two feet high with a front opening, like a doghouse without a roof. Maverick and Hunter strode straight to it, so Kennedy followed.

"This is what's known as a whelping box," Maverick said, kneeling down at the opening.

"Whelping?" Kennedy said, standing beside him.

"Whelping is what the canine birth process is called," he said.

"Barley's been making herself comfortable," Hunter said. "In preparation to deliver." He stood on the other side of his brother and stared down at the mom-to-be.

She had golden fur and pointy black ears. Her bedding looked pawed at and she gazed at Maverick as if to say, *Please help me get this over with*. A stack of towels and a laundry basket lined with a blanket were also inside the whelping box.

There was no one else in the house. No sign of a

veterinarian, which meant... "Are you delivering the puppies?"

"I'm here if Barley needs me," Maverick said in a soft voice, so composed that Kennedy couldn't help but admire the way he stared back at his dog. Man's best friend was definitely in play. "Female dogs know what to do by instinct, so she'll do most of the work. We know she's ready to go into labor because the sixty-four days or so of gestation are up, she hasn't eaten all day, been restless, and before I picked you guys up, she was licking herself."

"Mav might not have graduated vet school, but he finished enough of it," Hunter said with pride and a gentle voice as well.

So he did go to vet school. Kennedy tucked that information away to ask about later. Tonight was about Barley.

"Is this her first time giving birth?" Kennedy asked quietly.

"Yes," Maverick said, shifting to sit down with his leg bent in front of him. Hunter got on his knees and draped his arms over the edge of the box.

Both brothers kept their attention on Barley, their expressions full of adoration. Kennedy's stomach fluttered when her gaze caught on Maverick's enraptured profile. She'd watched dads give support to their wives during childbirth, but none had ever captured the slightest bit of regard from her. This side of Maverick appealed to every part of her as a woman.

She darted her gaze back to Barley to cure herself of that unwelcome thought.

"Bear—that's the golden on the ranch next door—got

frisky with Barley when we weren't looking," Hunter said.

"Barley and Bear, that's cute," she said, then, "oh my gosh, what is that?"

"That grayish sac," Maverick said, "means the first puppy is on the way soon."

Kennedy dropped down next to him, hand on his jean-clad knee to steady herself while she got situated. It was an unconscious move, but when their eyes met—for one second, two seconds, three seconds—awareness burned through her and she'd swear it swept over Maverick, too. They both looked away.

"How many puppies is she going to have?" she asked.

"With a dog her size, it's usually between four and seven."

"And how long does labor last?"

"We should see the first puppy within an hour. If not, we'll call the vet to decide if we should bring her in. After that, it goes fairly quickly."

"Mav's helped several mamas, so I doubt we'll be going anywhere," Hunter said. "Mind if I grab a drink?"

"Go ahead," Maverick said.

"Anyone else want one?"

"No, thanks," she and Maverick answered.

"I never get nervous in the ER, but I'm nervous now," she admitted. "I don't want anything to go wrong for Barley or her puppies."

Maverick peeked at her out of the corner of his eye. "It's hard when you're not in control, huh?"

"Exactly. I've delivered many babies and never worried." She wrung her hands in her lap. "But this is completely foreign. I don't like it."

"Here we go," Maverick said suddenly, crawling into the enclosure. He petted Barley's back as she quietly squirmed, then licked herself—or rather the first puppy that popped out.

"I'm here," Hunter said, kneeling and leaning over the edge of the whelping box.

Kennedy watched in awe as Maverick described everything that happened. She wanted to kiss him for explaining the process.

"Puppies are born in a thin membrane," he said. "Barley is removing it as the puppy comes out... It's done." He showed her what looked like plastic wrap before discarding it. "Now she's licking the pup, which stimulates it to breathe and cry." A whine sounded.

"Music to my ears," Kennedy said, and Maverick looked up at her and grinned.

Grinned!

She almost fell backward at the shock of seeing his straight white teeth on full display, along with a pair of dimples that made her stomach quiver like a schoolgirl experiencing her first crush.

"You want to cut the umbilical cord?" he asked next, and come on, who was this sexy man letting her in on the action?

"Yes!" She crawled on her hands and knees to get closer to them.

Maverick instructed her on where to cut the cord, to crush it, rather than make a clean cut to reduce bleeding, and then he tied the cord off with heavy thread. His big, strong hands were a sight to see. He handed the puppy to Hunter, who put the little thing in the laundry basket.

"Newborn pups want to nurse immediately," Maverick said, "but that can't happen until whelping is finished. As long as Mama can see her puppies, all is well."

Kennedy stared at the newborn pup. So amazing.

Barley chewed through the umbilical cords of the remaining puppies, but on the last one, after she'd removed the membrane, she sagged in exhaustion rather than lick the pup.

"Shortcake, you're up again. I need you to rub the puppy vigorously with a towel until it starts breathing on its own."

For the first time ever—it must be the heat of the moment—she didn't mind the nickname and jumped right in to rub the little animal until its perfect whimpers filled the room. The sweet sound almost brought her to tears. Her eyes met Maverick's, and for a moment, time stopped. Sharing this with him...

"The number of placentas matches the number of puppies," Hunter said as Barley discharged one final placenta. Maverick had explained that sometimes the afterbirth didn't come out with the puppy, but for this litter, everything lined up.

"I'm going to take Barley outside to urinate. Be right back," Maverick said, breaking their connection.

Kennedy sat back on her haunches and watched him go. He'd remained incredibly calm and in control throughout the birthing process, and she wondered what had happened to prevent him from finishing veterinary school. He was a natural with animals.

As soon as they returned, Barley got comfortable with her babies so they could nurse.

"What happens next?" she asked from outside the

whelping box.

"Barley will keep the pups warm and fed. I'll keep a close eye on them tonight in case she can't supply enough milk or rejects any of the puppies."

"That happens?"

"Our mom tried to reject Maverick, but it didn't take," Hunter teased.

"Maybe now's the time to tell you, you were adopted," Maverick deadpanned.

"Is that all you got?" Hunter fired back with a grin. He had dimples, too, but they didn't do a thing to her stomach.

Maverick ignored his brother this time and said to her, "Yes, that can happen. If it does, I've got nursing bottles and supplements I can give them. I'll take Barley to the vet tomorrow to check her for any injuries or complications we can't see."

"They're so cute," Kennedy crooned, staring at the new family. Three boys and three girls. "Thanks for letting me be a part of it. I enjoyed every second."

"It's pretty special. I'm glad you got to see it," Maverick said sincerely. "And participate, too. It's one more thing to add to your list of accomplishments."

If he'd been closer, she would have hugged him. "Watching you in action was pretty great, too." She put her hand over her chest. "My heart is still racing." Possibly for more reasons than she'd care to admit. Maverick Owens did things to her. Good things.

"It's getting late," he said, clearing his throat. "I'll drive you guys back now."

"I'm gonna walk," Hunter said. "Need to stretch my legs. I'll see you tomorrow. Thank you for the assist, Kennedy."

"Sure thing."

Hunter closed the front door behind him, leaving her and Maverick alone. With the birthing complete, she took a minute to look around. Wood-burning fireplace, full kitchen, dining area, all decorated in neutral tones with a masculine slant. A picture of the entire Owens family sat on an end table next to a sectional couch.

"Nice place," she said, wanting to drag her feet. She wasn't ready to go back to the inn. She was wide awake, energized. In Nancy Drew mode, interested in knowing more about her college nemesis.

"Thanks. You ready?" Apparently his feet were already out the door. All the more reason to stay put.

"Could I trouble you for a glass of water?" She really did need something to wet her dry throat.

"Sure." He ran a hand along the back of his neck. "Sorry I didn't offer sooner."

She followed him, taking a seat at one of two barstools at the kitchen island. "How long have you lived here?"

"Three years."

"Does your whole family live on the property?"

"Yes." He placed a tall glass of water in front of her.

"This is the stage of the program where you decide you've had enough chitchat, huh? You're contemplating how to get rid of me and how long it'll take."

"There's a certain nice ring to getting rid of you." He grinned.

"Maverick!" She punched him in the upper arm.

"Drink," he instructed, like that would get her out of his hair faster.

She drank. But slowly.

His eyes moved to her mouth pressed around the rim of the glass. Then they slid down the column of her neck as she swallowed before he leisurely moved his gaze back up to her eyes.

When Maverick Owens watched a woman take a drink, it felt intensely personal. If he checked under her collar, he'd burn his fingers. She put the glass down on the thick wood countertop and kept eye contact.

They'd played this game too many times to count, and she'd won nine times out of ten. She'd win now, too, no matter how much his baby blues threatened to drown her in unwelcome pleasure.

"Did you know your left eye is slightly lighter than your right?" he asked.

"Did you know there's a speck of green in your right eye and not in your left?"

"Did you know if someone stares at your pupil, it starts to look like the center of a daisy?"

No, she did not know that. Was that because no man had stared deep enough into her eyes to tell her? Or because Maverick had a way with words that snuck under her skin?

"Did you know a person's pupils dilate when they look at something they like?"

"What are you suggesting, Shortcake?" he asked evenly.

"Not suggesting. I can see it with my own two eyes. You like me, Maverick Owens, even though you don't want to."

"I'll admit you intrigue me, Kennedy Martin."

"Is this a new feeling or a carryover?"

He didn't answer her right away, and the sounds of puppies suckling filled the space. The nursing grew louder.

And at exactly the same time, they did two things: pried their eyes from each other to look across the room at the noisemakers, and laughed.

If she thought Maverick's dimples were dangerous, combined with a laugh, he might just kill her. That he seemed to have no clue how sexy he was made him that much more attractive.

"I don't think you're going to need those bottles," she said.

"Maybe not, but I'll still be on watch."

"Want some company?"

His brows did a nosedive.

"I'm not tired and this is pretty exciting stuff that I will probably never witness again, so I could keep you company. Not that I want any of the puppies to have difficulty feeding, but if one did and I got to bottle feed them, I might have to admit *again* that ranch life has its pluses. And wouldn't you love that, cowboy?"

"I don't need your validation to know how great ranch life is."

She opened her mouth to say she didn't mean to insult him, but he beat her to the punch.

"But," he added, "far be it from me to deprive you of a once-in-a-lifetime chance to be with newborn puppies on their very first night."

She grinned. "Thank you! I promise I'll keep any further questions I have to a minimum."

"Do you ever not ask questions?"

"Rarely. I just have this thirst for knowledge that needs to be quenched."

One corner of his nice mouth perked up, giving her a

tiny peek at the sexy indentation in his cheek. "Well, if I'm stuck with you, might as well get comfortable." He picked up her glass of water, grabbed his own, and walked to the couch. She sat next to him, leaving about a foot between them.

They had a perfect view of Barley and her puppies and for several comfortable minutes watched in fascination.

"Can I ask you something?" One more question, then she'd stop.

His head lolled forward in exhaustion. His chest rose and fell. He wore a pea green T-shirt tucked in behind his belt buckle but otherwise loose, and light-blue jeans that looked as soft as pajamas. His arms were tanned and sinewy. He really had it all going on.

"What happened to keep you from becoming a vet?" she asked. His tiredness didn't beat out her curiosity.

He lifted his chin. His stubbled jaw tensed before it relaxed and he said, "Life."

"Could you be more specific?"

Crossing his arms, a clear sign he wanted to close himself off rather than open up to her, he once again took a deep breath.

"I shared my story with you, and I'd really like to hear yours," she said softly. She hoped that appealed to his sense of fairness, but more than that, she genuinely wanted to know what had happened. He'd been so determined to become a veterinarian. So excited when he'd gotten accepted to the doctorate program at UC Davis, if she remembered correctly.

Rather than answer her, he got up to check on Barley and the puppies. She fought the urge to follow him for a closer look, deciding to give him some space. A couple of minutes later, he sat back down.

"How about I get you a beer? Would that help?" Surely he had some in the fridge.

He chuckled. "Probably."

"Done." She jumped up and grabbed a couple of beers. They clinked bottle necks and each took a healthy sip.

"I wouldn't have taken you for a beer drinker," he said pensively.

"There's a lot you don't know about me, cowboy."

"And a lot I do," he offered in a tone she couldn't decipher before he drank down the rest of his beer, his throat a nice place for her eyes to land while he did so.

She seriously had to stop thinking the word "nice" in connection with him. It blurred all the frustrating memories of him too much.

"My first year in graduate school, I met a girl," he said, staring out at the room. "*The* girl. Her name was Nicole."

Kennedy stayed quiet. She barely moved a muscle. She wanted to soak in whatever he gave her without any interruption.

"She wanted to be a vet, too. We started dating, fell in love. She was amazing. Smart. The kind of person who always put others before herself. And she got as excited about animals as I did. Then the summer before our third year, she got sick."

"No," Kennedy whispered so quietly, she didn't think Maverick had heard.

"The night I'd planned to propose to her was the night she told me she was diagnosed with ALS."

"Oh God, I'm so sorry, Maverick." There was no cure for

ALS. The disease made famous by Lou Gehrig killed everyone it met. Maverick didn't need to explain further, not to her. The progressive loss of muscle control that took away a person's ability to walk, talk, eat, and eventually breathe had a two-to-five-year life expectancy rate after diagnosis.

"We had talked about traveling after we graduated and before settling into marriage and our careers. Nicole had a bucket list two pages long of places she wanted to see. Weird foods she wanted to eat. Languages she wanted to hear firsthand. So instead of finishing school and risking missing out on that, we quit school and traveled."

"How much longer did you get with her?"

"A little over two years. The last few months we were here, of course. Her parents wanted to be with her, too, and she needed medical attention." He'd yet to speak *to* Kennedy, his focus somewhere else in the room.

"Did you marry?"

"No. I proposed, but…"

"I'm so sorry," she said again, taking his incomplete thought as a signal he didn't want to elaborate.

"Thanks. She was amazing through it all, waking up every morning with a smile, and she never felt sorry for herself, so I didn't either."

"She sounds really special."

He nodded. "She was."

"I'm sure she was grateful she had you."

At that, he finally looked at her. Pain and melancholy were etched in his temples, the corners of his eyes slanted downward. "That's the nicest thing you've ever said to me."

"I know." She leaned the side of her head against the

back of the couch. She *almost* reached out to touch him. "Don't get used to it or anything."

"I won't."

Did that mean he didn't want to hear her talk sweetly to him? Or that he planned to keep his distance as much as possible? She didn't know why, but both bothered her. The latter more so.

They settled more fully, him slouching and putting his feet on the coffee table, her bringing her legs up and snuggling with a couch pillow in her lap.

"Thanks," she said. *For telling me all that.* She'd been trusted with something he held close, a gift she wouldn't take lightly.

"We're even now," he told her.

Which should make her happy, but it only fueled her desire to challenge him again and again until she got everything she desired out of him. The question was, what exactly did she desire? And why was her heart once again beating faster than it had in a very long time?

Two years ago…

Dear Nicole,

Today is the day three years ago that I proposed to you and you said no. You looked at the ring in my shaking hand and told me to take my question back. To save it for someone who could say yes.

But you could have said yes. You could have been my wife for however long it lasted. But you said it was better this way. That you loved me and we didn't need a piece of paper to prove it. I said okay because all I wanted was for you to be happy, but your refusal broke my heart. I hated how logical you were sometimes. "Save the ring for your forever someone," you said. Well, that's not going to happen.

I tossed the ring in the lake today. Cole told me I was being ridiculous and should have returned it a long time ago. How could I return something that meant everything to me at the time? You said no, but that didn't mean I wanted to take back the gift. I wanted it between us, even tucked away in my sock drawer, as a tiny symbol of how deep our love was. The wound was also my lifeline. Until today.

Miss you like crazy,

Maverick

CHAPTER TEN

Four days until the wedding

Maverick woke with something soft and cozy attached to his side. A female something that filled his chest with warmth. She smelled good, too. He wrapped his arm more tightly around her in case she got any ideas about moving.

This was the most peaceful he'd been in forever.

His eyes flew open. The woman curled against him wasn't Nicole. Instead, she had wavy blond hair, freckles that made her look sexy, courage to be admired, and she stood only an inch or two above five feet, not just under six. She was healthy. Distracting. And they didn't typically get along.

You got along last night.

He lifted his arm, guilt warring with contentment at the position he found himself in. He'd let a moment of vulnerability get the best of him last night, but not today. Kennedy had five days left on the ranch. She was temporary. Crashing a wedding because she thought, what? The groom shouldn't go through with it?

He heard her on happiness, but he didn't want her causing unnecessary trouble and damaging the inn's good name. The couple looked in love, but... He'd never known Kennedy to be impulsive. That she came all this way to check on Reed, for whatever reason, did speak to the kind of person she was. She saved people—in and out of the ER, apparently.

She stirred as he tried to maneuver out of their too-close-for-comfort position.

That last part was a lie. He'd been plenty comfortable.

"Morning," Kennedy said, sitting up and seemingly unconcerned with the way they'd just been huddled together.

"Morning." He stood, eager to put space between them and to take a closer look at Barley and her puppies. Mom and babies had done well during the night, and he and Kennedy must have fallen asleep around one. The vintage clock on the mantel now read six thirty.

"How does everyone look today?" she asked from the couch.

"Good." He kept his back to her, pretending to stare inside the whelping box when he was really trying to figure out what this new, feels-good relationship between them meant. He didn't want to be rude, but he craved time to himself before he started on his tasks for the day.

Slowly, he turned around, the perfect idea hitting him. "I should get you back to the inn. How about I drive you to Baked on Main first?" He'd survive ten extra minutes with her if it meant a Kennedy-free day after that.

Only, when he looked at her gentle eyes and tousled hair and soft, rose-colored lips, the urge to scoop her up and take her somewhere special, where just the two of them could get to know this newer version of themselves better, hit him like a force of nature.

"Okay," she said quietly. "If that's what you want."

If that's what he wanted? What did that mean? Didn't she want to get away from him, too? They'd spent more time together in the past two days than they would have during two weeks of college. They'd spoken way more words. Stared at each other way too much.

Shared more than he thought himself capable of.

"What do you want?" he asked. He had no idea where the question came from.

She straightened her back and shifted to the edge of the couch, hands pressed into her lap. "Okay, don't laugh, but I had a dream last night." When he didn't respond, she continued. "I was riding a horse!" She grinned.

He raised his eyebrows. That didn't tell him much.

"It wasn't a real horse." Now this was getting interesting, and he couldn't help the slight curve taking over his mouth. "It was a horse on a carousel. I think I was at an amusement park or something. But the thing is, I hate carousels. I fell off one when I was four and broke my wrist and I've been afraid of them ever since."

He still failed to see where this was going and how it concerned him.

"So…I think this means I'm supposed to get 'back on the horse.'"

She gave him a cautious smile this time, and hell if it didn't stir some protective, give-her-everything-she-wants instinct in him. Not that she wasn't perfectly capable of taking care of herself, but as much as she liked helping people, he did too. He just did it far more quietly. And preferably without notice.

Not that much went unnoticed in Windsong. He'd left ten bales of hay for Texas Tom before the sun had risen a few weeks ago, and by midmorning the old man had driven over to thank him. The bales had been unexpected, so

Maverick had no idea how he'd known it was him.

"Roosters talk," his grandmother used to say. He'd started to believe her.

"You want to go horseback riding?" he asked.

"Not really, but I think I should."

"I think *want* trumps *should* in this case, but if you're dead set on it, we can see if Hunter has some time today."

"Oh." She dropped her gaze to the hardwood floor. "Okay."

"If we hurry, we should be able to catch him at the barn."

She nodded, and a minute later they hopped in his truck, made a pit stop at the bakery, and pulled up to the barn at seven a.m. on the dot. As Maverick cut the engine, Hunter ambled out of the barn looking like he had a fight in him—Maverick *was* late this morning—until he saw Kennedy slide out of the truck with a wave in his direction.

Then Hunter's face practically split in two. "So this is how it's going to be the rest of the week," his brother said.

Maverick had no idea why he kept getting himself in these situations with Kennedy and nosy members of his family. He knew better. "No, this is how it is this morning only. You have time to give Kennedy that riding lesson you mentioned to her?"

Hunter looked between him and Kennedy, deep in thought—too deep for Maverick's liking. Which meant his younger brother was about to say something wildly inappropriate or try to bargain with a chore or two, and Maverick wasn't in the mood for either.

"Actually, never mind," Maverick said. "I've got this."

"Awesome," Kennedy said, chiming in before Hunter could say anything. "Let me just take my doughnuts to my room and do a quick change of clothes and I'll be right back."

"I hadn't meant—" Too late. She moved to the truck to grab her food and then toward the inn like she was trying to shave several seconds off her time. He hadn't meant right now, but she'd made the decision for him.

Hunter slapped his thigh and laughed. "She's got you wrapped around her little finger."

"No, she doesn't."

"You are even more clueless than I thought if you can't see she likes you and you like her."

"There is no liking."

Hunt put a hand on Maverick's shoulder. "There is a lot of liking and I'm glad. It's past time you allowed yourself some fun."

He shrugged off his brother. "We're not having fun, either."

"Well, whatever you want to call it. Nicole has been gone for three years and you've been living like a monk ever since. You're leaving in less than two weeks to fulfill the promise you made to her. From now until then, have some non-fun with a gorgeous, smart woman who is under your skin whether you admit it or not."

Maverick scrubbed a hand over his jaw. His brother didn't know everything. He'd had hookups here and there, just nothing more than one night.

"Don't think too hard about it. Go with your gut. That's what you've always told me. What is your gut telling you right now?"

His own words coming back to bite him in the ass didn't feel very good. Because the truth was he did like Kennedy.

She challenged him in a way no one else ever had, and he hadn't realized how much he'd missed it until she'd stood in front of him with heels sinking into the grass and a fiery expression on her face.

"Right now it's telling me to get her on a horse."

"*A* horse?"

"My horse. You got things covered for the next couple of hours?"

"Absolutely." Hunt sauntered away but turned after only a few feet to add, "I'll let you know what you owe me later."

The damn guy had already won the puppy pool with a guess of six; what more did he want? "You do that." Maverick wasn't too worried. His brother forgot to collect payment more often than not. He owed the lucky skunk at least a dozen wagers.

Stepping inside the barn to greet Magnolia and outfit her, he rubbed down her neck. "Morning, girl. We've got an extra passenger today. You cool with that?" Her tail lazily swished back and forth, telling him *yeah*, she was good with that. He'd never admit it aloud, but he looked forward to taking Kennedy on her first-ever horseback ride.

She kept surprising him. Kept him on his toes. Kept him wondering what she'd say or do next. When had the enemy become something unique and different?

"This is her first time on a horse," he told Magnolia a few minutes later. "So we'll take it nice and slow."

"Do you always talk to your horse?"

Maverick startled at the sound of Kennedy's sweet voice but kept his back to her while he finished getting Magnolia ready. "I do."

"Does she understand what you're saying?"

"Some. My tone of voice and body language help a lot with comprehension."

"We had a dog growing up, Coco, and she didn't listen to anything I said, no matter how I said it. She was still a great pet, though."

He smiled to himself, then turned, ready to go, but when he laid eyes on Kennedy, he needed a moment. Standing where she was, with subdued rays of light filtering into the barn behind her, she practically glowed, and the sight of her had him swallowing. Hard.

It's Kennedy. The biggest pain in your butt. Trying to ignore her, however, proved futile. He couldn't look away. She had on the same jeans, he'd guess, but the new white T-shirt was frayed around the collar and ends of her short sleeves and did little to hide the color of her bra. *Pink.* He immediately wondered if her underwear matched, then mentally slapped himself for caring.

She'd collected her hair up into a neat bun on top of her head, leaving the column of her neck bare, and he noticed a few more freckles there. But what really got to him where it hurt—in a good way—was the footwear. She'd put on the pair of boots again. Girly, but boots nonetheless.

He never in a million years would have thought he'd be face-to-face with Cowgirl Kennedy.

He liked it as much as he hated it.

"Is something wrong?" she asked, glancing down her body. "I thought jeans and boots would be best for riding."

"You look great."

Her head popped back up. Yeah, she was as shocked as he was by the compliment.

He quickly changed the subject. "This is Magnolia. She and I are ready to go." He led them out of the barn.

"What about George?"

"I thought we'd ride together so I don't have to worry about you falling off. Plus, I never made it back out to the trees yesterday, so we can take another look this morning."

"I think there was an insult in there, but I'm going to ignore it."

"Good idea." He grabbed his Stetson hanging on the wall and dropped it on his head as they exited into the soft sunshine spilling over the mountains. Mornings were great for rides. The temperature cooler, the air fresher. And today the fog had stayed away.

"I'll get on first, then have you hop on behind me."

"You make it sound so easy. Magnolia, did you hear that?" Kennedy cupped her hand around her mouth and leaned closer to his horse. "He thinks I can hop on like it's no big deal."

She was talking to his horse. Like they were friends.

Something stirred inside him.

"All you have to do is place your left foot in the stirrup like this"—Maverick put his foot in—"then pull yourself up and swing your right leg over like this." He moved in slow motion so she could see how simple it was to get seated on a horse.

She looked up at him with appreciation he felt in the middle of his chest. "I never thought I'd ride a horse, let alone ride one with you." Her friendly voice sounded new and open-ended, like she had no intention of going back to the way things were between them. He could relate. A switch had been flipped and while a part of him still wanted her far away from his ranch, another part wondered what else they might do together this week.

"Right back at you." That she stood here now was some kind of fantastic fluke.

"What if I miss?"

"Then you fall and try again."

"All right." She took tentative steps closer. Her tongue darted out to sweep over her bottom lip. He left her plenty of room to sit in the saddle behind him. "Here I go, Magnolia."

"Left foot first," he reminded her.

She took a huge breath in, her chest rising but not falling, and put her foot in the stirrup. Once her boot fit snugly in place, she whooshed out a breath, took his offered hand, and pulled herself up and over.

"Maverick!" She almost slid all the way over, but he caught her by snaking his right arm behind her and catching her around the waist. His shoulder grumbled at the strain on his muscles as he pushed her back into place.

"Grab onto me," he instructed.

She latched on tight, her arms wrapping around his middle like she was trying to squeeze him to death. Maybe she was.

"I think you're okay, so you can relax your hold a little."

"Do not tell me how tight I can hold on."

He fought a smile. Well, if he was going to die, there were a lot worse ways to go than on his favorite horse with a pretty girl's warm breath on his neck and her breasts crushed against his back. In fact, he could feel every press and release of her chest, every quick beat of her heart.

"You okay if we start moving?" he asked after a few

long beats of silence.

"Can you give me another minute?"

"Sure." He held the reins in one hand by his hip and rubbed Magnolia's neck with the other. Given Kennedy's thirst for knowledge, he supposed talking her through this would be a good idea. "Balancing on a horse does take practice," he said. "You have to get used to the motion and movements of the horse, but luckily you'll be doing that while attached to me."

Her chin moved up and down against his back.

"You don't have to worry about doing anything but enjoying the scenery. I've got the reins, and that's how Magnolia knows to turn or stop or trot or gallop. She and I have ridden together thousands of times and know each other's body language with our eyes closed."

Kennedy eased up on her death hold, lifted her head. "Okay, I'm good to go now. Thanks for giving me a minute."

"No problem. We'll start nice and slow, but if you ever feel uncomfortable or scared, just let me know and we can take a breather."

"Sounds good."

They walked down the dirt path toward the trees, moving slower than molasses, but oddly, it didn't bother him. Time had a way of getting away from him, so right now he chose to enjoy every minute.

"You doing okay?" he asked over his shoulder.

"Yes. It's so peaceful out here." Her grip on him remained steady, but her voice held less trepidation.

"You picked a good time to barge your way into a ride."

"I didn't barge," she argued.

"Whatever you say." They continued off the beaten path

toward the lake, across an overgrown pasture, and through wildflowers.

"How many acres do you own?" she asked.

"Just under a thousand."

She shifted, sliding closer if that was even possible, but loosening her arms so they draped around his middle instead of crushing it. "I bet you had the best time growing up here."

"Are you feeling okay back there? I think that was another compliment about the ranch."

"I'm just saying there was probably a lot to do outside, and boys like that kind of stuff."

"And girls don't?"

"I'm sure plenty do, but I didn't. I liked shopping malls and movie theaters and the library."

"You never played outside?"

"Not really, unless it was to lie out in the sun at someone's swimming pool."

"No sports, either, I take it."

"I chose to work out my brain instead. I read a lot of books, studied things I found interesting. PE was always the worst. No one ever picked me for their team, and I always came in last on things like the mile run. When it came to debate and the academic decathlon, though, everyone wanted me on their team."

That's pretty much how he would have pictured her. She was fit and moved with confidence, but her focus lay on mental challenges.

"I do like long walks," she added.

He gently pulled back on the reins and pressed his leg against Magnolia's body with subtle pressure.

"What are you doing?" Kennedy asked in a panic, obviously sensing his slight movement and not liking it.

"I'm just telling Magnolia to turn left. She takes her cues from me on which direction we should go."

"Oh. Okay."

"I promise you're safe," he said.

"I know. I trust you. Most of the time, anyway. Oh, wow, look at that."

He let the trust thing slide and assumed she'd noticed the lake that had come into view. "That's Boone Lake. It's man-made and named after my great grandfather. It was originally open to the public, but about ten years ago my father closed it."

"How come?"

"To save the fish and other wildlife that make their home there. Pollution from small boats and people's trash was slowly killing off the ecosystem. Now it's just for guests of the inn. And we allow only canoes or kayaks, nothing with an engine."

"Do people swim in it?"

"They can, yes."

He gave Magnolia the signal to turn right, and this time Kennedy did just fine with the change in direction. Her body relaxed against his, the tension that had rolled off her like a heat wave earlier lessening considerably. They moseyed in amiable silence until the trees came into view.

"The landscape here is truly breathtaking," she said, leaning ever so slightly around him to get a better look at the valley covered in pine trees. "I've never seen anything like it."

"It is," he agreed. "A lot different than the city."

"You can say that again."

"A lot different than the city," he repeated.

She swatted at his chest, releasing her grip on the front of his T-shirt for a second.

"Haven't you *ever* ventured to the country or mountains? For a vacation or something?"

"No. We couldn't really afford vacations when I was young, so my parents would plan staycations, and we'd go to an amusement park and museums and movies. By the time my parents could afford it, they were getting a divorce and things were different and very tense, since my mom and dad didn't get along anymore. I actually lived with my dad while my two younger sisters stayed with our mom. My mom still hasn't forgiven me for it, but I couldn't handle all the bickering and meanness that came from my sister Victoria, especially after my surgery. Dad was easygoing and pretty much left me alone. Don't get me wrong, I do love my family, but I didn't know how to process everything that was happening, and I've always been fine on my own."

They meandered down the aisles of trees, Maverick doing a quick study of each. His childhood had been vastly different from Kennedy's. He and his siblings had kept each other company constantly, laughing and teasing far more often than fighting. His parents argued on occasion, but they loved one another fiercely to this day. He, Cole, Hunter, and Nova had fished and climbed trees and played hide-and-seek for hours. The family vacationed at mountain resorts and fancy campgrounds, tropical islands, and the jungle of Costa Rica.

"Then, when I was an adult, I didn't have time to travel,"

she continued. "Too busy with school and then my residency."

"Does travel appeal to you?" he asked, wishing he could take the question back as soon as the words left his mouth. Travel was his and Nicole's thing.

"Honestly, I've never given it much thought."

Good answer—she didn't have any hint of wanderlust, not like he did, and a sense of relief filled him. In less than two weeks, he'd be on an airplane to fulfill not only Nicole's wish, but his own desire to escape, leaving behind any preoccupation with a certain ER doctor.

CHAPTER ELEVEN

Four days until the wedding

The second Kennedy's feet were planted firmly back on the ground at the barn, she wrapped her arms around Maverick's shoulders in thanks. "That was wonderful. Thank you!" If anyone had asked her a week ago if she saw herself riding a horse, she would have said, "Not in a million years." Yet, here she stood, staring up into the face of a handsome cowboy after doing just that. Funny how life had a way of throwing curve balls. Thankfully, this one had turned out well.

"You're welcome," Maverick said, his hands on her waist, keeping them connected for longer than necessary.

Her stomach dipped. His fingers practically burned through her clothes. And his eyes held something new. Something different. She couldn't put a name to it, only that his usual annoyance seemed to have slipped into something less indignant…and much more tender.

Was he feeling this new energy between them, too?

On a scale of one to lethal, riding a horse with her front pressed against his back, his confident, controlled stature keeping her safe, had been much more dangerous than she'd imagined. The reasons were numerous: He had muscle everywhere. He was patient. He talked to her like an equal, even though she'd never been on a horse before. He was a good listener. He wore a cowboy hat way sexier than she had known cowboy hats could be. He talked to his horse like Magnolia was his best friend. He smelled incredible.

Kennedy stopped the inner monologue there and lifted onto her tiptoes. To do what, she didn't know, but some magnetic pull tugged her mouth closer to his.

He blinked, dropped his arms, and took a step back, breaking the spell.

"I'm glad you enjoyed the ride," he said, turning away to lead Magnolia back into a stall.

Disappointment filled her. She'd wanted to kiss him. She'd wanted *him* to kiss her.

She banished the ridiculous thought from her mind. It had been a silly moment, a blip she'd already forgotten.

"Did you?" she asked, not quite ready to say goodbye.

"Yes."

"Well good, because…" She couldn't admit she liked the ride so much that she'd consider doing it again. "I'm having a good time here."

"It's only Tuesday," he countered, effectively ruining whatever vibe she thought they had going on a minute ago. She got the message: he had things to do now that didn't include her.

"Lucky me!" She turned on her boot heels to take her leave. "I guess that means I'll see you around, cowboy." The reminder that they could bump into each other around the next corner ought to keep him on his toes.

She inwardly smiled all the way back to her room.

She found Andrew exactly where she'd left him earlier, sprawled on his stomach on top of the bedcovers in his boxers and a T-shirt. "Time to rise and shine," she said, opening the shutters before lifting a yummy glazed doughnut out of the white paper bag she'd left on the counter of the kitchenette. She jumped onto the bed next to her best friend, earning a grumble. He'd sleep until noon if she let him.

"I have a problem," she said.

That got his attention, and he opened his eyes to look at her. "Where'd you get the doughnut?"

"Since you're shirking your doughnut duty this morning, I got it for myself." Via a cowboy.

"Sorry. After you texted you were staying the night at Maverick's, I hit up a wine bar in town with Liam and a few other people and crashed late."

"It's okay. Have fun?" she asked.

"Yeah. Be right back." He rolled off the bed to use the bathroom. On the return, he noticed she'd brewed the in-room coffee and he made a beeline for a cup. "Bless you." He brought two cups back to the bed with him, handing her one before he situated himself beside her, pushing his pillow upright and leaning against the headboard. "How was the dog thing?"

"Amazing. She had six puppies."

"That's cool." He took a sip of his coffee. "So, what's the problem this morning?" He glanced down her body. "I like that the boots are becoming a regular thing."

She wiggled her feet. "Right? They're way more comfortable than I would've guessed. So, back to my problem. Maverick is being weird and I don't like it."

"Define weird."

"Open, then closed off. Sweet and not so sweet. Sexy and charming."

Andrew raised his eyebrows in interest. "Tell me about the sexy and charming. That's all I care about."

She pushed him in the thigh.

"Kidding! Kind of. That man is one fine specimen, no matter what."

"He was never like this in college. I don't know how to beat this Maverick."

"What are you trying to beat him at?"

"Everything."

"Why? You aren't in competition with him anymore. You're a doctor about to start working at one of the country's best ERs. You've accomplished everything you set out to do."

Almost. She still hoped to hear from Dr. Weaver with the news they wanted her in Boston for a final interview. "You're right. I don't know why I'm carrying this silly rivalry with me."

"My guess is it's because you want to be around him."

"No, I don't."

"You like him."

"Not even a little."

"You are a terrible liar, Kennedy Martin, and you know it."

She put her coffee down on the bedside table and crossed her arms. "Okay, fine. I don't *want* to like him."

"Because…"

"Because he's…" She huffed under the heavy load of emotions she hadn't prepared for. She'd always planned, studied, mapped out her future so she could remain in control as much as possible. She didn't need sticky notes or phone reminders or any other prompts. Everything was in her head, right where she liked it.

Maverick had been locked away in her past.

He wasn't supposed to collide with her present without a hcads-up.

Looking back, he was the only person who had ever truly challenged her. Who had made her work harder. Who had sparked a strong desire to succeed inside her.

"It's hard to put into words," she said, chickening out of saying anything incriminating.

"Let me do it for you, then." Damn her best friend and his knowing her better than she knew herself. "Maverick is your equal, whether you want to admit it or not, and he always has been. You hated him because you were afraid of him."

"No, I wasn't."

"You were afraid he could break your heart."

"That's not true. I hated him because he pushed all my buttons. On purpose. And besides, he had plenty of attention from girls, and it never bothered me."

Andrew narrowed his eyes at her. She tried to recall if they'd ever talked about Maverick in a romantic way. They hadn't, because she didn't think of him that way.

"For someone so smart, you can be so clueless when it comes to your own life."

"I'm not—"

He waved his hand to stop her. "You're also stubborn and have to figure everything out on your own, so I suggest you just let it go while we're here and you try to talk to Reed."

"Speaking of…" She glanced at the clock on the nightstand. "We need to get to the golf course. I'll jump in the shower first."

"Do we really have to crash this?"

"Yes." She got to her feet and glanced at the wedding itinerary. "It's for the guys only, so it's the perfect chance for me to talk to Reed without Elle around."

Andrew looked dubious. "And *you* won't look out of place or anything."

She pushed the mattress up and down to jostle him. "Don't be hating on the plan now! We've got this."

An hour later, with Andrew behind the wheel of their golf cart, they arrived on the golf course pretending they hadn't broken every courtesy rule to get to the third hole behind Reed and two other men.

She and Andrew exited their vehicle and each pulled a golf club from the bag they'd rented. Andrew looked golf-ready in plaid pants and a white golf shirt he'd bought in the pro shop. She looked decidedly less prepared in her shorts, T-shirt, and white sneakers. They weren't anywhere near the right spot on the course to be in, but they were in close proximity to her target.

Reed settled into position to putt. He'd golfed from a young age, so she had no doubt he'd make the shot. While he did so, Kennedy took a few practice swings with her club. Not that she knew anything about swinging a golf club. Besides miniature golf as a teen, she'd never played the game.

On the first swing, the golf club accidentally flew out of her hands. It spun through the air and almost hit Reed in the head before landing on the green.

"Oh my gosh, I'm so sorry!" She covered her mouth and nose with her hand.

"Kennedy?" Reed said, responding to her not-so-subtle entrance. He looked at the men with him. "Give me a minute." He picked up her ill-behaved club and walked it back to her. "Hey."

"Hi. Sorry to interrupt."

"No, you're not." Reed smiled at her. "Hey, Andrew."

"Hi, Reed. I'll just be over…" He trailed off, stepping away to give them some privacy.

"Sorry I haven't texted," Reed said. "I haven't had a chance."

"No worries. Crashing your golf game to have a minute to talk is like a normal Tuesday for me."

He winced. "I wish you didn't have to crash anything."

"Me too. But, since I'm here, I need to make sure you want to get married. Because if you don't, I can help."

Reed let out a slow breath. "I know what I said the other night, but I was hoping I'd slurred it or something and you'd misunderstood."

"There was a little extra emphasis on the vowels, but I heard it clearly." She glanced back and forth between his eyes, trying to get a good read on him. "It's a problem if you even thought it, Reed."

"I know. I guess that night, I felt like she didn't trust me, and the truth is…" He swallowed. "I'm not sure I want to go through with it."

Her stomach knotted. "What do you need in order to be sure?"

He stared off somewhere behind her. While he contemplated his answer, she recalled his short attention span with women over the past several years. His revolving door of dates and the trail of half-broken hearts he left behind.

Reed was smart and focused and dedicated to his profession. Before he'd gotten engaged, she would have bet money on him staying married to his career. Elle had changed that.

"I don't know." He ran the back of his hand along his jawline. "A conversation with Elle for sure. We've just been so busy, and she's so excited. Our friends and family are here, and I don't want to be the bad guy. I don't want to hurt her."

"An honest conversation is always a good idea," she said.

"I do love her, but trust is essential, and sometimes she's…" His eyes searched the grass like the answer to his doubt hid in the blades.

"How many times over the years have we said that medicine isn't an exact science?"

"I don't know. A hundred?"

"Love isn't an exact science, either. Sometimes you have to take a leap of faith." Trusting their instincts was something they'd talked about often over late-night study sessions and long residency hours. She noticed the scar on his arm from the knife wound he'd received when he'd come to her rescue in the ER. Now it was her turn to save him if he needed it.

He nodded. "I'll talk to Elle and then touch base with you."

"Reed! You ready?" one of his golf mates said.

"Yeah," he called back, then squeezed her arm in thanks. "Stand by?"

"You know I will."

"Thanks." He handed over her golf club. "Maybe wait until we've cleared the area before swinging again."

"What? Like I'd do that again? I needed your attention and I got it."

"Riiight." He walked away, she hoped feeling more confident than he had before she arrived.

Andrew moseyed back over to her, his attention on Reed. "That man has one fine —"

"Hey, eyes over here," she motioned to herself. "We should hurry out of here. Come on." She climbed into the golf cart, glad to have had a minute with Reed and cautiously optimistic that clarity would come to him soon. She knew from her experience with Trevor how important and fragile trust was.

"Sucks having doubt," Andrew said on the drive back to the clubhouse.

"You heard all that?"

"Of course. Someone's got to have *your* back."

She leaned over and kissed his cheek. "Thank you."

They returned the golf cart and clubs and drove back to the inn. They were barely out of the car when Bethany approached.

"I'm so glad you're here," she said. She wore cute black capri pants and a white polo shirt with Owens House Inn printed on the breast pocket. "Doc called, and he was hoping you could help him out at his office."

Kennedy's heart started beating a little bit faster. "Did something happen?"

"His nurse is home sick with a fever and he's got his hands full, I guess, including a head injury."

Kennedy didn't need to know anything further. "Of course I'll help. Let me just change clothes really quick."

"Great. I'll drive you when you're ready. His office is just in town."

Ten minutes later, she walked through Doc Choi's office

door. A thirty-something woman wearing funky eyeglasses that matched the color of her red hair greeted her.

"Dr. Martin, right? I'm Georgie, Doc's office manager. Thank you for coming so quickly. We haven't been in a predicament like this in a long time and appreciate the assist."

"My pleasure. What can I do?"

"Follow me." She led Kennedy through a main door and down a hallway to an exam room, lifting a chart out of a file holder on the wall. "Leah arrived fifteen minutes ago. She—"

A child screamed from inside the room across the hall.

Georgie winced and handed Kennedy Leah's medical chart. "That's Billy. He's six and hates needles. He's here for his immunization shots. I should…"

"Go ahead. No worries here," Kennedy said. "I've got this." (Kennedy loved that Doc still used handwritten charts, given most everything had moved to electronic software.) Eyes on the medical chart and the notes written there, she stepped inside Leah's room, clicking the door shut behind her before raising her head. "Hi, Leah. I'm Doctor…" To her surprise, Leah wasn't alone. Maverick sat in the visitor chair beside the exam table. "Martin. It's nice to meet you." She didn't have time to address the cowboy in the room because Leah held a blood-soaked towel to the top of her head. *Hello, head injury.*

Kennedy quickly dropped the chart on the small work counter and donned gloves. "What happened?"

"Hi, Dr. Martin," Leah said. "I was delivering flowers to the inn and was in a hurry. The trunk of my car closed on my head."

"Ouch." She stood in front of Leah and nodded at the towel. "May I?"

"Of course."

The head bled a lot, so it could be anything from a small cut to a larger gash. Kennedy lifted the towel to take a look. Leah's blond hair, matted with blood, made it more difficult to see clearly, but thankfully the bleeding had stopped.

"I feel so foolish," Leah said.

"I've seen and heard a lot worse," Kennedy told her, separating the strands of hair so she could view her scalp. "This may hurt. I'll do my best to be gentle."

Leah flinched when Kennedy found the laceration just above her hairline but said, "It's okay."

"The cut is deep enough that I think we should suture it. Did you at any time pass out or feel nauseous?"

"No."

"Feel dizzy or experience blurred vision?"

"No."

"I was there when it happened," Maverick said, reminding her he was in the room. "The back of the SUV closed right on her head and then she took an unsteady step back."

"I also cried like a baby. Thanks for leaving that part out, Mav."

Mav? Kennedy darted a quick glance at him before focusing back on her patient. Just how well did these two know each other?

"She started bleeding right away," he said, his tone neutral. "But otherwise seemed fine. I put her in my truck and drove straight here."

"It hurt worse than anything I'd ever felt before, and it's throbbing now."

"That's normal." She looked Leah right in the eyes as she spoke, conveying warmth and self-assurance. "Give me a minute to find what I need, and we'll have you fixed up in no time."

She removed her gloves and searched the cupboards above the sink. Finding everything for the minor procedure, she placed each item on a stainless steel surgical tray and then put on a new pair of gloves.

"Let's lie you down," she said, pressing the button to lower the back of the exam table. Once Leah was comfortable, Kennedy got to work. "You're going to feel a sting as I numb the area." As gently as she could, she injected local anesthetic around the injury. Leah fisted her hands in response.

"Take a slow breath in and then slowly let it out," Kennedy instructed. "Good. One more time. Great. The hard part is over. We'll wait a minute or two for the lidocaine to take full effect and then get started."

She replaced the safety on the needle in case she needed to add more local.

"So you were delivering flowers. Are you a florist?" Kennedy asked.

"I am. My sister and I own a shop just down the street."

"How long have you been in business?"

"Going on five years now. We inherited the store from our grandmother."

"Oh, I'm sorry."

"She's still with us, just retired. Although she likes to show up on a daily basis to make our lives more interesting."

Kennedy smiled. "I'm guessing that's a nice way of putting it."

"Uh-huh. It doesn't matter that I've worked at the shop since I was sixteen; she still likes to tell me how to do things." Leah's eyes wandered over to Maverick. "Remember when she told me I'd made my own corsage wrong?"

He nodded.

Did they go to a dance together? Date in high school? A twinge of jealousy pricked her stomach.

Kennedy got back to work, touching around the wound with the needle holder to check for numbness. "Do you feel anything?"

"No."

"How about here?"

"No."

"Great. Let's stitch you up."

"How many do I need?" Leah blinked up at her.

"I'm guessing three or four. Do you arrange flowers for the inn often?" Kennedy asked, purely to keep Leah's mind off the suturing, not because she was fishing for more info on how often Leah saw Maverick.

"We do all the big events at the inn. Weddings and other large parties. Nova keeps the property looking gorgeous on all the other days. There's a wedding this weekend and I was meeting with the bride. I'd brought a couple of samples with me to be sure we were on the same page. Elle, the bride, loved our designs online, but it's often different when you see them in person."

The wedding. The entire reason for Kennedy's visit to Windsong.

"Did she like them?"

"She did. And I've never met a nicer bride."

"That's good to hear." She hadn't doubted Elle was a kind person. She'd captured Reed's attention, after all. But a good marriage required more than that. Kennedy tied off another stitch. Two more to go. "Have you always lived in Windsong?"

"Yes. Maverick and I both." She glanced at him again, affection clear in her regard. "In fact, I think the only other time I've been hurt, you were there, too."

"When Red Star threw you," he said.

"Red Star?" Kennedy said.

"My horse," Leah clarified. "He got spooked and caught me off guard. Mav saved me then, too. Luckily, I only sprained my wrist and scraped up my legs and arms."

"When you landed in poison oak."

"Oh my God. That's right." Leah grinned at Maverick, and Kennedy had to peek at him to see if he was grinning back.

He was smiling that killer smile of his. Kennedy quickly returned to her last suture, not liking the sting of jealousy that stabbed her in the chest this time.

Leah looked back at Kennedy. "He refused to help me up, the big jerk."

At that, *Kennedy* grinned, grateful to be back in Maverick territory she understood. "Sounds like him."

"You two know each other?" Leah asked, confused.

Oops. She hadn't meant to say that out loud. "We went to college together."

Maverick stood. "Looks like you're almost done."

"She is," Kennedy said.

"I'll grab you an iced coffee, Lee, and meet you out front.

She can go after this, right?"

"Yes."

"Thanks, Kennedy." He put his hand on her shoulder, then left the room.

Left her body humming from the brief touch and the sincerity in his gratitude.

Leah sighed. Kennedy knew exactly what kind of sigh it was, too. Her sister made the same one when she crushed on a classmate. (And off the record, Kennedy almost sighed, too.) "That man is so frustrating."

Tell me about it.

"I wish… Never mind."

"I'm in town for only a few more days," Kennedy said. "You could tell me your wish and no one would be the wiser."

"I wish he saw me as more than a friend, but he never will."

"It sounded like you guys dated in high school."

"No. He was a year ahead of me, and my senior year when my boyfriend dumped me the day before prom, Mav happened to be home that weekend, and he stepped in and took me."

Kennedy removed the draping from around Leah's head, a funny tickle in the back of her throat over hearing about Maverick's good deed. "Let's have you sit up slowly." She brought the table back to a chair position. "How do you feel?"

"Good."

"Sit still a minute and then I'll have you stand. Right now the area is numb, but as soon as the anesthetic wears off, it's going to be sore and tender to the touch. You can take some over-the-counter pain relief if you need to. No shower until the morning, unfortunately, and no shampoo. Just rinse your scalp with warm water until Doc removes your sutures. Take it easy for the rest of today, too, and if anything starts to concern you, give me—I mean give Doc a call."

"Thanks, Dr. Martin."

"You're welcome. Any questions?"

"Knock, knock." Dr. Choi poked his head inside the room before entering fully. "How we doing?"

"Hi, Doc," Leah said. "We're done."

"Fantastic. Thank you for taking care of my patient, Dr. Martin."

"It was my pleasure. Leah, you ready to stand up?"

Leah stood without trouble, gave Doc and Kennedy each a hug, and left with instructions to return on Monday.

"You want to stick around a little longer?" Doc asked her. "I have a patient in Room Two who decided to lodge a fishing sinker up her nose."

"Oh no." Kennedy said.

"It's been one of those days. There must be a full moon coming tonight."

"I'm happy to stay as long as you need me to." She walked down the hallway with an extra bounce in her step. Every day that she got to practice medicine and help someone was a great day.

"Appreciate it."

They stopped at Doc's office. The room held a sleek glass desk with two armed leather guest chairs for sitting, and a bookshelf lined with medical books, cards, and knickknacks. Doc opened the top drawer of a filing cabinet and pulled out a stethoscope.

"Here you go, Doctor." He handed her the stethoscope and retrieved a lab coat hanging on the back of the office door. "Now you're part of the team. Let's do this."

Kennedy slipped her arms through the coat and placed the medical instrument around her neck with a huge smile on her face. She worked beside Doc and she worked on her own, meeting townspeople of all ages, hearing gossip, and being asked a million questions about herself. She now had several people crossing their fingers for her to get the job in Boston.

At around two o'clock, another wave of patients stopped by the office. Doc saw walk-ins on Tuesday afternoons, another reason he needed Kennedy in his nurse's absence. Typically, he saw a handful of people, but looking out at the crowded waiting room today, he said, "You're good for business, Dr. Martin."

"Do you think they're all sick?"

"No, I think they're all nosy, with the exception of Mrs. Freed. She's been fighting a sinus infection. Why don't you start with her?"

"I can take the heat," she countered, not afraid of more prying. Being interrogated took her mind off cowboys, grooms, and a dream job across the country.

CHAPTER TWELVE

Four days until the wedding

A few hours later, Kennedy rubbed the tiny glass ladybug Mary Rose had given her between her fingers. The gift meant more to her than she could say, and right now she needed some good news—she needed the ER job on the other side of the country so she'd have distance from her family.

She stared down at her phone. At the text her mom had sent a few minutes ago, wiping out Kennedy's happy mood from an afternoon spent in Doc's office.

Andrew sat back down in the cushioned chair next to hers on their patio and handed her a freshly baked chocolate chip cookie from the inn's kitchen.

"Thanks," she said without lifting her head from her cell.

"Staring at it isn't going to change it."

"You want to try?" She held the phone up to his face.

"You know I'd make those words disappear if I could."

"I know." She dropped her arm, took a big bite of the soft cookie. It tasted delicious, and it helped make her feel a little better. "I can't believe them. I can't believe this is happening."

"I'm sorry."

"There are three hundred and sixty five days in a year and they have to pick *my* birthday to get married?"

"It sucks."

"I'll be reminded of their wedding day every freaking year when it should be a day for me. Not to be selfish, but come on. This is completely insensitive given the circumstances. Not that I care about them getting married anymore—I'm over it. They deserve each other. But it isn't fair for them to ruin my birthday, too."

"No one said life was fair."

She glared at him.

He raised his hands in defense. "Just saying. And you know, it goes both ways. They'll be reminded of your birthday every year on their anniversary."

"We both know that's not true." Her self-centered sister cared about one thing: herself. She probably didn't even realize February twenty-fifth was Kennedy's birthday. Kennedy wasn't sure if that made it better or worse. "And what happened to getting married next summer?"

Andrew shrugged, sympathy written all over his face.

Kennedy stared off toward the mountains and the setting sun. "My mom could have at least called me rather than texted. I love how she gives me news like this as if it's no big deal, an afterthought, even. She still resents me for living with my dad a million years ago, and that's never going to change." Blowing out a big breath, she sank deeper into the chair and finished her cookie. "This is why Reed shouldn't get married unless he's one hundred percent sure. Divorce sucks."

"Agreed." Andrew stretched out his long legs. "How about we stay in tonight and play cards?"

"That's nice of you, but I know you want to go to the hoedown. I think I'll take a walk instead and then a hot bath. You have fun and when you get back, you can fill me in."

"Are you sure?"

"You look too handsome to miss it."

He jumped to his feet. "I do. Don't I?"

Jeans, a light green collared shirt, his dirty blond hair combed to the side, he could definitely pass for a Hemsworth.

"I'll see you later," she said.

As soon as the door clicked shut behind him, she exchanged her heels for sneakers and slipped out the small patio gate. She had maybe an hour of sunlight left, so she took a walk across the neatly manicured grass, the sound of country music in the distance. She wandered in the opposite direction, toward the stable, then strolled inside the dimly lit building, the air cool with both the front and back doors open. She admired the animals from afar, then resumed walking. Down the private well-packed dirt road lined with evergreens, toward Maverick's house. She told herself it was because she wanted to see the puppies.

His truck was parked near the horse fence and lights were on inside. She had no idea what she was doing until she bypassed the front door and tiptoed around the house and through the sloped flowerbed to peek through the living room window. Apparently she'd turned into a weirdo who couldn't muster up the courage—or maybe it was strength—to talk to the owner of the puppies. It made her mad, yet she didn't backtrack. Instead she bumped her forehead on the glass as she tried to see Barley and her babies.

There they were, cuddled together without a care in the world. Must be nice.

She stood there like a peeping Tom as guilt and

embarrassment wormed their way inside her head. She was being ridiculous.

At the sound of a twig breaking, she whirled around. And bumped right into a hard body. Just like the other day, she lost her balance, and Maverick caught her to keep her steady. This time, though, they were chest to chest, his arms around her waist. On the sloped ground, his handsome face was *right there*.

Neither of them spoke. Their cheeks brushed. Kennedy turned her head slightly, grazed her nose against his. His breath mingled with hers. She swallowed the thick bundle of nerves coating the back of her throat.

Their eyes held, his a stormier blue than she'd ever seen before. She didn't know what kind of storm, only that she didn't mind it. Not one bit. She enjoyed every reaction she got out of him.

One centimeter farther and their mouths would meet. She'd get to feel his lips on hers, discover if he'd kiss her in frustration or because he wondered what she tasted like, too. Her heart hammered and she was curious if he felt it. Maybe if she didn't say how much she wanted to explore this connection between them, he wouldn't deny her. Although words had never seemed to sway Maverick Owens, one way or the other.

"Um…" she muttered, figuring she should at least acknowledge she'd been caught snooping.

Maverick looked into her eyes, that storm she saw in his baby blues waging a battle. She held her ground. Willed her muscles to relax. Not a hard thing to do when she wanted to melt against him.

"What are you doing here, Shortcake?" His voice, deep

and low, resonated with more than one meaning. He knew. He knew, even if she didn't, that she was here for more than one reason.

"I, uh…" she breathed out. Speaking when they were nose to nose proved difficult. *Just kiss me and put us both out of our misery.* He read minds, right?

"You, uh…?" He intended to make her say it, damn him.

Or *she* could just kiss *him.*

Yeah, that sounded like a much better idea than answering his question.

Slowly, carefully, purposefully, she brushed her lips against his. His piercing gaze made her shiver, but she'd started this expedition and she planned to finish it. Whether he liked it or not.

And he'd like it.

She pressed her mouth more firmly to his, testing the waters. Ready to drown if he'd just give her the sign. And then he did. *He* moved his mouth against hers. Eyes wide open, he kissed her. Watched her. Kissed and watched her as their lips connected in a slow dance of getting-to-know-this-part-of-you. Her hips moved of their own accord, rubbing against his body. Closer. She wanted to be closer, to crawl inside him and stay there until all his walls came crashing down.

He kissed her like she was something new, something breakable, and she *was* both those things. Because the last forty-eight hours had been unexpectedly welcome in a way she'd never known. Or anticipated.

But just as they were about to get to the good stuff and part their lips, he pulled back with a pained expression on his face. "What are you doing here?" he asked again.

They disengaged farther, space swelling between them. He took a step to the left and she took a step to the right. She guessed they were going to pretend the kiss never happened. She guessed, sadly, he might already regret it.

"I wanted to see the puppies."

"And you decided to sneak around because…?"

"Honestly, I don't know. I suppose I wanted to get a peek at them and then leave without having to see you, too." Which did nothing to explain why she also wanted to kiss him. This situation confused the crap out of her.

"Okay, you good to go, then?"

No. She wasn't good to go, and she most definitely wasn't good to go and let him win this tug-of-war. "Well, since I've been caught, mind if I come in for a better look?"

He combed his fingers through his hair like he wanted to pull the thick locks out. "Next time just knock, okay?"

She drew an X over her heart. "Promise." An easy guarantee, since she didn't plan on visiting him again anytime soon. He'd left his front door open and gestured for her to enter before him. "How did you know I was out there? I thought I was exceptionally quiet."

"I saw you the second you walked up. There's a window in the kitchen with a view of the road. When you didn't knock right away, I figured you were up to no good."

She swatted him in the arm. "Thanks a lot."

He closed the door behind him. "I was right, wasn't I?"

Rather than answer him, she wandered over to the dogs. "How are they doing?"

"Good, for the most part." He took the spot right beside her, their arms brushing. "I just got back from the vet and Barley checked out well."

"*But…*"

"But one of the pups was restless earlier. She's having a hard time feeding, so for the next day or two, I'll help out."

"I could, too, you know." When he didn't say anything, she added, "I mean, if you're busy with work around the ranch, I'm happy to stop by to bottle-feed her. I've fed many babies in the hospital and feel confident I could handle it." So much for not visiting him again.

"I'll keep that in mind." He was just appeasing her, the big lug.

"I'm assuming the different colored ribbons around their necks are so you can tell them apart?" All the puppies had fluffy, golden fur and pointed ears like their mama.

"Exactly. Pinky there is the one I'm a little worried about."

The sweet concern was such a juxtaposition to Maverick's rugged stature that she was once again reminded he had layers she knew nothing about.

They watched the sleeping family in silence until Maverick turned and headed into the kitchen.

She walked back toward the front door. "I guess I'll be go— Is that sushi?" she asked, veering away from the door and into the kitchen where two take-out cartons sat open. Recently opened, by the fact that they looked untouched. "Since when do you like sushi?"

"Since always."

This new information made no sense. He was a steak and potatoes kind of guy. Right? She leaned against the counter across from him. She loved sushi. "Windsong doesn't seem like a sushi kind of town."

"It's not." He filled a glass with water from the dispenser

on the front of his fridge, then a second glass, and carried them to the counter.

"Thanks." She accepted the tumbler he handed her. "I'm sorry I interrupted your magical dinner, then."

His lips curled slightly. Lips she would never look at the same way again. "Nice" did not do them justice anymore. She absently touched her bottom lip, remembering the way her body had tingled when they'd kissed.

"Cole had an appointment in Rustic Creek and grabbed it for me."

"So he's the nice brother." At Maverick's raised eyebrow, she continued. "Cole is nice. Hunter is outgoing. And you're…you're prickly."

"You sure that's the word you want to go with when you're hoping to share my dinner? Not to mention I'm the one who knows you haven't been invited—"

"Okay, fine. You're nice, too."

He bit back a smile, darn it. No dimples for her. But he did grab a couple of napkins and push the containers of sushi to the center of the counter. "Have at it."

She didn't need to be invited twice.

They stood at his counter, ate spicy tuna rolls and some delicious crab-shrimp combo roll, and let the silence guide their thoughts. There was something intimate about eating this way, simply standing in his kitchen and using their fingers to share a meal. When Maverick focused on his food, she took in the open space with high ceilings, noticing for the first time a passport and travel guide for Europe sitting at the end of the counter.

"Are you planning a trip somewhere?" she asked.

His face pinched like he wished he'd put away the

evidence out in plain view. "How'd it go with Doc today?"

"Do you want to talk about it?" she asked.

"Do I want to talk about what?"

"The reason you answered my question with a question that had nothing to do with travel."

"I think it's obvious." He popped a piece of sushi into his mouth. When he'd finished chewing he said, "I *don't* want to talk about it."

"Why not?" At his pained expression, she decided to take pity on him. "Okay, how about this: we exchange information."

"There's nothing I need to know," he said plainly.

"There's absolutely nothing else you'd like to know about me? Gee, thanks."

"You're welcome."

She ate her sushi and scowled at him. A minute of painful — although introspective — silence later, she'd figured out the reason for his grumpy attitude. "I think the trip has something to do with Nicole and that's why you don't want to talk about it."

He choked on his spicy tuna.

"Sorry. You know I can't let things go. And for what it's worth, I do care about your answers; I'm not just trying to irritate you."

He took a long pull of his water. "And yet—"

"Stop." She held up her hand. "No need to finish that thought. I'm only trying to make conversation, and your passport *is* right there, so you can't really blame me for asking. How about we Rock Paper Scissors?"

"For what?"

"If I win, we talk, and if you win, you pick what we do."

"What we do?" he asked, amused.

"Yep." Let him stew on that one-word answer. She had no place to be and had no problem wearing out her welcome. Not with him.

"Best two of three?" He put out his fist.

She made a fist and extended it. "Sure."

"On three," he said. "One…two…three." He made a rock. She made paper. He immediately counted again. On three, she did a repeat of paper. He made scissors. Dang it. They were tied now. They studied each other for a moment. She didn't know why, but she felt certain he planned to do paper, which meant she needed to do scissors.

And that's what he did.

Yes! Rather than gloat out loud, she grabbed another piece of sushi and contemplated her next question. To his credit, Maverick took the loss in stride, eating another piece himself and then waiting for her. Like he knew her mind was at work.

"Are you going somewhere Nicole wanted to go?"

"Yes."

"By yourself?"

"Yes."

Okay, time to ask a question that didn't have a "yes" or "no" answer. "When are you leaving?"

He leaned his elbows on the counter, leading her to believe her questions exhausted him and he needed the support. His forearms were strong. His hands big and masculine. "In twelve days."

"Oh wow." She hadn't expected that answer. "So soon."

"It's been planned for a while."

They reached for pieces of sushi at the same time, their

fingers brushing, and a shock of electricity skated up her arm. "How long are you going for?"

"Two to three months." Another answer she hadn't considered. "So, a job in Boston?" he asked, changing the subject.

"Fingers crossed." She lifted her free hand and crossed her fingers. She really hoped to hear from Dr. Weaver before the end of the week.

"You haven't applied anywhere else?"

"No. This position came up and I really want it."

"It's a long way from home."

"That's part of the reason I want it."

"The engaged sister thing," he stated, obviously good at reading between the lines.

She touched her finger to the tip of her nose. "I don't know how to be around her or my mom anymore, and it stresses me out when we're together. I will miss my other sister, Ava, though. She's starting her senior year at UCLA next month. And Hugo and Andrew."

When Maverick didn't say anything else, she steered the conversation back to him. "Are you excited for your trip?"

"Yes."

"Are you going back to favorite places or visiting new ones?"

"Both, but mostly..." He glanced at his passport. "I made a promise to Nicole to visit the places we didn't get to see together, so those are at the top of the list."

"How long ago did she pass away?"

"Three years."

His voice, tinged with sadness, penetrated down to Kennedy's bones. She'd witnessed patients passing away numerous times in the ER, but this one hurt the most. Hearing Maverick so *defeated* hurt. He obviously still had unresolved feelings. "Did you ever think about going back to veterinary school? There's no reason why you couldn't, right?"

"There're reasons," he said, leaving her to wonder what they were. "You want the last one?" He pointed his chin toward the spicy tuna.

"No, thanks. The rest is all yours."

He ate the last piece of sushi while she gazed out the kitchen window. Dark now, there was nothing to see, but she kept looking nonetheless. One of the puppies whimpered, pulling her attention toward the living room. "Is that Pinky?" she asked hopefully.

"Sounds like it. Why don't you go have a seat on the couch and I'll grab a bottle for you to give to her."

"Okay." She practically skipped into the other room, grateful to Pinky for breaking the silence in the kitchen and for being hungry while Kennedy was still there.

Maverick put the tiny little thing in her arms and then handed her a bottle. Pinky immediately took to it. "She's so cute," Kennedy cooed, unable to take her eyes off the soft, sweet animal.

"You're a natural with her."

"Was that another compliment, cowboy?"

"Just stating a fact."

"Good to know. If you start giving me compliments all the time, I really won't know what to do with you."

Except kiss. She'd like to kiss him until the cows came home. That was a ranch saying, wasn't it? And kissing him meant no talking, only feeling, and boy had she felt a lot of pleasure when they'd kissed.

She noticed out of the corner of her eye, however, that his attention was on his phone, not on her at all, like she'd hoped it would be.

"Everything okay?" she asked.

"My mom just texted that George is loose somewhere."

"Is that a problem?"

"It could be. George likes to wander and always comes back, but with the hoedown happening, he may get frightened or frighten someone. Hunter's in town, so he asked if I could track George down and return him to his stall before anyone's the wiser."

"I'm fine here with Rumi if you want to go."

"Rumi?"

"Is it okay if I name her that? Rumi was a famous thirteenth-century poet. He's a favorite of mine, and I think it's a great name for a pet. Not that this little angel is mine. You can change her name after I leave."

"You like Rumi?"

"More like love." One of Rumi's quotes hit her just then. She knew Maverick would appreciate it. "'Silence is the language of god…'"

"'All else is poor translation,'" he finished for her.

Her jaw dropped. "No way."

"I know Rumi quite well."

This time, their staring contest wasn't about who could beat whom. It was about realizing a magnificent piece of treasure you never knew existed had been right under your nose this whole time.

Rumi's lyrical poetry was breathtaking and beautiful and spoke of celebrating union. This newfound piece of

Maverick made her want to test the glittering waters further… "'In your light I learn how to love. In your beauty, how to make poems.'"

"'You dance inside my chest where no one sees you, but sometimes I do, and that sight becomes this art,'" he finished once again.

The room spun. He'd just blown her mind, and she didn't know whether to laugh or cry.

Who was this man? And who was she for suddenly thinking him the sexiest man alive?

He quickly stood. "When she's done eating, go ahead and put her back with the others. I won't be too long."

Kennedy simply nodded before focusing back on Rumi. She didn't lift her head until she heard the front door shut.

Talk about an epic surprise. If Maverick threw one more pleasant unknown at her, she might have to rearrange her entire view of him, and that wouldn't do. Because once she did that, her only reason for getting under his skin would be to make him change his view of her in return. And she'd prided herself on not caring what he thought of her.

Rumi finished her bottle and Kennedy petted her and held her close before gently placing her back in the laundry basket. She wondered if Maverick planned to keep all the puppies. Certainly Jenna would want one. But were the rest spoken for? Would Maverick give the others away to local families?

She moseyed back into the kitchen to rinse out the bottle and get a drink of water. If it weren't pitch-black outside, she'd walk back to the inn by herself. Not that she was afraid of the dark—just the creatures that might be lurking unseen. Like bats. Or spiders. Or snakes. She'd seen many patients in the ER because of animal bites and preferred not to join their ranks.

The takeout containers were still on the counter, so she cleaned up their dinner mess and put their glasses in the dishwasher. Hoisting herself up onto the counter, she sat with a clear view out the window over the sink. She'd see Maverick's truck lights coming down the drive any minute, she supposed.

She stretched her arms and her fingertips accidentally touched his passport. She contemplated the small book for a few seconds before picking it up to check out his picture. Underneath it, she discovered, was a second passport, and her pulse sped up. Same blue cover. Same binding. She knew it was an invasion of privacy to look at either one of them, but she couldn't stop herself. The first passport was Maverick's. Of course he took a good picture. The second passport belonged to Nicole Morisette. She was pretty with dark hair and a full mouth.

An ache filled Kennedy's chest. Both passports were filled with stamps. Venezuela. Argentina. Greece. Their pages matched. Pages that told a story only the two of them knew. Secrets and memories and shared adventures.

Kennedy had never been out of the country. She'd barely been out of the state.

A tiny piece of paper slipped from Nicole's passport. *Don't unfold it. Don't unfold it.* She unfolded it. The words were written in Maverick's writing, she guessed, the penmanship more masculine than feminine.

It was her favorite Rumi poem.

I want to see you.

Know your voice.

Recognize you when you
first come 'round the corner.

Sense your scent when I come
into a room you've just left.

Know the lift of your heel,
the glide of your foot.

Become familiar with the way
you purse your lips
then let them part,
just the slightest bit,
when I lean in to your space
and kiss you.

I want to know the joy
of how you whisper
"more."

She closed her eyes and silently recited the poem from memory. When had Maverick given this to Nicole? Had she whispered "*more*"?

A flash of light behind her eyelids had her opening her eyes. Maverick was back.

And because she'd never get the chance to do it in reality… "More," she said softly to the empty room.

CHAPTER THIRTEEN

Four days until the wedding

Maverick pulled up to his house, the headlights flashing across the kitchen window and catching Kennedy's glossy blond head. It looked like she was sitting atop the counter before the vision of her vanished.

Tonight hadn't gone at all how he'd planned. After Cole had dropped off dinner and stuck around long enough for a quick conversation about the puppies, Maverick had been about to sit down and eat when he'd caught sight of Kennedy walking toward his house. She had on a plum-colored sundress and sneakers and was a prettier sight than any one person had a right to be. He'd watched her until his view of her disappeared, then he'd waited a beat for her to knock…only she never did.

When he found her snooping, he'd almost laughed out loud. She kept him on his toes, that was for sure, and his need for isolation dimmed considerably when she was near. How could it not when she always invited an interesting war of words?

And then he'd done the unthinkable.

He'd kissed her.

And liked it.

Her lips made a man think impure thoughts. Made a man want to stray from his convictions. Kennedy Martin, with her smart, sexy mouth; intelligent eyes; and perceptive mind wore him down.

Holding her close had been heaven. She'd fitted inside his arms like she'd been made to be there. And she smelled amazing, obliterating the scent of horses and hay and pine trees and narrowing it down to her. Only her.

He'd caught himself, though, before the kiss went beyond the point of no return. Kennedy wasn't a one-night stand kind of woman. She was dinners and movie nights and reading poetry on the porch.

This Saturday marked the three-year anniversary of Nicole's death. It also marked what would have been her thirtieth birthday. The day she'd entered the world, she'd left it, a sick joke he hated to dwell on. Before she passed, she'd asked him to finish their travel list before that milestone birthday, and he hated that he was a little late in delivering. Obligations to his family and the ranch had warred with his promise to Nicole, but better late than never. He was a man of his word, and this trip was long overdue. He had to stay focused on that.

Before he could turn off the truck's engine, Kennedy bounded out the front door and hopped into his passenger seat. "Mind driving me back to the inn now?" she asked, slightly out of breath.

Earlier, he couldn't wait for her to go, and now it seemed she couldn't get away from him fast enough.

"Sure. Everything okay?" He had a sneaking suspicion she had mischief on her mind again.

"Everything's fine. I'm just tired, and the bathtub in my room is calling my name. Did you find George okay?"

Great. Now he was picturing her in the bathtub. Water sluicing over her small shoulders and pert breasts as the faucet filled the tub. His jeans grew tight behind his zipper.

This visceral reaction to her had to stop.

He stepped on the gas pedal a little too roughly. "Sorry," he said, grateful it took less than two minutes to drive to the inn. Then, "Yes, George is back where he belongs."

They stayed quiet after that, and as quickly as she'd jumped into his truck, she jumped out when he came to a stop. "Thanks!" She caught the car door just before it shut all the way and added, "For everything. It was a fun night."

"You're welcome."

"There's one more thing. I accidentally on purpose looked at your passport. And Nicole's. I shouldn't have, but I did. I'm sorry."

Appreciation overtook the flash of anger that tensed his jaw. She owned up to her mistakes and believed in honesty. The deed done, he could hold it against her or move on, and forgiveness left him feeling a lot lighter as he nodded. "Thanks for telling me."

She gave him a small smile and nod in return before beelining it to the inn.

Once she'd safely entered the inn, he put the truck in drive. Sharing a meal with her in his kitchen *had* been enjoyable, even with all her questions. She'd gotten him to open up more in the past three days than he had in the past year. Partly because he didn't want to let her win their battle of wills.

But another part of it was *her*. She was easy to talk to.

And now that he knew she loved Rumi, he felt a kinship he hadn't felt with anyone else. Not even Nicole. She'd loved when he whispered poetry to her, but she didn't feel it deeply enough to be moved to distraction or remember the verses. Nicole was more practical. Even about love. After her diagnosis, they'd loved each other deeply, but she'd held a piece of herself back. The piece, she told him, she wanted him to have from the woman he fell in love with next.

Next.

That was a tricky word he tried not to overthink because he couldn't predict *next*.

He'd certainly never imagined seeing Kennedy again.

Or thought he'd lose Nicole when he had. Life held no certainties. He'd learned that more than once.

He walked into his house and found Barley and her puppies sound asleep and his kitchen clean, the baby bottle and nipple drying separately on a paper towel beside the sink, the passports exactly as he remembered leaving them.

Kennedy not only spoke her mind and invited conversation, she had class. She was gracious. In college they'd been so competitive with their schoolwork, they'd never taken the time to learn anything personal about each other. With age came maturity, though, and he'd be lying if he said he didn't like this new version of their friendship. If you could even call it that. "Kennedy Martin" and "friend" still didn't exactly go together.

You were friendly enough to kiss each other.

That she initiated the contact was the reason why—he wasn't sure he would have followed through on the urge. It was one more thing he liked about her. She was no shrinking violet.

Needing to get his mind off the beautiful and fascinating doctor, he grabbed his laptop and sat on the couch to do some work. His family had no idea he had a meeting with a friend interested in investing in his non-toxic pesticide. During his travels with Nicole, they'd met a winemaker in Italy. Marco and his wife owned a vineyard, and they'd hit it off on their visit there. So much so that Marco had kept in touch over the years.

Maverick had been thinking about mass-producing his pesticide as a means to add further financial stability to the ranch, and Marco wanted in. The older man saw potential; he just needed documentation.

Maverick opened the business proposal he'd been working on for the past several months. The numbers were there. The action points. If this happened, Maverick could hire help for the ranch and build a small processing plant, then take a step back. Knowing the ranch and inn would not only survive, but thrive without him twenty-four seven meant he could go back to veterinary school.

He worked late into the night putting the finishing touches on the project, and then before he could change his mind, he emailed it to Marco. This would give the man plenty of time to go over the proposal before Maverick arrived. And take the weight off Maverick's shoulders sooner rather than later.

Falling asleep took all of two minutes, an image of Kennedy standing in the middle of bright green grass in bare feet and a sundress, a mischievous smile on her face, sending him off to dreamland. If he thought he had even a chance of keeping his mind off the beautiful and compelling woman, he was sorely mistaken.

· · ·

The next morning, some sixth sense told Maverick to check on the trees. He hadn't observed them carefully enough during the past two visits with Kennedy as his sidekick. She had a way of hijacking his attention. Whether silent or talking nonstop or staring at him, it didn't matter what she did—if she was near, he couldn't fully concentrate.

And he had to be sure the trees were in good condition before he left town.

He drove the electric utility vehicle through the far edge of the farm as the sun rose over the mountains. The smell of the salty air and views of the ocean popping in and out between the hills made this location unique. Their ranch held the distinction of being close enough to the coastline to swim in the Pacific and ten minutes later stand in a forest of pine trees. The ocean breeze carried away the dust and grime found on most ranches and left behind bright surfaces and shining scenery.

This morning though… "Damn it."

He parked and took a closer look at the trees. Several of them had dead, diseased, or damaged branches. Others oozed sap from multiple holes, a sure sign of insect damage.

"Damn it," he repeated. The last thing he needed was an insect problem this late in the growth cycle and with only days until his scheduled flight out of the country.

If fault lay with his pesticide, he was screwed.

Crawling on all fours, he dug into the soil with his bare hands, checked the irrigation lines, looked for bacteria or fungi under the tree bark.

It took until noon, but with help from Hunter, their cousin Miles, Uncle Tim, and their groundskeeper, Jerry, they inspected every single tree with a careful eye.

Maverick lifted his cowboy hat and wiped the back of his hand across his forehead, wiping away the perspiration.

"You're right," Hunter said. "The problem is isolated to the southeast corner only."

"With no clear explanation as to why," he grumbled. What made that area vulnerable when it hadn't been before? Why the hell today and not a month ago when he would have had plenty of time to figure it out? He may have learned quite a bit about trees over the past three years, but he wasn't an arborist, and right now he wished his dad hadn't let go of their tree manager, albeit for financial reasons.

Pressure built in Maverick's shoulder blades. They probably wouldn't figure out what caused the problem, but at least they'd caught it before any permanent damage had been done.

"Jerry's coming back with a small crew," Hunter said. "I'll stay with Uncle Tim and Miles and we'll prune the affected trees so you can do what you need to do."

"Be sure everyone uses rubbing alcohol between cuts to disinfect the tools."

"We will."

"I'll owe you a beer later." Maverick put his hat back on his head.

"You'll owe me at least two," Hunter said around a smile. "And a cheeseburger."

Maverick patted his brother on the back and left to do what he needed to do: spend the afternoon in his greenhouse shed doing quality control on his tree food and then double-checking the delivery system hub. The small slice of solitude where he worked on creating his special mixture normally kept his mind sharp. Focused.

But not today.

Today he worried about the proposal he'd sent to Marco. He needed his investment. Needed to make this new endeavor a reality if he had any hope of returning to vet school. But more than that, for helping to secure his family's financial well-being.

Like a certain doctor, he had plans for his future.

Fourteen months ago…

Dear Nicole,

Jenna rode George all by herself today. The kid is a natural with animals and I couldn't help but think that our kids would have been, too. Jenna's joy was contagious, thank goodness, because I'm sad to say Bethany had another miscarriage. She and Cole are such amazing parents that I don't understand why this is happening to them.

Then again, I didn't understand why you got sick, either. I'm dwelling less on that, though, and remembering all our good times. You asked me to do that, and I've been slow on the uptake. Whenever Jenna catches me looking sad, she says, "Uncle Mav, turn that frown upside down." If I don't listen immediately, she takes her little hands, squeezes my cheeks, and tilts the corners of my mouth up. She does the same with her dad and mom. Although less with Bethany because Beth is strong like you were, and focuses on the one amazing child she is blessed with instead of dwelling on her losses. To keep from thinking too much about the bad stuff, I'm watching and learning and spending every waking hour to make the ranch better.

One day, things will be different. They have to be, right?

Miss you like crazy,

Maverick

CHAPTER FOURTEEN

Three days until the wedding

Dr. Weaver wanted her in Boston.

Dr. Weaver wanted her in Boston.

DR. WEAVER WANTED HER IN BOSTON!

Kennedy read the email one more time to be sure her eyes weren't deceiving her. She had an in-person interview on Tuesday. Six days from today. One hundred and forty-four hours.

She did a happy dance, then called Ava to tell her the news. Her sister didn't answer, so she texted, *Have good news! Call me!* When Ava didn't call back right away, Kennedy ran out of the room to search for Andrew.

She was bursting with excitement and in such a hurry that she shut the door behind her without taking the key, *and* she bumped into someone in the hallway.

The someone being Elle.

"I'm so sorry!" Kennedy said as the pitcher of lemonade in Elle's hand slipped out of her grasp and crashed to the floor, spraying them both with pale yellow liquid before it landed with a thud.

The two stared at each other in shock.

They looked at the floor and the clear plastic pitcher lying in a puddle on its side surrounded by several matching cups.

They glanced back up...at the wet marks on their

shirts…and laughed. They laughed so hard they slid to the floor, seated across the hall from each other, to…Kennedy wasn't sure to do what, but the moment seemed bigger than them walking away from each other.

"I'm sorry," she said again. "I was in a hurry and not watching where I was going."

"It's okay. I was on my way to one of my bridesmaids' rooms. We were going to add some vodka for a little cocktail hour."

Kennedy leaned over to gather the cups and right the pitcher. "I'll get you a new pitcher and cups and deliver it." Right after she found a mop to wipe up the spill so no one slipped and fell.

"That's nice of you, but…" Elle said sincerely. "Mind if we just sit here for a minute?"

It sounded like Elle had something on her mind, and they were alone in the hallway, so Kennedy didn't see why not. "Okay."

"I've seen you around, but I know you weren't invited to the wedding," she said.

Kennedy should have read *Wedding Crashing for Dummies* or at least googled what to do in this type of situation. She never shied away from confrontation, though, and prided herself on being a straight shooter— until this week at least—and she felt this accidental run-in had happened for a reason.

"I'm Kennedy. It's nice to officially meet you."

Name recognition shined in Elle's green eyes. "You're Reed's friend and ex."

"Yes, but please don't be upset with him. He didn't know I was coming."

"Why are you here?" Her voice wobbled. "Wait. Don't answer that. I'm not sure I want to know." She looked down at her lap. "He's been distant since his bachelor party and I'm afraid…" She lifted her head. "Are you why?"

"No," Kennedy answered quickly. She didn't want Elle to doubt Reed's faithfulness for a second. "We're friends, that's all."

Elle sniffled. "Okay. I'm hoping it's just cold feet, then. I'm not the best at sharing my feelings, and the last couple of weeks, I know I've been clingier than Reed likes. Than anyone would like."

Over the years, many patients had talked to Kennedy, confided in her about things that were easier to share with a stranger than a family member or friend. Every person had a right to their feelings, and Kennedy never judged. Her coworkers, especially the attendings, told her it was one of the things that made her a good doctor. People felt comfortable talking to her.

"Is there a reason why?" she asked.

Elle let her eyes close for a moment. She had thick, dark eyelashes. A friendly oval-shaped face. A long side braid and a cute off-the-shoulder blue top, even with lemonade on it. "There is. Or was. It's not an issue anymore, and so I thought things would go back to normal, but they haven't." She met Kennedy's concerned expression with equal parts shame and apology. "There's something I've never told him and I should have."

Kennedy stayed silent, hoping Elle would continue.

"He thinks I kept calling him the night of his bachelor party because I didn't trust him. But that wasn't the reason at all. It's true I'm insecure now and then, like when he wanted to invite you to the wedding and I said I wasn't comfortable with it. But aren't we all a little bit? Relationships are hard and precious, and occasionally my confidence wavers." She ran a finger over her engagement ring. "Reed's bachelor party was supposed to be a day on the golf course, but then his brother changed the plan and I panicked. I panicked because I was worried something might happen to Reed."

"Like an injury?"

"Or worse." Elle waved her hand like she was being ridiculous. "The thing is, my mom was engaged before she met my dad. On the night of her fiancé's bachelor party, my mom got this terrible feeling. She knew something was wrong and she was right. He died in a bar fight."

"Oh my God."

"When she met my dad and they got engaged, she worried that if he had a bachelor party, he'd die, too, so he didn't have one."

"Why didn't you tell Reed this? I'm sure he would have understood."

"I don't know. The day of golf seemed safe to me, and I didn't want to ruin the tradition for him. But then when his brother changed the plan, I couldn't bring myself to spoil it for him. So that night I kept calling to make sure he…he was still alive. Naturally, he thought I was checking up on him, and I was, just not for the reasons he believed. I planned to tell him the next morning, but we're staying in different rooms, and family arrived, and I just didn't get around to it."

"Elle." Kennedy touched her arm. "You need to tell him. This is an easy fix. He'll understand, and then you'll both feel better."

"I feel so silly."

"You're getting married! Of course you're not going to be rational all the time."

A small smile brightened Elle's face. "He's asked me more than once to tell him when things are bothering me. It's caused problems before and I'm afraid he's going to... going to walk away. Decide I'm not worth the effort."

"You are." Kennedy considered herself a good judge of character, and she liked Elle. A lot. The warm, kind vibes Elle gave were impossible to ignore. "And so is Reed. Secrets are hard to share sometimes, but if it impacts your relationship, you have to. You have to trust Reed will love you more because you're being vulnerable."

"Thanks, Kennedy. I am lucky to be marrying him."

"You definitely are, and I say that as a compliment to you, too, because I never thought he'd get married. That you've captured his heart is a big deal. He'll never let you down, Elle."

"You're right. And I plan to keep his heart safe and sound for the rest of my life."

"I'm happy to hear that." Kennedy wanted nothing more than for Reed to be loved, and Elle had just reassured her of that.

"I'm sorry for not inviting you to the wedding. I truly am. Will you please join us on Saturday?"

"Oh, uh..." She'd love to accept the invitation, but she'd lost track of the various characters Andrew had played and dragged her into. She didn't want to get caught in a lie *at* the wedding...

"Please." Elle got to her feet, so Kennedy picked up the

pitcher and cups and did the same, careful to avoid the puddles of lemonade. "Having you there would mean a lot to Reed. And me."

"Elenore Carson!"

Kennedy and Elle looked down the hallway to the man sticking his head out of a door.

"We were about to send the wedding police after you! Get your butt in here!"

"On my way!" Elle turned back to Kennedy. "That's my brother and man of honor."

"I'll grab you a new pitcher. And thank you, I'd love to attend the wedding." Bottom line, she really did want to be there. She'd just cross the identity crisis line when she got there.

"Wonderful. Please feel free to bring a guest, too. And you're welcome to join us now if you want."

"I think I'll let you celebrate without me. I was actually on my way to track down a friend when I bumped into you."

"Oh, right. Of course. Tall blond guy, right? He and my brother have been talking a lot," Elle added with a smile. "And don't worry about the lemonade." Elle took the pitcher and cups from Kennedy's hands. "I'll grab it if you don't mind letting someone know about the spill on the floor."

"Deal."

Kennedy planned to wipe up the spill herself, but she ran into Cole and he said he had it. He also had a master key to her room and opened the door for her so she could change her shirt.

Then she went in search of Andrew. She found him on

the second floor veranda enjoying—you guessed it, lemonade. Small platters of bruschetta and cheese, crackers, and red grapes were also set out. She made herself a plate and poured herself some lemonade before joining him and the two women who looked captivated by everything he said. It took super-human strength not to immediately drag him away to share her job news, but going on looks alone, one of the women had to be Elle's mom, and Kennedy didn't want to be rude.

"This is my best friend Kennedy," Andrew said, no Aussie accent. And *yay* for finally telling the truth.

The women introduced themselves. It *was* Elle's mom. Her name was Bea and the other woman was Bea's best friend, Melanie.

"Andrew was just telling us about his job as a water slide tester," Bea said.

"Oh?" Kennedy choked on a grape.

Andrew patted her on the back. "You okay?"

She swallowed and gave the universal sign of "okay" with her hand. Not another persona!

"As I was saying…" Andrew smiled at the women, charming them so much with his winning grin that it didn't matter what came out of his mouth. "Every time an amusement park or hotel or other tourist locale adds a waterslide, they need a quality control person to make sure that it's both safe and fun. And that's where I come in. I check on things like how much water is in the slide and how long it takes me to slide down. Then I write up a report, outlining any concerns or safety issues."

"What a fun job!"

"It is. And I've lost my trunks in the water only a few

times. And not from sliding, if you get my drift."

Kennedy rolled her eyes.

Bea and Melanie laughed.

"Would you mind if I borrowed Andrew for a minute?" Kennedy asked, taking his arm and leading him away. Once they were alone she said, "I got the interview!"

He lifted her feet off the ground in a brotherly hug. "That's fantastic! When is it?"

"Tuesday."

"So you'll fly out Monday? Stay overnight?"

"Yes. Dr. Weaver is going to have someone make the arrangements and email me the itinerary." Clouds played peek-a-boo with the sun, but at the realization there was a very good chance she'd be moving across the country, her face grew warm.

"Do you need to head home sooner?" Andrew asked.

"No, we can stay. I actually just ran into Elle, and we had a nice chat."

"Do tell."

She gave a summary of their conversation. "So, once she talks to Reed, I think he'll feel better, and staying to see them get married would be great."

Andrew kissed her cheek. "Awesome! Now, how about you and I head into town for a celebratory cheeseburger and fries? You're one step closer to your dream job, and I'm damn proud of you."

• • •

They sat in a corner booth of The Couch Potato. The restaurant and bar reminded her of a modern-day saloon, given the dark wood but contemporary chandeliers, tables, and chairs. The sleek bar gleamed under the lights. Two bartenders, one male and one female, wore cowboy hats. Servers were dressed in denim attire more trendy than country.

"Don't look now, but Tall and Hunky times two are coming our way," Andrew said.

"Hey, Kennedy, mind if we join you?"

She turned her head to find Hunter with a ready smile and hand already held out to Andrew. "Hi, I'm Hunter," he said.

Trailing behind Hunter with a decidedly less happy look on his face was Maverick.

"Andrew," her best friend said, scooting over as he spoke.

"We saw you sitting here and, since there're no other tables available, we thought you might not mind company." Hunter slid into the booth beside Andrew.

Which left the spot beside her for Maverick, his thigh brushing hers as he scooted in. "*We?*" he said.

"Ignore my brother. It's been a helluva day."

"Is everything okay?" she asked at the same time Andrew said, "You aren't twins, are you?"

Hunter shook his head. "I'm two years younger and much friendlier. But you're not the first person to ask that. And once we down a couple of beers, everything will be A-OK."

A waitress appeared, eyeing Maverick like he was the chocolate sauce on her vanilla ice cream. "Hi, Maverick. Hunter. Are y'all ready to order or do you need a few minutes?"

"Hi, Lys. A cheeseburger and fries for me," Maverick said.

"Make that two," Hunter said.

Kennedy shared a look with Andrew and said, "We'll have the same."

When asked what they'd like to drink, they all settled on beer. "So how do you two know each other?" Hunter asked her.

"Andrew and I have been friends since high school."

"Nice." He glanced at Andrew. "Did you go to the same college, too?"

"I did. Transferred from a junior college, though."

"What do you do now?"

"I'm an actor." He gave Kennedy a quick wink. On the way here, she'd asked him not to assume any more personas. She'd hit her max, especially now that they were invited guests to the wedding.

"That's cool. Have you been in anything I might've seen?"

"Your brother's in trouble now," Kennedy said quietly. "Andrew can talk about acting for hours."

"Must be tough for you," Maverick said.

"What do you mean?"

"When do you get to talk?"

"Ha ha. I am a good listener, too, you know."

"I do know. I'm just giving you a hard time." He also gave her little flutters. Everywhere. He smelled like good old-fashioned soap and man, but he looked like a Hollywood movie star with his finger-combed light brown hair and chiseled jaw. And he had that air of mystery about him that made a girl want to know everything going on in his head.

Kennedy had uncovered some of his secrets, but she

wanted to know more. The country air was definitely messing with her sensibilities.

"So what happened today?" she asked.

The waitress dropped off their beers, and he took a healthy drink before saying, "Some of the trees needed attention, that's all."

"If I'd known, I would have helped." She meant it. She'd enjoyed being among the trees and imagining how fun and festive it must get at Christmastime.

"Those hands"—Maverick dipped his head toward her hands wrapped around her beer glass—"are meant for more important things than trees."

She took the compliment to heart, studying her fingers, her short, clear polished nails, and the skin that often dried out because of the constant hand washing. "I miss it," she admitted.

"The ER?" Maverick asked.

"Yes."

"Was there a reason you didn't stay at the hospital where you did your residency?"

"My ex and future brother-in-law is a doctor there."

"Got it."

"The asshole doctor?" Andrew said, overhearing them. "He was never good enough for our Kennedy. She absolutely dodged a bullet."

"I did," she agreed.

Their food arrived, and the conversation turned to regular, superficial stuff. Kennedy happily let Andrew and Hunter do most of the talking. Sitting so close to Maverick, catching the rise and fall of his chest beneath his black T-shirt, feeling warmth emanate from his strong body, and noticing that he ate two fries at a time had her a little off-balance. She wasn't sure she could form a complete sentence that sounded neutral.

And don't get her started on his biceps. They bulged every time he lifted his beer glass. She'd had to sit on her hands so she didn't reach out and touch them.

Something about Maverick had her tongue-tied and butterflied.

Something new. Different. Appealing in a way she couldn't stop thinking about. His quiet intensity called to her. His explanations and stories called to her. She'd thought she could fight her attraction to him, but every minute they were together made it harder and harder to remember why she'd ever disliked him.

Maverick paid for dinner, refusing to take the money she and Andrew offered. Hunter thanked his brother and, noticing a woman waving at him from the bar, asked if Maverick wouldn't mind waiting a minute.

"Go, take your time," Maverick said, "I'll walk back."

"Andrew!" Liam called out, two seats over from the woman getting Hunter's attention.

"Mind?" Andrew asked, giving her a hopeful face.

"No. I'll walk back with Maverick." She turned to make sure that was cool, but the cowboy was already halfway to the door. "Bye!" she said to Andrew over her shoulder.

"Maverick, wait up." She caught him on the sidewalk in front of The Last Word Bookstore. The stylish store with books and stationery in the window looked right up her alley, and she made a mental note to return before leaving Windsong. "Can I walk with you?"

He slowed his steps, and they walked in companionable silence.

"It smells like rain," she said after they'd left Main Street and were on the road toward the inn. Darker here, sizable trees on both sides created an archway over the two-lane street. Old-fashioned iron columns with hanging lamps provided light, but they were spread far apart, so moonlight glowed in between. There were other people out, walking to and from the inn, their conversations and laughter echoing through the treetops.

"Good observation. If we don't pick up the pace, we may get wet. Summer storms aren't uncommon this time of year."

She didn't pick up the pace. In fact, she may have slowed a bit. "Are you afraid of a little rain, cowboy?"

He laughed. It hit her square in the chest, and she wished they were under a streetlight so she could get a good look at his dimples.

"It's not me I'm worried about."

"You think I can't handle getting wet? Because I can. Contrary to what you might think, I won't melt." She only did that against him. With his arms around her. Which couldn't happen again if she hoped to spare herself any more unwanted feelings.

CHAPTER FIFTEEN

Three days until the wedding

All Maverick heard was "getting wet" and his mind immediately went to the gutter. He pictured Kennedy in his house. In his bed. Where they'd put their mouths to good use on each other's bodies, no talking allowed.

He gave a little shake of his head. No sense in going there. Besides the fact that they simply liked to goad each other, she'd be gone in a few days and his life would go back to normal. Normal being his quiet, controlled existence. No smart, interesting blondes allowed.

"I'm sure there's nothing you can't handle, Shortcake." Truth right there. She'd been through not one, but two life-saving surgeries, dealt with her parents' divorce, a jerk of an ex-boyfriend, and become a doctor. All with a positive attitude, as far as he could tell.

She glanced up at him in surprise. Yeah, he'd just confessed he thought highly of her. A compliment was due where a compliment was due. Especially after his somewhat chauvinistic remark about getting wet.

"Why do you do that?" she asked.

"Do what?"

"Act closed-off one minute and accessible the next. It's really annoying."

"You confuse me," he said honestly. This was what a cold beer and delicious burger did to him: made him drop his guard. The sultry air and gorgeous woman who was an open book might have something to do with it, too.

And maybe, just maybe, he'd finally tired of fighting with her.

"You confuse me, too," she admitted.

"Something we agree on," he said lightly, even though his stomach tightened in anticipation of what their honesty meant.

"We have more in common than we thought." Her statement was a simple one, but man, did it feel heavy. Significant. Because they did. And he wasn't sure how he felt about it, other than still confused.

"Let's not get carried away," he teased, hoping to diminish the impact of her observation.

She laughed. "Okay, cowboy, I'll be sure not to yank on your country card."

"My *country card*?"

"Man card. Country card. Same thing in your case. And then I arrived and baffled you with my endearing city personality."

It was his turn to laugh. Again. She said some funny things—things that made him feel lighter and apparently led to him smiling more. "It might surprise you to know I don't think all city girls are bad." Nicole had been a city girl. One he wouldn't have allowed himself to fall for if it hadn't been for Kennedy.

"Just me, then?" she teased.

"You do own a distinct place in my memory bank."

"Spank bank?" she said, loud enough to be broadcast to anyone within a mile radius.

Looked like his mind wasn't the only one diving to

extracurricular activities. "I said *memory* bank."

"Oh!"

"I like yours better, though." And he liked the blush on her cheeks as they walked by a streetlight.

"Do you now?" she fired back.

He should have known she wouldn't shy away from any topic. He imagined she'd been in all sorts of interesting situations in the emergency room. But that didn't intrigue him nearly as much as her personal life suddenly did.

"I'm all for fun between two mutually consenting adults," he said.

"You and fun? I'd like to see that."

"Are you implying you want me to spank you?"

"No!" She gave him a playful push. "I like my bottom left alone, thank you very much."

"What do you like, then?"

"We are not having this conversation."

"Why not? You always want to talk."

"Not about this." She sounded so unwavering, he couldn't decide if he wanted to push her further or let her off the hook. The latter was definitely easier, but the former had him wondering if he made her nervous. Had she thought about their kiss outside his house as often as he had?

"I was spanked once," he said.

Her eyes narrowed like she didn't believed him.

"I was seven and it was my birthday party. I didn't want to do it, but Cole called me a baby, so I did. Seven swats and one for good luck."

She giggled. "I thought that tradition died a really long time ago."

"Yeah, I'm pretty sure it was something my brother cooked up. I got him back on his birthday, though. My mom made him an Oreo cookie cake the night before, and I snuck out of bed and replaced all the cream fillings with toothpaste. It took a long time but was the best revenge ever."

"You little devil. Was your mom angry?"

"She was. I had to buy him a new cake with my own money, but it was worth it."

His hand brushed hers, and he fought the urge to lace their fingers together. To further connect them. This wasn't a date. It wasn't anything special. Yet the air rustled around them with potential…because he didn't normally do this. He didn't spend a lot of time alone with women other than his mom and sister.

The hermit thing is getting old, Hunter had said the other morning. And while true, it didn't change the person he was: a loner with wanderlust. He couldn't wait to hop on an airplane next week for a myriad of reasons.

It's past time you allowed yourself some fun, Hunt had told him, too.

"What's your favorite kind of cake?" Kennedy asked, the intrusion on his thoughts welcome.

"I'm more of a pie guy."

"What's your favorite pie?"

"Apple."

"I had a feeling you'd say that. You seem like a traditional guy. I bet you like it cold without any ice cream."

She was right. He shrugged. "What's your favorite?"

"I'm a cake girl all the way. White cake with buttercream frosting."

"A traditional cake girl," he said.

Their eyes met. "Yeah, I guess I am." A raindrop plopped onto her cheek. Then another. "Uh-oh."

In the time it took to blink, sheets of rain started to pour down on them. He took her hand and ran for quick cover. The bright lights of the inn shimmered too far away, so he aimed for the giant weeping willow at the foot of the property. Most storms this time of year lasted all of ten minutes, so they could wait it out there. There was nothing like getting stuck in a rainstorm on a warm summer night, and he imagined it a first for Kennedy.

She kept up with his pace without complaint, not an easy feat in her boots. The boots and her knee-length sundress were a killer combination. One he'd tried to ignore, but now the dress stuck to her body, outlining every gorgeous curve. He refocused back on the sidewalk in front of them, fearing he might trip over his own feet.

They reached the tree slightly out of breath, humidity making it harder to take in oxygen. Or maybe that was just him and his reaction to her.

Under the canopy of the willow, they caught their breath. She put a hand on the tree trunk for support, and he couldn't help himself—he looked her up and down, lingering on the material clinging to her thighs, her breasts. He didn't even care that she caught him blatantly checking her out.

Drenched from head to toe, she looked magnificent.

And when she returned the favor, her gaze remaining on his chest and abs before taking a leisurely stroll back up to his face, he'd had enough. He couldn't think straight around her and he didn't want to.

All he wanted was to be closer to her.

She stood on a wide, thick tree root, placing them at similar heights. He erased the space between them slowly but surely, giving her time to retreat. She didn't. Not even a little. Instead, she slicked her wet hair away from her face and twisted so that she leaned back against the tree, her arms spread against the trunk behind her.

An invitation.

Encouragement.

Temptation he could no longer deny himself.

He caged her in with his body, one hand going to her waist, the other to her chin to tip her face up exactly where he wanted it. Their first kiss had been tentative. Their second kiss would leave no doubt as to how much he desired her. He might never admit it, but he could show her...

Hidden under the pendulous branches of the weeping willow while the sound of the rain trilled its sweet yet powerful tune, he could show her how much he craved her.

"Mav," she whispered. She'd never called him by his nickname before.

His blood pounded at the tender sound of her voice, at the confirmation that she wanted him, too. Knowing that whatever he felt she echoed demolished any doubt about what he planned to do.

"Kennedy," he whispered back. There was more to say. Things like, *You're beautiful. You make me forget everything around me. I'm sorry for treating you like I did in college.* But there was no point. They had right now. A couple more days. And then they'd never see each other again.

"Kiss me," she said.

He slid two fingers to her mouth, gently rubbed them across her soft, full lower lip, parting the top from the bottom and bringing a sigh from her he felt all the way down to his toes. He'd never heard anything sweeter.

With her eyes locked on his, he traced her cheek next, the tips of his fingers tingling from the gentle contact. One second passed. Two. And then his lips descended on hers like she was the only thing to satiate his desire. His need. He lightly bit her bottom lip, tugged and teased, before sliding his tongue inside her mouth.

As expected, their tongues dueled for dominance, for control, for the freedom to finally let go and surrender to each other. This kiss was unlike any other he'd ever experienced. Openmouthed. Powerful. Unforgettable. Rain fell around them in sheets, and he hoped it never let up.

Tomorrow he'd blame the weather.

Tonight he'd forget there was a tomorrow. The only thing that mattered to him right now was Kennedy and her mind-blowing kiss.

Her hands slid up his pecs and over his shoulders. He cupped the back of her head. Her body pressed against his and then she jumped up, wrapping her legs around his waist. He somehow managed to keep his balance as he wrapped an arm around her and stepped back onto even ground. The new position left them exposed to the rain.

They didn't care.

They kissed until the rain stopped.

As if the time limit on their make-out session expired the second the rain did, Kennedy lifted her head, unlocked her legs, and slid down his body, righting the skirt of her dress once her boots hit the ground.

His heart pounded, and for some reason, he wanted her to know that. He took her hand and placed her palm on his chest. Water droplets clung to her eyelashes. Her honey-comb irises glittered.

She took his hand and placed his palm on her chest. Their heartbeats were in sync. A perfect yet flawed rhythm. They stood like that, frozen in time, in their own heads. Staring. Back to playing one of their favorite games.

Maverick looked away first.

By unspoken agreement, they resumed walking toward the inn as if that kiss hadn't just rocked their world. It happened, but whatever thoughts they might have on the matter were to be kept private.

He was fine with that. Appreciated it.

"What are you doing tomorrow?" he asked, running his fingers through his wet hair to comb it off his forehead.

She fanned her dress away from her stomach. "No plans that I know of. Except…"

"Except what?"

"I got the interview in Boston. It's on Tuesday, and I thought I might do some research on the hospital so I'm more than prepared for anything they might throw at me."

His heart took a little beating at the news. He'd…miss her. Ridiculous, given she was leaving the ranch regardless of the job. "Congratulations."

"Thanks. I'm beyond excited."

"I'm happy for you, Shortcake."

"Okay, that's enough," she chided good-naturedly. "I can't take any more irresistible Maverick tonight. What's going on tomorrow?"

Irresistible, huh? "I thought we could go out on the lake, but if you're worried about jumping my bones again, we can skip it."

"I did not—" She caught herself and he chuckled. Because she *had* just climbed him like a tree. Not that he was complaining. "Do you mean canoe?"

"Yes. If you want the whole ranch experience, canoeing on the lake is part of it."

"You're not going to tip it over or push me out, are you?"

"You do know how to swim, right?"

"Yes, I know how to swim."

"Then what are you worried about?"

"You didn't answer my question."

"No, I won't tip it or push you out. Now, if *you* tip it or accidentally fall overboard, then I can't be held responsible."

"Maverick!"

He loved riling her up. "Hey, just stating a fact. I'll do my part, but you've got to do yours."

"Meaning?"

"Follow my directions. Think you can do that?"

"How about this? I drive my own canoe and you drive yours."

He *almost* burst out laughing. "You don't drive a canoe, you paddle it. And if you think you can handle one on your own, that's fine with me."

"I absolutely can," she asserted, her determination so damn attractive, he couldn't wait to see her in action. Did *he* think she could manage it on her own? Not necessarily. But only because she was a complete novice. She'd do great for a minute, maybe two, before her arms grew tired. And if he wanted them to paddle out to the sand bar in the middle of the lake, well, that might be pushing it. He'd play it by ear.

The inn rose in front of them like the brightest ornament on a Christmas tree. Voices floated from inside, and he pictured his mom's homemade desserts spread out in the living room for guests to enjoy before bedtime.

"Thanks for walking me back," she said, coming to a stop near the foot of the staircase. "And for dinner. I have to admit, the food in Windsong is really good."

"You're welcome." He grinned. "Eleven a.m. tomorrow— meet me at the lake. It's about a ten-minute walk from here to the small dock where the canoes are."

"Okay." She zeroed in on his wet T-shirt before her attention bounced back up to his eyes. The thin cotton remained plastered to his torso. Much like her clothes were. Hands down, she won sexiest look.

Not that he was memorizing every curve and angle of her womanly shape or anything.

"Okay," he said back to her.

Neither made a motion to move, though, until she shivered. It wasn't because of him. She was cold, damn it, and he stood there staring at her like a damn teenager.

"Guests don't know this, but my mom makes a mean spiked hot chocolate. I bet she'd whip one up for you. Let her know I recommended it."

"Mmm. I will, thanks."

"'Welcome. See you tomorrow." He forced himself to walk away.

"Good night," she called out.

He waved over his shoulder, not daring to turn around and be tempted to join her in a drink. Or another kiss. Because she might be a good swimmer, but *he* was in danger of drowning.

CHAPTER SIXTEEN

Three days until the wedding

"All right. Spill everything right this minute," Andrew said, barging into the bathroom without knocking. Thankfully, the frosted shower door kept her hidden, not that he'd care to look if it wasn't. "Rumor has it Maverick Owens was seen kissing the bejesus out of a blonde wearing cowboy boots with her legs wrapped around his waist like a python. And yes, that's a direct quote."

Kennedy spit out the shampoo bubbles that had slid into her open mouth. How in the world had news of her kissing Maverick traveled so quickly? And who had witnessed it? She hadn't noticed anyone around them.

That's because all you could see was him.

Kissing obliviousness, the state of being so engrossed in a kiss with another person that everything else disappeared, was obviously a real thing. She'd find it in a medical journal somewhere, right?

Okay, not really, but she'd never experienced a kiss like the one she'd shared with Maverick. It wiped away every other kiss she'd ever had. Whoever she kissed next would have a hard time making her feel the same electrifying way Maverick had. As if all her nerve endings were sparkling like flawless diamonds.

She had flaws…but with him they…

"Well?" Andrew prodded.

"We kissed in the rain," she said dreamily.

"And…"

"It was incredible. The best kiss I've ever had."

Andrew whistled. "I knew if you guys ever gave in, it would be hot."

Ever? What did he mean by that? She ran her hands over her head to rinse off the rest of the shampoo. "It was."

"What happened after?"

"He invited me to go canoeing with him tomorrow." To say she was excited about that would be an understatement.

"Wow, Ned. What does this all mean?"

"I have no idea, so I'm taking your advice and living day by day. Having some fun. How was the rest of your night?"

"Good, but let's get back to you. I need more details."

She chuckled, turned off the water, and pulled down the towel resting over the top of the shower. She ran the soft cotton over her body, then tied it around herself. Steam filled the bathroom when she stepped out of the enclosure.

Andrew sat on the closed toilet lid, a look of contemplation on his face. "I think this means you've answered the question, 'can enemies become lovers?'"

"We're not lovers."

"*Yet*."

She wiped her palm in a circular motion on the fogged mirror, butterflies filling her stomach at the thought.

"I don't know," she said calmly. "We're definitely enjoying each other, but I'm hopefully moving to Boston, and he's actually leaving soon to travel for a few months." She brushed her hair. "And even if that wasn't the case, it's *Maverick*."

"Meaning?"

"Meaning whatever this is, I can't trust it. He's just lonely, and I guess I am, too, and we're familiar with each other, so we gave in to the spark between us."

"He's *lonely*?"

Kennedy poured some lotion onto her hand and rubbed it up and down her arm, then switched to the other. She hadn't told Andrew about Nicole, had she? She filled him in now.

They moved to the main room, and she slipped on her nightgown while Andrew kept his back to her.

"Damn," Andrew said, sympathy clearly steeped in the one word as he turned around.

"Right?" She flopped down on her bed, thinking about the hot chocolate Maverick had mentioned. She'd been chilled to the bone when she'd walked into the inn and needed a hot shower before anything else. Now she was too tired to move. Closing her eyes, she replayed their kiss. His warm tongue inside her mouth, his hands everywhere, his arms holding her plastered against his solid muscles.

"Hey! Knock it off."

Her eyes flew open.

Andrew pointed a finger at her. "No dreaming about him when I'm right here and wishing for my own tongue lashing from Liam."

"Sorry," she said sheepishly. Then yawned. "Do you want to canoe with us tomorrow?"

"And interrupt the sexy vacation vibe between you two? No way. We could walk into town for doughnuts and coffee, though, if you have the time first."

"I always have time for doughnuts."

• • •

"Good morning, Dr. Martin. Andrew," Claudia said from behind the counter of Baked on Main the next morning. "Get you the usual?" Claudia owned and operated the bakery and apparently remembered everyone's name and order. Even out-of-towners.

"Please," Kennedy said.

"Looking good this morning," Andrew said, drawing a blush from Claudia before he handed Kennedy a twenty and walked away to claim the last available table by the window. Kennedy didn't know if he meant Claudia or the pastries. Probably both, given he loved to flirt.

Claudia wore her red hair in a high ponytail, her skin was free of makeup and impossibly smooth, and her hazel eyes were bright and cheery.

Before Kennedy handed over the cash at the register, she quietly said, "Would you mind adding Maverick's favorite in a separate bag?" He hadn't ordered anything the other morning when they'd stopped in, and while he probably would have eaten breakfast by the time they met up at eleven, she wanted to bring him something anyway.

"Sure." Claudia smiled like she and Kennedy were sharing a secret, which they kind of were. Whether it stayed that way was beyond Kennedy's control.

Gossip had never bothered her. Rumors and whispers were commonplace at the hospital, especially after her breakup with Trevor. The only time a mean or unflattering word stung was if it had to do with her abilities on the job.

"Dr. Martin?" a woman asked from over Kennedy's shoulder.

"Yes?" Kennedy met the friendly face of a thirty-something woman wearing scrubs.

"I'm Savannah, Dr. Choi's nurse. I just wanted to introduce myself and say thank you for helping out in the office when I was sick."

"Oh, hi! It's great to meet you. And it was my pleasure. I take it you're feeling better?"

"Much, thank you. I understand you had a super-busy day."

"Just how I like them," Kennedy said around a smile. "I'm used to a busy ER, so it wasn't anything I couldn't handle. And it was nice to get to know some of the townspeople. Everyone had a story to share and made me feel welcome and appreciated."

"Here you go," Claudia said, splitting Kennedy's attention between the two women.

"You left quite an impression on everyone," Savannah said sweetly. "I'll let you go. Thanks again and have a great day."

"Thanks. You too. And please call me Kennedy." At Savannah's nod, Kennedy turned back to the register.

"Maverick has two favorites," Claudia said softly as she accepted the twenty-dollar bill from Kennedy. "Apple turnovers and ginger scones."

"Those both sound really good."

"They are." Claudia handed over Kennedy's change and then the food and coffees. "Happy Thursday!"

There were several tables between Kennedy and the table where Andrew sat, but everyone this morning knew her by name and said hello. She recognized only one person, Mrs. Freed, who said her sinus infection had all but disappeared.

"Looks like I'm eating with the most popular person in Windsong," Andrew said, taking his coffee and the white bag with their pastries inside.

"Jealous?" she teased.

"Of course I am," he joked back. "You know how I like all eyes on me."

At that exact moment, the strangest thing happened. She felt eyes on her. And not just any eyes—*his* eyes. How she knew it was Maverick, she didn't know, but when she looked out the window, there he was. Standing on the sidewalk, staring at her, an unreadable expression on his face. She gave a little wave. The gesture seemed to wake him up from whatever trance he was in. He walked into the bakery and straight to their table.

"Morning," he said.

"Good morning." Andrew's cheery voice rang a little over the top.

"Hi," Kennedy said, feeling a touch shy all of a sudden. Bright sunlight spilled into the bakery, highlighting Maverick's soulful azure eyes and the golden highlights in his brown hair.

"Want to join us?" Andrew asked.

"I got you something." Kennedy held up the bag in her hand.

Maverick smiled, his dimples coming out to play, and she almost forgot how to breathe. "You did?"

"*You* did?" Andrew said.

She ignored the fact that her best friend had paid for

their food and focused on her new friend. "I was going to bring it to you later but, since you're here..." She gave him the bag.

He peeked inside it. "My favorites. Thanks."

"You're welcome."

"Okay, you two, enough already," Andrew said amiably, pulling his croissant out of the bag. "Go canoodle already."

"Andrew," she warned.

"What? I said go *canoe*." He handed her the bag with her doughnut, acting like he hadn't accidentally on purpose made a play on words. "I'll be fine here." He eyed her meaningfully. "Really."

"Okay, but it's not even ten." Still, she folded the bag over, implying she was ready to leave for the lake if Maverick was. An extra hour with him? Yes, please.

"I'm ready to go if you are," Maverick said, echoing her thoughts aloud. She liked being on the same wavelength as him.

"Okay. Thanks, Andrew. I'll see you later." She got to her feet and followed Maverick out of the bakery, turning every single head in the shop. If their kiss hadn't made the morning news yet, then their leaving the bakery together would.

Maverick swept his gaze over her when they were safely outside and out of view. "You good to go or do you need to stop at the inn?"

"I'm good." Her shorts, T-shirt, and sneakers were perfect for a day on the lake.

"You have sunscreen on?"

Call her ridiculous, but the question made her heart flip-flop in her chest. He cared. "No, actually."

"Dr. Martin, that isn't very responsible of you. Luckily, I've got you covered, since I need to stop at my house and change clothes." Too bad, considering his jeans, cowboy boots, and cowboy hat were growing on her.

Maverick not only supplied her with sunscreen but a faded blue baseball cap to keep the sun out of her eyes and *protect the freckles across your nose*. She'd blushed hard at that and let him win their staring contest. No man had mentioned her freckles before, let alone preserving them.

And when he wasn't looking at her, she definitely enjoyed looking at him. He'd changed into black board shorts, athletic shoes, and a light gray T-shirt. His calves were toned, his stomach flat, his shoulders broad. Whether a cowboy or a boater, he made it difficult for her to look away.

They stood on the bank of the lake, two canoes ready and waiting for takeoff. They were the only two people there, the silence golden, the lake beautifully placid. The sky and mountains were vivid shades of blue and green. A lone, two-story house he said belonged to Cole sat on an empty bank to the northeast.

"See that sandbar out there?" Maverick said. "Think you can paddle that far?"

The closest she'd come to being in a boat was the pedal boats at the Disneyland Hotel, but he didn't need to know that. "That U-shaped thing? Sure."

He cracked a small smile. "It's not too late to change your mind and take a tandem canoe."

"Worried I'll beat you across the lake?" Tough words hid doubt, right? She *could* beat him. Miracles happened.

"Suit yourself." He picked up a life vest. "Let's get this on you. On the water it's known as a PFD or personal flotation device."

Grateful she'd be protected if she did fall into the lake, she didn't argue when he fitted it over her head and tightened the safety straps to his satisfaction.

"What about you?" she asked.

"I'm good." He stepped toward the shorter and narrower canoe and lifted a paddle out. "This is your ride. It's strictly for recreation, so very stable and durable. You've never been in a canoe, right?"

"Right."

"Okay, so you can either sit down on the raised seat or kneel in front of it, whichever you feel more comfortable doing. This end of the paddle"—he touched the rubber blade—"is what goes in the water."

"Or over your head if you don't stop talking like I'm in kindergarten. I'm familiar with how a paddle works, Mav."

He grinned. "I wasn't sure, given your city girl status," he teased. Then more seriously he said, "You don't need any further explanation?"

She supposed there was a correct way to move the paddle with her body and, since she did want to prove to him she could do this independently, she nicely said, "What else do I need to know?"

"Two things." He handed her the paddle and retrieved his own out of the other canoe. "Rotate your torso when you paddle using your upper body to provide the power needed to move the canoe. And keep your arms within your field of vision, so always in a square or box shape. Like this." He demonstrated, and she copied him. "Looks good. You ready to give it a try?"

How hard could it be? She sat in the canoe and paddled. She had good balance, above average intelligence, and a life jacket on. She was raring to go. "Yes."

He took her elbow and helped her inside the canoe. "Get comfortable and then I'll push you into the water."

She sat on the raised seat, feeling pretty relaxed. "Okay."

Mav moved to the back of the canoe and pushed her off. The second she landed fully in the water, though, she was anything but relaxed. The canoe wobbled! Her paddle hit the water with a splash and little else. And she had zero control over her direction.

A few seconds later, Maverick's canoe slid beside hers and his big, strong hand gripped the edge of her canoe to help steer her. "Relax, Shortcake. Take a breath and settle into your seat, and your lower body will keep the canoe stable."

She did as he said, intentionally settling her weight into her bottom and sitting more confidently. Her canoe stopped rocking. He released his hold but continued to float at her side.

"Now, plant the paddle in the water and pull the boat toward the paddle, rather than the paddle toward the boat."

It took a different kind of concentration than she was used to, but she did it. She was finally canoeing across the lake. "I'm doing it!"

"You are," Maverick agreed, making it look easy as he paddled around her in a circle before moving parallel to her on their way toward the sandbar.

If she weren't so focused on staying straight and keeping her balance, she would have loved to stare at

Maverick's muscled arms as he paddled. Maybe on the way back, she'd be able to.

"Ducks at nine o'clock," he said.

"It's a family!" She stopped paddling to watch them. Four baby ducks floated on the water behind their mama. She tried to recall if she'd ever seen baby ducks in the wild before, and she didn't think so. She'd spent so much time focused on school and becoming a doctor that she'd missed out on basic beauties of nature. Being in Windsong had opened her eyes to many things this week: small-town camaraderie, the smell of pine and earth, the joy of horses and mules, the awe of bringing newborn puppies into the world, and now this.

The front of her canoe drifted to the left as she stared at the ducklings, so she put her paddle back in the water—and something hit it. It startled her so badly that she let go of the paddle.

"What was that?" she shrieked. "Something in the water just hit my paddle." And oh, crap, where did her paddle go? It was sinking!

She started to move onto her knees to lean over the canoe and grab it, but the canoe wobbled, so she sat right back down and focused on keeping her balance. She didn't need the paddle that badly.

Well, she did, but...

Maverick's laughter caught her attention. He'd turned his canoe around so he faced hers.

"It's not funny," she said. "There is something big and strong in the water. You didn't tell me about that," she accused. "And why in the world doesn't my paddle float? You'd think a novice canoer would get an appropriate paddle. Aren't you going to jump in and get it for me? What kind of guide are you?" She huffed out a breath.

"Are you done?" he asked pleasantly.

"Yes."

He regarded her like he found her amusing, but also fun and interesting, so she didn't mind his laughing. In fact, she suddenly found herself laughing, too. She amused herself, to be honest, so why not the gorgeous man who'd decided she was worth a few firsts this week?

Once she stopped laughing, she said, "Sorry about the paddle."

"It's okay. I should have brought a backup." He floated closer. "The paddles sink because they're made of metal. The something big and strong in the water is a largemouth bass. We keep the lake stocked with them for people who like to fish."

"Oh."

"I should have mentioned them."

"It's okay."

"Good job avoiding tipping over." He pulled his canoe beside hers. His still pointed toward the shore while hers pointed toward the sandbar.

"I really wanted to make it to the sandbar," she said.

"No problem. Climb in."

Taking a closer look at his canoe, he'd claimed a tandem model with a second seat inside the hull. "Really?"

"Unless you'd rather float around aimlessly until I go get another paddle and bring it back to you."

"What about the canoe?"

"Hunter and I can get it later. Believe it or not, you're not the first person to lose an oar and abandon a canoe."

She straightened her neck, lifted her chin. "That makes me feel a lot better."

"Get over here already."

Their canoes were touching, so really it should be no big deal to climb in. "Don't move," she instructed.

"I wouldn't dream of it." The mischievous quality of his deep voice worried her, but…

One…two…three. She dove into the other canoe with as much grace as an ostrich on roller skates. Righting herself on the seat, she looked over her shoulder and smiled at Maverick. She didn't care what she looked like, she'd done it.

"Nice move," he said easily enough.

"Thanks. Want me to paddle us?"

He blessed her with dimples that almost knocked her overboard. "I think I'll hang on to the paddle, but thanks for asking." He released her canoe.

Before he started to paddle, she turned on the seat so that she faced him. There was no reason they had to face the same direction if she wasn't paddling, right? This way she got a great view of him and his arms, as well as the scenery. All without tiring herself out!

Unless she considered the workout he gave her eyes.

"Hi," she said.

"Hi," he said back.

"This is nice." It took all of two seconds for her body to completely decompress as they glided across the lake. Sunbeams danced off the water. Ducks flew overhead. Greenery surrounded them in the distance. And Maverick's bare knees almost touched her bare knees.

He rowed with a gentle rhythm, barely causing the lake

to ripple. His faded red ball cap shaded his eyes and nose. Stubble lined his angular jaw and circled his mouth. It was the first time she'd seen him unshaven.

And she liked it.

"It is," he agreed.

She scanned him top to bottom. Left biceps to right biceps. Moved her gaze to the water, then back to him.

"My view is better," he said, looking his fill of her in return.

"I never knew what a smooth talker you could be."

He shrugged a shoulder. "I never knew you to give such blatant perusal. Probably because you always had your nose in a book."

"Or I didn't like you."

"That too."

"I do willingly admit to books getting my undivided attention. Now, though, my world has expanded. I don't have to hide in medical journals and textbooks. I've almost accomplished what I set out to do, and so, for the first time, I can live outside that box." Sage words she needed to start living by more frequently.

"Almost?"

"Once I have the job in Boston, I'll be set."

"I never doubted you'd reach your goals. You were a big reason I worked so hard to reach mine. Or rather, you were the motivation I needed."

"I could say the same about you. I hated the thought of losing to you."

"Right back at you." He looked beyond her. "Get ready to land." With one big paddle, their canoe hitched up onto the sandbar.

He jumped out first, his shoes getting wet, and pulled the canoe higher onto the sand. She took his offered hand and stepped out of the canoe, his warm, calloused palm covering her small, delicate one with ease.

The sandbar was a U-shaped bank about the size of a playground at the park, and she wanted to bury her feet in it. She slid off her shoes and socks, wiggled her toes. The grains were soft and cool, and sent a wave of serenity up her body.

Maverick sat down, his legs bent at the knees. She took the spot next to him, taking off the life jacket and placing it beside her. "There are so many peaceful spots on your ranch," she said.

"Agreed."

"And good places to think."

He peeked at her out of the corner of his eye. "You're right."

"Is that what you do out here and in the trees?"

He lay back, legs remaining bent, and looked up at the sky. "Sometimes. It's easier to work things out when I'm alone with nature."

"I get that." She lay back, too, pulling down the bill of her hat to block the sun from her eyes. "No distractions, just your own brain telling you what to do."

"You must get exhausted."

"You're hilarious." She stretched out her legs. Closed her eyes.

He did have a point, though, so she let her thoughts about work and weddings and ranches fade away and instead focused on her body. On letting her limbs soften into the sand, her muscles completely relax. She placed her hands on her stomach. Breathed deeply.

About to drift off for a quick nap, she felt something tickle her foot. She pressed her heel into the sand and moved her leg side to side. When that didn't work, she wiggled her toes. And when that didn't work, she lifted up onto her elbows to take a look.

"Ahh!" She scrambled backward as fast as possible, away from the reptilian creature staring at her. Wait…it was only a…small turtle? At her sudden movement, the animal hid inside its shell.

Maverick placed the turtle in his palm, *his* stare full of mirth before he looked down at the creature. "It's okay, Digger, the pretty doctor is mostly harmless and more afraid of you than you are of her."

Okay, where to start with that sentence? Maverick's calling her pretty twisted her stomach into a delicious knot. She never knew exactly what to think when his eyes were on her, so knowing he liked what he saw on the outside was a welcome bit of information. Of course, he probably wouldn't have kissed the bejesus out of her if he wasn't attracted to her, but, since she'd never been caught up in the heat of the moment like that before, she didn't know if looks had factored in. Hormones were potent all on their own.

And then there was the *mostly harmless* comment. What did he mean by that? Because if she was given truth serum and had to spill the beans on how Maverick affected her, she'd say there was nothing safe about the new emotions creeping in and changing her opinion of him. Did he feel the same way?

Lastly, how cute was the name Digger?

"I think you've shocked her silent," Maverick said. "Good job, buddy." The turtle poked his head out from his shell like Maverick's voice reassured him it was safe.

"Hey! I'm just assessing."

"Assessing?" he asked. "Please don't tell me this is the first turtle you've been up close to."

"Okay, I won't tell you." She leaned forward on her hands and knees for a closer look.

"Shortcake, what am I going to do with you?"

Her eyes jumped from watching the turtle emerge fully out of his shell up to Mav's incredibly blue eyes. "That's kind of a loaded question." She sat back on her haunches with what she hoped was a sexy smile.

He smirked. (Which for the record was quite sexy.) It was hard to believe this was her life right now. Stuck on a sandbar in the middle of a lake with her college nemesis and a turtle named Digger.

"How about you start with telling me about Digger. Did you name him?"

"Jenna did." He put Digger down on the sand. "She found him and his girlfriend." He nodded toward something off to Kennedy's left. She turned her head to find another turtle climbing out of the water. "That's Scooter. They're red-eared sliders."

"How can you tell them apart?" They looked identical to her.

"Males sport a thick, long tail while females have a short, skinny one."

Kennedy watched as Digger walked to meet Scooter. The red stripe behind their eyes must be where they got their name. Their shells were olive colored with yellow lines. "Do they bite?" she asked.

"No."

"Scratch?" Digger had elongated front claws she'd rather not get acquainted with.

"Not on purpose. They're docile creatures who, when threatened, hide inside their shells."

"Much like people." "Threatened" meaning anything uncomfortable, uneasy, awkward… Kennedy didn't hide often, only when it came to her mom and sister. And she hated that. Hated that they made her retreat instead of communicate. *No more*, she thought to herself.

"I suppose so," he said, taking off his baseball hat, flipping it around, and putting it on his head backward.

The switch made him even sexier. It added a boyishly handsome quality to his ruggedness she found appealing on every level.

"What?" he asked.

"Nothing." She practically pulled a muscle in her neck looking away from him. Silently scolding herself to cool her jets, she rubbed the muscles where her neck met her shoulder.

"Whatever you say, Shortcake." He so knew she was not immune to him, damn it. "How about a race?"

"What kind?"

"The Digger against Scooter kind. Jenna and I race them all the time."

"Sounds interesting." Losing her paddle had taken some wind out of her sails, and she was more than determined to prove herself. "I'm in, and there should be a prize involved." She flashed her straight, dentist-whitened teeth at him. (It helped to know other doctors who gave steep discounts.)

"Of course."

"Who usually wins?" she fired off.

"If I told you that, you'd have an unfair advantage."

"But *you* know."

"True, so I'll hold the turtles behind my back and you can pick a hand."

"Can I make the track?" She felt at a disadvantage no matter what, and this gave her some level of control.

"Sure. They usually race from the sand down to the water."

While Maverick walked over to pick up the turtles, she did a quick study of the terrain to locate an even decline. Finding it, she shuffled over on her knees and drew a start line in the sand. "Is this distance okay?"

"Should be." Maverick's shadow loomed over her. "Pick a hand."

She stood up, tapped her chin. "Hmm...left."

He brought his left arm out from behind him. "Looks like it's girls against boys."

"Perfect." She gingerly accepted Scooter in both hands, worried she'd drop the turtle otherwise. She wasn't much bigger than Kennedy's palm, but still. Her guiding principle was to keep everyone safe.

They put their turtles down behind the start line but didn't let go entirely. The animals, obviously accustomed to being held, strained their legs for release.

"On three," Maverick said. "One, two, three."

CHAPTER SEVENTEEN

Two days until the wedding

Digger and Scooter both hit the sand running—or rather fast walking. It was usually hit or miss as to who won their races, and seeing the look of pure delight on Kennedy's face, Maverick hoped Scooter won. He always hoped whichever turtle Jenna had picked won, too. Being the precocious seven-year-old that she was, though, she told him it built character to lose once in a while. *No one wins every single time, Uncle Mav.*

"We forgot to pick a prize for the winner," Kennedy said, bouncing up and down. "Go, Scooter, go!"

Bouncing drew his gaze right to her perky breasts. Luckily, she didn't notice, her attention solely on the turtles. Which meant he could take his time checking her out, raking his eyes up and down her body in complete fascination. That she couldn't resist a challenge added to her allure.

The best way to get Digger and Scooter into the water was to meet them there, so he tore his eyes away from Kennedy, tossed off his shoes, and walked down the bank. "What do you want to bet?" he asked over his shoulder. They were in his domain. There wasn't anything he didn't mind doing.

"I don't know." She noticed him moving toward the water and did the same.

There was never a guarantee this worked, but the playful side of him that Kennedy pulled out with ease chose right now to surface and perform. He stepped into the cold water up to the tops of his shins and splashed the fresh water onto the shore by kicking his feet. "Down here, Digger!"

Kennedy's eyes widened. Never one to be outdone, she immediately strode into the lake, her body shivering at the contact, and kicked water right at him instead of the sandbar. "Down here, Scooter!"

"Hey!" He splashed her back.

She grinned and continued splashing him, an arm and leg involved now.

"If I win, you camp out with me tonight," he tossed out without much thought beyond she'd hate the idea and he... liked it. "And if you win, you don't."

"Or if I win you...you..." She spit out water that had gotten into her mouth. "You go to the wedding with me."

They both stopped splashing.

"I've been formally invited, and Andrew told me this morning he has his own invite and..." She wiped hair from her face. "I think it would be fun to go with you."

Honored she asked, and relieved her crashing days were over, "okay" sat on the tip of his tongue. As a rule, though, he didn't attend weddings on the ranch. He'd pictured his own wedding here and since that didn't happen, he couldn't bring himself to watch someone else's.

"Do we have a deal?" She moved closer and splashed him with both hands.

His hands were much bigger, and thus his splashes more powerful. He retaliated and drenched her. Not that she seemed to care, if the smile on her face was any indication. His own cheeks started to hurt from smiling throughout this friendly competition.

"We do." He'd tell her the truth *if* she won, and ask her to pick something else.

The splashing got serious after that. They laughed and sprayed each other, kicking their feet up and swiping their arms through the cold water. For someone much smaller than him, she gave as good as she got, never letting up. Water went in his mouth, up his nose, inside his ears.

She advanced on him. He dodged left. She pivoted with little effort and heaps of determination on her face. He hopped right, let his arms rest for a moment. Not because he was tired, but so she could get a good, solid splash in without immediate reciprocation.

"Don't you dare let me win this!" Her hands went to her hips.

Big mistake.

He splashed her full force, never thinking for a second he had the upper hand or would *let* her win. What Kennedy lacked in size compared to him, she more than made up for in tenacity. She was heart, guts, and attitude all rolled into one impressive package.

She spewed water out of her mouth and grumbled her dislike of him. He laughed, not at her but with her. He didn't think she saw it that way, though, and spurred on even more now, she went full-court press on him. So much so that she lost her balance.

He caught her before her backside hit the water and instead, he brought her toward his chest. She didn't fight him. She grabbed the front of his soaked shirt and helped heave her body closer to his, causing them to crash together, her arms sliding around his waist. Him wrapping one arm around her shoulders and securing the hand on his other arm firmly on her bottom. Totally involuntary. Mostly.

If points in time were measured in pure pleasure, then this one neared the top of the list. Everything around him faded away (this was becoming customary with her), narrowed down to a simple, albeit complicated, look between them. Droplets clung to her long eyelashes and her lips parted slightly as she caught her breath.

He wasn't sure how long they stood that way. It could have been a minute. It could have been ten. He did know he relished their position and had no plans to let her go.

"The turtles!" she exclaimed, jumping back and breaking the spell she'd cast over him.

Digger and Scooter were no longer on the sand. Nope. They were swimming in the lake away from him and Kennedy.

"Shoot! We didn't see who won," she said. "This is your fault."

"My fault?"

"Totally. You were the one who started splashing."

"Not at you. I was splashing toward Digger when you decided to launch an attack on innocent me."

"That's because you didn't tell me you had a secret weapon in your pocket, which makes you far from innocent."

"Okay, true, but it took you all of a second to figure it out, which I knew would happen." He smiled at her, earning him a spot back in her good graces by the way she tilted her head and pressed her lips together, the corners of her mouth lifting anyway.

"I guess we'll have to call it a tie," she said.

"Sounds fair."

"I'd still like you to go to the wedding with me."

He stroked the side of his neck, then to deflect said, "I'd still like you to camp out with me."

"Okay."

"Shit." She wasn't supposed to be so agreeable, not when his nerves were shot at the prospect of watching two people get married on his family's ranch.

"What?" Her brows furrowed in confusion.

"I thought you'd say no." *So that I could say no.*

"So you don't really want me to camp with you?"

"No, I do. But the wedding…"

She looked down and away. "You don't want to go."

He tucked a finger under her chin and brought her gaze back to him. "It has nothing to do with you, but can I think about it? I don't usually attend weddings here at the ranch."

She contemplated him, those light brown eyes of hers soft, sincere, and assessing. "Of course. In the meantime, what does camping out involve exactly?"

"A campfire, sleeping bags, stars brighter than any you've ever seen before."

"We sleep on the ground?"

"If that's roughing it too much, I could supply a blow-up mattress to lay your sleeping bag on."

"No tent?"

"And block the view of the sky?"

"That's true." They walked back to the sandbar. He kept his attention above her neck, not an easy task when once again her wet clothes showed off her curves. "What about wild animals?"

"None you have to worry about."

"Meaning you will?"

"Meaning the fire will keep them away, and I'll bring Magnolia. She'll alert us to any potential trouble. Not that there is any, really."

Kennedy buried her feet in the sand, fastening herself in place. He kept a safe six feet away, lest he get any out-there ideas about reaching over and touching her.

"Is this as weird for you as it is for me?" she asked.

"This?"

"Us."

"You think we're weird?"

"I think…" She chewed her bottom lip. "I think we're unexpectedly drawn to each other."

That she admitted something so vulnerable made him care for her even more. And no way would he leave her alone on that ledge. "Agreed. You're a pleasant surprise, Kennedy Martin."

She beamed. "Fair warning: this truce could have lasting effects."

He chuckled. "Such as?"

"I am pretty great," she said with a wink. "And I'm leaving in three days and we'll never see each other again. You'll definitely miss me."

"No doubt," he said honestly. She'd livened up his days, and if it weren't for his upcoming trip, he'd probably be more upset about their parting ways.

"By the way, if anything happens to me while I'm sleeping under the stars, you're going to be in big trouble."

"Noted." A ridiculous amount of pleasure swept through him at their plan for tonight. These past few days had reminded him how it felt to be alive again. Not that he didn't appreciate time with his family. He cherished it, despite how it sometimes looked on the outside. He knew how fragile life was—as did Kennedy. "You ready to head back?"

"Yes." She slipped her life jacket on, grabbed her shoes, and barefooted it to the canoe.

He followed, tossing his sneakers into the boat so he could push it off and then jump inside from the water. Kennedy kept excellent balance on the takeoff, facing forward instead of toward him. He missed her face.

And quickly told himself to get over it.

Her abandoned canoe floated off to the west, and he dreaded having Hunter fetch it with him. His brother would no doubt find the whole situation amusing and pester him with annoying comments. Brotherly love and all that.

"You're awfully quiet back there," Kennedy said.

"Just watching the water bug crawling up your back."

"What?" She furiously wiggled her torso. "Get it off! Get it off!"

Guilt crawled up his spine. He really shouldn't tease her like this when he knew she hated bugs. He gently swiped at the nonexistent insect. "All gone."

She calmed down. "Thank you. Are water bugs common on the lake?"

"Umm…"

She glanced at him over her shoulder, scowling. "You did it again, didn't you?"

"Guilty," he said with an apologetic shrug. Then with

cheerfulness added, "I'm sorry I can't seem to stop myself from teasing you."

With the careful precision of a doctor, she did a one-eighty without causing even a tiny list to the canoe or taking her gaze off his. Once completely turned, her eyes slid down to his chest and widened. "Uh, Maverick."

"Yes?" He kept his eyes up. If she thought him that easy to get back, she was sorely mistaken. Until a slight movement below his neck and just outside his scope of vision snagged his attention. He dropped his chin to look down. And there it was.

The one creature that creeped him the ever-loving hell out.

"That is the coolest worm I've ever seen," Kennedy said, completely unfazed by this particular animal.

He stopped paddling and willed himself not to squeal like a baby and ask her to get it off him. It was a mere two inches in size! But he'd disliked the tiny, squishy invertebrate since he found one in his swim trunks at four years old.

"Its skin is transparent," she said, leaning forward for a closer look. "I can see its internal organs! So cool. May I?" She made a motion to free it from his shirt.

"G-Go for it." *And please hurry*.

She placed the common aquatic worm on her palm, releasing him from his discomfort. Mostly. He was still too close to the worm for his liking, but seeing Kennedy completely fascinated made it easier to take.

"Did you know that Charles Darwin studied worms for over thirty years?" she asked, looking absolutely riveted. "And that he published a book on them?"

"I did not know that." He resumed paddling, in no rush to get to the other side even though his most feared animal (don't laugh) lounged mere inches away.

Kennedy lifted her hand so the worm was at her eye level. "My favorite fact about worms is that they have five single-chambered aortic arches that pump blood through their tiny bodies. They're located near the head."

She studied the worm, trying to see those hearts, he guessed.

"Want a closer look?" She extended her arm and he literally almost jumped out of the canoe.

"Nooo," he voiced with conviction. At his sudden retreat—he was leaning so far back he may as well lie down—she rolled her lips together to keep from laughing.

"Is the great Maverick Owens afraid of worms?" She sounded genuinely concerned as well as amused, her eyes full of tenderness.

"Yes," he admitted.

She tossed the worm overboard. One quick flick of her wrist and the creepy critter landed back in the water where it belonged. Boom. Just like that.

"I hate uninvited guests," she said.

He wasn't sure he liked how much her reaction made him want to lean over and kiss her. It took him a minute to wrap his head around her protectiveness, her easy respite from their typical ribbing. She'd just been handed a simple jab, but when it came to the real stuff, Kennedy put other people's well-being above all else.

Not that he didn't already know that. He just hadn't allowed himself to fully absorb it. The two of them thrived on taunts and teases, but this week they'd turned a corner into brand-new territory. Land he'd explore to the fullest if things were different.

"Thanks, Shortcake."

"Don't mention it."

"Oh, I won't."

"I might. But only when others are around to hear it."

And they were right back on course. Perfect.

It wasn't like he didn't deserve a little payback, her brand of revenge one he'd gladly suffer because…

Don't go there, man.

Because he enjoyed every single thing about her.

"Dish it out however and whenever you want, Shortcake. I can take it."

She let out a deep breath before raising her face to the sky. "I know you can. Otherwise I wouldn't do it."

The baseball cap he'd given her shielded her eyes and nose from the sun, but not her lips, which she currently wet with the tip of her tongue. He had a better cure for her dry lips—his. But no way would he make a move without her seeing him coming and accepting his advance. Instead, he studied her chin, the long column of her neck, how cute she looked in a life jacket, and committed it all to memory.

"Hey, watch where you're going!" a new voice yelled out.

At the sudden verbal warning, he blinked himself back to the task at hand. "My mistake!" He straightened his and Kennedy's canoe and focused on the bank of colorful canoes ahead of them.

Kennedy dropped her chin. "I leave you alone for one minute and you almost get us in a three-canoe pileup." She gripped the edges of her life vest. "Good thing I'm wearing a PFD."

He got them back to land safe and sound, took care of the canoe, then drove the electric cart toward the inn to drop off Kennedy. They passed the gazebo where preparations were beginning for thc wcdding on Saturday.

"Hi, guys!" Leah called out with a wave as Maverick slowed to a stop.

"Hi, Leah," Kennedy said. "How are you doing?"

"Good," Leah said, walking closer and looking none the worse for wear after closing the trunk of her SUV on her head.

"The flowers are absolutely gorgeous," Kennedy said, referring to the decorated columns and arch of the gazebo. Leah always made events at the ranch photo-worthy.

"Thanks. We're just getting started, though. Wait until you see the final look."

"I look forward to it. If I wasn't a doctor, I would have been a florist. I love going to the flower mart back home and putting together arrangements for my apartment."

"You're hired," Nova said. Maverick's sister, medical shoe on one foot, tennis shoe on the other, hobbled by with a large rod of tulle. Yeah, he knew what tulle was. There had been enough weddings on their property for him to properly name everything.

He hopped out of the cart to relieve her of the fabric.

"I got it," she argued, not letting him help. "It weighs nothing."

"What am I hired for?" Kennedy asked with interest. "If it has to do with flowers, I'm in."

"It does. Meet me in the main room of the inn in an hour?"

"I can do that." She slid out of her seat. "Thanks for the

canoe ride, Maverick. Good luck with the flower arranging, Leah. And I'll see you shortly, Nova." With that, she walked away.

Leah got right back to work, but Nova looked at him expectantly. "Canoe ride, huh?"

"It was nothing," he said by rote.

"Yeah, and I'm the tooth fairy. It's good to see you enjoying some leisure time with the opposite sex."

"Who said I enjoyed it?"

"It's written all over your face, big brother." She turned to go. "See ya around, lover boy!"

He scrubbed a hand across the back of his neck. For once, he had no comeback.

Twelve months ago…

Dear Nicole,

I got a package from Marco today. He and Isabel sent me a bottle of our favorite wine in honor of Cabernet Day. I guess there's a wine holiday every month and this one reminded them of us. I haven't sipped a glass of wine since our last night in Italy, but it would be rude not to drink this, right? I know you wouldn't want me to waste it. My mom's been bugging me for some mother/son time, so I think I'll invite her over for dinner and we'll toast to you.

I can't believe how fast two years has gone by. I still expect to see your face and hear your voice, but less often than I used to. It's true time heals, but I can tell you this: I'm not going to fall in love again. It's not worth the risk of experiencing the all-consuming pain of losing that person. Or watching them suffer and not being able to do a damn thing about it. Jenna was sick last week with strep throat, but it started with her complaining about swallowing, and I completely lost my cool, my mind going to the worst-case scenario. I rode Magnolia over every square inch of the ranch to get my head on straight. Logically, I know I overreacted, but I love that little girl so much. I love you, too. Now and always.

Miss you,

Maverick

CHAPTER EIGHTEEN

Two days until the wedding

"I could not keep a diaper on him to save my life," Mary Rose said, adding baby's breath to the flower arrangement in front of her on the pine worktable. "Needless to say, Mav was the youngest of my kids to be potty-trained."

Kennedy added another pink rose to the glass vase at her fingertips; Nova stood beside her doing the same. They had a dozen crystal vases to fill—the Owens family's contribution to making the wedding weekend even more beautiful. The arrangements were meant to spruce up the inn for the special occasion.

They were set up in a corner of the kitchen, flowers and greenery strewn about the table. Kennedy had been given carte blanche to fill her vases however she wanted, and the floral smell, camaraderie, and stories about Maverick and his siblings kept a permanent smile on her face.

"I bet he was pretty cute running around like that," Kennedy said.

"He was," Mary Rose agreed. "That little tushy of his made it impossible to be upset with him."

"You've never been mad at Mav," Nova said. "He's your golden middle son."

"And you're my beautiful baby." Mary Rose bumped her hip against her daughter's.

"Was it hard growing up with three older brothers?"

Kennedy asked Nova.

"Yes and no. They could be overprotective, but then I protected them right back. My best friend Callie and I would give them the honest truth about the girls around town, which they sometimes listened to and sometimes didn't, but at least we tried."

"They've got stubborn streaks, that's for sure," Mary Rose said. "But I was happy they protected both you girls from boys who wanted only one thing."

Nova swept a piece of light brown hair off her forehead. "I *wanted* to give one of those boys that thing!"

"But aren't you glad you didn't?" Mary Rose asked, even though it really wasn't a question.

A sudden sadness burned Kennedy's eyes. She'd missed out on a strong mother-daughter bond, and the comfort and ease with which she stood in this kitchen made her wish for a split second that Mary Rose and Nova were her family.

"Do you have a boyfriend now?" Kennedy asked, blinking away her emotions. She had Ava. And Andrew. Hugo and Maria.

"No." Nova sighed, reaching for a white rose. "It's hard in a small town, you know?"

She didn't know but nodded anyway. "If you ever want to come visit me in L.A., I'd love to have you."

"But rumor has it you're moving to Boston," Nova said.

Lost in thoughts of family, Kennedy had momentarily forgotten about the job back east. "That's true. So Boston, then. You can visit me in whatever city I'm in."

"Thanks. I'd like that."

"We could do a mother-daughter trip," Mary Rose piped

in. "I've never been to Boston and I'd like to see you again, too, Kennedy. And," she added just as Nova's mouth opened to say something, "I promise to let you two have a few nights out without me. How's that?"

Sounded wonderful to Kennedy.

Before she or Nova could respond, a noise from over their shoulders drew the attention of all three of them. There, caught with her hand in the proverbial—and nearly literal—cookie jar, stood Jenna. In this instance she was frozen, cookie mid-swipe off the plate on the kitchen counter, her nose scrunched up and eyes squeezed shut.

"We can see you, Jenna Wenna," Nova said.

Jenna kept the cookie but dropped her arm. "Drat," she said in the most adorable voice ever. She had on her yellow rain boots again, which was also cute.

Mary Rose chuckled. "Get your bottom over here and give me a hug and we'll call it even."

"Winner, winner, chicken dinner. Thanks, Nana!" Jenna skipped over to embrace her grandma. On the release, she smiled up at Kennedy. "Hi, Dr. Martin."

"Hi, Jenna."

"Hey, where's my hug?" Nova asked.

Jenna hugged her aunt and then, catching Kennedy by surprise, the little girl stepped to the side and wrapped her arms around Kennedy, too. "My daddy said Uncle Mav likes you. Do you like him back?"

Kennedy put her hands on her thighs and bent over to look Jenna in the eye. "I do, but don't tell him I said so, okay?"

"It's a secret?" Jenna took a bite of her cookie, eyebrows raised.

"Yes, well, maybe. I don't know for sure, but can we keep it between us girls anyway?"

Jenna nodded, but Kennedy had the sinking feeling Jenna was about to run back outside and head straight for her uncle to tell him what had just been said.

"One for the road?" Jenna asked Mary Rose, a hopeful expression on her adorable little face.

"Okay." Mary Rose ruffled Jenna's dark wavy hair.

"Thanks, Nana. Love you!" she called out, snagging another cookie. "Love you all!" She disappeared through the kitchen door and into the shards of sunlight bisecting the doorway.

Kennedy turned back to flower arranging, a warm sensation in her chest. She reached for another rose but paused when she noticed Nova and her mom weren't moving. They weren't moving because they were regarding Kennedy with raised eyebrows in obvious curiosity.

"Let's forget I said anything," she told them sweetly. It didn't matter if she and Mav liked each other *like that* because in less than seventy-two hours, Kennedy would be on her way back home. Then on a plane to Boston. Then working on the opposite side of the country, living her dream.

"A word about the Owens family," Nova offered. "We don't forget anything, but we do know how to give someone their space."

"And in my case, bite her tongue," Mary Rose said as they resumed their tasks.

"How's Jenna at keeping a secret?" Kennedy asked.

Mary Rose and Nova laughed in unison. "She's actually a steel vault," Mary Rose said. "No worries there. Unless you tickle her, then she caves."

"Don't we all?" Kennedy said, thinking about her ticklish places.

Conversation turned to everyday things after that, the afternoon passing by in happy unity. Kennedy almost didn't want their time together to end.

But she had a date with a handsome cowboy and a starry night, and nothing could keep her away from that.

• • •

She dressed in jeans, a T-shirt, tennis shoes, and the cardigan she'd smartly packed in case the evenings in Windsong were chilly. She hoped the lightweight sweater was enough to keep her warm before her mind wandered to the best way to ward off the chill: pressed against another person's body.

Did they make two-person sleeping bags? Did she want to cuddle up next to Maverick all night long? Did he have any designs on them sleeping inside the same bag? Would he remember to bring the blow-up mattress? Why did he always smell so good?

Smell was the oldest sense, and arguably the most important, because the nose was capable of driving a person to romantic distraction. True story. It did it by sensing complex mechanisms like sexual compatibility even when the conscious mind was unaware of it.

"You're pretty deep in thought there," Maverick said, breaking into her runaway train of thoughts.

She jumped up off the front steps of the inn, ready for him to whisk her away. He looked ruggedly handsome in faded, well-worn jeans and a dark blue long-sleeved ribbed shirt. Clean-shaven jaw. Hair neatly styled.

"Nope. Not thinking about anything." *But you.*

"You ready to go?"

"Yes." She walked beside him to the barn, where he saddled up Magnolia.

"We're riding to the campsite?"

"We are. I've got it set up already, and it's only about a five-minute ride. Is that sweater all you have?" At her nod, he pulled a denim jacket off a hook and handed it to her. "Bring this just in case."

Wanting her hands free when she rode with him on Magnolia, she slipped the jacket on. It was super soft and... she couldn't help but sniff it. *I'm doomed. Now I'm* wearing *Maverick's smell, too.*

They rode toward the setting sun with her arms wrapped around his waist. The measured cadence of Magnolia's steps had Kennedy's front rubbing against Maverick's back, a wonderful friction she'd gladly endure anytime.

Tandem horseback riding definitely had its perks.

"Are we headed to a special camping spot?" she asked.

He didn't answer right away, and she wondered if he'd heard her. "It's a spot on the property I really like."

"You mean there's spots you don't like?" she asked playfully.

"No, there's spots I just like more than others, Miss Nitpicker."

"So I'm not getting the spot you *love.*" She huffed out a dramatic sigh. "Seems unfair, since I'm here for only three more nights, and one of those is the wedding."

"I can turn this horse around if you want, Shortcake." He did something with the reins to make Magnolia begin to circle.

"No! Don't be silly."

Maverick made a clicking sound and Magnolia resumed course. "Good, because we're here."

She leaned out to the side to see around Maverick's broad shoulders, and the sight before her nearly took her breath away. His setup had layer upon layer of butterflies fluttering in her stomach.

"Mav, this is amazing."

The grassy area included two Adirondack chairs, a blow-up mattress with a sleeping bag and pillow on top, an unlit campfire inside a medium-size brass bin, a red-checked blanket and picnic basket, and several battery-operated tiki torches lit up in a circle around the site.

"I'm glad you like it."

"I love it," she corrected. She did. It looked like a picture out of *Sunset* magazine. That Maverick went to so much trouble to make her first camping experience special meant a lot to her.

He dismounted first, then helped her down. She moseyed around their cozy campsite while he tied Magnolia to a tree. There was a second sleeping bag rolled up tight, a couple of flashlights, and a pair of binoculars. He'd thought of everything.

Without a word, he lit a match and started a fire, stoking the twigs and wood until it blazed brightly.

Kennedy sat in one of the chairs to watch him. The final wisps of daylight painted the sky a dark orange, the shapes of the trees around them fading into darkness. "Have you always camped?" she asked.

"Yeah." He took the chair beside her. "Par for the course when you live on a ranch. Mother Nature has a way of capturing your attention and keeping it, especially when you have the chance to unwind from the daily grind."

"I never realized how much I'm indoors until this week. I'd work at the hospital, go home to my apartment to sleep, eat, and read, then go back to the hospital."

"Well, hopefully when you're in Boston, you'll take a little more time to enjoy the outdoors."

"I'm definitely going to make a point of doing that." She brought one knee up, wrapped her arms around her leg.

"You know, you fit in here, just like you do in the city."

"Don't let what I'm about to say go to your head, but I think you're right."

He smiled. "Usually am."

She rolled her eyes. "You got along well in the city, too. I may have bugged you relentlessly about being a country boy, but you had more friends than I ever did, and you took everything in stride."

He leaned forward, elbows on his knees, eyes zeroed in on her. "I didn't know you paid that close attention to me."

"I pay close attention to everything," she launched back, lest he think himself special or something.

His smirk told her he knew she thought highly of him. And okay, fine—she did. But he didn't need to have confirmation.

"You hungry?" he asked.

"I could eat." She'd snuck in a doughnut an hour ago, needing to get her fill of the best glazed doughnuts ever before going home. She'd splurged way too much this week, but that's what vacations were for.

They sat on the blanket, close but not too close. Maverick pulled large ready-made turkey sandwiches loaded with everything out of the picnic basket. She took hers and unwrapped the cellophane. "Thank you."

Next came napkins, cans of soda, and bags of chips. Barbecue potato chips—her favorite. They chatted about the ranch while they ate.

"Wow, so George is named after George Washington?" she asked. "I had no idea our first president bred mules."

"It started when he received a gift of large Spanish jack from King Carlos the third of Spain in 1775, then a couple others from French General Lafayette in 1786. From there he started breeding mares and created America's first quality mules, prized for their mixed breed."

"Is there special meaning behind Magnolia's name?"

"I guess you could say so. My mom named her after one of her favorite flowers on the property."

"Your whole family rides?"

"Yes." He took a sip of his drink.

"It's nice that you work together *and* have fun together. That's what Reed and I have—or had. I miss it." She took a bite of her sandwich. "Have you given any more thought to going to the wedding with me?"

"Not yet." Maverick's profile gleamed in the firelight.

"I hope you say yes," she whispered. Time was running out for them, and she didn't want any regrets.

He turned his head to look at her. His handsome face and undivided attention did pleasurable things to certain parts of her body. "I am glad you crashed it and landed here."

"Me too. I feel like if I hadn't, Elle and Reed might not be walking down the aisle." She held Maverick's gaze, the crackle of the fire and the hoot of an owl the only sounds.

Kennedy's phone rang, disrupting the pleasant vibe they had going on. "Sorry," she said, pulling it from her pocket and looking at the screen. "It's Ava, so I need to answer."

"Go ahead," he said easily, focusing back on his sandwich.

"Hey," Kennedy said into the phone, the device at her ear.

"Hi! You are never going to guess what happened. That guy from school I mentioned to you? Derek? He asked me out for coffee! For tomorrow. *Tomorrow*, Ned. And you're not here to help me decide what to wear!"

"Your pale yellow sundress you bought at that vintage store on Melrose with a pair of sandals," rolled off Kennedy's tongue.

"You think?"

"I know. And *yay*, by the way."

"I'm so excited. I really like him."

"Call or text me after, okay?"

"I will. How's it going there? Any more kisses with Maverick McDreamy?"

Kennedy cut a glance to Maverick, hoping he couldn't hear Ava through the phone. Her sister tended to have one volume: loud. But thankfully he didn't appear to be listening.

"Could you lower your voice a little?" Kennedy whispered.

"Oh! Is he there with you? What are you guys doing?"

Turning so the back of her head was to Maverick, Kennedy said quietly, "We're camping."

"*What?*"

That one little word could no doubt be heard through the trees a mile away. Kennedy shut her eyes and took a calming breath. "We'll talk tomorrow and catch up."

"I can't believe *you* are camping. Are you in a tent?"

"Ava. I'll tell you everything tomorrow."

"Okay, but don't get eaten by a bear or anything."

Kennedy chuckled. Ava's city-girl blood rivaled her own. "I won't."

"Oh, and will you please take a picture of him and text it to me? Pretty please? I'm dying to see what he looks like."

"No, I can't do that."

"Pleeeease? Just ask him. I bet he'll say yes. And besides, you owe me for taking care of Mrs. White's fish. Her apartment smells like something died in it. I'm not equipped for that sort of thing, Ned."

Kennedy feared if she didn't at least ask Maverick, Ava would text annoying emojis all night, so she turned and said, "Would it be okay if I took a picture of you for my sister? She'd like to see you."

"You could take a selfie with both of you!" Ava shouted through the phone.

Maverick heard it, his smile growing larger. "If she's half as tenacious as you are, Shortcake, we'd better take the picture."

"Shortcake! Oh my God. He has a nickname for you!"

"Please stop shouting," Kennedy said firmly into the phone, pressing it to her ear in hopes of muffling any further comments.

"Will do," Ava said, calming down in order to get what she wanted.

"You don't mind?" Kennedy asked Maverick.

"Not at all." He spread his arm wide, indicating she should come on over.

She moved to kneel beside him, tucking herself under his arm. Holding the phone in front of their faces, she snapped a photo.

"Take two just in case someone closed their eyes!" came through the phone loud and clear.

"Don't blink," Kennedy said before taking a second shot. She scooted back to her spot to look at them. Both were good, and to her surprise, Maverick's wide grin matched hers.

"How do I look?" he asked, his eyes twinkling in the firelight.

"Eh," she said with a shrug while her mind shouted, *Amazing! Hot AF! Dimples to die for!* She concentrated on her phone in case her face gave away the truth. Then, bringing the phone back to her ear, she said, "Picture sent. I'm hanging up now."

"Love you. Thank you!" Ava said. "Holy—"

Kennedy hung up before she could hear the rest of whatever Ava wanted to say. Two seconds later, though, a text came through with a string of smiley faces with heart-shaped eyes emojis. She put her phone on the blanket, facedown.

"Thanks for indulging her." She picked up the last bit of her sandwich.

"No problem. I know how younger sisters can be. Once Nova decides she wants something from me, there is no wrangling out of it."

They finished eating and returned to their chairs. The fire kept Kennedy toasty warm. So did the simple act of looking at her cowboy. *The* cowboy. Sheesh. He wasn't hers. "You were right. The stars are so much brighter out here."

"Yeah, without any commercial lights, you get a crystal clear view. Want a closer look?" He handed her the binoculars.

"Thanks." She held them up to her eyes. "Is this the part of the evening where you spout your knowledge of astronomy to impress me?"

"Afraid not. I don't know anything about the stars. Only that they're nice to look at."

Kennedy lowered the binoculars. Mav's eyes weren't on the stars; they were on her. She gulped at the intensity she saw shining back at her.

"Have you ever seen a shooting star?" she asked, putting the binoculars on the ground and tucking her hands inside the pockets of Maverick's denim jacket.

"Many. You?"

"Once, I think. A long time ago. I've never looked for them, but I imagine out here, people like to stargaze and without really trying, you see a shooting star or two."

He stretched his legs out in front of him, crossing one ankle over the other. Rested his hands behind his head and looked up. "I suppose."

"Do you ever—"

"Kennedy," he interrupted.

"Yes?"

"This is the part of the evening where you just take it all in. Without speaking. Listen, look if you want to, and feel everything around you."

He closed his eyes. His chest rose then slowly fell.

She followed suit. Let in the smell of pine, the fresh air, the sound of peace. She'd tried meditating. Tried yoga. Tried listening to music to clear her mind. None had worked. Maybe because she hadn't devoted enough time to reap the benefits.

But this? Being surrounded by nature, sitting beside a man she trusted implicitly. In a small town she never in a million years thought she'd enjoy. This got through to her. She lost herself to this exact time and place. Her pulse slowed. Her muscles loosened. She heard the slight rustling of leaves, the occasional crackle of the fire. When she opened her eyes and stared up at the sky again, the stars shined even brighter.

Time passed.

Maverick's hand coaxed hers out of her pocket. He laced their fingers together. His touch warmed her from the inside out.

She rolled her head to the side at the same time he did. Their gazes connected, blazed. She didn't consider herself an expert on men, but she knew an invitation when she saw one. Keeping hold of his hand, she got to her feet, stood in front of his chair. He tugged her down at the same time she moved to straddle his lap.

Wiggling her bottom, she got comfortable as he wrapped his arms around her waist beneath the jacket. She shrugged out of the denim, letting it fall to the ground behind her—she certainly wasn't cold anymore. Then she placed her hands on his shoulders.

"I have no words," she said softly. None to do the

evening justice.

A sigh slipped between his lips. Or maybe it was a catch of his breath. She couldn't tell for sure, but whatever it was, it rang with admiration. He understood that being here in the middle of nature took her breath away. "That's good," he whispered back.

And then he kissed her.

Lightly at first. Softly. Sweetly.

The gentle touch told her he enjoyed having her here with him. She wound her arms around his neck and melted against him, hoping he got the message she enjoyed being here, too. Under the stars. Just the two of them.

He escalated the kiss after that, fusing their lips together until finally, he slid his tongue inside her mouth, cupped the back of her head with one hand, and deepened the kiss, moving to a level she'd never experienced before. "Possession" was the best word she could come up with to describe it. Deep, caring ownership, like he wanted to erase every other kiss she'd ever had before.

She was on board with that.

Drop the paddle and float around forever on board with that.

Kissing him triggered all sorts of feel-good chemicals, like dopamine, serotonin, and oxytocin, to go hog wild inside her. Euphoria took over—all the pleasure centers in her brain stimulated at the same time.

Maverick moaned, the sound amazing, and just what she needed to get out of her head and the doctor analysis and back to the pure physical pleasure of kissing him. She didn't want to miss anything by analyzing it.

His mouth took over hers with skill and affection. The

hand on her waist tightened. The hand behind her head held her right where he wanted her. Their lips molded together in perfect harmony.

He delved inside her mouth, pulled back to drag her bottom lip down before he dove right back in. Her entire body went liquid pressed against his, her arms wove around his neck, her fingers playing with the soft strands of hair at his nape.

"Maverick," she murmured against his lips.

He smiled in return, the feel of his upturned lips against hers a victory she'd treasure forever. She got to him. It made her feel powerful and humble at the same time. He pulled so many welcome emotions out of her. And in a matter of days, he'd made her feel capable of more than she'd thought.

She cupped his face, looked into his eyes. They took a much-needed breath, a moment to say everything without a word spoken before kissing again. And again. The kiss went on and on, his tongue stroking hers. She'd enjoyed kissing in the past, but no other kiss compared to this. No other kiss tunneled under her skin and straight to her heart and head.

She was falling hard and fast for Maverick Owens. And the timing sucked.

They kissed until the moon hit the highest point in the dazzling night sky and then he tucked her inside her sleeping bag. Kissed her forehead in good night. She didn't take her eyes off him as he spread his sleeping bag beside her and climbed inside. He lay on his back, hands laced behind his head. She lay on her side, hands under her pillow, on the edge of the mattress so they could enjoy a few more minutes of gazing at each other.

She'd never consistently spent so much time with a guy before. A dinner date, a movie, an occasional museum, but never hours camping out, or on a horse, or in a canoe, or birthing puppies and crashing on the couch. She didn't regret her total focus on work and her career, but this prompted a turning point. She could be a doctor and have more. She just needed to own it.

And right now, she wanted to throw all caution and reservation aside and climb in Maverick's sleeping bag with him.

So she did.

"I don't want you to be a gentleman," she said, slipping out of her sleeping bag and landing on top of his with a soft thud.

He *oof*ed before saying, "What do you want me to be?"

She unzipped his sleeping bag enough to comfortably wiggle inside, all while he continued to lie there with his hands behind his head, a sexier-than-should-be-humanly-possible smile, and eyes that gleamed with yearning. She straddled him, leaned her elbows on either side of his head so their chests touched and their faces were only inches apart. "Inside me."

"Kennedy." He murmured her name with velvety reverence she felt between her legs. His hands moved to her waist. His hips pressed against hers, the hard, thick bulge in his jeans giving away his desire. For her. The chemistry, the emotion, the connection—all of it and more had brought them to this moment, and she was grateful they were on the same page.

"I've never had sex outside before." She rolled her hips,

unable to stop from rubbing over his firm, solid ridge. God, they'd just started and she couldn't remember ever being more turned on.

"Is that so?" He slid a hand underneath her T-shirt and cardigan, his palm warm and slightly calloused, and unhooked her bra with one flick of his fingers.

"Not your first rodeo, I see." She figured as much, but a wisp of air left her sails.

"No, but it's been a while." He lifted his head to brush his lips against hers. An open-eyed, openmouthed kiss followed. "I'm glad it's you here with me," he whispered.

"Me too." She touched her forehead to his. "I can't believe—"

"Believe it." He claimed her mouth, this time with hunger and urgency. The time for sweet nothings over, he made quick work of removing her sweater and shirt, kissing her while he did so.

She lifted his shirt over his head next. Kissed his neck, his collarbone.

He brought her face back to his. "Lose the bra."

It took her an extra few seconds because he distracted her by slipping his hands underneath the material and cupping her breasts. Rubbing his thumbs over her nipples. "Better than I imagined," he whispered.

"You pictured my boobs?"

"When we got caught in the rain."

"You're better, too." He'd obviously lifted a million bales of hay, his chest and abs strong and defined.

"There is so much I want to do to you." He traced his finger between her breasts, up the side of her neck, and around her ear, leaving a trail of tingles behind the soft touch. He landed on her bottom lip, dragged it down.

She sucked his finger into her mouth and she swore he grew even thicker inside his jeans. It made her lightheaded to know she affected him this way.

Without warning, he flipped their positions inside the sleeping bag, taking care to cushion her back with his arm before crushing his mouth to hers and unbuttoning her jeans. He slid his hand inside, effectively lowering her zipper, and grazed his palm over her most sensitive spot.

Two could play the in-the-pants game, so she undid his jeans. Pushed them—and his underwear—down his hips and freed his straining erection, hot and heavy in her palm. She made breathy sounds when he slid lower, along her very wet panties.

After that, they kicked off their clothes and kissed and laughed their way to total nakedness as quickly as possible. Sex had never been this much fun.

Except right when Maverick was about to get to the best part and slide inside her, he stopped.

"What's wrong?" she asked.

"I don't have a condom."

God, she'd been so enamored with him, so anxious to lose herself to him, she'd forgotten about anything else. "I'm on the pill and healthy," she offered.

"I always use protection, so I'm safe, too."

She smiled up at him. "Then what are you waiting for, cowboy?"

"Are you sure?"

"I'm positive." She slid her hands over his tight, round glutes for encouragement. She trusted him implicitly.

He spread her with his fingers and, with his breathtaking blue eyes locked on hers, slid unhurriedly inside. When she completely surrounded him, he stilled, seated so deep inside her, they both had to catch their breath.

And when he moved, when *they* moved, in perfect sync, their bodies slick with sweat, nothing else existed but the two of them. He whispered in her ear how good she felt. She whispered back for him to never stop. She cried out the first time he made her come.

Being the incredible lover he was, he didn't stop there. He continued to move inside her with slow, measured thrusts until a second orgasm rocked her. This time he followed right behind, spilling inside her with one final push before going absolutely still to enjoy his climax.

"Wow," he said, keeping them connected.

"Times two." She gave him a quick kiss on the lips. In thanks. In surrender. In bone-deep affection. Falling for Maverick? In only a matter of days?

Best mistake of her life.

CHAPTER NINETEEN

One day until the wedding

Maverick woke before Kennedy did. It didn't matter the day of the week or where he'd slept, his internal clock had him up early, rain or shine. This morning, the first thing he saw held beauty and intelligence and maybe a piece of his heart.

Last night had been incredible. They'd stayed inside his sleeping bag long enough for two rounds of sex before he'd tucked her back inside her own sleeping bag, cleaned up, and dressed. She'd fallen asleep near the edge of the mattress and there she remained, her cheek pressed into the pillow, her lips slightly parted.

He gazed at her, his mind and body inundated with warm feelings.

He never imagined having heart-to-heart conversations with her. Poking fun at each other with fondness. Letting his walls down, and kissing her like he'd never kissed anyone else. Like he was consumed. Possessed. Unable to get enough. She'd tasted like barbecue potato chips and he didn't care — they were his new favorite food. The smell of her skin his new favorite scent. Feeling her from the inside and being as close as two people could get, the best thing to happen to him in years.

His surrender came at her honesty, her pluck, her insatiable curiosity. Her kindness and beauty — inside and out. He liked who he was when with her. He liked…

Don't get used to it.

Kennedy's whirlwind appearance had an expiration date, he reminded himself. They had very different roads ahead of them.

Swallowing that thought, he looked away. Tomorrow's wedding had landed her at the inn, and the day after that she'd be gone. Back to her life as a big city doctor. He had no doubt she'd do great things. Save lives. Find someone to love her the way she deserved.

He rubbed at the sudden ache in his chest, unsure if the pain stemmed from the idea of Kennedy loving someone or from the pain of losing the woman he'd once loved. Three years. Nicole had been gone three years. Sometimes that felt like forever and other times like yesterday.

A week from tomorrow, he'd be on an airplane to honor her. He didn't have a return flight scheduled. Didn't have hotel reservations or train tickets or car rentals lined up. Just a promise to keep so he could finally move on when he got home.

Today…today he'd do his chores, then spend whatever time he could with Kennedy. She'd eyed the bookstore in town—maybe they'd go there. Or maybe he'd get her on George. Whatever she wanted, because making her happy made him happy.

He climbed out of his sleeping bag and rolled it up. Extinguished the remaining embers in the fire. Gathered the blanket, picnic basket, flashlights, and binoculars. His movements woke the sleeping beauty. She sat up.

"Good morning," she said.

"Morning."

"Looks like you're getting ready to go." She stretched

her arms above her head.

"If you don't mind. I've got some work to do this morning, but I thought we could meet up after that."

"I'd like that." She slipped out of the sleeping bag, raised up on her toes a few times to stretch her legs. "What can I do here?"

"Nothing. I'll take care of it later."

"A girl could get used to this special treatment, you know." Their eyes met briefly before she gazed up at the clear sky, the sun on the rise.

She put on her shoes, slipped on his denim jacket, and his breath caught in his chest. In the morning light, after the amazing night they'd shared, he liked her in his clothes way too much. Liked the idea of her even keeping the jacket, wearing it in Boston.

She followed him over to Magnolia, where they mounted the horse for the ride back to the inn. With her arms around his waist, he could feel her more at ease riding behind him. Bone-deep pleasure filled his chest now. He'd taught her to be comfortable on a horse.

He took them through the magnolia trees, near a ridge that offered views of the ocean. When the fog stayed away, the spectacular sight was incomparable. Kennedy let out a sigh of awe.

Veering away from the hilltop, the air immediately warmed a degree or two.

"Are those carvings in that tree?" Kennedy asked, missing nothing as they passed by the familiar landmark.

"They are. My dad carved his and my mom's initials after they married, and my brother carved his and Bethany's after they tied the knot."

"A family tree," she said.

"Yes." He slowed so she could take a better look.

"Are there other traditions in your family?"

"A slew of them. My mom's big on rituals. And before her, my grandmother started a few, too."

"Like?" she prodded.

"Like reading aloud *The Night Before Christmas* on Christmas Eve, playing touch football on Thanksgiving, having weekly family breakfast, my mom cooking 'good luck' dumplings whenever someone needs extra support, and—you'll like this one—kissing the last page of a book. My mom taught us there's nothing wrong with showing affection to a good story."

"That's really nice."

"How about you? Any traditions?"

"No," she said quietly.

He hated hearing the sorrow in her voice. "Well then, I officially pass to you the tradition of kissing the last page of books. You can share it with Ava, and it will grow from there."

She squeezed him. Pressed her soft lips to the side of his neck. "Thank you. I will."

A minute of comfortable quiet later, they arrived at the barn to find Hunter grinning from ear to ear at their appearance. "Good morning, lovebirds," his pesky brother said. "How was the campout?"

"It was great," Kennedy said, thankfully ignoring the "lovebirds" comment. She hopped off Magnolia without Maverick's help.

Maverick dismounted and shot his brother a warning look.

"Really? My brother didn't bore you to death with his motormouth?" Hunt slapped his hand on his thigh and barely stopped himself from cracking up.

Kennedy waltzed past him, a skip in her step. "Your brother has much better things to do with his mouth than talk," she tossed over her shoulder. "See you later, Mav."

Hunter flashed a proud, albeit slightly surprised grin. "I knew you had it in you, big brother." He lifted his palm for a high five.

"I am not high-fiving you," he said. "Let's get to work."

"Wait. I need details."

"When have I *ever* given you details?" He rubbed Magnolia's neck, then closed the gate on her stall.

"Exactly. Today's a good time to start. I'll tell you all about my night, too. You go first."

"Hunt, I'm not saying anything, but I'm happy to hear about you."

"Damn it, Mav. You need to get it off your chest."

He stopped walking in the doorway of the barn. "What are you talking about?"

"I know what tomorrow is—we all remember the day. And with Kennedy here, that's got to change things for you."

"It doesn't change anything."

"But—"

"But nothing. I'm going to the city like I always do. Alone," he added at the altruistic look on Hunt's face. "And whatever you think is happening between Kennedy and me, stop. She'll be gone in two days, and she won't be back."

"How do you know that?"

"Because she doesn't live here."

Hunter crossed his arms over his chest. "You could invite her."

"We both know I won't."

"That's what I'm talking about. If you get all the crap you've been accumulating the past few years off your chest, then you can move forward." He put a hand on Maverick's shoulder. "I want you to be happy again, and from what I can tell, Kennedy makes you happy."

Maverick knew his brother had only good intentions, but he was in no mood for brotherly love at the moment. "Let it be," he said firmly.

Hunt dropped his arm, shook his head. "Just tell me one thing. Do you feel something more for her?"

"Yes," he answered instantaneously. He couldn't help himself.

"Good. Then there's hope for you yet."

His brother made life seem so easy. Hunter's worst problem was a case of unrequited infatuation—he'd never watched the woman he loved take her last breath after suffering through an incurable disease. Those last few months with Nicole were awful and gut-wrenching and Maverick never wanted to go through that again.

And now he'd reconnected with a woman who had beaten death twice, once as a newborn and then as a teenager. What if that wasn't the end of it? What if Kennedy got sick again?

Even if they were on the same path, he couldn't afford the risk.

· · ·

Kennedy sat on the bench where she'd told Maverick about Hugo and her own life-saving surgery at fourteen. Big, beautiful trees provided shade from the late morning sun, and a warm breeze carried the scent of jasmine. She watched in the distance as Leah and others added more flowers to the gazebo and set up a white-carpet aisle for Elle to walk down. Other employees were setting up folding chairs. Still others were assembling round dining tables and a dance floor under a large white tent.

She lightly ran her finger over her bottom lip, remembering every sensation Maverick's touch had elicited. Last night had been unforgettable, and she couldn't wait to see him again. Her body heated at the mere thought of the quiet intensity in his blue eyes and the skill with which he used his body. With each passing day, the awareness between them sizzled brighter and the tight leash he held on his emotions diminished.

The animosity between them had finally fizzled out.

"Hey."

Kennedy looked up at Reed, quickly placing thoughts of Maverick in the back of her mind to bring out later. "Hi. Thanks for meeting me."

He sat down next to her. "I'm pretty sure our texts crossed at the same time."

"Great minds…"

"Yeah." He tapped his elbow to hers. "I owe you an apology and my gratitude."

"What are you sorry for?"

"Calling you like I did. I was having doubts about getting married and your nature is to immediately jump in and save people. Subconsciously, I knew you'd rescue me if

I needed it, when what I should have done is talked to Elle."

"You've talked now, I take it."

"We cleared the air last night, and we're more solid than we've ever been."

"I'm so happy to hear that."

"It's in large part thanks to you. I'm glad the two of you had a chance to talk."

"I am, too. She loves you a lot, and from the glimpses I've gotten of the two of you together, you feel the same way, even with your temporary doubts."

"I do. She makes my life better, and I'd be lost without her."

"Looks like my work here is done." Kennedy smiled at him.

"It was pretty awesome of you to come all this way ready to do whatever I needed."

"You'd do the same for me."

"I don't know," he teased. "I think you better promise you won't call me drunk from your bachelorette party."

She laughed. She'd never given much thought to her own wedding. But now…she could see herself having something small and intimate. "I promise."

"After the rehearsal tonight, we're meeting in the parlor for drinks and hors d'oeuvres. You should come. Everyone's welcome."

She wondered if Maverick had any plans for them. "Thanks. Maybe I will."

"Andrew will be there," Reed said, getting to his feet. "He and Elle's brother seem to have hit it off, although I'm hearing conflicting stories about what Andrew is doing for work now...and that the two of you are siblings *and* coworkers?"

Kennedy stood, put up her palm with an exasperated laugh. "Don't ask."

"Should I be worried? I think I heard him talking in an Australian accent, too."

"You can ask him yourself." She nodded over Reed's shoulder with a grin, where her best friend walked toward them with a beach towel hanging over his arm.

"All good here?" Andrew asked.

"Yes," Kennedy said. "But Reed's wondering what your story is, since he's gotten several different reports. For the record," she said to Reed, "I only agreed to us pretending to be boyfriend and girlfriend."

"Bro, don't sweat it," Andrew said, placing his hand on Reed's back in a reassuring manner. "I'm still acting, and I'm doing some method work while I'm here. I promise it won't interrupt your wedding."

"It better not," Reed stated, crossing his arms, but he broke into a grin, too.

"Are these reports in distress or happiness?" Andrew asked around a good-natured smile.

"Okay, point made," Reed said before turning to give Kennedy a hug. "See you later."

"See you later." She waved goodbye.

"Glad to see all is well in Wedding Land," Andrew said.

"Me too."

"I'm going to hit the beach for a couple of hours. I'll see you tonight, though? There's a cocktail party in the parlor."

"I think I can be there."

"Good," Andrew said before they went their separate

ways. She stopped inside the inn and asked Bethany to let Maverick know she'd walked into town and to meet her at the bookstore.

"If you want to give him my cell number, you could do that, too." Kennedy shared her digits as Bethany wrote them down. "Thank you."

She strolled leisurely into town, retracing the steps she and Maverick had taken the other night. In the light of day, she took in every tree (especially the one they'd sought shelter under during the rainstorm), every lamppost, the white picket fencing, the sounds of birds chirping, the smiles on the faces of everyone around her. She turned the corner onto Main Street a few minutes later.

Continuing to take her time, she absorbed everything about the traditional three-block row lined with shops and restaurants and massive oak trees. The charming architecture with a historic feel delighted her in a way she hadn't expected.

"Hello, Dr. Martin," a woman she'd never seen before said as they passed each other.

"Hi." She smiled back.

The sense of community also pleased her. No one in Los Angeles knew her name outside of the emergency room and her immediate neighbors. And she was lucky when those neighbors said hello.

"Dr. Martin, that dress is darling on you," Claudia said, passing by next.

"Thanks." She did feel good in her wildflower sundress. "How are you?"

"I'm great. Just stretching my legs while there's a lull at the bakery. Be sure to stop in later. I've got a special batch of glazed croissants coming out soon."

"Thank you, I will. You know I can't resist glazed any-thing."

They smiled at each other in goodbye and then Kennedy walked inside The Last Word Bookstore. It was decorated with white furnishings and comfortable looking, blue cushioned chairs, and she took a moment to look around. Besides books, she noticed stationery and other writerly gifts, candles, and small potted plants. Every nook included something. In the back was a café with a few small round tables and chairs. She quickly went in search of the poetry section, hoping to find a book of Rumi's writing to give to Maverick as a thank-you gift. She wanted to have it bagged before he arrived.

"Dr. Martin, hello!"

"Hi, Dr. Choi," she greeted cheerfully before making it to the poetry section. "It's nice to see you out of the office."

"My lovely wife pulled me away today. Maggie, this is the young doctor I told you about. Dr. Martin, this is my wife, Maggie."

"It's so nice to meet you," Maggie said.

"You too. And please call me Kennedy."

"My husband can't stop singing your praises. It's been a long time since he's had the pleasure of working with a young physician like yourself. He misses his days mentoring talent like yours in the hospital."

"You worked in a hospital?" she asked, assuming he'd always done family practice.

"In the ER." He winked at her. "I left to start a practice here when our sons were born. Maggie was having triplets and she needed me close by with a schedule I had more control over. Not that that worked out, exactly, being the only doctor in town, but we made it work."

"Triplets. Wow. How old are they now?"

"Thirty-six," Maggie said. "All married with children of their own. We're here to buy some books for two of our grandchildren who have birthdays coming up before grabbing some lunch in the café. You're welcome to join us if you're hungry."

"Actually, she has a lunch date." Maverick's deep voice sent delicious shivers down her spine. His palm on the small of her back magnified it times a million.

"Hi," she said a little too breathlessly. By the look on Maggie's face, she knew exactly what kind of effect Maverick Owens had on her.

"Hi, Doc. Mrs. Choi. I hope you don't mind if I keep Kennedy to myself."

"Not at all," Maggie crooned. "It's nice to see you enjoying some time off the ranch."

"I'll second that," Dr. Choi said. "Kennedy, you be sure to keep in touch, okay?" With the way word spread, everyone in town must know her departure date.

"I will." A sharp pang of regret pierced her chest. She'd miss Doc.

She'd miss a lot of things about Windsong.

She and Maverick stepped away. "Did you want to look around?" he asked. His beige shorts and blue T-shirt fit his tall, muscly frame very nicely.

"I was headed toward the poetry section when I ran into Doc." She couldn't surprise Maverick with a book now, but they could still look.

"Looking for anything special?" he asked knowingly.

"You know I am." She fingered the shelf of poetry books, deciding if she did find one she wanted, she'd buy it anyway. "Aha. *The Love Poems of Rumi*." She slipped it off the shelf for a better look.

Opening the book, she chose a random poem to read. "'You were born with potential. You were born with goodness and trust. You were born with ideals and dreams. You were born with greatness,'" she read aloud.

"'You were born with wings,'" Maverick continued from beside her, their arms touching. "'You are not meant for crawling, so don't. You have wings. Learn to use them and fly,'" he finished.

Holy inferno of hotness. Reading together from their favorite poet moved the earth beneath her feet. She didn't dare look at him, afraid he'd see affection and admiration written all over her face.

There had been a time in college when she'd wondered how she'd ever survive Maverick Owens. It didn't come close to how she was going to survive him *now*. Or rather survive *without* him. Logically, she would, of course. Maybe they'd even keep in touch. But deep down, she suddenly yearned for their lives to be different. For their plans to somehow meet in the middle.

She closed the book. "Sold."

He plucked it out of her hands. "Allow me."

"What? No, I can get it." She wove her way around the store to keep up with his strides toward the front of the shop.

"I know you can, but I'd like to buy it for you."

The young woman at the cash register had stunning green eyes, dark hair with streaks of purple, and wore a

T-shirt that read, Romance isn't dead…it's on my book-shelf. "Hi, Maverick."

"Hi, Willow." He put the book on the counter.

Willow's eyes slid to Kennedy. "I'm guessing you're Dr. Martin."

"You guess right. It's a little unnerving how everyone knows who I am."

"Right?" Willow said. "When I took over the bookstore two years ago, the same thing happened to me."

"But I'm only visiting."

"But you've done your doctor thing. And"—she cut a glance at Maverick—"your Maverick thing."

"Okay, that's enough," Maverick said. "Doesn't this town have anything better to do than gossip about me hanging out with a friend?"

The "friend" description didn't exactly feel right, but Kennedy had no better word to describe their relationship at the moment, either.

"Whatever you say, dude." Willow returned Maverick's credit card and placed the book in a cute brown bag with a twine handle. "Here you go, Dr. Martin. Enjoy."

Kennedy took the bag. "Thanks. I love your store, by the way."

"Thank you. I hope that means you'll come back again sometime."

Since Kennedy had no good answer to that, she simply nodded.

Maverick ushered her out of the store and led her straight to his truck parked in front.

She thought about torturing him with a request to stay in town, but bit her tongue. Her days of tormenting the cowboy were over. "Thanks for the book. Where are we off to?"

"How does fishing sound?" He put the truck in drive.

"I've never fished before, so good. But don't you use worms for bait and aren't you afraid of them?"

"You remember that, huh?"

"I remember everything." She pointed to her temple.

"That's too bad," he said with a straight face.

"Will you need me to bait your hook for you? Save you from the terrifying creatures with soft bodies and no limbs?" She gave him a giant grin.

"I appreciate the offer, tough girl, but we're going jig fishing."

"What's that?"

"A jig is a type of artificial bait. It's a hook with a metal head molded to it and skirted with rubber. They get bass to bite, more so than other fishing lures."

"Got it." She picked up the smooth, oval rock still sitting in his cup holder and rubbed her thumb across it. "Do you use this often?" Worry stones worked for some, not for others.

"Not so much anymore."

"So, it helped at one time? I'm always curious about different health remedies I can recommend to my patients."

"Do you want the answer I gave my mom or the real one?" he asked, not taking his eyes off the road.

"The real one. Always the real one."

"Not really. Now I just keep it there as a reminder."

"A reminder?"

"That I've got a family who cares. Sometimes they're a burr under my saddle, but I know it comes from a good place, and a lot of people don't have that."

She giggled.

"That's funny?" he asked good-naturedly.

"'Burr under my saddle' is. Somctimes you say things that remind me of how differently we were raised." She put the rock back in the cup holder. "The rest of what you said is really nice. You're lucky. My family isn't like yours."

He reached over to squeeze her hand as he drove down a dirt road, through the trees, toward his grandfather's lake. Kennedy rolled down her window to feel the wind on her face.

They parked near the bank of canoes, her eyes scanning the boats with fondness. She remembered every moment of their time spent on the lake with perfect clarity. She'd thought about other, more intimate, times spent together, too. The memories made this week — wedding related and Maverick related — would keep her company for years to come. Andrew being a bounty hunter and stunt man and dance therapist and water slide tester and her trying to remember who knew what and where she fit in...plus Maverick being unexpectedly *everything*.

From a shed he grabbed two fishing poles, a tackle box, and a khaki short-brimmed hat with a chin-cinch toggle. He plopped the hat on her head. "Gotta protect those freckles."

The hat did nothing for her outfit, but she cinched it nonetheless — how could she not when he wanted to protect her face? — and followed him down a short dock. His calves were tan and well-defined. His butt well-built and sexy. He glanced over his shoulder like he'd felt her perusal, and she quickly looked away. Streaks of sunlight glistened in the water. A few people paddled canoes, talking and laughing.

"Have a seat," he said when they'd reached the end of the wood planks.

She tucked her sundress under her bottom and sat with her legs dangling. Maverick slid off his shoes and socks before taking the spot *right* beside her. Their hips touched, then their arms. His feet disappeared under the water with a small ripple.

"Mav, what are you doing?" She wiggled in alarm. "Won't the fish bite your toes?"

"It's possible, but doubtful, near the shore like this. They usually swim deeper." He opened the tackle box, handed her a bottle of sunscreen. While she applied lotion to her arms and legs, he removed a couple of jigs and attached them to their lines. He demonstrated with his pole how to throw the line into the lake. It took her a few tries, but she finally did it. She appreciated his patience and confidence in her.

"Now what?" she asked, back straight, excited to be doing this.

"Now we wait. Jig fishing is all about feel and sensitivity, so pay close attention to your pole. It also takes time."

"How much time?"

He lifted the pair of sunglasses hanging on his shirt collar and put them on. "Sometimes hours." All calm and cool, did he have any idea how hard it was for her to sit still doing nothing for hours? "If a fish bites, it feels like a light thump traveling up the line."

"So fishing is kind of boring."

"Says you. A lot of people find it just the opposite and

enjoy the peacefulness."

"I can't figure out if you brought me here to shut me up or get me to talk." She rested her head on his shoulder.

"How about whichever you want."

"Okay, tell me the one thing no one else knows about you and then we can meditate on our fishing poles."

"I'm hoping to brand and market my chemical-free pesticide."

She lifted away so she could look at him. "Really? That's great."

"I'm meeting with a potential investor in a couple of weeks."

"Won't you be traveling then?"

"This investor is in Italy. He's a winemaker. Nicole and I met him and his wife when we were there, and we became friends."

She couldn't see his eyes behind his sunglasses, but she'd gotten pretty good at reading him, and he appeared both nervous and hopeful about the prospect.

"You haven't told your family?"

"No. I don't want anyone to get their hopes up."

"Yours are, I can tell."

His lips turned slightly upward. "I know I have a good product and a sound proposal. But the pesticide's been tested only here, and there was a health issue with some of the trees the other day. I cleared it up, but soil variance, air temperature, humidity, precipitation, and different types of pests all play a factor."

"You've got this." She put her hand on his knee. "You were the only person to get a better grade than me in chemistry, and you wouldn't even have approached this investor if you weren't confident in its value and success rate. Plus, I've seen your trees. They looked perfect to me."

"Thanks for the vote of confidence. I appreciate it." He covered her hand with his, laced their fingers.

"Do you see making the product here or in Italy?"

"Here."

"Well, I hope it works out. You'll have to let me know. Send me a postcard from Italy with the good news." She dropped her gaze to their hands.

"I'll do that." He brought her hand to his mouth and kissed her knuckles. Was that a promise? To keep his word on the postcard? She hoped so, because she suddenly realized that the last thing she wanted was this trip to be the last time she saw or talked to him.

Eleven months ago…

Dear Nicole,

Today was a good day. Hunter and I mended a few fences, mucked out the stables, and then had a beer with lunch while I listened to him talk. The poor guy still has a thing for Callie, and she is oblivious to it. Then I crashed on the couch and played fetch with Barley. She's been sneaking off onto the neighbor's ranch more and more lately, and Bear, the neighbor's dog, has been over here. Then there's George, who I'm pretty sure thinks he's a dog. A big dog with no bark. Ha.

Jenna started first grade and loves it. She's by far the smartest and funniest six-year-old there is. She insists on wearing her yellow rain boots everywhere and has already informed us she wants to be The Mandalorian for Halloween. Cole and Bethany are going out of town for a long weekend and she's asked to stay with me. She has a list of things for us to do together, including playing veterinarian. It's her favorite game for the two of us. And while it used to make me uncomfortable, it doesn't anymore. Sometimes I even think about going back to vet school. Time is definitely healing, at least that's what I tell myself.

Miss you,

Maverick

CHAPTER TWENTY

One day until the wedding

"Have you been down to the beach yet?" Maverick asked, not quite ready to leave Kennedy's side. Fishing had lasted approximately one hour before she'd declared the "fish are not *jiggy* with it today" and they—Kennedy and him, not the fish—should find a better use for their time. He didn't care what they did, as long as they were together, so standing in front of the inn now, the pathway to the beach called his name.

"I haven't. Want to walk down there?"

"You read my mind."

"Uncle Mav! Uncle Mav!"

Maverick turned just in time to catch Jenna as she launched herself at him. She wrapped her little legs around his waist and squeezed his cheeks with her hands. "Can you get me out of here?" she asked.

If Jenna weren't smooshing his face, he'd smile. "What's up?" he asked, but it sounded more like "Wasshhup" with her crushing his cheeks.

She released her hold. "Uncle Hunt wants me to pick up poop and I don't wanna."

Kennedy covered her mouth with her hand, finding his niece as entertaining and wonderful as he did, he suspected.

"Well, we can't have that, can we?"

"Nooo." She shook her head, her pigtails whipping

around her face.

"Let's go put our feet in the ocean, then," he said, taking quick strides in order to evade his brother.

"Yay!" Jenna said, crawling from his front onto his back for a piggyback ride.

"Do you have certain chores you need to do?" Kennedy asked her.

"Yes. I have to make my bed and brush my teeth every morning and night. I have to make sure the animals have water. And I have to pick up my toys and put them away. One time Daddy stepped on a Lego, and he was really mad."

"Jenna is a genius with Lego kits," he said. "She reads the instructions all by herself and does a great job."

"I'm better than you, right?" she said.

"You sure are."

The second his feet hit the sand, Jenna squirmed out of his hold. "Last one to the water is a rotten egg!" She quickly shucked her shoes and made a run for the placid waves.

"She keeps everyone on their toes, doesn't she?" Kennedy asked, removing her shoes and placing them on a nearby log.

"She definitely does. In the best possible way," he added. He put his shoes next to Kennedy's, then took her hand to walk down to the water. The feel of her small palm inside his relaxed every muscle in his body. Soft sand, a few seagulls overhead, the salty air, a winning combination all around.

When they reached the ocean, Jenna wormed her way between them so she could hold each of their hands.

Glancing at his niece and Kennedy, he experienced a punch to the gut. For a split second, he pictured this future. A daughter. A wife. His heart full.

Kennedy laughed at something Jenna said, and he yanked himself free of such notions.

"Will you swing me, pretty please?" Jenna asked. "When the wave comes."

"Sure," Kennedy answered.

In perfect sync, he and Kennedy lifted and swung Jenna when the wave came onto shore. "Whee!" Jenna sang. Followed by, "Again!"

After numerous times, his niece finally tired of the game and insisted the three of them look for treasure.

"What kind of treasure?" Kennedy asked.

"Any kind!"

Over Jenna's head, Kennedy smiled at him. He smiled back, his face muscles getting a good workout this week.

"Did you know Uncle Mav gave me my first treasure?" Jenna picked up a broken shell piece and put it in her pocket.

"He did?"

"Uh-huh. It was this." She reached inside the collar of her princess T-shirt and pulled out the necklace he'd given her for her fifth birthday. She lifted it for Kennedy to get a good look.

"It's beautiful," Kennedy said of the tiny silver sand dollar.

"I never take it off. Ever." She tucked it safely back inside her shirt. "It's my most prized possession." She skipped ahead to pick up a piece of driftwood.

"I'd say you win favorite uncle," Kennedy said.

"No doubt. Which bugs the crap out of Hunter. He wanted to get her a pony to one-up me, but Cole said not until she's ten. Buys me a few more years of favoritism."

"You'll still be her favorite." Kennedy rocked sideways to bump his arm.

"What makes you say that?" he asked, genuinely interested.

"Hunter will always be the fun uncle, I suspect, but you'll be the one who pulls her heartstrings. And that's a pretty powerful place to hold."

The words that came out of this woman's mouth.

He pulled her to a stop and, not caring if Jenna took notice, kissed Kennedy square on the mouth. Lips, tongue, he poured his soul into the kiss before lifting away.

Her dreamy expression told him mission accomplished; his thanks and gratitude were well received.

They resumed walking, hand in hand. A few sunbathers dotted the sand, including Andrew, who, by the grin on his face and the thumbs-up, had witnessed their kiss. Kennedy groaned. "I guess I forgot to mention Andrew was down here."

"Wouldn't have mattered."

She gazed up at him in surprise.

He couldn't say it aloud, but boy did she throw him off-balance. She made him forget everything but her, and kissing her just then had been on instinct. Necessary. Important. "I doubt I'm the only guy he's seen you kiss," he said instead, *hating* the thought of her kissing anyone else.

"True," she tossed out breezily.

Touché.

He released her hand to pick up a flat gray rock.

Brushing the sand off, he placed it in his palm.

"It's shaped like a heart," Kennedy said keenly.

It was. And because his own heart was off-limits, he gave her the rock. "For you. A treasure to remember today."

CHAPTER TWENTY-ONE

One day until the wedding

"You've fallen for the enemy."

"No," Kennedy lied.

"You're such a liar," Andrew said, knowing her too well. "That kiss on the beach today was hot as hell. Not to mention there's The Sleeping Bag Sexcapade."

"Shut up." Her cheeks heated at the memory. "And I can't help it if *he* kisses me." Sitting on the edge of the bed, she slipped on her heels, head down, so she could replay the beach kiss in her mind without further scrutiny. Maverick had taken her breath away. Every kiss from him took her breath away.

"You don't have to kiss him back, *ma chéri*." Andrew fastened the belt on his slacks, not paying her any mind.

There was no denying anything with her best friend. She didn't know why she even tried. *Because the truth hurts. You're leaving for a life far away from Maverick's.*

"Fine. I like him more than is advisable."

"Hey, what happens in Windsong stays in Windsong."

"You're such a goober," she said, even though truer words had never been spoken. She stood, ran her hands down her wraparound dress.

"Yeah, but I'm *your* goober." He checked himself in the mirror. Handsome as always, he turned to her and added, "You look great."

"You too."

"Let's go cocktail it up." He put out his arm for her to take.

Her phone rang as she slipped it inside her purse. She caught Hugo and Maria's names on the screen and thought about answering before deciding to let it go to voicemail. She'd call them tomorrow morning when she had more time. Tonight she was anxious to see Maverick. He'd agreed to meet her in the parlor at seven, the entire Owens family included in tonight's party, and it was currently three minutes after.

Slipping her arm inside Andrew's, they walked to the gathering. Finding it in full swing, Andrew made a beeline for Liam while she strolled over to the bar for a drink. To her disappointment, Maverick hadn't arrived yet. "A glass of wine, please?"

She turned to check out the room while she waited for her drink. Reed and Elle were talking with friends; other people she'd noticed around the inn and property were gathered in small groups. Several of the vases they'd arranged decorated the room.

"Here you go, miss," the bartender said.

"Thank you." She lifted the glass for a sip just as a man sidled up beside her.

"Hello, there. I don't think we've met. I'm Jared." A groomsman, if her vague recollection of Reed mentioning him was correct. His friendly demeanor drew a smile out of her.

"Hi. I'm Kennedy."

"Friend of the bride or groom?"

"Groom."

"Huh. Beer please," he said to the bartender. "I'll have to talk with Reed about not introducing us sooner." He accepted his drink and lifted it in the air. "Cheers to getting to know you, Kennedy." They clinked glasses. She didn't want to be rude even though she had no intention of getting to know Jared any better.

"Hi, sweetheart, sorry I'm late." Maverick appeared out of nowhere and wrapped his arm around her in a possessive hold. Kissed her cheek. Sent Jared a glare to end all glares. She almost laughed.

Instead she melted against him. "Hi. Maverick, this is Jared."

"Hey," Maverick said, always a gentleman with inn guests, but not offering his hand. "Thanks for keeping my girl company."

His girl? *His* girl. What the heck did that mean?

"No problem," Jared said good-naturedly. "You two have a good night." He backed away before turning to join other guests.

She turned on the cowboy. "Your girl?" she inquired. How could she not? They hadn't spoken about what this was, and if she wanted to go hang out with Jared, she could. Not that she wanted to. Not in the least.

He took her hand and led her to a quiet corner of the parlor. "For tonight. Am I wrong?"

The sincerity in his blue depths floored her. He didn't usually give away much, but tonight he was.

"No, you're not wrong."

"You look incredible." His gaze slid up and down her body like a caress. He'd seen the green wraparound dress before, but he made her feel like it was the first time.

"Thanks. You look very handsome." He'd traded jeans for a pair of black slacks and a light blue button-down, loose around his neck. His hair was neatly combed, his jaw cleanly shaven. She took a sip of her wine to cool the flash of heat coursing through her body.

"I like to clean up occasionally." He eyed her wine. "You good there?"

"Yes, thanks." She wasn't much of a drinker. One and done for her.

"Don't move. I'll be right back."

She watched him walk to the bar and order a drink. The bartender chatted him up like they knew each other, and she reminded herself they probably did. Mav knew everyone at the inn and on the ranch. He had a family here who extended beyond his parents, siblings, and niece.

He had a place where he belonged. Where friendship bloomed, even quietly.

Kennedy wasn't sure where she belonged. In an ER, yes. But she didn't currently have that, and the feeling of being untethered suddenly made everything inside her hollow. Tuesday's meeting in Boston couldn't get here quick enough. She needed an answer about her future.

She wanted a place to call home.

She slid into a nearby high-back chair with a window view of the pond and white-painted bridge, rose bushes adding a splash of pink and red. She had this. An in-person interview meant they were serious about her.

"How do you think he is?" a woman asked from behind the chair.

"I don't know. How do we ever know? He won't talk," a man responded.

It sounded like Nova and Hunter. Were they talking about Maverick?

"He seems to really like Kennedy. That's good, right?" Nova said. "Means he's moved on."

"I don't know," Hunter said.

"Which part?" Nova asked.

Kennedy got to her feet. It was definitely Nova and Hunter, and it was wrong to eavesdrop.

"The moving-on part. He won't admit it, but he's wrecked about tomorrow."

Tomorrow? What was tomorrow?

"That's understandable," Nova said. "But after his trip, he better be ready to get on with his life. Otherwise, we need to do an intervention."

"Hey," Kennedy said when they hadn't noticed her. She stepped around the chair. "Sorry, I was sitting here and overheard you talking."

"Hi," Nova said, her eyes wide. "We didn't realize you were there."

"I know. It's my fault. Please forgive me."

"There's nothing to forgive. What we said isn't really a secret." Love mixed with worry in Nova's tone.

"But maybe keep it to yourself," Hunter said. "Mav can be a little prickly."

"I totally understand." She almost asked what tomorrow was, but bit her tongue, thinking if it was important for her to know, Maverick might bring it up later.

Hunter nodded. "I'm off to the bar. Care to join?" he asked both of them.

"Yes," Nova said. "A fruity cocktail is exactly what I need to help with the lingering pain in the bottom of my foot."

"I recommend some Tylenol," Kennedy said lightly, "and I'm good here, thanks."

Nova gave her a quick hug. "See you later."

Kennedy watched them greet Maverick at the bar just as his eyes caught hers from across the room. She swiftly looked back out the window to process what she'd heard.

Maverick still had some healing to do, and she wasn't sure where she fit in with that. Which meant the best thing for her to do would be to enjoy his company without allowing any more of her heart to get involved.

He came up behind her, his warm breath brushing the side of her neck with a goosebump-raising, featherlight touch. "Sorry to keep you waiting," he said softly.

"It's okay." She gulped down the rest of her wine.

His brows pinched. "Everything all right?"

"Fine."

"Can I have everyone's attention?" Mary Rose announced from beside her husband at the parlor's entrance. The room quieted. "John and I would like to thank Elle and Reed and their families and friends for staying with us this week and trusting us with their special day. We've very much enjoyed getting to know you all."

"You too!" someone shouted in return.

Mary Rose smiled. Maverick got his dimples from her. "Thank you. It's a tradition here on the ranch that the night before a wedding, the bride and groom add their thumbprints to our book of celebratory trees." Mary Rose opened a thin leather-bound guestbook to reveal a white page with a tree drawn on it. In place of the leaves were different-colored thumbprints. She placed the book on a table and opened three different colored ink pads. "Please come on over and write your name or initials inside or beside your thumbprints."

Reed and Elle walked to the table and added their personal stamp to the scrapbook. "Another tradition," Kennedy whispered to Maverick.

"Yes."

"Did Cole and Bethany get married here?"

"They did. Their thumbprints were the first ones in the book."

Bride and groom hugged when done and thanked Mary Rose and John. Liam made the next announcement. "It's time for one last wedding game to see how well you know our happy couple." He and one of Elle's bridesmaids handed out paddles. One paddle had a headshot of Reed, and one paddle had a headshot of Elle.

"Raise the correct paddle to answer the question," Liam said. "First question: who knows all the words to 'I Will Always Love You'?"

Kennedy raised her Reed paddle without hesitation. "He has a thing for Whitney Houston," she told Maverick.

Mav played along, raising his Reed paddle.

Liam raised his Reed paddle in confirmation. Most of the room had guessed Elle.

"Who said 'I love you' first?"

Again she answered with Reed. "He told me it was the first time he ever said it," she whispered. She'd only ever said it once, too. To her rat fink ex after he said it to her. She wished so badly she could take those words back.

And again, she was correct.

"Who drove across the country and slept in a van?"

Kennedy looked around the parlor. Some people stood,

some sat. The paddles in the air leaned toward Reed. Maverick raised his Elle paddle. So she went with the consensus and raised Reed's.

Liam lifted the Elle paddle.

Surprise rippled through the room. Elle shared the story about when and why. Liam asked several more questions before declaring the game over and saying, "Let's dance!"

Music played through hidden speakers, and while there was no official dance floor, an area had been cleared for dancing. Servers holding trays with mini cheesecakes, fruit tarts, and brownies circulated the room.

She and Maverick mingled some (thankfully avoiding the guests Andrew had introduced her to), their bodies constantly touching in some innocent way that felt anything but. He didn't offer much in the way of conversation, and she found herself appreciating everything he'd shared with her this past week more and more. When a slow song began to play, he asked her to dance.

Instead of joining the group of couples in the designated area, he led her to the much quieter veranda. It was like he had a sixth sense and knew she needed to steer clear of people, lest she mix up which persona she was supposed to be with which guest.

Faint notes of music reached her ears as he took her in his arms. She wrapped hers around his neck, laid her head on his shoulder.

It felt so right being together like this that she wanted to cry. She'd never experienced this sense of completeness before: a deep-rooted affection on the cusp of the forever kind of love. If only they'd reunited under different circumstances. And Maverick wasn't still working through his loss.

Kennedy had been beside many people who had lost loved ones. It sucked. It hurt. It devastated. The younger the deceased, the deeper the pain. A woman in her twenties like Nicole should have had decades in front of her.

"Shortcake, you're thinking too hard again."

"Isn't it ever difficult for you to turn off your brain?" she asked candidly.

"Sometimes. The secret is distracting yourself, and you're the best distraction I've ever had."

She lifted her head to gaze up at him. "You know you're really good at sweet talk."

"I'm glad you think so." He dropped a soft kiss to her lips.

"I think a lot of things about you," she confessed, their bodies swaying to the soft melody coming from inside.

"Right back at you."

"Should we compare notes?" Talk about playing with fire. Why say anything meaningful to each other when it didn't matter? When she knew her heart beat harder and faster than his.

"No," he said sweetly. "Not because you aren't something special, Shortcake, but because you are."

"What does that mean?"

He looked away, hiding from her once again. His body, though? His strength and passion continued to wrap around her without uncertainty, his head and heart obviously at odds.

"Can we not?" he asked, meeting her eyes.

"Not what? Talk?"

He nodded.

She couldn't even be mad at him. His request said volumes. His silence spoke louder than any explanation. He'd always been a man of few words—the times he'd opened up had been wonderful gifts she'd practically coerced out of him. She laid her head back on his shoulder. She didn't want to spend their remaining time together at odds.

The slow song ended, and Maverick led her to a cozy outdoor couch for two. Through the open French doors, they had a perfect view inside the parlor. For a quiet minute, they watched the goings-on.

"I love to people watch," she said. "Sometimes on my hospital breaks I'd go to a nearby coffee shop, sit outside, and make up stories about the people walking by."

"Yeah? Tell me about that guy in the striped blue shirt." Maverick lifted his chin toward a trim middle-aged man with dark hair.

"Oh, he's a duke from England. His wife is American and his family was terribly disappointed that he didn't marry a duchess, but she won them over when she served her famous apple pie on a silver platter."

He smiled at that.

"Your turn," she said. "The woman in the yellow dress."

"She's a lottery ticket winner from Oklahoma. She gave away half her winnings to a horse charity and the other half she spent on jewelry." A great backstory given the enormous diamond around her neck.

"See that guy there?" Kennedy lifted her chin toward

one of Reed's friends. "He's a jewel thief, and later tonight he's going to steal Oklahoma's diamond necklace and replace it with a forgery."

Maverick gave a *nice one* nod and then waved toward a server weaving through the crowd. The woman immediately smiled when she spotted him, like she'd been searching for him. "There you are," she said. "Two hot chocolates as requested."

"Thanks, Tanya." Maverick accepted the two glass mugs on the tray, handing Kennedy one. "Careful, it's hot."

"Enjoy," Tanya said, taking her leave.

"Is this your mom's special recipe?" Kennedy blew on the drink, the decadent smell of chocolate reaching her nose.

"It is."

"This is a nice surprise. Thank you."

Maverick took a sip of his hot chocolate, a bit of whipped cream remaining on his upper lip.

"You've got some—"

He leaned over and kissed her, effectively erasing the smudge from his mouth. "You were saying?"

She smiled and licked her lips before surveying the parlor again. "Your turn again."

"The man in white with the bow tie," Maverick started, "he's the heir to the Charmin fortune, which is why he's never in a crappy mood."

Kennedy laughed so hard, hot chocolate shot up her nose.

"Sorry. You okay?" Maverick handed her a cocktail napkin.

"I'm fine." She gathered herself, none the worse for wear.

"Now be quiet for a moment so I can take a proper sip." She sipped. She sighed. "This is the best hot chocolate ever."

"I'm glad you think so."

"Okay, see that lady standing next to Andrew and holding a cocktail in her hand? She's a beekeeper and loves to get buzzed." Kennedy grinned, waiting for Maverick to crack up.

He barely smiled, the big jerk!

"Hey, that was funny!"

"You can't *try* to be funny. You either are or you aren't." His playful tone and sparkling stare were more than enough to curb her complaint.

"I hear you and I raise you a hot chocolate," she said.

His upturned lips and dimples were the least funny thing on the planet, and instead so sexy and appealing, she had to look down at her heels for fear of rubbing up against him like an animal in heat.

"Deal." And did his voice have to be so deep and seductive?

Maverick had effectively rendered clear thinking impossible, so she recycled some information that popped into her head. "See that tall man with the blond mustache? He's a bounty hunter and his last bounty was a…was a woman with amnesia and she told him…" She paused for dramatic effect. "'I don't know what you're talking about.'"

He laughed. "Okay, you win."

"Just like that?" She had a feeling he'd gifted her the win out of the goodness of his heart.

"You came through on the spot, and that counts for double."

She pressed her lips together in an appreciative smile. What a difference seven years made. In college he would have one-upped her without hesitation, or at least tried. They'd battled so often back then. Clashed at every opportunity. She hadn't taken any time to understand him or see his good qualities—she'd disliked him and his know-it-all attitude at first glance. Had they given each other more courtesy and less attitude, would they have been friends? More than friends? She'd never know.

They sipped their hot chocolates in easy silence until a yawn snuck up on her.

"Tired?" he asked.

"A little. All the fresh air and sunshine this week have really relaxed me. I have a tan line for the first time in forever, even with the sunscreen you so kindly supplied me with."

"Really? You sure? Maybe I should double-check those lines." He regarded her with a lopsided grin.

"I'll show you mine if you show me yours," she fired back, unable—and unwilling—to stop the physical pull between them.

He quickly stood with his hand out to help her up. "Let's go."

She loved the urgency in those two words. The desire and intensity in his gaze.

Rather than leave through the parlor, Maverick held her hand and led her across the veranda. They entered the inn through the living room and arrived at her room less than a minute later.

Once inside, butterflies kissed her skin. She struggled to maintain her composure. She had the sexiest cowboy alive in her room and a bed three feet away. What would they do with all that extra space compared to a sleeping bag?

The door clicked shut, and the two of them stood in the middle of the room staring at each other. His eyes touched on every inch of her body as he took his time running those baby blues from her head to her feet and back up. She did the same, committing every inch of him to memory.

"Ladies first," he said.

She didn't hesitate. Just untied her dress, wiggled her shoulders to free the material, and let it fall to the floor.

Maverick sucked in a breath, his clear appreciation turning her nipples into hard points.

"Your turn," she told him.

He peeled off his shirt with one arm and tossed it aside. Next, he lost his pants, kicking off his shoes and socks in the process. His boxer briefs did little to hide how much he wanted her. The man had it going on and then some. Wet heat blossomed between her legs.

"The rest," he said, his voice deep, husky, demanding. She loved it.

She removed her bra and panties, his hawklike stare watching her every move.

"Heels, too."

"You don't want me to leave them on?" Didn't all men have dreams of a naked woman in heels?

"No."

She slipped off her shoes at the same time he eliminated the distance between them and scooped her into his arms. "I like you just as you are."

"Short?"

"And stunning." He placed her on the bed, positioning

himself above her.

Hard muscles against her soft ones.

Sun-kissed lips against the shell of her ear, down the column of her neck. To the valley between her breasts. He sucked on one nipple, then the other. Kissed down her stomach, spread her legs, and licked her to oblivion.

Clutching the comforter, she screamed his name.

"Delicious," he said, rising to kiss her lips. To share her taste.

She reached down and took him in her hand. Guided him to her entrance. With one sweet surge, he sank into her.

"Jesus," he whispered against her temple.

They moved in tandem. His warm breath coasted over her hairline. He whispered sweet things. Dirty things. And this time, they came together.

He collapsed beside her. Brought her under his arm to rest her head on his chest. She curved her body against his in satisfied bliss.

"Nice tan lines, by the way," he said.

She pressed a smile against his smooth skin. "Thanks."

"How about a quick shower and then I'll tuck you in?"

"Sounds perfect." She led him to the bathroom, where they soaped each other under the warm spray of water. Maverick washed her hair, something no man had ever done before. She almost fell asleep standing up.

After a quick towel dry, she slipped on her nightgown and crawled under the bedcovers. Maverick dressed and then joined her, sitting on the side of the bed. He fiddled with the sheet, taking his tuck-in duty seriously, and she laughed.

"Hey, watch it. This service isn't for just anyone."

She laughed harder. "S-service? You're so funny."

Her laughter ignited his own, and this, *this* right here would forever mark her thoughts of him. Laughter. Joy. New things learned and shared. Freedom. He'd challenged her to step out of her comfort zone and she'd surpassed her expectations. His too, she imagined.

Their laughter died down. He cupped her face in his calloused hand. "Thanks for making this a week I'll never forget, Shortcake."

She pressed her cheek to his palm. "I won't, either."

His smile didn't quite reach his eyes, but he followed it with a kiss that would have melted her panties if she'd been wearing any. His mouth moved over hers with perfect pressure and unmistakable affection. And that was enough.

It was enough to know she meant *something*.

The kiss ended when they needed to catch their breath. "About the wedding…" he trailed off.

"Yes?"

"I'd love to go with you. I've got something to do most of the day tomorrow so I'll meet you there. I'll be the guy with eyes only for you."

Be still her heart. "It's a date."

"Great. Good night." He pressed a soft kiss to her forehead, then turned to go.

"'Night," she whispered back.

Even after he shut the door behind him, she saw him standing there clear as day. Would he ever leave her mind? She doubted it.

Five days ago…

Dear Nicole,

There's something I never told you. Someone I never told you about. When we met and you accused me of being a pompous jerk and pushing you away, you were right. I did that because you reminded me of my college nemesis, a woman named Kennedy Martin. She was a city girl, like you, and we hated each other on the spot. Because of that, I wrongfully mistrusted you. After you called me out on my foolishness, I realized I'd never given Kennedy the benefit of the doubt either, writing her off and pushing her buttons instead. She poked me, so I poked back.

But in hindsight, she was also my equal. She was intriguing. And damn smart. So I apologized to you, and the rest was history. If it hadn't been for Kennedy, I don't think I would have pursued you. She's the reason I fell in love with you. And now guess what? She's here on the ranch. I'd planned to be as scarce as possible this week, but thirty seconds after being with her, we're arguing and disagreeing like it was yesterday. I hate that she's here. I hate the reaction she gets out of me. I hate that she makes me feel things I'm not sure I'm ready to feel. If only she'd arrived two weeks from now, after I'd left to finish our travels. Talk about bad timing.

Miss you,

Maverick

CHAPTER TWENTY-TWO

The day of the wedding

With the rose-pink light of dawn and the ranch in Maverick's rearview mirror, he focused on the road in front of him. The drive to San Francisco took about ninety minutes but always felt like forever. He didn't know if that was because he dreaded this day or because he couldn't wait to talk to Nicole.

He visited the cemetery only once a year…and this year would be his last.

He'd decided that when he'd booked his flight for Europe. Today and his upcoming trip were about letting go and moving on for good. Not that Nicole would ever leave the corner of his heart or mind reserved just for her, but because three years had been long enough to mourn. To hold on to anger and unfairness. He'd loved her with everything he had, and even though she couldn't communicate with him near the end, he saw the love in her eyes reflected back at him.

Nicole's blue eyes had always held some kind of emotion. She didn't wear her heart on her sleeve, but in her expression.

Kennedy's light brown eyes with flecks of gold hold depth beyond compare.

Not for the first time since waking this morning, Kennedy drew his thoughts away from everything else and he wondered what if… What if he told her he wanted more? Wanted to make her his, even long distance? Could he do that? Could he put his fears aside and risk his heart again?

Kennedy breathed new life into his own. She made him optimistic about the future.

She didn't know it, but she'd helped with the onslaught of memories that had plagued him leading up to this morning's drive. He'd been dreading today, and instead of anticipating sadness, he'd been wrapped up in her. Instead of focusing on what he'd lost, she'd easily kept him focused on only her.

Her smart, sexy mouth.

Her curiosity.

Her endless questions and genuine interest.

Her ambition.

Her selflessness.

Her touch and scent and sound.

He blinked her away to save it for the drive back to the ranch.

Easier said than done, so he turned up the volume on the radio. Glanced over at the roses he'd picked to lay on Nicole's gravestone. Looked for the… *Damn it*. He'd forgotten the letters he'd written to Nicole over the past three years. He wasn't sure what he wanted to do with them, but he'd meant to bring them to share with her in some way, as well as to let them go.

Turning around to get them would set him back an hour, at least. And he'd risk being late to the wedding or seeing his family. He'd escaped early for a reason; he didn't want any more sympathy or condolences. He'd had enough to last him a lifetime.

And so he kept driving.

CHAPTER TWENTY-THREE

The day of the wedding

Kennedy woke from a dream about her and Maverick making out in the sand, rolling around with the waves at their feet like a scene from a movie. She smiled sleepily, loving the way her mind worked this morning. She normally dreamed about medical emergencies and saving the day, and this ranked *so* much higher.

Pushing herself to a sitting position, she found Andrew sprawled out facedown on top of his bed with his pants around his knees. She bit her bottom lip to keep from laughing out loud. She hadn't heard him come in last night (amazing sex completely tired a girl out), and apparently he'd had such a good time that he couldn't be bothered to undress all the way.

This had "blackmail photo" written all over it. Not that she'd ever do something like that, but it would be fun to tease him with it when necessary. She looked at the nightstand for her phone so she could take a picture before remembering she'd left it inside her purse.

Even though Andrew slept like the dead, she tiptoed across the room to retrieve her bag off the couch. Pulling the phone out as quietly as possible, she snapped shots of him from every angle before leaping back into bed like nothing had happened and checking her phone for missed calls or texts.

There were three more calls from Hugo and Maria. Two voice messages. *Shit.* A heavy weight landed on her chest. She quickly listened to Maria's frantic voice.

"Kennedy, it's Maria. Hugo is in the hospital," she sobbed. "He fainted while swimming and almost drowned. Please call me back."

Second message: "We don't know if he's going to make it," she wept. "Please come if you can. We need you."

A loud, inarticulate scream tore from the back of Kennedy's throat as she jumped to her feet. *Not Hugo. Please, God, not Hugo.*

Andrew shot up off the bed and almost tripped over himself. "What's wrong?" he called out, catching his balance.

She could barely speak through her tears, but somehow he understood what she told him about Hugo. "I ha...I have to go," she muttered.

"Of course you do," he said, his calm voice helping to settle her down. She forced herself into doctor mode: composed, analytical, helpful. Hysterics did her no good.

"Driving will take too long. I need to fly," she said.

"You pack and I'll find out where the closest airport is and get you a ticket." Andrew's fingers flew across his phone.

"Thank you."

Five minutes later, packed, dressed, and ready to speak without losing it, she called Maria back. The doctors hadn't given Maria a prognosis, but Hugo's brain had been deprived of oxygen for several minutes. Kennedy told Maria to tell Hugo she was on her way and that she expected a magic trick when she got there.

Her hands shook as she put the phone down. She'd lost patients before—it came with the job. But Hugo had seamlessly moved from patient to friend to family, and she'd never lost someone so special before.

The soonest flight was in two hours, which left time for her to find Maverick and say goodbye. The inn and grounds were a hustle and bustle of wedding activity, and because of that, Kennedy stayed silent. She'd momentarily forgotten what day it was, and out of respect for Reed and Elle, their family and friends, and the Owens family, she kept her distance. She didn't need to bring anyone down with the reason for her sudden departure.

After searching for Maverick around the inn and at the barn, she asked Andrew to drive by his cabin on their way to the airport. He didn't answer the front door when she knocked, so she tried the handle. Finding it unlocked, she let herself inside.

"Maverick?" she called out.

No answer. No sound at all.

She said a silent goodbye to a sleeping Barley and her puppies. Tears pricked the back of her eyes as she wandered into the kitchen to leave Maverick a note. There would be no hug or kiss or *keep in touch*. The end had come, and she stood there alone.

On the kitchen counter sat a stack of loose paper. She found a pen, and upon closer look at the papers, discovered they were letters. Not just any letters. Letters to Nicole. Written by hand and signed by Maverick. She would have ignored them, had she not caught a glimpse of her own name.

There was no date, but the letter had obviously been

written sometime this week.

Hated each other on the spot... She's the reason I fell in love with you... I hate that she's here... If only she'd arrived two weeks from now...

Kennedy briefly glanced at the letters underneath. Maverick's sweet, tender words brought tears to her eyes. She wiped them away with the back of her hand as she reread his most recent letter.

The one where he'd wanted her gone.

Heartbreak replaced sympathy. His words killed her. Filled her with grief and doubt and an uninvited stab in the middle of her chest. Had she completely misread him? Was she a game to him? Was spending time with her some sick way of dealing with his loss?

She pressed her fingers against her sternum to stave off the sharp pain and let out a breath. Her legs, already unsteady because of concern for Hugo, shook even more. Leaning against the counter for support, she sobbed.

Then blinking repeatedly, she turned the letter over to write her own.

Dear Maverick,

No worries. You never have to see me again.

Respectfully,

Kennedy

Her heart and head devastated by his thoughtlessness, she didn't have it in her to say anything more.

• • •

Hours later and sick to her stomach with worry, Kennedy raced into the hospital to see Hugo. She knew the space like the back of her hand and rushed to the pediatric ICU, taking the stairs instead of the elevator to avoid the line of people waiting for it and to work off the extra tension thrumming through her veins.

With each step, a sense of comfort edged out her anxiety. The hospital was her safe place—she knew exactly how to be, how to help, how to trust in the competency of the staff. She breathed in the antiseptic scent and felt at ease. She took in the white walls and shiny flooring and light wood accents and tried to de-stress.

The second floor PICU was laid out so the highly trained staff could always have an eye on their patients, and Kennedy took just a second outside Hugo's room to observe him and Maria while she caught her breath and gathered her strength.

Maria turned her head and met Kennedy's eyes through the window. The unmistakable relief that washed across Maria's face made Kennedy glad she'd rushed to get here to be bedside. She'd made it in time to offer support to her dear friend and whisper in Hugo's ear that he better fight with everything he had.

"Kennedy," Maria said, wrapping her arms around Kennedy in a motherly embrace. "Thank you so much for coming."

Kennedy had never hugged anyone tighter. "There's no place else I'd rather be."

They broke apart, and Kennedy excused herself to talk to Hugo's nurse for an update. Brain hypoxia—oxygen deficiency to the brain—could be mild or severe. Brain cells began to die after just five minutes of oxygen loss, and Kennedy prayed emergency medical personnel had gotten to Hugo before then.

According to the nurse, Hugo had displayed only mild symptoms (thank God!) when brought in: problems moving his arms and legs, inattentiveness, and some memory issues. Because of his long QT syndrome, doctors remained concerned about his heart as well, though, and elevated his status to critical. His pacemaker had failed, and chances were high he'd need a replacement. But first they had to make sure he had proper brain function.

Because of Hugo's heart disease, he was on a ventilator and receiving IV fluids that included medications for seizure control and blood pressure. Kennedy squeezed Maria's hand by Hugo's bedside as she explained what she'd learned from the nurse.

"He's going to be okay," she whispered.

He had to be.

Then she gently held Hugo's hand and told him to fight. She told him he had a birthday party coming up and he was the star of the show. She told him no one did magic tricks like he did and so he'd better get well so he could do them. She told him he was the bravest kid she knew and stronger than he realized.

"Why don't you go home for an hour or two?" Kennedy said to Maria. She'd been at the hospital all night, and while Kennedy knew Maria wouldn't go home to sleep, she could grab a hot shower and something to eat. Food and drink weren't allowed in the PICU. "I won't leave his side," she added, sitting in the chair next to the bed. "I promise."

"Okay," Maria said with reluctance. "Thank you. I won't be long."

Kennedy settled more comfortably into her seat, eyes glued to Hugo, prayers for a full recovery playing on repeat in her head. She sent Reed a short text explaining her absence and wishing him a happy wedding and wonderful honeymoon.

Hugo's cardiologist came into the room, and Kennedy greeted him warmly. He was happy to see her again but wished the circumstances were different. He told Kennedy several brain scans and cardiac tests had been ordered and, once Hugo stabilized, they'd most likely replace his pacemaker. Hugo had a tough couple of weeks ahead of him, but if he could get through this, he'd get through anything.

He was young and resilient, and for the next hour she watched him sleep, zero doubt he'd kick butt.

Visiting hours ended at seven p.m., and while she could have probably stayed longer given her previous employment at the hospital, Maria urged her to go home and return in the morning.

Walking out the sliding glass doors of the hospital felt like leaving the Arctic and entering the rain forest. The humidity was a welcome change, and she paused by the large potted plant to peel off her sweater and put her travel bag down so she could text for a ride home.

Phone in hand, she heard a giggle she'd recognize anywhere and looked up. Her sister Victoria stood across the way laughing at something Trevor had said. They were walking arm-in-arm in the direction of the doctors' parking lot, him in his scrubs and Tori in a pretty light blue sundress. Kennedy hadn't missed seeing them together. But she also didn't suffer any ill will. A strange but welcome sense of indifference settled over her instead.

They were happy together.

Long live their happiness.

Because Kennedy had been reminded how fragile life could be. And she knew deep down that Trevor had never made her happy. Their relationship had been built around convenience, a shared profession under the same roof with similar goals and pressures. Victoria made his face light up in a way she never had. She brought something else to his life.

The betrayal Kennedy had suffered might always linger, but it wasn't because of Trevor and a love lost. It was because of the difficult relationship with her sister.

As they disappeared from view, she wiped a single tear off her cheek. It had been a heck of a day. A day, she suddenly realized, without a word from Maverick. Had he seen her note? She rolled her lips together to keep more tears from falling. Did she even want to hear from him?

"Hey, Blondie! Need a ride?" a familiar voice called out.

She turned to the street to find her best friend waving from the driver's seat of his car through the open passenger-side window. Warmth and love engulfed her. *Relief.* She picked up her bag, jogged over, and hopped in. "What are you doing here?" She thought he'd be at the wedding, dancing with Liam and moving smoothly between accents and occupations.

"I hit the road shortly after you left." He pulled away

from the curb. "No way was I going to let you deal with this by yourself. I know how important Hugo is to you."

Another tear slid down her face. This time she knew exactly why: Andrew was more than her best friend. He was her family. The one she got to choose.

"I love you," she said.

"I know." He grinned. "I love you, too. I'm sorry you missed the wedding."

At mention of the wedding, and knowing Hugo was likely to be okay, she couldn't hold her feelings in any longer. "I am, too. I was counting on you to tell me about it."

"I'm sure you'll get details from Reed."

"Not about…" The man who broke her heart. The man she couldn't get out of her head and who, despite what he'd written and what she'd written, she wished she could see one more time. She missed him even though she was unbelievably hurt by him.

"Maverick," Andrew said, finishing her thought aloud.

"I can't stop thinking about him. I've never felt this way before, and the timing sucks. I've got Boston and he's got Europe and feelings to sort out, and I'm afraid I'll never see him again, and saying that out loud hurts. It hurts so badly."

"I'm sorry." Andrew squeezed her hand. "There is something you should know about him, actually."

"No, thank you. He hurt me and the best thing to do right now is focus on Hugo."

A look of indecision crossed Andrew's face before he said, "How is he?"

Kennedy shared everything she knew until they pulled

to a stop in front of her apartment building. "Do you want to come in and crash here?"

"Thanks, but I think I'll head home. I'll check in with you in the morning and go to the hospital with you if you want."

She gave him a kiss on the cheek. "Sounds good."

Her key was barely in the lock of her apartment when Ava flung the door open and hurled herself at her, wrapping Kennedy in a one-sided hug. "I'm so glad you're home!"

"Me too," Kennedy said, grateful for the mega-squeeze. She'd texted Ava a few times to keep her up to date on Hugo and her ETA.

"I made you a sandwich," Ava said, releasing her hold and ushering Kennedy inside. "Sit down and I'll bring it to you."

Kennedy collapsed onto the couch. "You're the best," she said.

Ava delivered the food on a plate and included a glass of apple juice. She sat next to Kennedy, an expectant look on her face.

"Nothing new to report," Kennedy said, lifting the sandwich. "Hopefully he'll show signs of improvement tomorrow and we'll go from there."

"He's tough. He'll be okay."

Kennedy nodded, then took a few bites of her sandwich. She didn't have much of an appetite, but Ava had been nice enough to make her something, and she hadn't eaten anything all day, save for a granola bar at the airport.

"You didn't tell me how you left things with Maverick," Ava said after Kennedy put her plate on the coffee table.

"It…it just ended."

"What do you mean *just ended*? Like he said he doesn't want to talk to you again?"

"We didn't say goodbye. I couldn't find him before I left."

"Can't you text him?"

"I don't have his number." A little silver lining in all of this: she wouldn't be tempted to get in touch with him.

"How hard can it be to find? Just call the inn."

Tempting, but…

Ava narrowed her eyes. "Something happened. What was it?" She crossed her legs in her lap, settling in for a discussion.

Kennedy knew her sister, and if she didn't give her some explanation, she'd bug her relentlessly. She also knew herself, and if she didn't talk through the letter she'd found, she'd be up all night thinking about it.

"When I went to say goodbye to him this morning, he wasn't home, so I let myself in to his house to leave him a note."

"Okay."

"I found some letters he'd written to Nicole on his kitchen counter, and in one of them he mentioned me."

At Ava's frown, she added, "I think he wrote the letters to stay close to her and to cope with his feelings. Which is admirable, and I'm ashamed I peeked at them. I shouldn't have. But maybe they were left out for a reason. So I could feel his love for someone else and be reminded that Maverick isn't the first man to—"

"Stop right there. Maverick is nothing like our soon-to-be brother-in-law the asshole."

"I know," she agreed. Deep down she knew that, but on

the surface, it helped to think otherwise.

"You said one of the letters was about you. What did it say?"

Kennedy had memorized most of it, so she recited what she remembered. When finished, she let out a deep breath. "Was I a joke to him?"

"What are you talking about? For someone so smart, you are really dense sometimes."

"Excuse me?"

"He called you intriguing and smart and his equal, Ned. He said you're the reason he fell in love with Nicole."

"So?" She crossed her arms over her chest.

"So! He was in love with you." She didn't need to say, "Duh." It came through like a bullhorn.

"Don't be ridiculous. We hated each other."

"There's a fine line between love and hate."

"Now you sound like Andrew."

"It's true! He basically admitted he had feelings for you he never acted on, so when he met Nicole, he realized he'd been pigheaded and didn't want to miss another chance at being with someone amazing."

"But he hated that I was on the ranch. He wished I'd arrived after he'd left."

"Because his feelings came back! Probably worse because you're even more incredible now. You freaked him out and he didn't know what to do, so yeah, he might have wanted you gone, but that was before you guys spent time together! From what you've said, he sounds like a man with integrity, and there's no way he'd toy with your emotions if he didn't genuinely like you."

Kennedy let that sink in. She allowed her mind to go to

how wonderful it had felt to be with him—on outdoor adventures, birthing puppies, in a bookstore, eating sushi at his kitchen counter, slow dancing, and wrapped in each other's arms.

He'd shown her he cared. Whispered it, too.

"He said he planned to be scarce, and then you showed up and he was around all the time, right? That's because he *wanted* to see you. He might not have been willing to admit it out loud, but his actions speak for themselves."

Could Ava be right? Had Kennedy misinterpreted certain parts of the letter he'd written because *she* was scared? Because leaving on bad terms was much easier than leaving on good terms and wondering what if things were different?

"You need to get his number and call him."

"I don't know."

"I do. I may be younger, but I know what I'm talking about."

"It's too late, and right now I need to stay focused on my career."

"You can have a boyfriend and a career."

"Whatever, Miss Expert. Let's talk about you and your potential boyfriend instead." Ava's coffee date had been, to quote, "like the best scene out of a rom-com."

And just like that, her sister switched topics. She spoke nonstop for a solid five minutes and Kennedy soaked it up, loving the enthusiasm in Ava's voice and the happiness written all over her face.

The minutes reminded her of standing in the Owens's kitchen with Mary Rose and Nova. She reached into her pocket and rubbed her fingers over the glass ladybug she'd kept on her since receiving it.

"Can I ask you something?" Kennedy said when Ava took a breath. "Did you ever talk to Mom about personal stuff like sex?"

"*Eww*. No," Ava said, nose wrinkled in disgust. "Did you?"

Kennedy shook her head.

"She isn't that kind of mom," Ava said. No, she wasn't. Not like Maverick's mom, who talked openly with her daughter. She put people at ease and had such a warm and welcoming manner about her that Kennedy had easily shared parts of herself she didn't normally divulge with someone she'd just met.

"You never asked me about it."

"That's because you were in med school and I didn't want to bother you. I did think about asking, though."

"I'm sorry."

"Don't be. We talk about everything now."

"Did you talk to anyone?"

Ava smiled. "I talked to Andrew. He told me everything. Bought me condoms. And said I should never feel pressured to go further than I was comfortable with."

"He never told me that," Kennedy said, once again beyond grateful for her best friend.

"Because I asked him not to. I didn't want you to worry about me. And don't say you wouldn't have, because that's a lie."

"I knew he looked out for you, but not quite that much." Making it much easier for Kennedy to focus on her studies.

"He's the best big brother a girl could ask for."

"We owe him dinner."

"We owe him, like, fifty."

"He drove home today. Picked me up at the hospital."

Ava gave a closemouthed smile. "I know. He texted me. He's got a thing for us Martin girls."

"That he does." She laid her head back, her eyelids suddenly too heavy to keep open. She did have an amazing man in her life, and maybe one was enough.

CHAPTER TWENTY-FOUR

The day of the wedding

Maverick arrived back on the ranch a little later than planned. Already dressed in slacks and a button-down shirt, he parked his truck at the inn and hurried to the gazebo to catch the tail end of the wedding ceremony.

He stood at the rear and watched the bride and groom inside the elevated wedding gazebo ensconced in lush greenery and decorated with colorful floral arrangements and ivy. A white runner divided rows of folding chairs, and at the end of every aisle stood slender planters overflowing with more flowers.

Maverick searched the backs of everyone's heads for Kennedy. Today had been difficult, and he couldn't wait to see her. She soothed his nerves and got his blood pumping at the same time. They had one more night together. He didn't want to waste a second.

Someone in the wedding party chuckled, drawing his attention back to the main attraction. The bride looked stunning in a white off-the-shoulder gown with a train that trailed down the gazebo's three steps. The groom and groomsmen wore dark suits with white shirts and blue ties that matched the tropical ocean blue of the bridesmaids' dresses. The man of honor's blue shirt and white tie set him apart from the others.

The setting sun cast the special Owens Ranch glow over

the ceremony. They'd done enough weddings over the years to know the exact time to schedule vows for optimum photo opportunities. Speaking of which, the photographer took Reed's picture as he apologized for messing up his vows — earning more chuckles — before resuming his speech.

"I vow to trust and value you today and always," Reed said. "You're everything to me, Elle, and I cherish you with my whole heart…"

Maverick listened with half an ear, the love between Reed and Elle evident in the devotion on their faces and the way they leaned toward each other. He didn't know the details of what had transpired between Kennedy and Reed, but Maverick's gut told him her being here had influenced the couple in the best possible way. She'd made a difference in their lives. He smiled, thinking back to her crashing into his chest and her heels sinking into the grass and the look of determination on her face when he'd guessed she didn't have a wedding invitation.

Unable to find Kennedy among the guests now, Maverick closed his eyes for a quick nap on his feet and recounted the day: his last visit with Nicole. He'd never talked so much in his life and had a feeling Kennedy was the reason for that. She'd gotten him to open up more this past week than he had in a long time, and the floodgates had remained open while he sat beside Nicole's gravestone.

He shared the letters, what he could remember of them. He told Nicole he was sorry for pushing her away when they first met because she reminded him of Kennedy. He confessed to caring for Kennedy much more than he realized and never acting on those feelings. Not wanting to make the same mistake again, he'd changed his mind and let her in.

In hindsight, he should have gone all-in with Kennedy sooner. His heart had called to hers, but he'd been too stubborn—and proud—to admit it back then. That fate had brought them back together now was a gift he wouldn't take for granted. He'd been incredibly lucky to spend four years with Nicole, and he wasn't about to blow this second chance at a possible future with Kennedy.

"I now pronounce you man and wife. You may kiss the bride."

Maverick opened his eyes to witness the happy couple's kiss and walk down the aisle to the traditional wedding music. He'd enjoyed being part of the ceremony more than he thought he would, a peaceful mood replacing any lingering doubts about attending with Kennedy. He'd expected a stab or two of regret over his past with Nicole and wishing he'd had the chance to call her his wife back then, but instead he felt only anticipation. He couldn't wait to lay eyes on Kennedy.

Guests stood and cheered, and he once again searched for her without any luck. The bridal party followed behind Reed and Elle, then the rows of attendees filed out.

He waited off to the side to snag Kennedy's arms, to pull her against his chest and tell her he'd missed her.

But she never appeared.

Neither did Andrew.

Maybe they'd changed their mind about the ceremony. Maybe she was waiting for him back at his house so they could go to the reception together.

He hurried to his truck and drove home. Was her long

blond hair up or down? Was she wearing those ridiculously high-heeled shoes she loved so much? A new dress that hugged every beautiful inch of her?

"Hello," he called out, entering the house. A quick peek at Barley and the puppies told him they'd been well taken care of by Cole and Jenna and didn't need anything from him. He headed to the kitchen next to check for Kennedy there. She had a nose for doughnuts, and he'd bought some to have tomorrow morning. She looked at her glazed doughnuts like they were a work of art, and she had a similar look in her eyes when she glanced at him after they kissed. So, a win-win, in his mind.

"Hey," Hunter said, when Maverick rounded the corner into the kitchen.

Not the person Maverick wanted to see. "Hey. What are you doing here?" His brother sat at the kitchen island eating one of the glazed doughnuts, damn him.

"Did a quick check on Barley and the pups."

"And then decided to eat my breakfast?"

Hunter stopped mid-bite. "You want it back?"

Maverick gave him a look. Hunt smiled and continued eating the pastry. Dressed in his Sunday best, his brother's presence clearly had more to do with checking on him than the dogs.

"How was your day?" Hunter asked.

There it was.

"The first half was good." When he'd been alone to sit at the cemetery to talk to Nicole.

"And the second half?" Hunt washed his hands at the sink, then ran a hand through his hair at the same time Mav ran fingers through his own. Sometimes, looking at his younger brother really was like looking in a mirror.

"Nicole's mom and dad arrived, and that was hard." To see them. To talk to them. Nicole was their only child, and when Maverick had chosen to return to the ranch rather than stay in the city, they'd been hurt. They'd loved him like a son, but he couldn't take the place of who they'd lost. It was too much pressure, no matter how much he cared for them in return.

"Sorry," Hunt quietly said.

"I am, too. They're still grieving. With the love I feel for Jenna, I can't imagine losing a child. How *do* parents go on after that?"

"You just do. Sad things happen every day. To good people. It eventually gets easier, right?" Hunter looked meaningfully at him. *You've been dealing with this, too.*

For the first time since Nicole's death, Maverick felt confident saying, "Yeah, it does."

In the back of his mind, he'd always known today would be a major turning point, his upcoming trip the last promise. Suddenly his gaze caught on the letters he'd written to Nicole, stacked neatly on the corner of the counter. He reached over to pick up the top one, unfamiliar writing scrawled on a blank page.

Dear Maverick,

No worries. You never have to see me again.

Respectfully,

Kennedy

He turned the paper over to see the last letter he'd written to Nicole, on the night of Kennedy's arrival. Flipped it back to see the note from Kennedy. His throat tightened. She'd read the letter. She'd been here sometime today.

"Dude, you look like you're gonna hurl," Hunter said.

"Did you see this?" He waved the piece of paper in the air, a heated mix of anger and despair crawling up the back of his neck. He was upset she'd seen the letters, but it bothered him even more that she'd basically said goodbye in a terse note.

"No. I know not to go through your stuff."

Hunter didn't know about the letters—no one did. But he slid the paper over to his brother now.

"Why would she write this?" Hunt asked after scanning it.

"Read the other side."

Maverick fisted his hands while his brother read the letter. Why was she so upset about what he'd written? He'd admitted she'd played a part in his life even after college. Flattery like that usually pleased a person. The stuff about him not wanting her here? That had been at first sight. At the first uncomfortable stirring inside his chest. At her being on the ranch uninvited and crashing a wedding.

"You've been writing to Nicole?" Hunter smoothed out the piece of paper atop the counter. Maverick nodded. "It's helped you?" Mav nodded again. "That's good." He looked over Maverick's shoulder, out the kitchen window. "As far as Kennedy's note goes…"

Maverick turned, hoping he'd find her walking down the road toward him, eager to explain herself. A note wasn't exactly her style. Not when she had such a powerful voice.

There was no one there.

"I think she was having a bad day," Hunter said, drawing Maverick's attention back to him.

"That doesn't explain her rude goodbye. 'No worries'? Like we meant nothing to each other?" The more he thought about it, the more this felt like she was on her high horse again, having the last word and treating him like this past week hadn't mattered. "After today, we weren't sure we were going to see each other again anyway."

"It's human nature to focus on the negative rather than the positive. You ended the note wanting her gone, and that's what she took away."

"At the time, it was the truth." He wasn't going to feel bad for what he'd written. If anyone had asked Kennedy if she wanted Maverick gone that day, she would have shouted "yes," too.

"Women don't always like the exact truth."

"Says the expert on women."

"Dude, I've been with more women than you, so yes, I believe that qualifies me as the more skillful between us."

"Quality over quantity, little brother."

Hunter smirked. "You're looking at a man who's experienced both."

There was no winning this discussion. "Whatever. She's leaving tomorrow and I'm fine with it."

"You don't want to know why she was having a bad day?"

"Don't care." Not only had she left him a crappy note, she'd snooped in his kitchen first. *You know she didn't do it with malicious intent.*

"Would you care if I told you she already left the ranch?"

He crossed his arms. "What are you talking about?" Okay, so he could pretend he didn't care, but that would be a lie. "She's not here?"

"No."

His stomach clenched. "Is she okay?" *Please let her be okay.*

"I don't know. All I know is she flew home because a friend of hers was in the hospital. Andrew drove her to the airport, then came back to check out and drive to L.A. He told Cole and Bethany what had happened. Kennedy didn't say goodbye to anyone."

Maverick squeezed the back of his neck. She had left in a hurry without a goodbye to anyone…but him. She'd come looking for him. His mind spun with what she'd wanted to tell him when she walked through his front door before finding him gone.

He hadn't said goodbye because he thought they had tonight.

"I should call her," he said. Bethany had given him her phone number the other morning.

"You think? She was having a crappy day and then read your letter, so that probably explains her snappy attitude toward you."

He pulled his cell out of his pocket. Phone to his ear, his shoulders sagged when she didn't answer. "Voicemail," he said to Hunter.

Hunt made a circling motion with his hand, indicating *leave a message.*

The moment he heard the beep, he hung up.

"What was that?" his brother asked.

"I need to think about what to say." He leaned his elbows on the countertop. "If anything." Wanderlust and his promise to Nicole had him catching a plane to another country. *Countries.* For a significant length of time. Maybe it was best to let it be?

"Bro, that's cold."

"Thanks," he said, unsmiling.

"Okay, how about I coach you? Dial her again." He straightened his back and shoulders.

"I don't need you to do that."

"Apparently you do."

"I'm thinking it's best if we just leave it as is."

"With her thinking you're a dick?"

"Whose side are you on?" Was it a dick move to not call her? If she was worried about a friend's health, he didn't want to add any stress or impose on her to have a conversation with him. He could wait a few days, let their annoyance with each other die down.

"I'm on love's side," Hunt said matter-of-factly.

"Come again?"

"You two are wild about each other. I mean, have you seen your face when you look at her?" Hunter made what Maverick assumed was an exaggerated lovesick face, his eyes crossing and his mouth twisting.

"You don't know what you're talking about."

"Look me straight in the eye and tell me you haven't fallen for her."

"It doesn't matter if I have or not. We've been over this. She's going to Boston; I'm going on my trip and coming back here."

"Here's my take on the situation." Hunter looked him right in the eyes. "If you're lucky enough to meet someone extraordinary not once, but twice, then it's worth figuring out a way to make it work. You were planning to leave the ranch for Nicole. You can leave it for Kennedy. Do your pesticide thing in Boston."

"You know about that?"

"When I said I know not to go through your stuff, I meant some of the time." A grin that had gotten him out of more trouble than was reasonable spread across his little brother's face.

Maverick shook his head. Not angry, but relieved. He hadn't intentionally kept his family out of the loop with his business plan; it had just seemed easier.

Safer.

Ever since Nicole had passed away, he'd played it safe.

He took a seat on the barstool next to Hunter's to collect himself. He'd stopped playing it safe with Kennedy less than a day after seeing her again…and he'd never felt better.

"Look," Hunter said, "we don't need to get into your Lone Ranger attitude right now, but we should figure out the Kennedy sitch." At Maverick's frown, Hunter said, "Situation. Jeez, you're only two years older than me, dude. Get with it."

"Okay, *dude*." Maverick moved his gaze to his hands atop the counter. "Here's the thing. I don't *want* to leave the ranch. On the drive back today, I decided this is where I need to be, with my family. If things work out with the pesticide, we'll do it from here. And if they don't, we've got enough to keep us hard at work."

"We can't get rid of you?"

"No."

"That complicates things."

"Exactly." He reached for his phone. He wasn't a chicken, but more than that, he couldn't leave Kennedy to wonder about how he felt. "Hey, Kennedy, it's Maverick," he started after he got her voicemail again. "I'm sorry you had to leave the ranch like you did, and I hope your friend is okay. If you want to keep in touch, give me a call back. Or a text. Whatever you want. And good luck with your interview, not that you need it. I'm sure the job is yours already. Take care."

He hung up, placed his cell facedown on the counter.

"Not bad," Hunter said.

"I'm good with it." Mostly. He should have said, *Please* keep in touch. He should have said, *I wish I had a chance to say goodbye in person.* He wished they'd had one more kiss.

"And if she doesn't get back to you?"

Then his heart would privately break. "Then she doesn't. Nothing I can do about it."

"Man, I wish I had your composure when it came to love."

Maverick wished his brother would stop using the L-word. Because every time he said it, Maverick's pulse sped up. "Did something happen?" he asked, more than ready to switch the conversation to his brother.

"Just me running into Callie in town this morning and making moon eyes at her and her asking me if there was something wrong with me."

Damn. He hated the creases of anguish etched on

Hunter's forehead.

"So then I went and made an ass of myself with one of the bridesmaids before the wedding." Hunt slapped his hand on the counter. "That's it. I'm officially off women until further notice. Do not pass 'hello.' Do not look at them for longer than absolutely necessary. "

"With me leaving town in a week, you'll be plenty busy here."

"True. You have a return date yet?"

"No, but anytime you start to slip, call or text me and I'll straighten you out."

Hunter slid off his stool, and they gave each other a one-armed embrace. "Thanks. Mind if I crash on your couch? I think it's best I hide here and skip the reception."

"Go for it."

Maverick's phone pinged with a text. He quickly lifted it up, hoping to see Kennedy's name. Instead, disappointment swamped him at seeing a message from Cole. *Checking in to make sure you're okay.*

He debated what to text back. He wasn't okay, but normally he'd keep that to himself. Text an, *I'm okay* and forget about it. Things were different now, though.

He was different.

Thanks. I'm not, really. Come by for a beer later?

CHAPTER TWENTY-FIVE

One day after the wedding

"Have you seen my phone?" Kennedy asked, padding into the living room Sunday morning and dropping down on the couch next to her sister. "I can't find it."

Ava looked up from her magazine. "Where was the last place you remember having it?"

"Outside the hospital before Andrew picked me up. I slid it into the outside pocket of my bag."

"Maybe it fell out in Andrew's car?"

"Will you text him and ask?"

While Ava did that, Kennedy walked into the kitchen to make coffee. Sitting on the counter was a box of doughnuts from the grocery store, and her thoughts immediately slid to Windsong. To Baked on Main. To Maverick.

She didn't think it possible to miss someone after only a day, but she missed him. And she didn't like it. She wanted to be mad at him. She *was* mad at him, despite Ava's thoughtful and logical interpretation of his note. She hadn't known she could miss someone and be hurt by them at the same time.

"Andrew says your phone isn't in his car," Ava called out.

"Maybe it fell onto the ground," she said, walking back to the couch and pushing Maverick to the back of her mind. "Can I use yours?"

She called the hospital and sure enough, they had her

phone. Only it had been destroyed when a car pulling up to the hospital ran over it. She asked to be connected to Hugo's room next, and was glad to hear from Maria that things were status quo. She handed the cell back to her sister and covered her face with her hands. "At some point today, I need to get a new phone."

An hour later, Andrew showed up with breakfast burritos — he argued she needed something more substantial than a glazed doughnut if she planned to be at the hospital all day — and regaled Ava with stories from Windsong.

"On a scale of one to ten," Ava said, "how hot was Maverick?"

"With or without his cowboy hat?" Andrew asked.

Kennedy made to leave the room. She didn't want to hear anything about Maverick. He'd had all day yesterday to get in touch with her before she lost her phone, and the fact that he didn't told her everything she needed to know. They were done. He'd taken her albeit unpleasant note and respectfully decided to let her go without any further exchange.

Andrew stayed her with his hand on her arm.

"Oh my God. He wore a cowboy hat?" Ava fanned herself.

"I need to get dressed and head to the hospital," Kennedy said, reading the clock on the wall. Visiting hours started in thirty minutes.

"I know you do," Andrew started, "but there's something I didn't tell you yesterday."

Kennedy stiffened, unsure if anything else about yesterday mattered. Her usual curiosity, though, got the best of her. "What?"

"Before I left the ranch, I had a quick heart-to-heart with Bethany. She asked about our sudden leaving and I told her about Hugo. She was really upset on your behalf, and said she spoke for the whole family when she said she wished you the best and hoped Hugo would be okay. Then she told me about Maverick."

"What do you mean?"

"Yesterday was the anniversary of his girlfriend's death."

Kennedy's fist flew to her mouth as a rush of compassion overwhelmed her. "I didn't know."

"I didn't think so. It was also her birthday."

"No," she whispered, pressing her closed hand against her lips. As if Nicole's death wasn't tragic enough, she left the world the same day she entered it. "So, yesterday was…"

"A tough day for him. Bethany said every year he drives to San Francisco to spend the day at the cemetery and to see Nicole's parents. He refuses company and makes it a solitary thing."

"I would have—" She stopped herself. If she'd known, she would have gone with him instead of attending the wedding in a heartbeat. She would have wormed her way into his plan because she knew he could have used the support. And that's what a person did for someone they loved, whether they liked it or not.

She froze.

She loved him.

Ava gently took Kennedy's fist and lowered her arm. "Breathe," she instructed.

Kennedy took a deep breath. She loved him. With her

heart. With her soul. And she was overcome with sympathy for him. "He'd already left when I got to his house?"

"I think so." Andrew wrapped up the remaining half of his burrito.

"Do you think he even read my note?" She hoped not. Maybe a window had been left open and a gust of wind came through his kitchen and blew the piece of paper into a black hole. She hated the brief, unkind words she'd left him with, made much worse with this new knowledge.

"I don't know."

"I should call him." She looked around the room for her phone before remembering it was roadkill.

"Use mine," Andrew and Ava said at the same time, phones thrust at her.

She pulled a face, remembering she didn't have his number. "I need to call the inn." Her eyes darted back to the clock. "But I can't right now. I can't think about anything other than Hugo." She stood, threw away what was left of her breakfast. "I'll get a new phone later and reach out then." At the moment, she could only deal with one important person at a time.

In the privacy of her room, she leaned against the closed door and slid down to the floor. It felt like the walls were closing in on her. Hugo. Her interview in Boston. Maverick.

The day went by in a blur. She'd dressed, driven to the hospital, and remained by Hugo's bedside with Maria. When Hugo finally woke fully with his memory intact and much better mobility in his arms and legs, she and Maria literally jumped for joy. She'd never been so relieved.

Hugo moved out of the PICU and to a regular room. At

the request of Maria, Kennedy spoke with his doctors. Given the seriousness of his accident and his underlying health condition, they decided to keep him in the hospital until his surgery.

Left cardiac sympathetic denervation surgery. A big deal, but necessary given the failure of his defibrillator. She explained the procedure to Maria, assured her it was the best option, and promised to stop in tomorrow before her flight to Boston.

By the time she left the hospital, it was too late to head to the Apple Store for a new phone. She added it to her list for tomorrow, wishing she could wrinkle her nose and stop time for a couple of hours so she could catch up.

Ava and Andrew were waiting for her with pizza when she walked into the apartment, and she almost cried at the consideration. They watched a movie while they ate, but mostly Kennedy sat dazed and unfocused for a good chunk of time. Before the romantic comedy ended, she excused herself and fell into bed, bone-tired from the mental workout of the past two days. As was becoming habit, a slow-motion montage of Maverick played behind her eyelids as she drifted off to sleep.

The next morning she packed an overnight bag for her trip to Boston. She settled on a black knee-length skirt, light green blouse, and black pumps for her interview, linen pants and a comfy tee for the plane.

She had breakfast on the table when Ava wandered into the kitchen ready to go to class. "Morning, sunshine."

"Ugh. I'll be so glad when school is over. Thank you for this." Ava downed a plate of scrambled eggs, then buttered a piece of toast to take with her. "Have a good flight and kick butt tomorrow." She kissed Kennedy's cheek. "Call me tonight."

"I will. Love you."

"Love you, too."

At the knock on the door five minutes later, Kennedy glanced around, thinking Ava forgot her keys or a textbook or something. She opened the door wide. "What did you—?"

The rest of her sentence died on her tongue as she swallowed past the lump in her throat.

"Maverick?" She almost leaped into his arms.

Almost.

He looked equally happy to see her, his eyes a lively blue and his lips sliding into a slow, untroubled smile.

"Hi, Shortcake." His deep, friendly voice erased every ill thought she'd had about him over the past two days.

"What are you doing here? Is everything okay? Who's working the ranch? Don't you have a lot to do this week before you go?"

His dimples made a subtle appearance. "First things first, everyone's fine."

"That didn't sound very convincing."

"Probably because I left Hunter a note that I was driving here and would be back tonight and he's no doubt cursing my name and the day I was born and planning some form of revenge." He nodded inside her apartment. "Can I come in?"

"Yes, of course." She stepped aside to give him entry. His smell engulfed her, making her legs weak. God, he smelled good.

He stood in the middle of the room in jeans, a black

T-shirt, and boots and glanced around her apartment.

"I was just finishing breakfast. Can I make you some eggs and toast?"

"No thanks, I'm good," he said, finally meeting her gaze.

She couldn't stop staring at him, was lightheaded from the way he filled the space—her space—and from those earnest blue eyes of his.

"Kennedy?"

"Uh-huh?"

"Are you okay?"

"Yeah, sorry." She blinked away his mojo. "Just surprised to see you."

He made a motion for them to sit. With his broad shoulders, he took up a good portion of the couch, but she managed to situate herself on the opposite end and leave some much-needed space between them. She deserved a medal for the Herculean effort it took to resist touching him. *Does he have a magnet in his pocket with my name on it or what?*

"I didn't like how we left things, so I drove down this morning hoping to catch you. I tried calling but—"

"My phone broke," she interrupted.

"So you're not ignoring me?"

She shook her head. She feared he'd always hold a place in her head and heart. "Not on purpose." And wow. He must have left at two a.m. to be here now. "Don't move." She jumped to her feet and poured him a cup of coffee. "It's not Claudia's, but it's all I have," she said, handing him the kick of caffeine that tasted maybe half as good as the brew from Baked on Main.

His fingers brushed hers on the handoff. The usual

tingles danced up her arm.

"Did you leave me a message on my phone?" she asked, voice steady, thank goodness.

"A couple."

"I didn't think I'd hear from you again. What did they say?" Two days ago when she'd stood in his kitchen, their relationship lay in ruins at her feet, but now she hoped he was here to bring it back to life.

"I always planned on a proper goodbye, despite what I think you took away from my letter." He narrowed his eyes, not in an angry way but in a pleasantly annoyed way, and she understood—she *had* read it without asking. "What I wrote that day wasn't meant for anyone to see."

"I'm sorry. I shouldn't have looked at any of them." She ducked her head, ashamed of herself for invading his privacy.

He lifted her chin with his finger. "You're right—you shouldn't have. But I'm sorry, too, if I hurt your feelings."

They traded small smiles.

"So you came here to set the record straight?" Because nothing else had changed. She was still headed to Boston and he was still set to travel and return to Windsong.

"I came because I needed to see you in person. First, to wish you luck on your interview and safe travels. But more importantly, Bethany mentioned you yesterday afternoon, and when she said Hugo's name, I remembered how special he was to you and I wanted to make sure…" He quickly inhaled, then let out a sigh. "I wanted to be here for you."

She sucked in her lips to keep her emotions in check. And to stop herself from saying something foolish like, *I love you, Maverick Owens.*

"Is Hugo okay?" he asked when she didn't say anything.

"Yes. Or he will be. He needs surgery again, but I'm confident he'll come out of it better than ever. He's a tough kid."

"Like you were." If he didn't stop with the niceties, she feared she'd drag him to her bedroom. And keep him there for as long as he'd stay.

"Yeah."

"I'm glad to hear that." His gaze flitted around the room before settling on her carry-on bag. "Looks like you're packed and ready to go."

She jumped to her feet, having momentarily forgotten she needed to get a move on. "What time is it? I'm sorry to cut your visit short, but I need to get going. I told Hugo's mom I'd swing by the hospital, and then I need to go buy a new phone before I head to the airport for my flight this afternoon."

He stood, took her hand. "Would it help if I got the new phone for you and dropped it off at the hospital?"

His hand was warm, comforting. She focused on their joined fingers, the skin-to-skin contact setting her blood on fire. "That's really nice of you, but I can do it." The longer they prolonged their goodbye, the more it would hurt.

"I know you can, but—"

"No buts." She locked eyes with him. "Thank you for coming all this way. It means a lot. And I'm glad we cleared the air and can go our separate ways without regrets."

"If things were—"

"Different. I know." She had no doubt the romantic side of her would imagine the two of them together for a long time to come. She'd close her eyes at night and picture him leaving her poems from Rumi, stealing her breath with kisses, laughing with her, making love to her.

"It was a hell of a week, Shortcake."

"It was."

"If you ever find yourself in need of some R and R, you know where to find me," he said half facetiously, half wholeheartedly.

"I know where to find *the ranch*," she teased.

"Close enough."

"Safe travels to you, too." She tried to slip her hand free, but he held tight. "And good luck with the pesticide. I'm holding you to that postcard you promised."

"When you get your phone, text me your address."

"You're here, so don't you have it?"

"I don't have an address in Boston." He tugged her closer, wrapped his arms around her waist.

Time disappeared as they took each other in and she cupped her hands around his neck. This was it. Their last kiss.

Her body trembled and her eyelids fluttered as he canted his head and pressed his lips to hers. She absently wondered if this would have been the same kiss they gave each other if they'd said goodbye on the ranch. As his tongue slipped inside her mouth, she decided, no.

Because this kiss wasn't a given. He'd driven hours to make it happen. They'd apologized and shared a soft look, silently admitting they cared deeply for each other. Kennedy cared so much, she feared she'd never feel the same way again.

Feeling bold and unwilling to let this last opportunity

go by, she took his hands and moved them to her butt, fit her body closer to his. He groaned into her mouth, deepened the kiss. She felt exactly what this kiss did to him, and knowing he wanted her as much as she wanted him was both exhilarating and tragic. When he broke the kiss and stared down at her, his face creased in anguish, she desperately wanted to end this on a happier note.

"Did you know the longest kiss on record went on for over fifty-eight hours? A couple in Thailand did it to celebrate Valentine's Day," she blurted out. It was the first thing to come to mind. Kissing someone for that long was cause for happiness. And maybe she was implying she and Maverick could beat that record if given the chance.

"Did you know French kissing for just ten seconds can transfer eighty million germs from one person's mouth to another?" he asked in return.

"Where did you learn that?"

"In vet school. It came up when someone talked about kissing their dog."

"With tongue?" She made a face. She liked dogs, but that was gross. Dogs ate their own poop, didn't they?

"Yep."

"You win," she said with a smile.

And just like that, a sense of normalcy filled the air around them. A *new* normalcy. Because she never would have conceded before.

"Too bad I can't collect the prize I really want."

O-kay. Time to go before she canceled her life and took up a new one that included setting a new kissing record.

She stepped to the door and opened it. "I really do need to get moving."

They didn't take their eyes off each other as he made his exit. "Be safe and happy," he said with affection.

"You too." She closed the door and walked into the kitchen. But then quickly spun around, regret and sadness eating her up inside. She raced out the door to catch him. For one more hug. One more kiss. One more promise.

She found an empty hallway. *Too late.*

But...an envelope with her name on it lay at her feet. She picked it up and went back inside her apartment to read it.

Dear Kennedy,

As I walk away, all I want to do is pull your body over mine and whisper how much you mean to me. It's always been you, and maybe one day we'll meet again to pick up where we've left off. No matter what, though, I'll always want what's best for you. Good luck, Dr. Shortcake.

Love,

Maverick

CHAPTER TWENTY-SIX

Five days since they said goodbye

"Are you sure I can't come with you, Uncle Mav?" Jenna asked with pleading eyes, her hands clasped in front of her in prayer. She'd decided she'd get a much better education traveling with him than returning to school and sitting in a boring classroom.

He knelt down to her level. "You know your mom and dad would miss you too much. Not to mention George, Barley, and Rumi." He'd given his niece Rumi, asking her to take good care of the puppy for him while he was gone. The others were going to families in the area.

She scrunched up her nose. "Fine. Can you bring me lots of presents, then?"

"Jenna!" Bethany reprimanded. "That's not okay."

Jenna gave a small shrug like, *Sorry, Mom, but it's what kids do*. He hoped she didn't change too much while he was gone.

"I'll see what I can do, pipsqueak."

She flung her arms around his neck and gave him a kiss on the cheek. "Thank you."

He straightened and looked at his family. They'd gathered around the entrance of the inn to see him off. The week had been a busy one. After returning from L.A. late Monday night, he'd thrown himself into work around the ranch and spent a good amount of time riding Magnolia.

"I'll check in when I can," he said.

"No return flight yet?" his mom asked. Her question came from a good place, but it troubled him. He couldn't rush this trip with a good conscience. He understood his obligation to the ranch and his family, but he owed it to Nicole to do this right. To see the things she missed out on before putting their life together behind him for good.

"Not yet," he told his mom.

"Well, keep us posted and have a great time." She hugged him tightly. "I love you so much."

"Love you, son," his dad said next, embracing him with the same strong hold.

He hugged Cole and Bethany, then Hunter, who held on longer than necessary and said, "I'm gonna miss you, you jerk."

Nova came last. She squeezed him and whispered, "Don't forget to send Kennedy postcards."

"I won't." He wouldn't forget about Kennedy ever. Their last kiss was forever imprinted on his brain. Her smell and taste. The way she'd looked at him with love in her toffee-colored eyes. Whether he would follow through with the postcards, he didn't know. He'd left her a note and she hadn't replied. No call or text. She'd always been the smarter one, and she'd obviously decided to cut ties completely. Save them further pain.

A good thing, considering he'd fallen in love with her.

He'd realized it on the drive to see her. The second he'd laid eyes on her, he'd almost said it. Upon leaving, he'd almost said it again. Fear had stopped him both times.

A mix of regret and longing seized his stomach now. Maybe he should have texted her to check in. Ask about

Hugo and her interview.

Leah's SUV pulled up beside him. She had a flower show in the city and had offered to drive him to the airport. He put his suitcase and backpack inside the vehicle, hugged his mom one more time, and they drove away. If he'd been in the driver's seat, he would have looked in the rearview mirror to see his family for as long as possible.

"You good over there?" Leah asked.

"Yeah, how are you?"

"Grateful for the chance to escape to the city."

"Sounds like there's a story there." He'd be happy if she talked the entire drive so he didn't have to.

"Jackson's been in the flower shop every day this past week hoping to, I don't know what, but I keep telling him to leave me alone. We broke up for a reason and nothing is going to change that."

Jackson and Leah had dated for a few years before rumor had it he cheated on her.

"If only you'd liked me as much as I'd liked you back in high school, we could be married with kids right now," she said, a joking tone to her voice.

He shifted uncomfortably. Leah had never hidden her crush on him, and she often talked openly about what-if, but it was all in friendly understanding now. He thought of Leah like a little sister and had told her as much.

No, what made him uneasy was where his thoughts immediately raced to. Or rather, to *whom*. Kennedy. Did she want to get married one day? Have children? He pictured a miniature Kennedy running around, long blond hair and pale brown eyes, freckles, challenging anyone who so much as looked at her wrong. He chuckled.

"Thanks for laughing," Leah said lightly, bringing him out of his musings.

"Sorry. I was thinking of something else."

"Just what a girl wants to hear when baring her soul."

He gave her a headshake at hearing the humor in her voice. "You were always too good for that asshole."

She slapped the steering wheel with her palm. "Thank you! My grandmother thinks he deserves another chance, and I told her when they build airplanes while flying them at the same time, I'll consider it."

"I like those odds."

"Me too."

They drove in silence for a few minutes before Leah glanced at him out of the corner of her eye. "It looked like there was something going on between you and Dr. Martin."

"There was." He didn't plan to deny anything that concerned Kennedy. Besides, the whole town knew they were more than friendly. Apparently someone even took a picture of them kissing that night in the rain. Thankfully the grainy quality of the photo didn't reveal too much, at least according to Hunter. Maverick hadn't seen the evidence himself.

"Care to elaborate?"

"No."

She shrugged. "For what it's worth, I've never seen you look at anyone the way you looked at her. Not even Nicole."

He turned his head to stare out the passenger-side window. "How did I look at her?"

"Like you'd go to the ends of the earth just to see her smile."

"She has a nice smile." It was more than that, but he didn't need to share his deepest beliefs on the matter.

"Oh my God!"

"What?" He looked at her with raised eyebrows.

"I have never heard you sound so moony over a girl before."

"I did not sound moony." Whatever that even meant.

"You absolutely did. Are you going to see her again? I hear she's headed to Boston."

He sat taller. "She got the job?"

"Um, I have no idea. I know only what I heard before she left. But from your reaction, I'm guessing you have mixed feelings about her living on the other side of the country."

"Not mixed," he stated, hoping he sounded convincing. "It's reality. And she's a damn good doctor who deserves to land the job, so I'll be happy for her wherever she is."

"How polite of you."

"My mom raised me to have good manners."

"She also raised you to go after what you want. Let that sit for a while, Mr. Diplomatic."

Right now, what he wanted was to fulfill his promise to Nicole. To land a partnership with Marco. To live away from his normal life so he could forget about a certain gorgeous doctor.

Life might be about going after what a person wanted, but life was also about knowing when to let go.

CHAPTER TWENTY-SEVEN

Five days since they said goodbye

It wasn't supposed to be this way.

When Kennedy got on the plane to Boston five days ago, she'd left Hugo in good spirits and smiling in his hospital bed. He'd laughed at her corny jokes and told her he had a new magic trick to show her after he was released. He'd sat up with ease and coordination, devoured the chocolate chip muffin she'd snuck in for him, and said he'd felt *fine*.

Kennedy closed her eyes. She needed a minute—or a million—before she exited the car.

She'd arrived in Boston late in the evening. The first thing to pop up on her new phone when she'd switched off airplane mode was a text from Maria saying Hugo had had a good day and was sleeping peacefully. The news heartening, she'd taken a taxi to her hotel and fallen asleep within minutes of her head hitting the pillow.

The next day she woke, made the in-room coffee (which tasted *bleh* compared to California coffee), ordered room service for breakfast, and pumped herself up for her interview. *You've got this*, she'd told herself. Good luck texts from Ava and Andrew bumped up her confidence.

Composed and dressed for success (with the glass ladybug from Mary Rose and heart-shaped rock from Maverick in her pocket), she'd arrived at the sleek, modern hospital early for a look around on her own. Five minutes before her appointment time, she sat down in a small conference room and greeted Dr. Weaver and the other higher-ups with a firm handshake as they entered. The conversation flowed effortlessly. Kennedy felt she aced all their questions and concerns. Moving across the country would be a big change, they said. She assured them the opportunity to work in their distinguished facility outweighed any personal downsides. She was single, eager, loved a challenge, and ironically when she tried to joke around with a New England accent, sorta pulled it off.

She'd tucked that little surprise away to share with Andrew later.

On a tour of the hospital and emergency room, she met lovely staff members. Something about their accent actually made her feel like they were already friends. And the aura of determined chaos in the ER reminded her of long days side-by-side with coworkers she could count on. Her body hummed with excitement, the prospect of working in Boston taking deeper root.

Lunch across the street at a favorite restaurant of Dr. Weaver's proved to be another check in the pro column. The Asian food, heavy on ramen and garlic, had her taste buds doing a happy dance. (She'd smartly packed spearmint gum for post-meal.)

Afterward, the vibe of success clung to her as she headed to the airport for her flight home. Dr. Weaver had said he'd be in touch tomorrow, but the wink he gave her said to expect the offer.

She checked her phone while waiting to board the plane, and once again was happy to read that Hugo had no issues. She texted Ava and Andrew to tell them the interview went great. Then, because she couldn't help herself, she pulled up the photo of her and Maverick she'd sent to Ava when her sister had demanded one.

Ava was smart to request it. Kennedy didn't take many photos and wouldn't have his handsome face to stare at if not for Ava's tenacity. She should have asked him even more questions—gathered intel on *all* his favorite things to add to her memories of their escapades. *You'll always have his letter*.

Yes, she would. And in another life, they'd be together; she knew it down to her soul. She hadn't recognized his unique magnetism in college, but she did now.

An announcement came over the speaker stating she'd be boarding in five minutes. That gave her five more minutes to stare at her cowboy. So engrossed in his dimples, she almost dropped the phone when it rang. She didn't recognize the number, but the city the call came from made her heart speed up. *Windsong*.

"Hello?" she said.

"Hello, Kennedy, it's Dr. Choi. How are you?"

"I'm good, thanks. How are you?"

"Excellent, thank you. Do you have a minute to talk?" Given the time of day, she guessed he was on his lunch break.

"That's about all I have. I'm at the airport in Boston about to board my flight home."

"Perfect timing, then. How did it go?"

"Really well. Not to sound too confident, but I'm expecting the job offer tomorrow." She uncrossed her legs to place both her heels on the industrial carpeted floor.

"Congratulations."

"Thank you."

"I'd like to put a wrench in that offer if I may." His calm, fatherly voice put her at ease and thus his statement—not a question—was one she'd happily allow him to elaborate on.

"Okay."

"I'm retiring, and I'd love for you to consider taking over my practice."

What the what?

"I know this probably comes as a shock, and to be one hundred percent transparent, I did have another physician lined up to take over, but she has since decided to go in a different direction. When she told me, I immediately thought of you for the job."

Her left leg started bouncing up and down. She'd never bitten her nails a day in her life but suddenly brought her finger to her mouth. He wanted her to take over his practice? In the small town of Windsong? Where the best glazed doughnuts lived. And a beautiful inn. And friendly townspeople. And a puppy named Rumi. And a family she'd dreamed of adopted her.

And a handsome cowboy...

"Whether you want to believe it or not," he continued, "you fit in seamlessly here. You took initiative with Nova without second thought. Helped run the office when Savannah was sick. My patients and the townspeople love you. You developed quite a reputation here, and I'd be remiss if I didn't reach out and get your thoughts on the matter. I know firsthand that the ER life holds appeal, but moving into private practice was the best decision I ever made. I want you to have a choice, Kennedy. Picture yourself five years from now and think about what you want. Rest assured, I don't need an answer right now. I'm planning on retiring at the end of the year, but I would need you here sooner rather than later to gradually turn the practice over to you."

She didn't know what to say.

"I take it by your silence that you don't know what to say."

Didn't that comment right there speak volumes? This smart, mild-mannered doctor knew how she was feeling three thousand miles away. The little boy sitting on his mom's lap across the aisle from her picked his nose, and her thoughts jumped right to Jenna and her innocent, wide-eyed question about nose picking.

"I'm...I'm flattered and honored, Dr. Choi," she finally managed to say.

"That's a good start."

"But I never pictured myself in private practice." Or a small town.

"You picturing it now?"

"Um..."

"Too soon?" he asked with a chuckle. "I understand this is a big decision and one you never thought you'd entertain, but I'm hoping you will consider it. Yes, it's a far cry from emergency room medicine, but I promise it gives you the same high. The same sense of accomplishment. Only here, you get to form relationships with those you help."

Like Hugo.

"If attachment isn't your thing, then I completely understand. But I hope you'll think about this job and this practice from all angles, professionally and personally."

The announcement came for boarding the flight.

"Sounds like my time is up," he said, obviously hearing the notification in the background.

"I'm sorry; I do need to go. But I will think about your offer. I promise."

"That's all I ask. Have a safe flight and we'll talk soon."

"Thank you for calling." Her mind spun as she hung up. Emotions all over the map clogged the back of her throat. Could she take over his practice and be happy? She had to admit being her own boss sounded pretty great. But would she experience the same rush of adrenaline? The thrill of a fast pace and thinking on her feet during serious, unexpected, sometimes life-threatening situations? An ER was more than shears through a foot or a car trunk to the head.

She stood and picked up her bag. Overwhelmed by the surprise invitation, she put off thinking about it until tomorrow. As luck would have it, a very chatty woman sat next to her on the plane and talked nonstop, giving Kennedy something else to focus on.

When the next morning came, she heard from Dr. Weaver. He offered her the job in Boston. She should have jumped for joy but, wanting to keep her promise to Dr. Choi, she asked if she could have a few days to think about it.

Suddenly, the future she thought she wanted had some competition.

Between visiting Hugo and entertaining two job offers, she'd had time for little else.

Then Thursday came.

And she wasn't prepared. She'd been lulled into a false

sense of security. She'd looked into Hugo's dark brown eyes the night before and told him he was more awesome than a tower of glazed doughnuts. Smarter than any twelve-year-old had a right to be. And way more talented than any other amateur magician. She'd kissed his forehead, said, *Love you*, and walked out of his room knowing she'd see him after his early morning surgery.

He died on the operating table.

"Kennedy." The soft word broke her free of her recollections. She opened her eyes. "We should probably get to the gravesite," Andrew continued from the passenger seat of her car.

Through the windshield, she saw Maria and her family and friends gathering at the spot Hugo would be laid to rest.

It wasn't supposed to be this way.

Ava put her hand on Kennedy's shoulder from the back seat. "We've got you."

They did. They'd sat on either side of her during the service, helping to keep her up when all she wanted to do was slide to the floor and cry under the pew.

Slowly, she exited the car. She hated the sea of dark clothing and heads bent down in sadness. How dare the sun shine today. How dare the trees sway in a gentle breeze, carrying the scent of flowers and perfume.

Her first time to a cemetery sucked. Not that any visit would feel any better.

Andrew came around the hood and took her by the arm. Ava clutched the other, and together they walked closer to the gathering of mourners. They found a spot to stand under the white tent.

She weathered the next thirty minutes by sheer force of will. When it came time to pick up a shovel and help cover Hugo's casket with dirt, she wanted to jump down, open the much-too-small box, and do chest compressions until he came back. Until his heart picked up where it left off.

He was too young to die. It wasn't fair. He didn't deserve this fate. Neither did Maria.

As everyone dispersed, Kennedy did her best not to cry as she hugged Maria in condolence. Her best didn't come close. The two of them cried in shared pain, nostalgia, and failed wishes.

With each step back to the car, more tears fell, her throat felt raw, and misery stretched down her arms and legs, tight and uncomfortable. Lightheaded, yet heavy in her heart, she held on to Andrew's arm, grateful for the support. It had killed her to walk into the hospital to see Hugo's lifeless body. And it killed her to walk away from him today.

Somehow she managed to pull herself together when everyone gathered again at Maria's house. She even pulled off a magic trick in Hugo's honor. When she, Ava, and Andrew returned to the apartment, the three of them got good and drunk. Not a recommended sleep aid, but she slept through the night.

Sunday morning, rather than do her usual thing of padding into the kitchen to make coffee, she dozed off and on until Ava knocked on her bedroom door.

"It's almost noon," her sister said, clearly having just risen from sleep herself. She crawled under the covers beside Kennedy. "You feeling okay?"

"I'm not hungover, if that's what you mean."

Ava blinked in acknowledgment. Kennedy wasn't okay, but at least she didn't have a tequila headache.

"Want to stay in bed all day and watch movies?" Ava asked.

"Yes please." She didn't want to move or think too hard or face anything outside her bedroom door. That's what Monday was for.

"I'll go see what we've got in the kitchen." Ava slid out of bed. "And check if Andrew is still here." He'd crashed on the couch last night, per his usual if they drank or he was too tired to drive to his place.

Kennedy used the bathroom, washed her hands and face, brushed her teeth. Crawling back into bed, she lifted her phone off the nightstand. For the past week, her initial hope when looking at her cell was to see a text from Maverick. She didn't care what it said, only that it meant he'd been thinking about her. She hadn't texted him, though, not even a short response to his letter, so she couldn't really blame him for being silent, too.

And now he was an ocean away. In another time zone. Wrapped up in his promise to Nicole. She sighed.

There really wasn't a better man than Maverick Owens.

"Look out!" Andrew said, jumping onto the bed.

She put the phone back on the nightstand and braced for impact. "What are you wearing?"

"The question is what am I not wearing?" He waggled his eyebrows. "I forgot I left these here a while ago for morning-afters." The pajamas had Andrew's face all over them, sticking his tongue out. They were silly and fun like her best friend. And she knew what he didn't have on underneath, since he liked to go commando. TMI, she'd told him when he'd announced that years ago.

"They're…"

"Awesome. I know." He snuggled next to her, side by side. "So?" When she didn't answer right away, he said, "You okay today?"

"Not really."

"Good."

"Good?"

"Sadness takes a while to go away. Sometimes a really long while. Remember how long it took me to come out of my funk after Brendan died?"

Brendan had been one of his best friends growing up. "I haven't thought about that in a long time, but yes, I remember." She gave him a quick hug. "It never goes away completely, does it?"

"No."

"I feel like there's a hole in my chest." She put her hand over her sternum.

"It will close eventually."

"'My milkshake brings all the boys to the yard,'" Ava sang as she danced into the room clutching three tall glasses to her chest.

"'And they're like, it's better than yours,'" Andrew sang back.

"Milkshakes?" Kennedy asked, not sure that was the best thing to fill her stomach after one too many shots last night.

"That's not the line!" Ava and Andrew said at the same time.

"'Damn right, it's better than yours,'" she said, toneless.

Her sister and best friend frowned. What? She was not in a singing mood. She did appreciate them trying to lift her spirits, though.

"Ice cream, milk, and chocolate syrup was about all we had," Ava said, handing out the glasses. "And spinach. I dropped a couple leaves in so we can call it healthy."

"I'll order Chinese," Andrew said.

"Bless you." Ava smiled at him before climbing under the covers. Somehow the three of them managed to fit.

They decided on a Julia Roberts marathon. *Pretty Woman*, *Notting Hill*, and *I Love Trouble*. Ava rubbed her back. Andrew recited popular lines he'd memorized from each film. They flopped onto their stomachs, feet in the air. For a little while, Kennedy forgot about the sorrow chewing up her insides as she managed to lose herself in the stories on the screen. Her face even broke into a smile a time or two. But it didn't last long.

And when Andrew said good night and headed home and Ava went to her room to study for her upcoming final, Kennedy cried herself to sleep.

The next morning, she lay in bed to think. She owed both Dr. Weaver and Dr. Choi an answer. When she'd told Dr. Weaver about losing Hugo, he'd been kind enough to extend her decision date on the ER position. He understood that grief took over all rational thought, as well as a person's time, and a move across the country required careful consideration.

Staring at the ceiling, her mind drifted, as it often did, to Maverick. This time, though, to his letters. He'd used them as a coping mechanism. Maybe she could, too. She pushed herself to a sitting position. It didn't feel right writing a letter to Hugo. But…

She slipped out of bed and sat at her desk to pen a letter to the one person in her life who would understand.

Dear Maverick,

Hugo passed away four days ago. I'm devastated and sad and so angry. I'm not sure what I believe in, but when a smart, kind, funny boy dies, I wonder why I ever say a prayer or make a wish. How come good people leave us before we're ready? I know you've asked the same question, and Mav, I didn't know. I didn't know until now how much it hurts. I'm so sorry about Nicole. I'm sorry you lost someone you loved.

As I write this, you're traveling in her honor, and I hope you're finding peace. Happiness. She was lucky to have you love her. When I left to go to Boston, Hugo had looked good. He'd felt good. He was good when I got back, too. And then he wasn't. His heart stopped on the operating table, and they couldn't save him.

You lived with Nicole's illness for two years, knowing she wasn't going to survive it. Hugo was gone unexpectedly in the blink of an eye. I'm not sure which is better. Suffering is horrible, but your loved ones got to say goodbye. Hugo's mom, Maria, didn't get to do that, and I couldn't take away that heartbreak. I wish so much that you were here to hold me, to tell me it gets easier. I miss you. A lot. If it's possible to fall in love with someone in one week, then I fell in love with you, Maverick Owens.

I do hope we meet again.

Love,

Kennedy

She folded the letter and put it in an envelope. Wrote his name on the outside and held it in her hands. She'd mail it to him at the inn. *Maybe.* She had time to think about it. He didn't know it, but he'd been a source of comfort to her over the past few days. A happy memory in the middle of the crappiest week of her life.

He could have fought for you.

He could have said, "Let's see each other when I get back."

People who really cared about each other didn't give up so easily, did they? They figured out a way to keep in touch. To discuss possibilities. Not leave things to hope or fate.

Did she want a long-distance relationship with him? She gazed out her bedroom window, eyes unfocused. It didn't matter what she wanted; she'd fallen for a man currently unavailable, and she'd best remember that.

She had plenty of time for a romantic relationship later. Right now she had a career to launch.

The problem was, which one?

CHAPTER TWENTY-EIGHT

Three months after they said goodbye

Maverick stood outside his house knowing what waited for him inside. His family was about as stealthy as an elephant in a swimming pool. He'd caught movement through the window on the walk up, not to mention noticed the cute face belonging to his niece pressed against the glass.

"He's here!" he heard Jenna call out before disappearing from view.

The smile taking hold of his face felt good. He'd missed his family.

His mom flung open the front door. "Hi, honey! Welcome home!"

He rolled his luggage inside and stepped into her open arms. "Hi, Mom." If hugging were an Olympic sport, his mom deserved a gold medal.

On the release, he found the rest of his family standing side by side ready to greet him. Jenna launched herself at him first, Rumi right on her heels. He lifted Jenna off the floor and squeezed her while the playful pup with huge paws jumped on his legs, reaching close to his waist. "Hey, pipsqueak."

"I'm so gratified you're home," she said.

"Me too." He grinned over her head at his brother and sister-in-law. Gratified? That was a new one.

"On her vocabulary list this week," Cole said, proud as ever.

"Get over here," his dad said next. John Owens had a few more gray hairs on his head but, other than that, looked fitter than ever. Hunter had mentioned their dad and uncle were in some kind of fitness competition, and it appeared to be paying off.

"Looking good, Dad."

"You too, son." They embraced, and then came Cole and Bethany.

Nova had tears in her eyes when she wrapped her arms around him next. "Don't ever leave for that long again," she whispered.

"I won't," he whispered back. "I missed you too much." That got a smile out of her as she wiped the back of her hand across her cheek.

Last came Hunter, who took him in a brotherly bear hug. "Welcome home, bro. I missed your ugly face."

Maverick chuckled. "Missed yours, too."

"You hungry?" his mom asked. "We've got all your favorites ready, and you can tell us the highlights. You must be tired."

They moved into the kitchen where balloons and a handmade sign courtesy of Jenna greeted him. On the counter were several dishes of food—lasagna, roasted chicken, barbecued ribs, bacon-wrapped asparagus, choco-late chip cookies—plus plates, napkins, and utensils.

Hunter handed him a beer.

Jenna gave Rumi a dog bone to chew on. He quickly looked away, not quite ready to love on the dog Kennedy had named because then his thoughts would go straight to her. Three months had gone by and he still couldn't get her out of his head.

Not that he wanted to.

He filled his plate and took a seat at the table. Late-afternoon beams of sunshine spilled inside the room and cast a glow on everyone as they squeezed in around him, Jenna sharing a chair with Nova.

"First things first," his dad said, raising his drink. "A toast to OFO."

Maverick drank to that. Owens Family Organics had been born after Marco agreed to invest in the nonharmful pesticide company. Plans were almost complete for a near-by factory, Uncle Tim taking the lead on manufacturing. Mav may have used his chemistry background to create the product, but after a couple of virtual family meetings online, everyone knew he liked being outside with the trees best.

"What's OFO?" Jenna asked.

Cole gave a brief explanation, but Jenna was too busy sneaking pieces of food to Rumi to pay full attention.

"So you finished everything on Nicole's list." His mom tilted her head to the side in thoughtful consideration. "How do you feel?"

"Good." He meant it. He'd done what he set out to do and in the process released himself from his promise and the uncomfortable feeling of dragging his feet. "Really good. And relieved," he added. "I think I did it justice and that if she's looking down, she's happy."

"No doubt," Bethany said. She and Nicole had formed a fast and easy friendship, so her confirmation meant a lot to Maverick. "Does this mean you ate Creier pane?"

"I did. And just like Nicole said, 'fry anything and it tastes good.'" The Romanian dish consisted of boiled calf brains coated in flour, eggs, and bread crumbs, and then fried to a golden brown.

"Do I want to know what that is?" Cole asked.

"No," he and Bethany both said.

"Favorite place?" his dad asked.

"Patagonia," he said without hesitation. "The Andes Mountains were breathtaking, and the penguins that Nicole had wanted to see were fun to watch." He caught his mom's warmhearted expression. "What?" he asked her.

"This is the first time you've talked so freely about Nicole."

"It finally feels okay." He couldn't pinpoint the exact moment he'd been set free from the sorrow weighing him down, but he was pretty sure it started *before* he'd left for his trip and around the time Kennedy, in all her fun, fascinating, feminine glory, showed up on his ranch.

Kennedy.

He'd written her numerous letters and postcards.

And never mailed them.

Instead, he planned to give them to her in person. The time apart had done nothing to quell the love he felt for her. He'd told himself that, when he touched back down in California, if he couldn't picture life without her, then he'd do whatever it took to make her his, as long as that was still what she wanted. If they had to navigate cross-country trips to see each other, then so be it.

Because he was ready.

He hoped she was, too. He hoped he hadn't blown it with his silence, and he prayed some other ER doctor hadn't made a move on her.

"That's great!" Nova said, looking at him funny.

Talk turned to plans for Thanksgiving next week and hiring seasonal help for the month of December. Besides the bustling Christmas tree business they did, there were three weddings booked.

"Anything exciting happen here while I was gone?" he asked, taking his last bite of food.

Nova practically bounced Jenna off her lap as she said, "That depends."

"On what?" He looked around the table to find everyone's eyes on him like they knew a secret he didn't, which, given his absence, made sense.

"On your feelings about a certain doctor," Nova said.

"What are you talking about?" Had Kennedy visited Windsong?

"Uncle Mav, don't be dense," Jenna said. Then glancing up at her parents with wide, apologetic eyes added, "I'm going to take Rumi outside to go potty. Bye!"

Silence fell over the table.

"Is Kennedy…here?" he asked evenly.

"She's been here for two months," Nova said with an edge of excitement. "She's taking over Doc's practice." His sister could not have smiled any bigger if she tried.

Maverick's jaw dropped before he pressed his lips together, unsure what to say, if he could even speak right now. Shock registered, followed by annoyance. Someone should have told him sooner. Preferably Kennedy herself. But then she wasn't here for him; she was here for a job.

His mom reached across the table to cover his hand with hers. "We thought it best to wait to tell you."

"Did she ask you not to?"

"No." His mom shook her head. "She wouldn't do that, honey."

He looked around the table again. A mix of hopefulness and worry shaped everyone's expressions. Except Nova's. She had a look of pure joy on her face, and so Maverick focused on her.

"What happened to Boston?"

"She turned it down."

"Why? She said that was her dream job."

"I think she should tell you why."

He didn't like the uncomfortable feeling Nova's answer planted in his stomach. "She's good, though, right?"

Nova nodded. "Yes."

"Did you tell her I was coming home today?"

"She knows." Nova glanced at their mom and then Bethany. "But…"

"But…?" Jesus, since when did he have to pull teeth to get info out of his talkative sister?

"She said you haven't been in touch. At all. And…"

He was about to lose his mind. "Please just say it."

"I think she secretly loves you, and is waiting for you, but Nash Radcliffe is interested in her and so if you don't have a plan to whisk her off her feet, then you're in big trouble because Nash has it all going on."

Maverick gritted his teeth. Nash Radcliffe lived in Rustic Creek, the next town over. He'd liked the guy until right this second. "What's Rad doing in Windsong?" The pro football player should be with his team.

"I just told you."

"How did he meet Kennedy?"

"Rumor has it they had a meet-cute at the office."

"'Meet-cute'? What the hell is that?"

"Mav." His mom leveled him with a look that said, *chill out*. "There's nothing going on between them."

"Yet," Nova so kindly added.

He pushed back his chair with a little more force than necessary and stood. As tired as he was, he couldn't wait to see Kennedy. "Where is she?"

"Slow down, cowboy," Nova said. "You can't go see her guns blazing and piss her off. You need a plan."

"I have a plan."

Hunter laughed. "Dude, we're talking about Kennedy. You need a solid approach, not a two-second alpha-ass strategy that she will *not* appreciate."

He sat back down. His family was right. He'd done nothing to let Kennedy know a day hadn't passed that he hadn't thought about her. And given her stubborn, perceptive nature, he definitely needed a foolproof game plan if he wanted to win her heart. "Okay, I'm listening."

"Uncle Mav." Jenna came skipping back into the kitchen without Rumi. "There's someone here to see you."

"Where's Rumi?" Cole asked.

"Kennedy's playing with her." Jenna slapped her hand over her mouth. "I wasn't supposed to say her name."

His heart practically rocketed out of his chest at the same time his family dispersed from the table faster than he'd ever seen them move.

"We'll see you tomorrow!" Mom and Dad said.

"Don't screw this up," Hunter said.

"Good luck!" Bethany grabbed Jenna's hand.

"You got this," Cole said.

He blinked, and everyone but Nova had disappeared. "You still need a plan," she said.

"She's here," he breathed, not making any sudden moves. His sister was right, of course. He needed at least a minute to figure out what to say. How to say it.

"Yes." Nova stared at him. "And I'm pretty sure she's as nervous as you are."

"She doesn't get nervous."

"Not with her job, but you're a different story." Nova stood and pushed in her chair. "I'll tell her you'll be just a minute."

"Tell her ten. I'm making a *plan*."

He listened closely as the front door opened, his sister spoke, and finally he heard the voice he'd ached to hear again.

"Okay," Kennedy said. "I'll wait here on the porch."

He got to his feet and looked around for a plan, like he could pick one up off the kitchen counter. How was he supposed to do something romantic in a matter of minutes when he was jet-lagged, in shock that she lived in Windsong, and pissed at Nash for coming anywhere near her?

Think, Maverick.

Candles. There were a few in the cupboard. Useful over decorative, but they'd do. He gathered them all, placed them around the living room, and lit them.

Fireplace. Whoever had left logs in the hearth, he owed big time. He stoked the wood until a great fire flamed.

Flowers. He remembered her saying how much she loved them. He snuck out the back door to the jasmine shrubs and vines behind his cabin and cut a bunch. He didn't have any vases, so he filled a few Mason jars with water and arranged the jasmine inside. He put them around the living room, too, bringing in their floral scent.

The letters. Of course the letters. He rolled his suitcase into the kitchen, then opened it to retrieve the letters and postcards he'd written her. He found some string and tied it in a bow around the small stack. Placed them on the coffee table.

Lastly, he jotted down the two dozen or so words filling his head right now, tore the page from the notepad on the kitchen counter, and folded it in half to tuck inside his hand.

Time to seal the deal with his girl.

He stopped breathing when he saw her leaning against the porch railing. She had on light blue jeans and a soft pink sweater. Her hair, longer now, fell to the middle of her back. Sensing he stood in the doorway, she turned.

Their eyes didn't just lock. They sparked.

Well, hers did, and he found himself hauled right back into their bottomless shimmer.

"Hi," she said.

"Hi," he said.

They stared at each other, silent, getting used to seeing each other again, he guessed. God, being this close to her was better than he'd imagined. If she held a stethoscope to his chest, she'd get an earful, his heart pounding out of control. And then, like no time had passed at all, they broke into the same enthusiastic smile and he *knew*.

Their connection hadn't lessened in the slightest.

"Welcome home."

"Thanks. I hear it's your home now, too." He stepped onto the porch. It took superhuman strength not to haul her against him. "You gave up your dream job?"

"No," she said with a small shake of her head. "I found it here instead." He stayed quiet, waiting for her to continue. "I realized my dream was to connect with people and build long-lasting relationships where I could help keep them healthy *and* guide them through good days and bad days. Being here, I still get to help people of all ages with lots of different ailments, but I'm part of a community that extends beyond my medical practice." Her eyes softened. "I'm sorry I wasn't the first person to tell you. I was going to call or text, but then I decided to just come over. I didn't realize your family would still be here. I didn't mean to interrupt."

"You didn't." He stepped closer. He'd imagined Kennedy in all sorts of places and positions, but none like this. None with her leaning back against his porch railing with permanence etched around her eyes. She was the most beautiful thing he'd ever seen, and the cool evening air did nothing to diminish the heat flaming under his skin.

"I couldn't wait to see you," she said.

"Always needing a leg up on me," he teased, falling back into the easy banter between them. Three months suddenly felt like three minutes. "I couldn't wait to see you, either."

Her smug expression made him smile. "Don't do that."

"Do what?" he asked, genuinely confused.

"Show me your dimples. I'm not ready for them yet."

"What are you ready for?" He stood in front of her now, his fingers itching to reach out and touch her.

"To talk."

"Okay, but first—" He handed her the note in his hand. "Read this."

...

Kennedy didn't want to look away from Maverick's intense blue gaze. He was home! Standing a foot away from her! And seeing him in person rather than staring at the picture of him on her phone made this a million times better. She didn't want to seem obsessed with him, though, so she accepted the piece of paper and read it.

Goodbyes are only for those who love with their eyes. Because for those who love with heart and soul there is no such thing as separation.

Mother of pearl, he'd written down a Rumi poem. For her. She read the poem a second time, happy tears threatening to spill, before lifting her gaze back to his.

"Come inside?" He reached toward her cheek, then dropped his arm, as if thinking better of it.

She slipped the piece of paper into her front pocket, never breaking eye contact. She took his hand and brought it to her cheek, leaned in to his palm, relished the warmth and comfort. "I'd love that."

He led her into his house, shut the door behind them. Her breath caught at the sight before her.

"It's all I could do in less than ten minutes," he said.

"You didn't... Just having you..." She'd lost the ability to speak a complete sentence. "It's perfect."

She followed him to the couch, taking in the flowers and candles and stack of letters on the coffee table. The smell of jasmine filled her nose, along with the scent of wood from the fireplace. That he had done all this for her spoke volumes and calmed the nervous beat of her heart.

"Those are all for you," he said, pointing at the stack. "I needed the time away, Kennedy, but you were always with me. Here." He put his hand over his heart. "I did mail one letter yesterday. I thought I ought to follow through with at least one, in hopes you felt the same way about me that I feel about you."

Butterflies filled her stomach. "And what way is that?"

He brushed the hair off her shoulder and cupped the side of her neck. "You're going to make me say it before we've had a chance to catch up?"

"I've waited three months to hear your voice again. I think you can say it now *and* later." She fluttered her eyelashes at him.

"I love you." No hesitation. No doubt. Pure, genuine honesty.

Her heart exploded in her chest. She hadn't come to Windsong for him, but she had hoped in her heart of hearts that it would include them picking up where they'd left off, and hearing those three little words confirmed what she knew deep down: they were meant to be. "I love you, too."

His dimpled smile knocked the wind out of her. She grinned back.

"Say it again," he said.

"I love you."

"Please tell me I can kiss you now," he said.

"You could have kissed me two minutes ago, cowboy."

His lips were on hers a split second later, lighting up her insides like her feet weren't touching the ground. He pulled away far too soon.

"Best homecoming ever." He took her hands in his, rubbed his thumbs over her knuckles. Months away from the ranch had softened his skin

"It is. I wasn't sure…"

"Never, ever doubt how much you mean to me, okay?"

"Okay."

"Tell me what I missed. How is the job going?"

"It's great. I love every day I'm in the office, and some-times I even make house calls, which is so old-school, it's beyond fun." She glanced away for a moment. "You know, there is another reason I decided to come here."

He lifted his brows. "Me, right?"

"No, actually. Hugo. He…he passed away the day after I got the offer in Boston."

Maverick paled, his shoulders dropping. "Kennedy. I had no idea. I'm so sorry." He wrapped her in a hug and held tight until she drew back a full minute later.

She'd rehearsed what she wanted to say to Maverick when he returned, but seeing the sympathy written all over his face, the shared pain of loss, made it difficult to remember the speech she'd planned.

"Thank you." She glanced at the wood crackling in the fireplace, then focused back on him. "It changed everything for me. I realized how much I wanted to be close to the people I love, not live across the country from them. When Doc first called me about his practice, I told him I'd think about it, never believing I'd actually say yes. I thought Boston was my dream.

"But then I lost Hugo, and for a few days I could barely function. Then your mom called me. Bethany had told her the reason I'd left the ranch so suddenly, and she wanted to see if I was okay. My own mother hadn't even done that, and it struck me that a family like yours was a dream of mine, too. The people of Windsong. The sense of community that I've relied on a hospital for. I could have an amazing job *and* be with friends and only a six-hour drive from Ava and Andrew instead of a six-hour plane ride."

He stared at her with such clear adoration, she could barely keep herself from straddling his lap and fulfilling her naughtiest dreams of him. *We have time for that.*

"If I'd known…" he started.

"I know."

He seemed to wrestle with what to say next, finally settling on, "I'm unbelievably proud of you."

"Thanks. I'm ridiculously proud of you, too. I hear your pesticide is a big success."

"I feel at a distinct disadvantage here, Dr. Martin."

"Oh? How so?"

"I think I've got a case of Travelitis. Too much travel and not enough home. You know more about me than I know about you." He faked a cough. "I think I need a doctor to keep a close eye on me this weekend and talk my ear off, among other things. You up for the job?"

"Are you asking me to play doctor, Maverick Owens?"

"Absolutely."

"Hmm…" She tapped the side of her jaw, pretending to have to think about it. "I guess I could do that. I do like to talk."

"I like to listen."

"What exactly are the other things you need?"

"They don't involve talking at all." His eyes glittered with lust and his kissable lips hitched up at the corners. "And I should warn you, this is just the beginning, because I can't ever go without you again."

"I'm all for beginnings." She climbed into his lap, needing to be closer, to feel his body against hers "I missed you so much."

"I missed you, too. Missed everything about you." He twirled her hair around his finger.

"Did you have a good trip? Accomplish everything you wanted to? I did get info from your family, but not everything. I didn't want to pry too much."

"I'll tell you all about it tomorrow. Tonight I have other plans."

"As your doctor, shouldn't I be in charge?"

"I think you'll like what I have in mind."

"Really? And what is that?" She played with the hair curling around his ears.

"Loving every single inch of you." He kissed the side of her neck. "Showing you how much you mean to me."

"Well, I have some news for you." She dragged a fingernail along his chiseled jawline. "Absence definitely made my heart grow fonder."

"Mine too."

"We have so much to catch up on," she said softly, loving the renewed intimacy building between them.

"We have the rest of our lives, Shortcake. You're my today and all my tomorrows. My home base and my travel partner. I want to show you the world, if you'll let me. I should have said more to you before I left."

She pressed her finger to his mouth. "Let's not look back. Only forward."

He clasped her wrist, kissed each knuckle on her hand. "I can do that."

"I did appreciate the note you left on my doorstep. I've read it a million times. And when I moved here, I tucked it under my pillow. When we said goodbye that morning at my apartment, I never imagined things turning out this way. I never thought I'd be here when you weren't. I've heard stories about you from your family and friends, seen baby pictures, listened to Hunter revere you while trying to trash talk you at the same time. I've learned all about the secret good deeds you do."

"First order of business, invite Ava here to tell me stories about you."

She laughed. "She's visiting for Thanksgiving."

"Great." His eyes sparkled with mischief. No doubt he and Ava would get along famously.

"I've learned a lot about myself these past couple of months, too. Like how much I enjoy building relationships with my patients. How important it is to me to belong somewhere that isn't my workplace. I love the country as much as the city. And I also enjoy a slower pace, which doesn't mean boring, that's for sure. I'd tell you about it, but then I'd be committing HIPAA violations."

"The town is lucky to have you."

"I think I'm the lucky one."

"If we're going to go there, I'm the lucky one. At some point I should probably reach out to Reed and thank him for getting married on my ranch. If you hadn't crashed his wedding…"

"Your life would be so boring," she teased, a split second before he scooped her up into his arms. "Maverick! What are you doing?"

"We've done enough telling for tonight." He carried her

down the hallway toward his bedroom. "It's time for the showing part of this reunion."

She wiggled against him. "Finally."

"Forever," he whispered.

"Yes," she whispered back. "Forever."

Dear Kennedy,

I'm flying home tomorrow. It's been a fantastic trip and I don't think I would have accomplished all that I have if I didn't have you sitting in the back of my mind, pushing me to not miss a thing. To honor every detail Nicole left me. No matter how tired I was, or how lost I got (I should have brought a compass), you guided me, and for that I'm forever grateful. It seems you don't have to be with me to challenge me. And it's clear I'm up for anything and everything with your voice in my head.

The angel-slash-devil on my shoulder is you, and I mean that in the best possible way. When I wasn't being led around by Nicole and you, I did a lot of thinking. Earbuds in and music playing, I had time for introspection and future-self scenarios. Guess what I came up with? I am mad/nuts/crazy/wild about YOU. And when I see you again, I'm going to tell you.

YOU are the love of my life, Kennedy, and I want to ride the rest of our days together.

Get ready, because here I come.

Love,

Maverick

ACKNOWLEDGMENTS

There are some very serious subject matters in this book: ALS, long QT syndrome, death, miscarriage, family strain, and I did my best to portray these issues accurately and with sensitivity. For anyone who has experienced or is experiencing any of these difficulties, my heartfelt thoughts and prayers are with you now and always.

• • •

Big hugs and thanks to my editor, Stacy Abrams. I say it every time, but you always know exactly how to make my stories better and I'm forever grateful. xo

Thank you to the entire team at Entangled Publishing for everything you do, and a special shout-out to Elizabeth Turner Stokes for my amazing cover, Claire Andress for loving Maverick and Kennedy as much as you did, Nancy Cantor for your awesome copyedits, and Curtis Svehlak for your always quick and considerate production assistance.

Samanthe Beck, you're the best and I would be lost without you. Seriously. Thank you for everything!!

To Charlene Sands, Roxanne Snopek, Paula Altenburg, and Maggie Kelley, thank you for being such wonderful, supportive friends while I write my books. I am so lucky to have you in my life.

Thank you Rachel Hamilton for helping me with social media, but more importantly for being a friend and reader since the very beginning. I treasure our friendship so much!

To Robin Palm and Karen Begun, best friends since we were teenagers, you are my sisters, and your friendship, love, and support has literally gotten me through many days. Thank you. Love you!

Mom, you are the best, and I'm the luckiest girl on the planet to be your daughter. Thank you for teaching me strength, kindness, generosity, and for always being there for me. Love you so much.

To my cousin Shelly, thank you for our long talks and much-needed conversations. I have always looked up to you, and being close friends and family is a true gift.

To Claudia, Lorie, and Mayra, I love talking books and everything else with you girls! Your friendship brightens my weekdays, and I'm so grateful I get to work with you.

Lastly, to my funny, loving, kind, and generous hubby, through good times and bad, we're a team, and I love you so much. Thank you for always supporting my dreams and cheering me on. Let's crash a wedding together! ;)

The Wedding Crasher and the Cowboy is a sweet, sexy rom-com full of hilarious hijinks and ending in a satisfying happily ever after. However, the story includes elements that might not be suitable for some readers. Death of loved ones, life-threatening illness, and mention of a miscarriage in a character's backstory are included in the novel. Readers who may be sensitive to these elements, please take note.

Hilarity ensues when the wrong brother arrives to play wingman at her sister's wedding.

the
wedding
date
disaster

by Avery Flynn

Hadley Donavan can't believe she has to go home to Nebraska for her sister's wedding. She's gonna need a wingman and a whole lot of vodka for this level of family interaction. At least her bestie agreed he'd man up and help. But then instead of her best friend, his evil twin strolls out of the airport.

If you looked up doesn't-deserve-to-be-that-confident, way-too-hot-for-his-own-good billionaire in the dictionary, you'd find a picture of Will Holt. He's awful. Horrible. The worst—even if his butt looks phenomenal in those jeans.

Ten times worse? Hadley's buffer was supposed to be there to keep her away from the million and one family events. But Satan's spawn just grins and signs them up for every. Single. Thing.

Fine. "Cutthroat" Scrabble? She's in. She can't wait to take this guy down a notch. But somewhere between Pictionary and the teasing glint in his eyes, their bickering starts to feel like more than just a game…

New York Times *bestselling author Ginny Baird is back with another sweet, heartfelt, and unique take on the wedding genre.*

The
Matchmaker
Bride

Successful Boston matchmaker and television personality Meredith Galanes's reputation is on the line. During a guest appearance on a morning talk show, she's broadsided by questions about her own romantic attachments, just as she's trying to secure a syndication deal. Afraid to admit her love life is a total disaster, Meredith blurts out that she's seriously involved with a very special man—a boatbuilder in Maine. She never expects that small slip to get spun into a story about her supposed engagement.

Or that the paparazzi will track the guy down...

Derrick Albright is laid-back about many things. Being hounded by the press about some imaginary engagement to a woman he's only met once—and couldn't stand—isn't one of them. Then Meredith actually shows up at his cabin in Blue Hill, Maine, with an apology, a pot roast, and a proposal—play along until she secures her TV deal, and she'll help him win back his ex.

It's a simple plan, but if they have any chance of pulling it off, they'll have to survive each other first...

Don't miss the new sweet rom-com about returning a sleepy beach town B&B to its former tourist-destination glory.

A Lot Like
LOVE

by Jennifer Snow
USA Today Bestselling Author

When Sarah Lewis inherits a run-down B&B from her late grandmother in coastal Blue Moon Bay, the logical thing to do is sell it and focus on her life in L.A. But when she learns that interested buyers will only tear it down in its current state, she feels a sense of obligation to her grandmother to get it back to the landmark tourist destination it once was... even if that means hiring the best contractor for the job, who happens to be her old high school crush.

Wes Sharrun's life has continued to unravel since the death of his wife three years before. Now with a struggling construction company and a nine-year-old daughter, he sees the B&B as an opportunity to get back on his feet. Unfortunately, despite trying to keep his distance, his daughter has taken a liking to Sarah, and his own feelings are tough to deny.

As they spend more time together painting, exploring a forgotten treasure trove of wine in a basement cellar, and arguing over balcony placement, the more the spark between them ignites. But will saving the B&B be enough to convince them both to take a second chance at love?

AMARA
an imprint of Entangled Publishing LLC